That Deadly Space

A Civil War Novel

Gerald Gillis

Mills Street Publishing, LLC
Marietta, Georgia

THAT DEADLY SPACE

Copyright © 2017 by Gerald Gillis

Mills Street Publishing, LLC

ISBN–13: 978-0-692-84062-7

Cover: General Gordon Vows To General Lee, At Antietam 1862, 1991 (oil on canvas), Troiani, Don (b.1949) / Private Collection / Bridgeman Images

Book cover design by Jay Montgomery

Printed in the United States of America

This book is dedicated to:

My late mother, Evelyn Hughes Gillis, who instilled in me a love of reading and an appreciation of the power of the written word,

and

My English teacher at Atlanta's Druid Hills High School, the incomparable Margaret Davis, who was simply the best and most inspiring teacher I ever encountered.

Acknowledgements

That Deadly Space is a work of fiction. It is a story of service, sacrifice, and tragedy during the four bloody years of the American Civil War. While told from a Southern perspective, the story recounts the skill and heroism of both sides.

My appreciation is extended to my friend Don Spence who has been kind enough to review my draft manuscripts and provide his excellent feedback. Every writer should have such a resource.

A word of appreciation is extended to my family members who assisted with various portions of this project. Thanks to Debby, Steve, Suzanne, and Edie.

Thanks also to the acclaimed artist Don Troiani whose work is displayed on the book's cover. Kudos to the talented Jay Montgomery for his cover design.

Chapter One

First Manassas — The Inaugural

Oh Shenandoah,
I long to see you,
Away you rolling river.
"Shenandoah"

July 21, 1861

He had never killed anyone before, never seen a man die a violent death before, but he knew from deep within his innermost regions that he was about to experience the latter and quite possibly both. That is, of course, unless a sharpshooting Federal soldier from somewhere across the field beat him to it.

"Dear Lord," he said softly, "if my prayer from last night is just now reaching you—the one about allowing me to fight bravely and, if necessary, to die honorably—then kindly allow me to make the exact same request again, but this time with a bit more urgency."

Second Lieutenant Conor Rafferty, Army of the Confederate States of America, was at his post as the very first shots of the very first battle of the Civil War were fired in his direction. The cannon and musket fire commenced just after daybreak, shattering a peaceful silence that would not come around again for four long and grueling years. The twenty-one-year-old Georgian looked out across the green, undulating, Northern Virginia landscape and saw the masses of Federal troops in their blue-clad uniforms, their bayonets gleaming in the morning sun, their officers on horseback with sabres drawn, their regimental flags

1

uncased and flapping in the steady breeze. Puffs of smoke from the enemy lines of battle soon had .58-caliber lead Minie balls flying by the thousands in Conor's general direction, whizzing past his head like bees angered at the rough tampering of their hive. He felt unsurpassed levels of exhilaration and fear surging through his body in unison, causing him to feel more alive and more frightened than at any other time in his young life. The pungent smell of gunpowder quickly displaced the more familiar morning odors of wet grass, freshly plowed earth, and cooking fires.

Conor's mind suddenly flashed back to the night before he was to depart for military duty and the bitter confrontation with his father. Enraged over Conor's decision to join the army and fight in a war his father had warned would destroy their family, Conor was told he would never become a good officer, that he was too soft, too naïve, and too concerned with his own welfare to find success as a soldier in any army at war. His father had also told Conor that he was too much a thinker and not enough a doer. Finally, he had added that if the Confederacy was looking for competent officers, they would have to look elsewhere because Conor was doomed to become an abject failure. The elder Rafferty's harsh words and spiteful tone had devastated Conor. While his relationship with his demanding father had always been respectful but nonetheless complicated, his father's heated words had pierced hard into Conor, opening a gaping laceration of his spirit at a moment when encouragement and approval were so badly needed.

Conor came back to the present, drawing a deep breath and steeling himself as the dangers around him intensified. He would fight and fight hard, to the death if circumstances necessitated, and thus go to his grave as a brave, competent officer—a thinker *and* a doer. He would never please his father, he concluded, so he would concentrate on pleasing himself with his skill and bravery for as long as he was destined to live.

A Confederate soldier barely twenty feet away suddenly screamed and fell over when he was struck in the abdomen by a bullet. Other nearby soldiers were gasping, shouting, or sometimes falling without making a sound. Cannons were firing at the Southerners from three directions, and their own cannons were answering with equal fury, flinging shells above Conor's head with a distinctive ripping noise and into the advancing blue droves. Conor's horse, a five-year-old Saddlebred Gelding named Chief, was surprisingly steady as the noise of battle grew increasingly thunderous. Cannon explosions as close as twenty yards were flashing and kicking up dirt and debris, but Chief flinched only slightly. There soon appeared the ominous sign of several wide-eyed, riderless horses galloping in fright from across both sides of the field. Conor wondered for a moment if Chief could judge his own anxiety.

Conor was a courier with the 2nd Brigade of General Joseph E. Johnston's Army of the Shenandoah. His brigade commander, Colonel Francis Bartow, had selected the young lieutenant for his staff when he discovered that Conor had attended the University of Georgia, Bartow's own alma mater. Conor dutifully remained at Bartow's side, ready to receive his orders, determined to earn the senior officer's trust and confidence.

Conor glanced about at the bedlam and quietly observed, "So *this* is what it's really like." The noise was deafening, unlike anything he could have imagined, as the whole area was transformed into something as chaotic and menacing as a raging, out-of-control forest fire. Soldiers were firing muskets from every portion of the battlefield, a continuous rolling cascade of lethality. Cannon explosions came ever closer, and the shouting of orders along with the bloodcurdling screams gave the entire scene an otherworldly feel to it. Conor remained surprisingly calm until he scanned the adjacent ground and saw the bodies of fallen soldiers, some grotesquely torn apart by shot and shell, some still wriggling but many more lying motionless, either singly or in clusters. Everywhere there was smoke, often making it difficult to see ahead where elements of the Federal army were attempting to flank the Confederates. The acrid smoke was increasingly bitter, filling his nostrils so effusively that he briefly wondered if he would ever again be able to smell things normally.

By the time the lines of the 7th and 8th Georgia Regiments formed at Matthews' Hill, the Federals were pounding the Confederates with deadly accurate artillery. The Union lines extended beyond the Confederate flanks, and after taking heavy casualties the Southerners retreated to Henry Hill. From what Conor could see, the withdrawal was mostly orderly even with the Federals continuing to pour musket fire into the Rebel ranks. Conor stayed close to Colonel Bartow, receiving his orders and then passing them along to the regimental commanders.

It was near noon when Colonel Bartow pointed and shouted to Conor, "That looks like Jackson on the high ground yonder. Get over to him and tell him we need his support. Tell him to cover our movement back toward his position."

Conor spurred his horse and galloped to the ridge upon which General Thomas J. Jackson had positioned his Virginia brigade's infantry and artillery. Jackson sat up tall and straight on his horse, his sabre dangling to his left side, his cape sagging from his shoulders almost to his saddle. He was issuing a steady stream of orders to couriers and foot soldiers as he sat calmly, his penetrating blue eyes taking in the frenzied scene around him. He never flinched at the bursting Federal shells, never raised his voice, and never showed any outward signs of fear or self-doubt over the evolving situation.

Jackson turned and noticed Conor. "Do you have something for me, Lieutenant?" he called with a tinge of impatience.

"Colonel Bartow sends his compliments and asks that you cover his withdrawal, sir. General Bee and Colonel Evans are also moving this way," Conor replied.

"I will not be going anywhere but forward, sir. Advise Colonel Bartow to move to this ridge with all due haste."

Conor saluted, called out "Yes, sir," and rode away.

He had galloped perhaps one-hundred yards when Chief suddenly and noisily reared, almost toppling him. Conor felt the *thump thump* of two more balls penetrating the horse's torso while another struck near its left eye. Chief ran forward only a short distance before collapsing on its front legs and throwing Conor forward, out of the saddle and to the front of the large falling animal. Conor slammed the crown of his head when he hit the ground, and he was suddenly limp with starry white flashes in his vision. He remained on the ground for several minutes before he finally began checking his limbs for their working order. Apart from a slight nausea, he seemed largely intact. Nothing appeared broken, no bullet holes, no searing pain, just a mild disorientation.

"You okay? Hell, I thought you was shot dead."

Conor turned and saw a Confederate infantry sergeant moving toward him.

"That was quite a tumble, sir. You're gonna need yourself a new horse."

Conor rose, nearly falling over from wooziness but quickly righting himself, and then began dusting off his gray woolen clothing. If it was his fate to be killed on this field today, he concluded, he would do so in a proper uniform. He rose up straight, shoulders broadly squared, a handsome, muscular, soldierly example of young Southern manhood. At six-foot and one-hundred eighty pounds, he was an impressive physical specimen. His medium-length brown hair, bright blue eyes, and smooth facial features would have given him a boyish quality were it not for the dark moustache and goatee he had sprouted since joining the army. He checked to make sure his pistol was still in its holster, which it was, and he spotted his hat nearby. He glanced over at Chief who was beyond help, its eyes wide, tongue protruding, and the bullet holes to its brave heart leaking large volumes of blood. Despite his best efforts to appear otherwise, Conor still seemed to be in a sort of foggy haze.

"Anybody got a spare horse?" Conor asked, drawing a smile from the sergeant.

"I ain't got one on me, sir, but I'll bet there are plenty to choose from by now."

"What's happening here?" Conor asked, looking around in confusion. "Are we retreating?"

"If our soldiers moving away from their soldiers is a retreat, then that's what is happening here, Lieutenant."

Conor could not see the Federals in the distance, but it was clear they were pushing his fellow Confederates toward the ridge where he now stood.

Colonel Bartow's 2nd Brigade, along with the brigades of General Bee and Colonel Evans, were moving toward Henry Hill when General Jackson moved forward to stabilize the left and center of the Confederate line. When Conor finally spotted Colonel Bartow approaching on horseback, he waved and caught the commander's attention.

"I got the message to General Jackson, sir, but then my horse was shot out from under me and I haven't been able to look for another mount yet."

"Don't worry about a horse, Rafferty. I want you to find the Seventh Georgia's B Company and assume command there right away. The regimental commander is wounded, so I am giving you this order directly. The B

Company officers are all dead. You must go and find them on this field without delay. In addition, when you do find them, I want you to place B Company in reserve, to the rear of this ridge, and wait for orders from me. You must organize what is left of the company. They have been badly battered, but you have to get their mettle back into them so they can rejoin the line. This fight is not over. Do you understand what I've told you?"

"I understand fully, sir."

"Be damn quick about it, Lieutenant," the colonel called as he turned and rode away.

Conor's head was still slightly groggy when he looked at the sergeant who was standing nearby. "Sergeant, kindly help me with this one thing: Which company did the colonel tell me to find and take command of?"

"It was B Company, sir. Seventh Georgia."

"Yes, that was it. B Company. Thanks."

Conor immediately began working his way down the ridge on foot, against the flow of the retreating Confederate companies. He searched for Company B's guidon among the many flags in front of and passing beside him, but he couldn't locate it. The troops were moving hurriedly but without panic, and in the distance the Federal lines were moving toward them steadily, deliberately, like an animal stalking its wounded prey, stopping only to unleash deadly volleys into the backs of the Confederate ranks.

"B Company? Can anyone tell me where B Company is?" Conor shouted, by now more steady on his feet.

He kept moving among the men, calling out for what was now his new command. "Anyone know where I can find B Company? I'm looking for B Company."

A lieutenant passed and pointed with his thumb to the rear. "B Company's right behind me."

Federal bullets were still slicing through the decreasing distance. A wounded Confederate soldier dropped a battle flag but another quickly picked it up and continued. Dirt was flying up around Conor's feet, and men were dropping on all sides. Conor stepped over one dreadfully wounded young soldier who lay on his back in a bloody heap, calling out for his mother. Many of the retreating soldiers were exhausted to a point of near collapse, their reserves of adrenalin long since depleted, their desire to be someplace else evident in their faces and movements.

"I'm looking for B Company."

A stocky, red-faced sergeant approached, bathed in sweat and short of breath. "You've found us, or at least what's left of us."

"I'm Lieutenant Rafferty. Colonel Bartow has directed that I take command of the company. Are you the ranking sergeant?"

"I'm the ranking everything, sir. I'm Sergeant Rayburn."

"Our orders are to move to the far side of the ridge, reorganize there, and wait in reserve."

"I'm all too happy to obey that order, Lieutenant."

Conor turned and looked around at the retreating Confederates, hands on his hips, bullets passing ever nearer to him. When he surveyed the field to his front he could see the Federals in the near distance, moving their lines steadily closer, pausing only long enough to fire a volley before moving ahead again. He could hear the voices of their officers as they shouted commands to keep their ranks aligned. He briefly wondered what might be happening to his fellow Southerners across the unseen broader portions of the battlefield, but from what he could observe on this little piece of the field, the Confederates were being pushed hard.

"No, wait," Conor called to Rayburn. "This is the order you need to carry out: Stop the retreat of B Company now! We are no longer moving away from the firing. We will stand and fight here. Now get this company halted and in a line of battle."

"But according to what you just said, those aren't our orders, sir."

"I'm aware of what I just said, Sergeant. And I'm changing the orders based upon my assessment of the situation."

"But sir—"

"I have given you your orders, Sergeant. If you don't feel you can obey them, then bring me the next in line and move along. Do you understand?"

With their faces only inches apart, the unblinking Conor scrutinized the physically larger Rayburn before the sergeant turned and set about shouting at and collecting the men of B Company. After several minutes of gathering the remaining survivors of the diminished unit, Conor and Sergeant Rayburn quickly organized them into a line of battle. Some of the soldiers were grumbling and arguing with Sergeant Rayburn, but they all obeyed and began firing at the advancing Federals. Even though they were still heavily outgunned, the battered company kept firing, reloading, and firing again into the blue line. Conor noticed that the soldiers would occasionally steal a curious glance back at him, but the young Southerners stood their ground and kept shooting, despite their misgivings and their fatigue. One soldier fell, followed by another, but the Yankee line some one-hundred yards distant had far more of theirs on the ground.

Confederate soldiers from other companies were moving past B Company.

"If you boys would like to join us and fight," Conor shouted at them, "then find a place in our line beside the finest damn soldiers in this damn army. You can be one of those too, boys. But if you'd rather be shot in the back or the ass, then go right ahead and keep moving away."

Some stopped; most didn't.

"I didn't know Georgia boys were the retreating sort. My, what an unpleasant surprise this is. It's a good thing you boys weren't at the Alamo. The whole sorry lot of you probably would have taken off running to Guadalajara. *Adios y'all amigos.*"

Some hesitated; several officers stopped and looked at Conor as if he were a madman; some of Conor's own men were looking at him similarly.

"We're going to *stop* these people, right here on this ground. Join us, boys. We need you here, not back there where it's safe. What would your mommas and sweethearts think if they could see you now?"

More than two-dozen soldiers joined B Company and took a place in the line. Another thirty came running when they turned and saw what was happening behind them. Ten minutes later another forty joined, including a captain and two lieutenants. The captain fired his pistol and made no effort to usurp Conor's role as commander.

There was a fine officer's sabre on the ground nearby—expensive, Conor judged—and he picked it up and motioned toward the Union lines. Conor walked behind the men and shouted encouragement, stopping occasionally to unholster and fire his pistol.

"The retreating stops here, boys. Stack 'em up like firewood."

"Aim well, boys. Give 'em a volley for the friends you've lost today."

"This little piece of the field still belongs to us, boys. And by damn it's going to stay that way."

"Sergeant Rayburn?"

"Yessir?"

"If they roll over us here, they won't stop until they push us all the way to Georgia."

"I know, sir."

"So, Sergeant Rayburn?"

"Yessir?"

"That is *not* going to happen. Are we clear?"

"Couldn't be clearer, sir."

One of the privates in the line turned and shouted to Conor, "We're almost out of ammunition, Lieutenant. What happens then?"

"We'll charge 'em with bayonets," Conor shouted in return. "We will *not* leave the field to them."

The private rolled his eyes and muttered "Damn!" as he loaded his musket.

As Conor was walking behind the men, shouting encouragement, a nearby soldier was suddenly struck flush in the head with a musket ball. Conor's face was peppered with blood and shards of bone, but he calmly stepped away from the man's body and kept moving, kept shouting, making no effort to cleanse his face.

The fighting waged on for another twenty minutes as B Company continued to face down the far larger enemy force. Suddenly Conor heard the concussion of cannons behind him, followed instantly by the shells passing close over his head. A Confederate artillery barrage began ripping into the Union formation with devastating accuracy. The damage was swift as large numbers of Union troops began falling from the deadly bursts. Soon fresh Confederate infantry began arriving on either side of B Company, screaming wildly and moving aggressively toward the wavering Federal lines. Conor hadn't noticed the approaching reinforcements to the rear of his position, and their sudden presence on the field immediately shifted the momentum to the Rebels. Rather than breaking, however, the Federals began an orderly retreat.

"What are your orders, Lieutenant?' Sergeant Rayburn called. "We're all out of ammunition."

As Conor raised his sabre and pointed toward the ridgeline to the rear, a Union bullet dislodged it from his grip, breaking off the blade near the handle. Conor looked at and shook his hand, saw that it was uninjured, shook it again and then called out, "Move to the other side of the ridge," to Sergeant Rayburn. Conor then turned and threw the handle toward the retreating Union line, adding a few choice words to go with it before starting the trek back toward the higher ground.

Sergeant Rayburn found an area on the far side of the ridge that protected the company from direct musket fire. There were 36 men remaining in B Company, including two corporals and one sergeant. The unit had begun the day with a captain, two lieutenants, and 89 troops on the rolls. The young soldiers, their initiation into the brotherhood of warriors now attained, were exhausted from the exertion and emotion of the hard day. Some fell asleep while others appeared to be in a state of mild shock at fully grasping what they had just endured. Conor walked among the men, observing their condition but otherwise saying nothing. He allowed them time enough to eat what rations they had, mostly hardtack and salted bacon, since it was 3:00 pm and they had been without food since the very early morning.

Someone had built a small cooking fire and Sergeant Rayburn presented Conor with a tin cup filled with black coffee. "This right here is the last of the coffee my momma sent me from back home," he said with a chuckle.

They moved several paces away from the troops and took a seat on the ground, enjoying both the aroma and the taste of the thick, black coffee. Like Conor, Sergeant Rayburn was also from Atlanta where he had helped maintain the downtown hotel and restaurant his parents owned. He seemed saddened but not overly surprised at the casualties the company had suffered in the day's fighting thus far. Rayburn spoke of the relationship he had been building with the now-deceased Captain Byron Black.

"I think he would've been a good one," Rayburn said with a tinge of regret.

Rayburn then looked at Conor and laughed softly. "I gotta tell you, Lieutenant, what you did out there was the craziest damn thing I ever saw, I swear to God. I thought you were suicidal, that you would get the rest of us killed along with you. But you stopped cold a Yankee advance of probably eight-hundred men with our company of one-hundred, or so, counting the stragglers who joined us. The boys want to meet you, they want to know who the hell you are, so I would suggest you gather them up, introduce yourself, and say a few words."

Conor nodded. "I'd better hurry up and do it before Colonel Bartow has me shot for disobedience," he added as he took a dampened cloth and wiped the dried blood from his face.

At 4:00 pm, a courier came charging into their position on horseback. "Is this B Company?" the officer shouted.

Conor stood and approached the lieutenant. "Yes. Lieutenant Rafferty here, B Company Commander."

"Have your company ready to move to the front as soon as ordered. We are attacking across all fronts."

"Where is Colonel Bartow?"

"Colonel Bartow's dead on the field. Major Day now commands Second Brigade and Major Nichols now commands the Seventh Georgia. You will report to Major Nichols. Wait here and you will soon be given orders to proceed, but do not advance until you have orders."

Conor nodded his understanding as the courier turned his horse and quickly galloped away. Sergeant Rayburn and Conor glanced at one another. Conor still had a headache and felt slightly sick to his stomach from the earlier fall, or maybe from his near brush with death while leading his new company, but now the pounding in his head intensified over the shock he felt at the death of Colonel Bartow.

"What do you want to do, sir?" Rayburn asked.

"Better gather the men so I can address them."

Rayburn immediately turned and called, "B Company, on your feet. Quickly, boys. Form up on me."

The troops gathered around in a semi-circle, rifles and equipment in hand. Conor motioned for them to be seated and then took a moment to study the faces of those courageous, nameless young men. The hour's rest seemed to have refreshed them and brought them out of their stupor. Those with minor wounds had been bandaged and released to return to duty. They had refueled themselves with food and drink, perhaps even a quick nap, with time enough to inspect and clean their muskets. All eyes were on Conor as he stood before them.

"I'm Lieutenant Conor Rafferty. I have been assigned as the company commander here, and I will do all in my power to command B Company as effectively and aggressively as possible."

One of the young soldiers blurted out, "We noticed that, sir," and everyone laughed, including Conor.

"I realize," Conor said, continuing, "that this company has been hard hit today, and I will see about replacements in due course. Meanwhile, we have little choice but to fight with what we have left. You have fought well and bravely today, and I am impressed with your fighting spirit. I am honored to be a part of this company, to be in command of it, and I look forward to leading you into battle again. We are now awaiting orders to proceed, but until then just stand easy."

Conor then recognized a private near the back who raised his hand with a question.

"Are we going back to the other side of this ridgeline, sir?" he asked, turning and pointing to the nearby crest that separated them from the fighting on the other side.

"If I have anything to do with it, yes," Conor answered firmly.

The steely-eyed private nodded his approval, as did several others.

"Any other questions?" Conor asked, waiting several moments.

There was a sudden commotion from the ridgeline. Conor turned and saw a Confederate soldier on horseback approaching the company position at top speed, shouting and waving his hat. *"They're running! The Yankees are running!"* he screamed as he rode by B Company.

"B Company, on your feet," called Sergeant Rayburn, who then turned and looked at Conor expectantly.

Conor had no idea what to do. His heartbeat accelerated, and he had another fleeting spell of dizziness. He had twice been told to remain in this reserve position and await orders, and he was reluctant to ignore that directive again.

What are my possible choices? he kept thinking. Stay? Attack? Who should I ask? What should I do?

To his left, a Virginia artillery battery on the ridge was preparing to move forward. The noise of the gunfire ahead had diminished slightly, but it was clear the battle was still unfinished.

The little voice inside Conor's head was screaming, *Do something!* But what? he kept wondering. He said nothing until he could no longer tolerate his own silence.

Conor took a deep breath, cleared his throat and steadied himself. "Sergeant Rayburn?" he called in as forceful a voice as he could generate.

"Yessir?"

"Let's move out over this ridge and add B Company's muskets to the cause."

Many of the men began yelling their approval as the company formed up and began moving. Conor could see the Confederate infantry elements ahead, through the smoke, moving quickly to force the matter, perhaps even conclude it. The artillery battery soon passed on the left with teams of horses pulling the guns and wagons. The men were shouting, yelling, waving their hats in a celebratory way, eager to pursue the retreating Federals.

B Company formed a line and moved over the crest of the ridge.

There were bodies of men and carcasses of horses scattered all across the field. Wounded men from both sides called out to the B Company soldiers, but Sergeant Rayburn kept the line moving forward. The smoke and acrid smell of gunpowder hung over the battlefield in a low cloud, and the men kept a wary eye on the charred remains of a Federal ammunition wagon nearby. They walked through shell craters with the freshly disturbed soil only partially covering the grisly sight of severed arms and legs. Conor noticed that his splitting headache had mostly eased, finally, and his dizziness had cleared.

He was beginning to think he just might survive this day of madness.

They advanced perhaps 200 yards without incident before three officers on horseback approached. "Are you B Company?" a lieutenant called.

"We are indeed. I'm Lieutenant Rafferty, the commanding officer."

"I'm Major Nichols," spoke the senior officer. "I now command the Seventh Georgia. Were you the officer who stopped the advance of a full Federal regiment with your understrength company?"

Connor shrugged. "The credit goes to these brave soldiers, sir. They stayed and fought like a pack of wolves."

Major Nichols quickly climbed down from his horse, approached Conor, and shook his hand enthusiastically. "By God, I've already heard all about you and your soldiers. We need a few more like you, Lieutenant. Fine work, sir. Damn fine work."

The major then mounted his horse and glanced down at Conor. "Oh, and I'm curious, Lieutenant. When my adjutant came looking for you, he couldn't find you. So tell me, what were the latest orders you received?"

Conor swallowed hard. "To remain in reserve behind the ridgeline to our rear, sir, until further ordered."

Major Nichols' eyebrows arched. "Then may I ask, Lieutenant Rafferty, why is it you're out here and not back there?"

"Because this company very badly needed one more go at the people who killed or wounded fifty-six of their brothers today. It was my decision, sir. I'm the commander. I'm the one responsible."

The mustachioed Major Nichols was tall in the saddle, and his sitting atop a tall horse made him seem all the more imposing. He stared at Conor for a long moment, finally saying, "I like your spirit, Lieutenant, I really do. However, I'm afraid the Federals are moving back to Washington as fast as their feet will take them. It appears that we won't give pursuit, so I'm assembling the regiment back behind the ridgeline where you just came from."

"Understood, sir."

The major had the slightest of smiles on his face as he moved his horse closer to Conor, saying loudly enough for all the troops to hear, "And this time, dammit, *stay there*, Lieutenant Rafferty! That's an order."

The troops laughed raucously. Conor also laughed, releasing several hours of accumulated tension.

Major Nichols removed his hat, looked at the grimy, tired young soldiers, and added, "You did one hell of a job today, B Company. You helped us win a great victory on this field. This Virginia ground still belongs to us. I could not be prouder of you. The entire South is proud of you. God bless you."

The men began cheering and raising their rifles in celebration. Major Nichols waved his hat as he and his staff turned and rode away.

So, B Company did an about face and started back to the ridge once again. The battle was over and victory rested with the Southerners. It was bittersweet, Conor thought, what with all the Confederate and Union corpses within view. The nearby Henry House had been badly damaged, the Henry family nothing more than innocent bystanders who suddenly and sadly found themselves in the middle of a violent, indiscriminate firestorm.

The wounded were being moved to a makeshift regimental hospital behind the ridgeline. Many of the lesser wounded were walking or being assisted by others as they made their way to the tents for treatment. Ambulance wagons were collecting the more seriously injured.

Conor came upon a wounded Federal officer, lying on his back with his head propped against his dead horse. He was drifting in and out of awareness, his face as pale as a granite slab. He appeared to be in his late-thirties, dark-haired, bearded, and heavyset. His right arm just below the shoulder had been badly mangled by bullets and his left wrist had also been hit, partially severing his hand. He was among several dead blue-clad soldiers which Conor took to be troops of his own Union regiment.

"Can I offer you a drink of water, Colonel?"

"I'd be much obliged," he said in a tired voice.

Conor pressed his own canteen to the man's dry mouth and poured until he received an appreciative nod in return.

The colonel moaned slightly and shifted to his left, his acute pain apparent, his blood loss excessive and still seeping. He turned his head and spoke to his horse. "Sorry about this, Flatbush. Hell of a way to end the day, huh ole fella?"

"We'll collect you up and any of your wounded and get you to our regimental surgeon soon," Conor said after he had also taken a drink from the canteen. "It seems the rest of your army has skedaddled back to where they came from."

The colonel let out a loud sigh. "It wasn't supposed to happen this way."

"You might want to keep that to yourself, sir. There are plenty of us here who have a different view."

Conor noticed the finely crafted Colt Model 1860 pistol on the ground near the Union officer's feet. He leaned forward and took hold of the pistol, giving it an admiring glance and wiping the dirt off the barrel. He then took the old, well-traveled Starr revolver he had bought from another lieutenant in camp, and shoved it inside his belt, in the back. "Apologies, sir, but this will have to go with me," he said as he placed the Colt in his hip holster.

"It'll go with you only because I can't pick it up and shoot you in the damned forehead, Lieutenant."

Conor noticed the two cigars in the colonel's front uniform pocket, and when he leaned forward to claim them the Federal officer turned slightly to avoid his hand.

"Well since you're unable to shoot me in the damned forehead, sir, these will also have to go with me," Conor said, reaching around him and claiming the cigars.

Conor then eyed the colonel's fine leather boots.

"You're an officer, son. For crissakes start behaving like one," the colonel said brusquely.

Conor stared at the man for a moment and then realized with chilling, absolute certainty that only minutes before this Yankee officer would have killed him without hesitation or remorse, and with the same pistol that was now in his own possession. Despite the colonel's evident pain and the gray clamminess of his features, his face became stern, unblinking, like that of a schoolmaster eyeing an errant pupil.

"You're quite right, sir," Conor finally said, slipping one of the cigars back into the colonel's pocket.

Conor saw the colonel succumb soon thereafter from blood loss. The other cigar then came into the possession of Sergeant Rayburn.

It was over. The first battle of the war had ended in a stunning Confederate victory. The Union troops left the field in a panic that had spread like a virus throughout their ranks, something Conor had not observed in the Southern soldiers even though on several occasions early on they were in danger of being encircled. He had seen enough from the troops of the Union side to realize that their tenacity and resiliency would make this a difficult and strongly contested struggle. Only at the end did panic reach out and seize the Federals who had otherwise been heroic and skillful during the bulk of the fighting. Clearly, though, the fighting spirit of the Confederates had been awe-inspiring, in spite of the mistakes and inexperience of so many of its officers, Conor included. Still, he looked forward with great anticipation to commanding troops, his B Company troops, in the battles sure to come.

Now that the first shots had been fired, any hopes of compromise had evaporated along with the early-morning mist that had hung over the Manassas battleground. Both sides settled in for what they could now judge would be a difficult, bloody conflict. Lincoln called for 500,000 more troops while Jefferson Davis called for 400,000. The Confederates were filled with confidence and swagger, and Conor couldn't help thinking of his brother Sean's prediction that the South would win a quick and easy war. He very badly wanted to believe it, and certainly hoped it, but he had seen the Federal troops in action and he seriously doubted that neither quick nor easy would in any way factor into the final outcome. The boys in gray were in for one hell of a fight, and they damn well knew it.

And by now, so did the boys in blue.

***

Sunday, February 10, 1918
Even though he had lived it, Conor had never really taken an inventory of all the major battles of the Civil War he had participated in, all the heroism on both sides he had witnessed, and all the hardship he and his soldiers had endured. One afternoon his only grandson, Aaron, unexpectedly appeared at his Atlanta hospital bedside, a mere two weeks before Aaron was to ship out for his own army service in Europe during the Great War. As it were, Conor was sick and laid up, contemplating the very real possibility that he might soon cross over into that place up yonder, or at least the "up" being the stronger of his preference in yonders.

Aaron thus became a regular visitor, arriving at his grandfather's bedside just after sunrise and remaining until just before sunset each day for the next week. At first the nurses tried to shoo Aaron away, albeit halfheartedly, but he was so darned handsome and dashing as a U.S. Army captain that those sweet young flowers always relented and allowed him to stay. The older nurses just growled like parlor dogs but otherwise did very little. To Conor's great amusement, Aaron's care in that hospital became every bit the equal of his own.

Aaron told Conor that it was only when he had learned from one of his instructors—an Army historian at West Point—that his grandfather had been an illustrious Confederate officer who survived many of the war's most important engagements, that he decided to come to Atlanta. Aaron told Conor he wanted to hear of his experiences, about where he had fought, under whose command he had served, and what lessons he had learned about warfare, not only for his own personal interest but also for his professional benefit as an infantry officer soon to command troops in battle. And, of course, Aaron wanted to learn more about his father, Taylor.

Aaron, traveling from Virginia, hadn't known his grandfather was not well. Conor's old war wounds, the crotchety heart, and the normal stiffness of advancing age were pressing down hard on him, sticking to him like pine sap on the fingers, but sharing time with Aaron proved to be a better pain potion than even the best of Irish whiskies could match. Aaron's father, Taylor, who had been Conor's only child, had been killed in action with Theodore Roosevelt's Rough Riders at San Juan Hill in Cuba in 1898. Taylor had been just twenty-eight when he had died, leaving behind his young wife, five-year-old Aaron and a two-year-old daughter, Catherine.

When Aaron first entered Conor's hospital room on that blustery Atlanta day in February, 1918, unannounced and smartly dressed in his Army officer's uniform, Conor gasped and instantly thought he might be encountering the delirium that sometimes precedes death. Aaron was nearly an exact copy of his father, not just in height and body weight but also with his dark hair and bright blue eyes, his dazzling smile, and his chiseled chin. It took Conor's breath away and very nearly kept it, an astonishing sight especially for an old man who was quite certain he had seen it all by then. When Aaron introduced himself and then winced at seeing his grandfather's ghostly pale expression, he apologized for turning up so suddenly and suggested that he might best return at a later time. It took a moment for Conor's heart to steady, for his brain to catch up with and sort through what his eyes were seeing, but he soon recovered and warmly welcomed the grandson he hadn't seen in ten years. It was the biggest and best surprise his old memory could muster up.

Aaron stood up straight, like a man trained in the ways of the military. His hair was close-cropped and his face was clean-shaven, and Conor stole a quick glance to see if his shoes were highly polished, which of course they were. He looked first-rate, likely in possession of a first-rate mind, and appeared to Conor to be the sort who would reject outright any standard other than excellence from himself or from those with whom he held sway. His broad, muscular shoulders and flat stomach confirmed that he took his physical conditioning seriously. Conor briefly wondered how his own genes might have played a part in the making of such an impressive young man as the one who stood before him, but he promptly shelved the question when his own long list of defects came parading out of the unlocked closets in his brain.

So, Aaron stayed close to his grandfather, paper in hand, asking questions and making notes and showing amazement at many of the wartime events and observations Conor shared with him. It was the first time Conor had ever spoken with Aaron about his service in the war. In fact, it was the first time in over fifty years that Conor had spoken to *any* person about some of those experiences.

"Let's start at the top, Cappy," said Aaron. "Tell me what it was like to be a Confederate officer during the Civil War."

Conor smiled. Cappy was the name his son Taylor had begun calling him when a group of former Confederate soldiers paid a postwar visit and referred to Conor as "Captain," his rank at the time they served together. Two-year-old Taylor couldn't quite manage the full word, so he immediately dropped "Daddy" and henceforth called Conor "Cappy" from that point on. Now the nickname had passed to a successive generation.

"The War Between the States," Conor said, pausing to gather his thoughts, "surely must have been a foretaste of what it will be like when the world finally comes skidding

23

to an entirely unpleasant ending. Given that premise, were I to live long enough to experience the End Times, I would probably recognize enough of it from my war experience that I wouldn't be fully surprised. If offered a choice, however, I would rather not have survived one only to fall victim to the other. One was plenty enough for me. Anyway, I became an infantry officer and, as we'll discuss, I had a vast range of experiences. The war was a brutal, deadly business, and as such I shot other men, was myself shot by other men, all while participating in some of the truly consequential battles of the conflict. I led lots of men in lots of engagements, some of which our side won, some we did not. I met many of the highly acclaimed Confederate commanders of the war, even a few from the Union side, and I served under a man who would eventually come to command an entire corps. I squeezed a lifetime of events into those four years, Aaron."

And so the conversations began.

Two hours later, Aaron later looked over his notes and then put down his pencil. He sat back in the metal chair and sipped from the cup of coffee a young nurse had recently delivered.

"What was it like, Cappy, to win the opening big battle of the war? Did you think it would be over soon?"

"No," Conor replied, shaking his head. "I had seen for myself how the Federal troops had fought and died so bravely. They were well-organized and tough fighters, and they had large numbers of men and plenty of good equipment. They pushed us just as hard as we pushed them in the early going, maybe even harder, and it was our luck that we got additional people to the field at just the right time so we could concentrate on the Federal weak spots. Nope, I didn't think it would be over soon. If anything, I became convinced that it would be a long time before I ever got back here to Atlanta, if I ever got back at all. We were all pleased to have won that battle, sure, but most of us knew it was going to be a tough fight."

"What made you decide to stop your troops from retreating, and then to stand and fight?"

"I didn't like the idea of retreating. Somebody had to stop it and I was young enough and foolish enough not to know any better, so I just thought it might as well be me."

"You may have inspired the entire army, not just your company."

"That's an exaggeration of sizeable proportions, Aaron."

"Oh? The momentum of the battle shifted after you made your stand."

"That was just one little portion of a much larger battlefield."

"Yes, but you may have planted the seeds of doubt. Here's a speculative question for you: What do you think would've happened if the Confederate army had pursued the Federals all the way back to Washington?"

Conor couldn't help but smile. "Good evening, Mister Lincoln, sir. I regret to inform you that your house, your city, and what is left of your army are now in the possession of the Army of the Confederate States of America. President Davis will be along shortly to answer any questions you might have. Until then, I bid you and the Missus a very pleasant good evening, sir."

Aaron smiled, but then his expression changed. "Why did you join the Confederate army, Cappy?"

"It was simple: I never could have taken up arms against my home state of Georgia."

"Sort of like General Lee and Virginia?"

"I suppose so. But any comparison with me to General Lee ends there."

"Did it bother you when the Union was dissolved?"

"I was disappointed, yes, because it meant there would probably be no peaceful resolution. And if no peaceful means could be found, I knew we would soon be shooting at one another—American versus American. That didn't have a pleasant sound to it, but it seemed more and more probable we were headed that way."

"What were your feelings on slavery?"

"I was opposed to it. The South's economy was dependent upon slave labor, of course, but it was a morally bankrupt system that couldn't last much longer. The South would eventually run out of trading partners who would tolerate slavery. Its demise was inevitable, and my hope was that the Southern states would abolish it over time. Our family farmed crops and raised beef cattle, but we didn't own slaves. My father was adamantly opposed to it and I concluded early on in life that I would never own slaves."

"That stance didn't win you a lot of friends in the Confederate army, did it?"

"Well, very few of the troops I commanded owned slaves. But many of the officers I served with were slave owners. It made for some interesting conversations, that's for sure. I really didn't know any black people apart from the servants in some of my friends' homes or the workers at the stores where we traded. Slavery had been a part of this nation for generations, but only when I got to college did I really start to consider what it was doing to the people who were enslaved and to the people who were enslaving them."

"Why was your father opposed to slavery?"

"He thought it was immoral, that no man should be another man's property. He had an Irish sensitivity toward judging men by what they did rather than who their fathers were or what the color of their skin was."

"What did he think about the South fighting to maintain slavery?"

"He thought it was foolish for the agrarian South to fight a war against the industrialized North, no matter the reasons."

"You didn't agree?"

"No, I thought we would win. I wouldn't have volunteered if I thought we were going to lose."

"And by winning, the institution of slavery would have been maintained for some period afterward, correct?"

Conor took a long breath. "Probably so, yes. But what were my choices, Aaron? I could have become a traitor to my native South and either run away or joined the Union Army and fought against my own flesh and blood; or I could have waited to be conscripted into the Confederate army; or I could have volunteered, which I did. And if I was going to volunteer to fight, then I was going to fight to win. And my father detested me for it."

"Why?"

"Our relationship was stretched to the breaking point when I joined the army. I explained to Father that I didn't join the army to keep slavery, but to keep the Yankees out of the South so we could decide our own future course. And I hoped to have a voice in charting that course."

"Why was your relationship with your father so strained?"

"When my two younger brothers announced to Father that they had also joined up to fight, he got very angry. I had never seen him that angry before. Never in my life. This all happened the night before I was to leave for duty. Father blamed me for their decisions since they looked up to me and used my joining the army as their reason to do the same. He told me the South would have hell to pay, and that I would very likely bring destruction down on our own family by being such a damned impetuous fool. Father told me I was destined to become a miserable failure as an infantry officer because I was too soft, too naïve, and too concerned with my own personal welfare to find success as a soldier in any army at war."

"Why so harsh, Cappy?"

"I don't know," Conor answered with a sigh. "But I can tell you I was devastated. And I swore I would prove him wrong, even if it killed me."

"Then what happened?"

"Then he slapped me in the face and turned and walked away."

Aaron swallowed. "What did you do then?"

"I kissed my mother and told my brothers goodbye, and I left."

Conor stared at Aaron for a moment before saying, "I've only spoken to two people about what Father said to me that night, and those conversations took place back during the war. This isn't something I find easy to discuss. In fact, you're the first person to hear this in over fifty years."

Aaron nodded but said nothing.

Chapter Two

A Chance Meeting

Hurrah! Hurrah!
For Southern rights hurrah!
Hurrah for the Bonnie Blue Flag
that bears a single star.
"Bonnie Blue Flag"

May-August, 1862

After Manassas, Conor's army life was filled with small skirmishes, training, encampments, a harsh bout with dysentery, winter quarters, and still more small skirmishes. He was growing and gaining expertise as a leader of troops, and his B Company was rightly viewed as the finest-performing element not just in the regiment, but in the entire brigade. Conor came to be viewed by his officer peers with equal parts admiration and envy, and he was especially popular among his enlisted troops for his honesty and his concern for their welfare. His audacity in battle was highly regarded by his fellow soldiers of all ranks.

At Seven Pines near Fair Oak, Virginia, at the end of May, 1862, there was a nasty, merciless affair with over 11,000 casualties combined. Both sides claimed victory, but in truth the battle was tactically inconclusive in every way. The 7th Georgia was in reserve for almost the entire battle, much to the chagrin of its commander. Conor was now a captain who badly wanted to get his troops into the fight, which he eventually did when B Company moved into action late in the day.

Conor was leading a charge against a well-entrenched Federal force in what was literally the final hour of the battle when a Union artillery shell exploded near him, sending a jagged piece of hot shrapnel the size of a silver dollar into his hip. Luckily, it was slowed by his leather pistol holster before penetrating through and burrowing itself in his flesh. While the metal fragment did not shatter his hip, it did break off several small pieces of bone.

Conor was out of the fight almost as quickly as he had joined it.

The battle did provide a change in Confederate leadership that would influence the rest of the war in a significant way. General Joseph E. Johnston was wounded and replaced by General G.W. Smith, who was then replaced after the battle by General Robert E. Lee.

Meanwhile, Conor left by train for a hospital in Richmond.

His hip healed nicely while he was a patient at the large Chimborazo Hospital in Richmond. He walked with a slight limp and his hip still pained him much of the time, but his balance was fine and the doctors told him that the limping would subside over time. The hospital was admitting injured Confederate soldiers every day, from the walking wounded like Conor to the amputees and the gruesomely maimed. Since this was his first experience as a hospital patient, he discovered to his great satisfaction that the level of care from the doctors and nursing staff was entirely professional and compassionate. He also discovered that the food was mostly good, not always, but far better than the field rations to which he had become accustomed. His stomach noticed the difference, as well, and for about a week it reminded him daily in a not so delicate way that a wounded hip was not his only problem.

Conor was assigned to a ward with twenty other soldiers, both officer and enlisted. One of the poor fellows, a corporal from Mississippi, had been shot in the spine and paralyzed from the neck down. The rest of the patients were mobile enough to get out of their beds and move about, some easily like Conor, others more gingerly. The paralyzed corporal had a book of poetry from which several men began taking turns reading to him, and inevitably the corporal's eyes would fill with tears at the end of each session. Sadly, during the third week of his hospitalization, the corporal contracted pneumonia and died in his sleep. The next day another paralyzed soldier was assigned to the ward, and the men continued with the poetry readings. Somehow it made them all feel better, and while most had never been much for poetry, the soldiers came to appreciate, and look forward to, the readings.

Conor especially enjoyed the paradox of battle-hardened Confederate soldiers sitting around the hospital bed of a wounded chum, discussing the finer points of a particular poem. He led some of the discussions since he had studied poetry in several college courses. Mostly there was quiet contemplation but occasionally there would be spirited disagreement that always ran the risk of becoming loud, profane, or worse. The second paralyzed soldier lived but three days.

Conor eventually received letters from his mother, but there was never any mention of his father's interest in, or concern over, his son's wounding and convalescence. Did he care? Conor wondered. Would he ever care again? Conor could only suppose that, in the worst of cases, he no longer existed in his father's world, that his father had written off his eldest son, much like a cow sold at auction. Conor had a lot of time to think and reflect during his hospital stay, and the one firm decision he made was that he would never treat a son of his with the same heavy-handedness and estrangement that he was enduring. He simply never would, ever.

After his daily session of walking around the hospital grounds for nearly an hour to build his endurance, Conor heard the sudden piercing scream of a nurse as he came back to his ward. There, a truculent young patient from another ward was holding a surgeon's scalpel to the throat of a doctor who had been attending to an amputee. The startled nurse stood nearby, her hands over her mouth, fighting back tears of fright and panic.

"They're trying to kill me, so I'll kill them instead," the wild-eyed, gaunt, shaggy bearded man shouted.

The middle-aged doctor tried to remain calm, but the prospect of having his throat slit was making it difficult.

"They don't think I know what they're planning for me. The voices tell me. The voices tell me everything. They want to kill me, to get rid of me. And I won't let them."

The other patients in the ward watched but said nothing.

"Put the scalpel down, sir," Conor called forcefully, approaching to within fifteen feet. "Let the doctor go and put the scalpel on the ground."

"Who the hell are you?" the man said, his expression hard and threatening. "And try to take another step toward me and this here doctor will be dead before your foot hits the ground."

Conor stopped, noticing the additional pressure applied to the doctor's throat.

"Are you a soldier? Where did you serve? Were you in the battle at Manassas like I was?" Conor asked, softening his tone.

"Ain't none of your business. I'm here to get even with these doctors."

"Forget the doctor. Tell me about where you served. Were you there at Manassas like I was? Now that was one hell of a fight, wasn't it? I'll bet you were there. Am I correct?"

After a long pause, the man eased his grip slightly. "I was there. C Company, Second South Carolina. Captain Dan Remington was my commanding officer. Who were you with?"

"B Company, Seventh Georgia," Conor answered. "What's your name, soldier?"

"Grimes. Private Eric Grimes. This doctor here knows all about me. And he and his fellow butchers are trying to kill me. But today they'll lose and I'll win. It's a war with them. It's nothing but a damn war."

"Put down the scalpel, Eric. These doctors are not here to hurt you or kill you. They are trained to heal, not harm. And besides that, they're on our side."

"How the hell do you know that? Who are you, anyway?"

"I'm Captain Rafferty. We fought together at Manassas, you and I, on the same field. And you and I helped win a great victory that day. Put down the scalpel, Eric. You're a soldier. You don't hurt innocent people. That is your duty. This doctor is helping lots of soldiers here. That is his duty. You hurt him and we'll lose someone who is helping us, who is helping our fellow soldiers, and who won't be around to help those who will be coming here after us. Now put down the scalpel."

Two sergeants from a security detail, their pistols drawn and cocked, suddenly entered the ward, walking slowly and deliberately toward the scene.

"Tell those people to stay put, Captain, or I'll kill the doctor. Tell 'em I'll do it."

Conor turned and caught the attention of the two men. "Don't come any closer," he said in a calm, steady voice. "This is Captain Rafferty, and I'm ordering you to stay where you are and hold your fire."

"We've been ordered to stop this man and take him into custody, Captain."

"I've just put a hold on those orders for now. Stay where you are."

Conor then turned to Grimes. "There, Eric. They've stopped. Nobody's going to hurt you. I'm coming over there and I want you to hand me the scalpel."

The doctor's eyes bulged. Grimes stared at Conor but said nothing.

"You and I fought together, Eric. You're a soldier in a hospital, and I'm asking you as a fellow soldier to release the doctor, let him go home to his family tonight. If your mom were here, she would be saying the same thing. She would be telling you not to hurt anyone. Captain Remington would tell you the exact same thing. He would never want to hear about one of his C Company soldiers hurting an innocent man. Now give me the scalpel."

Conor took a step toward Grimes, then another.

"That's far enough, Captain," Grimes said as he released his hold on the doctor and shoved him away. "Go on, doc. Go on home to your family."

Grimes then plopped down on the floor and burst into tears, the scalpel still in his hand. The two soldiers promptly rushed Grimes, their pistols aimed at Grimes' head.

"No, don't shoot him," Conor called loudly.

"He's a crazy man," said one of the sergeants. "He's a danger to everyone here."

"He's a soldier, not a mad dog," Conor countered. "I'm ordering you, do not shoot him."

Conor calmly walked to Grimes' side and took the scalpel from his trembling hand, then patted him softly on the shoulder. Grimes looked up, his eyes wet with tears, a pleading expression on his face.

"I want to go home, Captain. Please tell them to just let me go home."

More soldiers from the security detail arrived. They brought Grimes to his feet, tied his hands behind him, and quickly whisked him from the ward.

The still-shaken doctor returned soon thereafter and thanked Conor.

Nothing further was ever heard about Eric Grimes.

During the latter stages of his convalescence, Conor received several day passes to visit a nearby tailor's shop and have another uniform made. After one such visit to claim his new gray uniform, he sat on a bench outside the hospital enjoying the unusually mild July weather. Birds were singing, roses were in bloom, and the wind gently stirred the leaves of the tall oaks that lined the street. Horse-drawn carriages with finely dressed men and women passed in that familiar *clippety-cloppety* rhythm, some nodding or tipping their hats to Conor. Elderly citizens strolled by on foot. Shops were open, a bell chimed in the distance, and children walked along with their vigilant mothers. An underfed stray dog ambled by nervously looking for a meal, reminding Conor that he had missed his own lunch. It was hard to believe that elsewhere in Virginia the celebrated Stonewall Jackson was driving the Yankees from the Shenandoah Valley as skillfully as Robert E. Lee was keeping the bluecoats away from Richmond.

Conor greatly hoped that this scenic, peaceful city of Richmond would never see the ravages of war. He also thought about his family back in Atlanta, and his two brothers who were elsewhere in the service of the Confederacy. He knew it would fall to those in uniform to make certain that no Yankee army would ever be able to capture and perhaps even destroy any of the key Southern cities. He had a hard time imagining such a condition as the capture of Richmond or Atlanta and the massive destruction and dislocation that would likely follow. We have to win, he kept thinking. We have to win no matter what.

Conor was about to return to the hospital to coax the kitchen staff into serving him a late lunch when he was approached by a lovely woman.

"Excuse me, sir, but do you work here?" she asked, nodding toward the hospital. She was dark-haired, slim, and attractively attired, and she seemed to be in her early thirties. She had a natural elegance in the way she walked and spoke and dressed, and Conor was instantly curious.

"No, ma'am. I'm actually a patient. I'm Captain Conor Rafferty," he answered, standing.

"Well, I'm very pleased to make your acquaintance, Captain. My name is Rebecca Gordon. And since you're a patient, I want to give you this," she said, holding out a small package. "There's writing paper and a small Bible inside. I'd like you to have it."

"You're very kind, ma'am. I appreciate it."

"Where are you from, Captain?"

"I'm from Atlanta, Georgia."

"Ah, what a small world. My husband and I are also from Atlanta. Maybe you know him. He's Colonel John Gordon. He practiced law in Atlanta before joining his father's coal-mining business. Now he commands a regiment in Robert Rhodes' Brigade. Have you two met?"

"No, I'm afraid not."

Mrs. Gordon looked toward the hospital. "Well, you'll get a chance soon. He should be along any minute now. We took the train this morning to pay a visit to one of John's officers and we didn't find out until we got to the hospital that he had died last night. It's been a difficult day, to put it mildly. John stayed to visit several others from his regiment, and some of those may not live to see another sunrise, God forbid. It's such a ghastly sight, some of those boys. I'm ashamed to say I had to step outside and breathe some fresh air."

"I understand, ma'am."

She nodded. "Of course you do, Captain. And we are all in your debt, sir. Were you badly injured?"

"A hip wound, from a shell. I'll be able to return to duty in a week."

Mrs. Gordon sat with Conor on the bench where they spent the next half-hour talking about many things, including the latest news from Atlanta. She was well informed, intelligent, and unpretentious for a woman of such high standing. She had a quick, rapier-sharp wit, and she didn't mind poking fun at several high-ranking Confederate generals whom she found pompous and ill-equipped to command troops. "He couldn't pour pee out of a boot," was the description she applied to one politician-general in particular whose name Conor didn't recognize.

Conor laughed aloud, and then reminded himself that it might be wise to avoid laughing at the mockery of a Confederate general from a Confederate officer's wife in the middle of the Confederate capitol. Then the image returned and he laughed out loud again. He was surprised to learn that she traveled with Colonel Gordon's Regiment, remaining dutifully in the rear when the regiment went into battle.

"I'm not going to let a little thing like a war get in the way of my being with my husband," she said with a catty smile, equal parts sassy and charming.

She looked at his left hand. "So you're not married, Captain?"

"No, ma'am."

"Anyone special back in Atlanta?"

"There was a young lady, Patricia Welch, a schoolteacher from Decatur, but I called things off when I joined the army?"

"Why?"

"I didn't think it would be a good idea to get married when I was about to be sent off to war."

"Not a good idea for her or for you?" she pressed.

"For both."

"Did you ask her what her thoughts were?"

"No ma'am, I didn't. Nor did I ever propose marriage to her."

"So you just packed your things and went off to the army?"

"Yes ma'am, pretty much. Me and thousands of others like me."

"Did she love you?"

"Yes, I believe she did."

"Did you love her?"

"I think so."

"Ah, then you did the right thing by not asking her to marry you, Captain. It would help to *know* so."

Conor laughed. "Of course."

Mrs. Gordon smiled and touched his hand. "John and I love each other a great deal, and we put up with each other's flaws because we *know* how much we love each other. When you finally find the right woman, and you know that you love her and want to marry her, then concentrate on the good things about one another and work on the other stuff. You will never find a perfect woman, Captain. And remember that any woman looking for a perfect man will never choose you."

"Thank you for that bit of wisdom, Mrs. Gordon."

Conor heard footsteps and turned to see a tall, thin Confederate officer approaching at a fast walk.

"Begging your pardon, sir, but are you attempting to endear yourself to my wife?" he said with a serious expression. "Am I interrupting something I wasn't supposed to see?"

"No sir, of course not," Conor replied, quickly standing.

"He's already endeared himself, John," Mrs. Gordon playfully interjected. "This is the endearingly delightful Captain Conor Rafferty from our wonderful city of Atlanta. Captain Rafferty, please meet Colonel John Gordon."

Colonel Gordon smiled and extended his hand. Conor saluted first and then shook the outstretched hand. Mrs. Gordon proceeded to inform her husband of Conor's wounding and his status as a patient.

"What regiment, Captain?"

"Seventh Georgia, sir. I command B Company."

"Ah yes, Dick Nichols. I know him well. Your regiment helped save the day at Manassas, from what I've heard. Thank goodness for the Seventh Georgia. Very well done, sir."

"Thank you, Colonel."

"So what did you do at Manassas?"

"I was a courier for Colonel Bartow before my horse was shot out from beneath me. Then the colonel told me that all of the officers of B Company were casualties, and I was to assume command of the company. So that's what I did."

"There was a story circulating about a brand new lieutenant taking over a retreating company and getting them back into the fight. The story I heard was he stopped a full Union regiment with something like one-hundred soldiers."

"That's pretty much right, sir."

"Ah, so was that you, Captain?" Colonel Gordon asked. "You're the famous one?"

"It was me, sir. But I'm hardly famous."

"How do you like commanding troops, Captain?"

"It's the best job in the army, sir. I haven't seen anything else I'd rather do. I'm looking forward to getting back to my soldiers now that my wound is nearly healed."

Colonel Gordon smiled and nodded his agreement. "There *is* nothing better. Leading these wonderful troops is the greatest honor of my lifetime."

Mrs. Gordon cleared her throat loudly.

Colonel Gordon grinned and added, "Second only, of course, to marrying my lovely wife."

Mrs. Gordon smiled at her husband, quickly blinking her eyes for dramatic affect.

"Captain Rafferty, do you have supper plans?" Mrs. Gordon asked.

"Dear, he's a hospital patient, not a tourist," said the colonel.

"Could you ask permission to meet us at the Spotswood Hotel for supper," she asked. "Send a note back with him, John, requiring his presence at an important military pow-wow, or something."

Colonel Gordon laughed. "He's a Confederate officer, dear. He can manage those sorts of things on his own initiative." He then turned to Conor. "We'd be honored to have you dine with us tonight. The least we can do is to treat one of our wounded fellow officers to supper at the Spotswood. And as far as I can gather, an exemplary gentleman from Atlanta, Georgia, to boot. What do you say, Captain? Can you make it by seven o'clock to join us?"

"I'll do my best to be there, sir."

Colonel Gordon leaned in and whispered, "I just came from a visit with Doctor McCaw, the Chief Surgeon. Tell him that I have given you a direct order to be at the Spotswood for supper at seven. Good officers strictly obey orders, right Captain?"

Conor grinned. "That's correct, sir. I'll be there. Thank you."

The nurses were not happy with Doctor McCaw for giving Conor permission to join the Gordons for supper, but Conor didn't care. His new uniform fit nicely, and he left and began walking to the hotel still with the limp that had yet to go away. By now he was starving since he hadn't eaten since breakfast, and then only some cornbread concoction broken up into a sort of mush with things in it he couldn't recognize but swallowed anyway. He made a vow to go easy on the alcohol since his stomach was empty. Besides, he didn't need to draw attention away from the fact that he looked strikingly handsome in his new uniform, in his own humble opinion.

Conor was prepared to walk the nearly two-dozen blocks from the hospital to the hotel at 8th and Main when a banker passing in a carriage kindly stopped, waved him over, and took him the entire distance. That Conor greatly exaggerated his limp when he heard the carriage approaching from behind may have influenced the offer of a ride, but he couldn't be certain of that.

Conor arrived well before seven, but Colonel and Mrs. Gordon were already in the lobby awaiting him. Once seated in the dining area, the colonel glanced at Conor over the top of the menu and asked, "Red wine or white?"

Conor hesitated a moment, remembering his pledge to go easy on the alcohol.

"Wine, Conor. Red or white?"

"I prefer red, sir," he said, caving with such ease that he surprised himself.

"Splendid. Our preference as well."

The beef was excellent, the French wine superb. The conversation was invigorating, ranging from battle tactics to politics to the principles of leadership. Colonel Gordon seemed to know something about everything, but he was also curious and attentive. He was easily the most intellectually adept man Conor had ever met. He was also inspiring and persuasive and forceful, all of which Conor concluded had surely made him a fine lawyer and businessman before becoming a field commander.

The colonel wanted to know how much direct participation Conor had in the training of his company, what disciplinary issues he had encountered and how he had handled them, and what he saw as the biggest obstacles to the Confederacy winning the war.

Colonel Gordon listened carefully as Conor answered his questions thoughtfully. Yet more wine arrived at the table, and yet again Conor threw caution to the wind. When Conor mentioned what he thought were obstacles to the South's winning the war—the comparatively limited industrial base, the smaller population size, the South's seeming inability to control its territorial waters—the colonel wanted to discuss further.

"Would you like to see France and England come in on our side?" he asked.

"Yes, sir. Either or both. Recognize us, support us on the seas, supply us with weapons, and buy our cotton."

"Do you think it will happen?"

"I don't know. I've read where slavery is a sore spot with the English. They began enslaving people before Roman times and officially abolished slavery thirty years ago. They are a deliberative people, those British. As for the French, I know little about them. Does anybody really know about the French?"

Colonel Gordon laughed. "Indeed."

The colonel referred to his wife as Fanny on several occasions during their time together, but Conor's reference to her was always formal. She asked about Conor's family, and he described their farm outside Atlanta.

"Does your family own slaves?" the colonel asked.

"No, sir. My father opposes it."

"Do you oppose it, Conor?"

"Yes, sir. I do."

"Do you have any opposition to anyone else owning slaves?"

"If we lived in an ideal world, I would say yes. But this wound in my hip reminds me every day that it's a long way from being an ideal world. And obviously, I come from the South where our economy depends upon slave labor. It's an established institution in our part of the world, and while I want no part of it myself, and I truly wish it

42

didn't exist, I'll leave it to others to make their own choices about owning slaves."

Colonel Gordon nodded his understanding.

"Let me give you a hypothetical, Conor. Tell me what you would do if I put you in charge of an infantry company that was the worst in the entire brigade. Moreover, they are the worst because their desertion rate is the highest, their discipline is the poorest, and their military skills such as shooting, marching, and navigating ground without becoming lost are deplorable. What would you do?"

The colonel filled Conor's wine glass.

"Tell me how Captain Conor Rafferty would fix this sorry mess of a company."

"Well, Colonel, first I would locate the best sergeants and corporals I could find and get rid of the current crop."

"Okay. What else?"

"Then I would lay out exactly what I expected of the enlisted leaders, and when I wanted everything done."

"Yes? And?"

"And then I would gather all the men and congratulate them, informing them that they have just become part of the best company in the regiment. And by the way, our training starts tonight. Pack all your things because we will not be back in camp for a long while. We will learn to move faster, shoot straighter, and fight harder than anything the Yankees have ever seen. We will move quickly into battle, but never quickly away from it. In addition, they will be able to count on me being up at the front, leading and making sure the sergeants and corporals are also leading. Our battle flag will set us apart as the best—the best fighters, the best looking, the most ferocious Johnny Rebs on the field. And as a result I will help save the lives of many of my men by our being better in battle than the people we oppose."

The colonel smiled. "Very well said. Yes, *very* well said. Now, if you got your hands on a deserter, would you shoot him to make an example of him?"

"No, sir. I would give him a rifle and tell him that I would rather use my ammunition on the Federals than him. I would tell him that his brothers will need that extra rifle when the shooting starts, so I am giving it back to him and letting him have a chance to earn back his self-respect. The men will know that I will never shoot one of my own, but I will remind them that cowardice in the face of the enemy will be a fate worse than death. If that same man stands his ground and fights with us, and is prepared to fight with us to the end, he will no longer be a deserter. He will be redeemed, a gallant soldier in the best company in the regiment. Such a thing might come in handy when he gets home to his sweetheart."

Colonel Gordon shot a quick glance at Fanny, who nodded slightly and sipped her wine.

"How can you know that the men will fight hard when they get into battle?" the Colonel asked.

"I won't know the answer to that question, sir, until I actually see how they perform once the shooting starts. Only then will I know for sure. However, I'll have a good idea, a really good idea, based upon the way they've trained. There's a strong connection between their preparation and their performance under fire."

"You should know, Captain. You've fought your own companies enough to test that connection."

"Sir, my experience in battle is somewhat limited."

Colonel Gordon blinked. "Limited in quantity but I would guess high in quality."

Conor blushed slightly. "Thank you, sir."

Conor noticed Colonel Gordon staring at him, as if he were fully digesting what the younger officer had told him. The colonel finally smiled broadly and extended his hand.

"Well, Conor, you have been a delightful supper companion, my dear sir. Fanny and I have thoroughly enjoyed having you dine with us. You may be aware that I had no military training prior to the start of the war, so I've been very interested in what you've had to say about leadership. I'm impressed, and I can say without hesitation that I've learned some worthwhile things from you this evening. I can only hope you've learned something as well. We should do this again sometime."

"I'd be honored, sir. Thank you for your kindness. And thanks to you also, ma'am."

The colonel arranged for a carriage and hotel employee to transport Conor back to the hospital.

Conor spent the next several days exercising and taking increasingly longer walks in and around the hospital in an effort to regain his endurance. He continued to limp slightly, the area around the wound was still numb and the muscles still tender, but the pain was manageable. He was eager to get back to take his place with 7th Georgia and B Company, and he wondered how the company might be doing without him. The hospital's patient population continued to expand, causing Conor to realize that the war was far from slowing. If anything, judging by the growing numbers of new wounded, the level of fighting was steadily intensifying.

Conor got more letters from his mother informing him that his brothers Sean and Daniel were serving in Virginia and Tennessee, respectively. His mother wrote that Sean had already participated in several battles, but that Daniel had made no mention of his experience to date. Once again, she did not refer to his father, but she hoped Conor's recovery was still going well. She wanted to know if he had received the shelled pecans and roasted peanuts she had earlier sent in a package addressed to him at the hospital.

Conor frowned. Several patients had already told him that foodstuffs sent to patients had about as much chance of reaching their final destination as that of a candle remaining lit in a Florida hurricane. Conor thought it despicable that some rogue mail clerk or orderly would steal from the wounded of the Confederacy, an act of treachery that should earn the offenders an immediate assignment to the front. Perhaps then, coming back as a patient, the thieves might understand the value that mail and packages had on the wounded men. Conor wrote his mother in return and thanked her for the delicious nuts, which he was sure were enjoyable to some nameless, shameless, dishonorable cheat.

Later, in the wee hours of the night, Conor posted a large handwritten sign in the hallway of the building which stated the following: "To the scoundrel who stole the package of nuts sent to me by my Dear Mother—I will make it a priority to find out who you are, and then I will enter your home in the dark of night and shoot you in both knees."

Another patient scrawled at the bottom of the sign: "As for the scallywag who stole my box of oranges—there will be an additional pistol shot from me, but I shall not tell you in advance where I'll aim it."

The sign didn't stay up long.

The day before his scheduled release from the hospital, Conor received the following written message: "To Conor Rafferty, Captain, 7th Georgia Infantry Regiment, CSA, Subject: Return to Duty. You are herewith directed to proceed without delay on or about 2 August 1862 and report to Colonel John B. Gordon, CSA, Commanding Officer, 6th Alabama Infantry Regiment, in the vicinity of Monocacy Junction, Virginia, for duty."

I'll be damned, Conor thought. He did it! Colonel Gordon had somehow appropriated him from the 7th Georgia to the colonel's Alabama regiment. Conor would be leaving B Company and assuming his duties in an unknown capacity with an unknown organization, but he was elated at his seemingly good fortune. The colonel really did it, he thought, laughing. He stole me away from my regiment. Did they object? Do they even know?

Conor was greatly excited for such an opportunity. He was healthy again, he had his orders for a return to duty and a new assignment, and he would be working for a splendid officer. Things were good, really good. He couldn't wait to report to his new regiment and see what Colonel Gordon had in mind for him.

He hadn't noticed the package on the floor at the foot of his bunk. When he picked it up and examined it, he discovered to his great surprise that it was the package from his mother containing the pecans and peanuts.

Yes, he concluded. It was a very good day, indeed.

***

Sunday, February 10, 1918

"You look tired, Cappy," Aaron noted. "Why don't we wrap it up for today and start again in the morning?"

"Yes, that's fine. Did you learn anything worthwhile today?"

Conor watched as Aaron considered the question for a moment.

Aaron put away his notes, took in a deep breath and then pushed back in his chair. "Several things caught my attention: First, how difficult it must have been for Robert E. Lee and other professional soldiers from the South to decide to leave the army they had given so much to, and join the Confederacy, even at the risk of being treated as a traitor. Second, how unbending the South was in maintaining its agricultural economy based on slave labor, even when doing so might result in war. And third, how odd it seems now that Americans from different regions of the country could have reached a point of mutual mistrust and contempt so intense that shooting and killing each other in massive numbers seemed the only viable alternative."

Conor nodded his agreement.

"But the one thing that stands out to me the most," said Aaron, incredulously, "is that it would have been virtually impossible for the people of either side to know beforehand just how devastating the war would actually become. Hardly anyone could have foreseen such a level of loss in lives and property. It had to be incomprehensible to many, if not most."

"I certainly didn't know. My father seemed to see into the future better than most, but I don't know how he could have grasped the full extent of the carnage."

"Thank you, Cappy. This is going to be an unforgettable week."

Aaron grabbed his overcoat and started toward the door.

"Good night, sir. See you first thing in the morning."

"Good night, Aaron. And thank you, as well."

Chapter Three

Bloody Sharpsburg

Avenge the patriotic gore
That flecked the streets of Baltimore,
And be the battle queen of yore.
Maryland! My Maryland!
"Maryland! My Maryland!"

September, 1862
Colonel Gordon assigned Conor to F Company, which the other companies in the regiment liked to joke that "F" was precisely the grade the company deserved. The general told Conor to put his plan into action for all the regiment to see, that there would be great interest in watching what F Company would become.

Conor went to work immediately. He transferred out the weakest of the junior leaders, and he found an outstanding sergeant who was new to the regiment and awaiting assignment. The sergeant understood exactly what Conor wanted to do, and Colonel Gordon made the transfer happen within hours. Conor and his new sergeant then went about training the company as hard and as thoroughly as the limited time permitted. Sergeant Gilbert Tanneyhill hailed from Mobile, Alabama—a tall, strapping, fearless lad, easily the best non-commissioned officer Conor had come across thus far. Sergeant Tanneyhill was dark-haired and dark-eyed, with a space between two front teeth that protruded slightly. He had a keen mind—a clear, insightful thinker with an ability to see shapes and patterns where

49

others saw only lines. The young soldiers responded well to his leadership. He was smart, tough, demanding, and fair.

Conor and Tanneyhill worked the men to a point where several considered running away, but the soldiers hung on and stayed together. Before long most began to see the worth of what their commander was attempting to do. The junior leaders assumed the strong leadership roles demanded of them, but they also saw they were being trusted to do their jobs. The mutual trust among the soldiers and their leaders eventually enabled a strong unit cohesion.

Conor knew F Company was making solid progress. None of the troops had deserted, none had experienced any disciplinary issues, and none had tried to dodge the harsh training by claiming to be sick or injured, which were all positive signs. The men began to take pride in their company and in themselves, unlike before. The other companies in the regiment also took notice. Colonel Gordon brought General Rodes, the brigade commander, to inspect F Company and the general said he thought the way the company was shaping up that it just might turn out to be the best in the entire brigade. Conor could see the pride in the men's eyes, and he was confident they were going to give a good account of themselves. He also knew that only when the men were tested under fire would their full progress be demonstrated.

Conor and his men began crossing the Potomac River into Maryland on September 4, 1862. His soldiers were lightly equipped, and his F Company was part of General Daniel Harvey Hill's Division that was protecting the right and rear of General Lee's Army of Northern Virginia. Conor marched at the head of his column along with Sergeant Tanneyhill as they moved along at a brisk, steady pace. The landscape was replete with rich farmland interrupted occasionally by a small town or village. The corn in the fields was tall, and there was lots of it. The curious citizens of the Maryland towns they passed through came out to see this highly publicized, mighty Confederate war machine for themselves. The young women would often smile and wave while the young Maryland men would just stare, some in admiration, others in disbelief. Sergeant Tanneyhill observed that the Maryland men were expecting well-fed, muscular giants of perhaps ten feet in height, given the Confederate exploits on the battlefield to date. However, what they saw were many barefoot, scarecrow-thin, shaggy Southern soldiers, some in gray uniforms, some in butternut-colored clothing, wearing a wide array of shapes and sizes in hats, and all of the men dirty and covered in dust.

"I'm bettin' they can smell us before they can see us," Sergeant Tanneyhill said laughingly.

"Do you think the Maryland men will join us?" Conor asked Tanneyhill. "Will they 'rally to the cause' and march off with General Lee and the rest of us?"

"Hell no, sir. Why would they want to do that?"

Conor began laughing. "I don't know. Maybe they're as crazy as we are."

"If we keep losing all these stragglers, F Company may be all that General Lee has left to fight the Yankees with."

"Then that would prove my point about how crazy we really are," Conor said.

They both laughed.

One of F Company's soldiers, Private Adams, who was marching immediately behind Tanneyhill, suddenly blurted out, "Will it be okay if some of those pretty girls rally to our cause, Captain?"

"I'm guessing we're talking about different causes here, Adams. But before she can rally to us for any cause she would first have to know how to fire a musket."

A nearby soldier quickly called out, "Adams couldn't shoot the balls off a bull at ten paces, Captain, yet he's out here with us."

"Then I'll modify the qualifications," Conor said, adding, "and we'll trade Adams for *any* girl who can shoot."

The laughter among the men was immediate and loud.

"You're all wrong, Simpson," Adams countered. "I could easily hit a bull's balls at ten paces. It's your balls I couldn't hit at even two paces because they're so damn small."

"And how is it you know about the size of my balls, Adams?"

"Why, your sweetheart back in Fairhope told me one night. One *really* good night. For her, I mean."

And so it was on. Other soldiers chimed in, and soon the comments were ribald and soon after that outright vulgar. It quickly became a contest.

Sergeant Tanneyhill and Conor looked at one another and shrugged.

Despite their ragged appearance, the Confederates moved along with a certain élan, a confidence in their arms and their commanding general that they would prevail no matter the odds, that when the shooting ceased, the field would be theirs, and fairly won. Lee's army had just recorded another victory, this one at Second Manassas, though the 6th Alabama had not participated.

The soldiers were being pushed hard enough on the march to understand that General Lee was in a hurry to find the Yankees and offer them battle. One of the regimental staff officers had passed along a newspaper account of the recent Second Manassas victory, and it brought back a flood of memories for Conor. Winning a stunning victory in Maryland might just alter the course of the war enough so that the European powers could then be enticed to join the Confederacy. The soldiers all understood how much was at stake in this campaign.

With Colonel Gordon's regiment bringing up the rear of the long column, Conor and Sergeant Tanneyhill began encountering large numbers of stragglers who had been unable to maintain the pace, or who were simply content to give up and go back to Virginia.

"Form up on us, boys," Conor would call to the clusters of laggards. "We are the rear of this army. Don't walk away or you'll regret it forever. Your musket can't help us if it goes back with you. Stay with us and do your duty. On your feet, boys. Come with us and fight."

Some would reconsider and reluctantly fall in at the rear of our column. Some would sit on the side of the road and wait for the others to pass with no intention of going any further. There were hundreds, perhaps even thousands, falling out. Several officers on horseback rode among the stragglers, alternately cajoling them to rejoin the column or threatening them with a firing squad for desertion. Whenever they took a short break from the marching, Conor would ask Sergeant Tanneyhill how many F Company soldiers had dropped out.

"None, sir," he reported each time to Conor's great relief.

On September 13, General Lee's Special Orders, No. 191, which detailed the disposition of his divided Army of Northern Virginia, fell into the hands of the Union commander General George McClellan, as if it were a divine gift. The orders, wrapped around a bundle of cigars, were found in a field and quickly delivered to McClellan, who could easily see that Lee's army was dangerously divided with Jackson at Harper's Ferry, Longstreet moving toward Hagerstown, and D.H. Hill guarding the rear. When General Lee found out from a Southern sympathizer that McClellan had possession of the orders, he directed that his entire army concentrate at Sharpsburg, Maryland, on Antietam Creek. Hill's Division, and thus Colonel Gordon's 6th Alabama Regiment, proceeded to South

Mountain to guard Crampton's Gap and Turner's Gap and its subsidiary Fox's Gap, thereby ensuring that the Federals would be unable to utilize those mountain passes to maneuver between Lee's forces and thereby destroy his army in detail.

There was a great sense of urgency developing among the senior officers. Generals Lee and Rodes rode among their soldiers several times to direct the men forward with great dispatch. There was a distinctive, familiar feeling that came upon Conor when a battle was imminent—that the die is already cast and there is nothing he can do about it—and that feeling resided in his belly so thickly that he had to force himself to eat, almost as if there weren't enough room for both.

The first shots of the Maryland Campaign were fired on the morning of September 14 at Turner's Gap and Fox's Gap. Conor's F Company was positioned north of Turner's Gap on the extreme left of the Confederate positions. Large numbers of Union infantry, supported by artillery, launched a furious attack in an attempt to gain control of those critical passes. Conor's soldiers resisted with equal fury, and for the first time as F Company's commander he was facing the enemy in battle. His men were pouring sheets of flaming musket fire into the blue lines, dropping their soldiers in large numbers but likewise taking casualties in return. The Federals kept coming, however, pressing the Confederates, trying to flank them, killing and wounding them in equally large numbers. A Federal officer on horseback, a man of about Conor's age, rapidly approached at a close range and fired a single pistol shot that sliced through the top of Conor's hat, barely creasing his scalp. Conor returned fire with his own pistol, striking the Union officer three times in the torso. The man lurched and fell sidelong from his horse, limp and unmoving, before two Federal soldiers quickly picked him up in a blanket and moved him to the rear. Several times

Conor grabbed the musket of a dead Confederate and began firing at the advancing enemy. The noise of the gunfire, the concussion of the exploding shells, and the incessant shouting were all so incomprehensibly loud that suddenly it was no longer loud, as odd as it seems. Everywhere men were suffering and dying, the smell of blood and powder in the air, the deadly projectiles, large and small, flying across and into what Sergeant Tanneyhill had termed "that deadly space."

Bullets were striking the trees near where Conor stood, as if someone behind him was pounding the bark with a hammer. An artillery shell flew by after skipping off the ground in front of him, striking rocks and leaving showers of sparks in its wake, decapitating the unlucky private who was standing next to Conor. He turned and gazed at the ghastly spectacle, a sight so grotesque that it very nearly brought him to a point of nausea.

The Confederates counterattacked on several occasions but could never succeed in accomplishing anything more than temporarily stemming the onslaught of the Federals, whose numbers were stronger on every part of the line. In addition, with each attack and counterattack Conor's F Company losses grew, as did those of the entire regiment. They were killing plenty of Yankees, to be sure, but the fighting was so close and intense that the exchanges of gunfire were mostly at distances of no more than thirty yards, often closer.

Colonel Gordon moved among his companies, shifting the men this way or that, shouting orders and words of encouragement, seemingly oblivious to the chaos enveloping them. "You are the end of the line, Captain Rafferty. This is the extreme Confederate left. You cannot allow them to flank you. Do what you must, but under no circumstances allow them to flank you."

"Understood, sir."

"Kill 'em, Captain. Keep them in front of you and destroy 'em. You cannot be flanked."

"You can count on F Company, sir."

When Conor explained to Sergeant Tanneyhill that their orders were to deny the enemy their flank, the sergeant took a deep breath and pointed toward the front.

"They ain't shrinking, Captain, they're reinforcing. If we don't do the same, they'll keep attacking us until they finally wear us down and then chew us up like a pack of wild dogs. I'm guessing our company's facing an entire regiment, and those ain't good odds, sir."

The unblinking Conor stared hard at Sergeant Tanneyhill. "We will not be flanked, Sergeant. Not now, not ever. Those are my orders and those are now your orders. Are we clear?"

"Yessir," Tanneyhill said, moving away quickly to check on the disposition of their troops on the exposed left.

The Federals attacked repeatedly, each one seemingly more determined than the last. F Company continued to take casualties, but they also resisted ferociously and in doing so inflicted enough losses to cause the Yankees to break off and reorganize before attacking again. Conor saw their repeated pattern of attack, retreat, reorganize, and attack again, and he expertly timed a counterattack to drive into their retreating line. The Federals were surprised by the quick strike and left the field in a much bigger hurry, but barely fifteen minutes passed before they were back again, attacking in force. At one point General Rodes and Colonel Gordon both appeared on horseback behind F Company's thinning line, shouting words of encouragement and firing their pistols at the approaching Federals.

"Give it to 'em, boys," Conor heard Colonel Gordon calling above the noise.

For several tense hours, Conor and his men remained in imminent danger of being flanked. Finally, at about 3:00 pm, General Longstreet's reinforcements reached the field. These additional troops bolstered Conor's left flank and added desperately needed depth all across the Southern positions. By 4:00 pm, yet even more Confederate troops arrived, allowing Conor to hold intact the F Company position until darkness fell. His company had begun the Maryland Campaign with a strength of 88 soldiers, but by nightfall the count had fallen to 59. Sergeant Tanneyhill did an admirable job of shifting the men around to fill in the gaps made by the casualties, and his personal leadership was both inspirational and skillful. More than once Conor drew strength from Tanneyhill's brave example of poise and professionalism under fire, and he was certain that many of the younger troops did likewise. As for Conor's own performance in command of his new company, he was generally pleased. His troops responded to his orders; his orders were timely and clearly stated; and he began to anticipate the moves of the enemy and could thus counter with moves of his own.

And, most importantly, he wasn't flanked. To say he was relieved about not yielding the line would be a significant understatement. He had never before experienced a day that had demanded so much of his energy, both mental and physical. He felt exhausted, but he somehow found additional reserves to keep him on an even pace with the events as they unfolded. This was going to be a long war, he kept thinking. Once again, he wished that his father could have seen the manner in which his "too soft, too naïve, and too concerned with his own welfare" son had led F Company in battle.

The regiment pulled out of its position at South Mountain and made a night march through Boonsboro to Sharpsburg. Colonel Gordon placed F Company at the front of the regiment after telling Conor that the 6th Alabama had lost one-third of its strength in the day's fighting, which was consistent with F Company's losses. The Confederate commanders were concerned that McClellan would push his Federal army to pursue them, but nothing of the sort transpired. After several hours, the regiment reached Sharpsburg and took up positions along Antietam Creek. The men were drained after days of marching and a full day of hard fighting, but the news that Stonewall Jackson had successfully captured the Federal arsenal at Harpers Ferry and was now moving toward Sharpsburg was reassuring.

Colonel Gordon asked Conor to sit with him at a campfire after the colonel had provided the next day's orders in a meeting with his company commanders. An orderly brought coffee, and Conor lit a cigar that General Rodes' adjutant, a new friend, had given him on the march over from South Mountain.

"We will be attacked here in this location, Conor, and I expect it to come in full force, and I mean with everything McClellan's got. He will have the advantage in numbers and firepower, and if he throws it all at us early, we'll have a fight on our hands. If he delays and deploys his units piecemeal, we can meet them and destroy them in detail. Either way, we're in for a hell of a fight here. I can see it coming."

"Maybe they'll turn tail and run when they feel the full weight of Southern steel again," Conor said, but then added, "although they didn't run today. If they're coming here tomorrow to go at us like they did today, then you're right, sir. We'd better be ready to fight."

"I think it's very likely they've been given specific orders to find us and destroy us. We're too close to Baltimore and Washington for them to do anything else. Which means, we'll have our chance to offer them battle on this ground, whip them, and maybe put an end to this war."

When Conor told Colonel Gordon that his mother's recent letter informed him that his brother Sean was with the 10th Georgia Regiment, the colonel pointed out that the 10th Georgia was a part of General Semmes' Brigade.

"I'll go look for him."

"Of course. Go and find him."

Conor got up and started to leave.

"Just one more thing, Conor," said Colonel Gordon. "I fully expect you to be the leader that I deeply believe you are, because we're going to need all the strong leadership we can get once this thing starts tomorrow. I know you'll be at your best, and you'll have to be. We all will. There's no other choice now."

Conor saluted and went off in search of the 10th Georgia amidst all the units scattered across the Sharpsburg landscape. It took some doing, but he finally located Sean asleep on the ground with other members of his company. A campfire provided ample light, and Conor stepped over several sleeping soldiers until he reached Sean, stretched out on his side with his pack and rifle beside him.

Conor leaned over his brother and tapped him on the shoulder. "Corporal Sean Rafferty, get your sorry carcass up and get on your feet. General Longstreet wants to see you. Now!"

Sean stirred only slightly. "Tell General Longstreet to send for me in the morning and I'll be happy to have breakfast with him. Otherwise, he can kiss my big Irish arse. I'm sleeping now, if you hadn't noticed."

"Get up, Corporal Rafferty. That's a direct order from Captain Rafferty."

Sean looked up in the dim light and then quickly sat up. "I'll be damned. I'll just be damned."

They both started laughing as they lunged into a long hug. For a fleeting moment Conor was home again, and it felt so good and so familiar that it warmed him as much as the campfire. They stood and talked for nearly an hour about home, about the action they had seen and the wound Conor had received, and about the jobs they were now doing. Eventually the other members of Sean's company told them for the umpteenth time to quiet down and allow them to sleep. They moved away and stood on the far side of the fire. Sean had seen no action at South Mountain, but instead had been on the road to Sharpsburg with Semmes' Brigade. The brothers had learned from their mother that their younger brother Daniel was serving in Tennessee with the 5th Georgia, but neither had any further word on his activities to date.

"He's just a kid," Conor said. "God, I hope he's okay."

"He's a Rafferty, remember? He'll be fine," Sean replied. "Oh, and I've got a funny story to tell you about Daniel."

"Yeah? Let's hear it."

"Right before I left for the army, I took a walk around the farm with Daniel and his girlfriend Paige. Remember Paige?"

"Sure. The pretty girl whose father owned the feed store in Atlanta."

"Yes, that's right. Anyway, the three of us are having a stroll near the northeast pasture. Daniel is holding Paige's hand and they're giggling like they always do. All of a sudden Daniel stops and points over to where a bull is busy doing his duty with a young cow. Daniel says, 'Ah, yes. That's what I'd like to do,' and then he looks over at Paige and grins. Well, she looks back at Daniel and says, 'Do you think the bull would mind?' Daniel's face turned as red as a ripened tomato, and I nearly fell over laughing."

The two brothers cackled so hard that yet another admonishment came from several of Sean's fellow soldiers.

"Heard anything from Father?" Sean finally asked.

"Nope, nothing. And I don't expect to. Have you heard from him?"

"Yes. He wrote to me recently."

"Oh?"

"Yes. He said he was concerned that he was going to lose all his sons to the war. He wanted to tell you that he was sorry, that he shouldn't have blamed you for me and Daniel deciding to join the army, and that you had always been the wise and solid one he knew he could count on. And now he was afraid that you would never want to see or speak to him again."

"Why the hell did he tell you that and not me?"

"I don't know, Conor. I wish I knew. Father has his ways, for sure. Know what I mean?"

"Yes," Conor said with a sigh. "Of course I do."

Sean cleared his throat and then hit Conor lightly on the shoulder. "Don't go and get yourself wounded again, big brother, even if you are a high and mighty officer. I see your hat has a hole in it, so be careful, please."

Conor grinned and put his finger in the gap. "Damned Yankee captain made a run at me and got off a shot before I blew him off his horse."

"Kill him?"

"Yeah, I think so," Conor said, nodding. "The dust flew off his chest three times when I fired."

"I can't wait to kill me some Yankees," Sean said with all the martial ardor he had often exhibited before the war.

"They'll be enough to go around, I'm sure. Take care of yourself, Sean."

"You do the same, Cap'n. I'll see you when this is over."

They shook hands, and then ended with another long hug. Conor wished for a moment that he and his brothers could all go home again. How good it would be to see their mother and fill the house with their laughter, their stomachs with her cooking, and their nostrils with the familiar smells of the farm. Conor had a huge lump in his throat as he left Sean and returned to his company. Then he thought of his father and the warm thoughts of home promptly dissipated.

The concentration of the Army of Northern Virginia was complete on September 16, with only General A.P. Hill's Division remaining at Harper's Ferry. The Potomac River was at the Confederates' back, and with only a limited number of locations shallow enough for infantry fording, theirs was certainly not an ideal strategic position. The thought crossed Conor's mind more than once that they could be destroyed by the superior Federal numbers if pushed hard enough, but he resolved that at least F Company would not allow such a condition to develop on its small portion of the battlefield.

Too, they had Robert E. Lee on their side.

The shooting started early on September 17, on the left of the Confederate lines. The Federals assaulted toward a wooded area, across a main north-south road, and came under intense fire from Stonewall Jackson's soldiers. Southern troops soon counterattacked through a cornfield where the volume of fire was so heavy and so concentrated that the corn stalks were literally shot away by the tens of thousands of flying bullets. The fighting was so close and desperate that entire rows of men of both sides remained where they fell. The corn stalks were not the only objects hit. The opposing artillery batteries were firing at the masses of infantry troops and the cannons supporting them. Conor noticed to his left an entire Confederate battery that was suddenly destroyed by counterbattery fire, men and horses alike, its guns now silent. There was an ebb and flow to the fighting, first one side gaining the advantage, then the other. Conor could see the troops under Confederate battle flags advancing toward the cornfield where the Federals under the Stars and Stripes were in an orderly, deliberate retreat.

Conor's F Company, with the 6th Alabama Regiment, was positioned on the unit's extreme right but near the overall center of the Confederate line. He could see nearly the entire field before him, with the slight waves in the terrain on either side of a narrow valley leading north to the cornfields. There was a small church to his left-front, surrounded on three sides by thick woods, off the main road and directly across from one of the Confederate artillery batteries. To his rear was the Potomac River, and to his immediate front was a sunken road, a dirt farm lane worn by years of wagon traffic and erosion. The road generally ran east-west until it bent sharply to the south, on his far right, after several hundred yards. D.H. Hill's entire division positioned itself along this road, some 2,600 men, all of whom could see the Yankees forming to their front to commence an attack. While no shots had yet been fired at the Confederates posted along the sunken road, the troops nevertheless piled fence rails on the embankment to provide cover while they awaited the arrival of the Federals. Conor and his men held the most advanced position on their part of the field, with no supporting lines behind them. Once again, to be flanked would endanger not just Hill's Division, but the entire army.

Conor saw puffs of smoke from the Federal artillery in the distance, only seconds before the shells began crashing around his position. Confederate artillery answered, and the duel of the cannons added to the level of smoke and noise enveloping the area.

At one point in the morning there was a lull on the left, and Generals Lee and Hill rode along the lines. They spoke to Colonel Gordon, advising him of the importance of holding his position at all costs. All were captivated by the sight of the gray-haired, gray-bearded, gray-uniformed General Lee, sitting straight and tall in the saddle atop Traveller. His powerful presence stirred the hearts of his soldiers, and his calm, self-assured demeanor instilled a confidence that every soldier very much wanted and needed. Conor had never before seen another human being in any endeavor have the sort of near-spiritual appeal to men of all types as did General Lee to the soldiers of his army. Always without fail, the troops cheered him wildly when he appeared on the battlefield.

Colonel Gordon was moved to the point of shouting, "These men are going to stay here, General, 'till the sun goes down or victory is won."

Both generals saluted Colonel Gordon when they heard his declaration.

At 9:30 am, just minutes after the departure of the two generals, the Federals moved into position with an assault front of four lines in depth. With bayonets fixed, the Union soldiers aligned themselves smartly and started moving toward the Confederate positions, their commander on horseback in front, sitting tall in the saddle with his sabre drawn. Colonel Gordon sent word that his soldiers were to lie down, take aim, and wait for his order to commence firing. Thus they waited as the Federal troops kept steadily advancing, coming ever closer with each step. The silence across the entire field was unnerving, and several of Conor's troops became anxious once the men in blue had advanced within rifle range.

"Steady, boys. Hold your fire," Conor said as he walked slowly behind his F Company troops with Sergeant Tanneyhill. "Wait for the order. Hold your fire, boys."

The Federals finally advanced to a point where Conor could read the "US" insignia on their brass belt buckles when Colonel Gordon suddenly shouted, "*Fire!*"

The first volley erupted into a sheet of flame across the entire Confederate line, their bullets cutting down the Federal front line almost in its entirety, with the Southerners quickly standing and pouring successive volleys into the brave but staggered Yankees. The Union soldiers had yet to fire a shot, and they were dropping into piles so fast that, for the Confederates, it was at once an exhilarating and obscene sight. Colonel Gordon shouted to Conor that they were attempting to break the line in a bayonet charge, but that the Federals would soon enough load and fire on them. Conor found it odd that they would expect to gouge the Confederates into submission. F Company kept firing, the Yankees kept falling, and soon the Union commander, whose horse had been killed, began an orderly retreat. Once he had reformed his men out of Confederate musket range, the resolute Union commander led another attack and was again repulsed. This sequence of retreating and reforming was repeated twice more before the Federal troops finally unleashed a terrific volley into the Rebel line. Conor couldn't fail to notice the large number of passing balls within a whisker's distance from him. The fighting was vicious and deadly, at a range so close that the troops of either side could hardly miss.

Conor looked out at yet another Federal line advancing toward him, and it was then he noticed the green flag with the harp symbol in the middle. It was the flag of the Irish Brigade, and Conor's heart sank when he realized that the deadly accurate bullets from his company were killing Irish immigrants, sons of Ireland much like the Southern commander who was opposing them. The casualties among the soldiers of the Irish Brigade were shocking, yet they kept coming. Oddly enough Conor was proud of them, of their astonishing bravery, for by now he was convinced that the Irish on both sides would all die in this place.

Conor was firing his pistol, reloading, and firing again. Men were lying prone all around him, and the Federals were bringing more men into the fray. It was slaughter at close quarters, a horrifying sight even to men who had become hardened by battle and bloodletting. He briefly wondered about Sean and what danger he might be facing. It was clear from what he had seen of the early fighting, now to include the struggle along this sunken road, that it would be an especially deadly encounter. He hoped for his mother's sake that she wouldn't receive the news of her two sons' deaths at this ruinous place. When

Conor glanced to his far right he saw the Federals maneuvering to get in position to flank his soldiers and create an enfilade fire down the length of the road. He called out, "Oh dear God, no! That will devastate us."

"No, no, no!" Conor shouted with a point to his right. "Stop them from flanking us. Push out and stop them."

None of the Confederate troops were moving toward the Federals on their right.

"No! Do not let them flank us," Conor shouted again, pointing, but to no avail.

Inexplicably, some of the Confederate soldiers under the command of an adjacent regiment were withdrawing from the road. By the abandonment of their positions they were enabling the Federals to begin their flanking maneuver. Nearby Confederate officers who saw the danger of the exposed flank were trying to retrieve the men, only some of whom returned. The others were in an orderly retreat, much as if they had been ordered to do so. It was a gift the Federals did not hesitate to exploit. Conor glanced behind him several times to look for reinforcements, but there were none. The bodies of the Southern troops were lining the floor of the sunken road so densely that one could have walked its length without setting foot on the bare ground.

A hand reached toward him as Conor stepped over the bodies.

"Captain Rafferty," a young private called in a raspy voice. "Captain Rafferty, sir."

Conor leaned over and grasped his hand. He was gutshot and ashen-colored, his breathing labored, his eyelids heavy. He was a new enlistee, and Conor remembered him as being a nineteen-year-old from Dothan.

Conor leaned in closer. "What can I do for you, soldier?"

"Please tell my momma I fought bravely. Will you do that for me, sir?"

"You can tell her yourself when you get well and go home. Tell me your name, soldier."

"It's Samuel Prescott, sir."

"Yes, of course, Samuel. Now I remember. And you should remember this: All those pretty girls in Dothan are counting on you coming back home and courting them."

The smile left the young private's face in gradations, as did the rhythm of his breathing, until soon there was neither.

Conor found a loaded musket and turned to seek a target. When he looked up he saw a Federal soldier taking aim at him from a distance of ten yards. The muzzle flash and the bullet's striking him were virtually instantaneous.

The ball struck Conor in the left shoulder, passing just above the armpit. He fell backward and hit the ground hard, like a bale of cotton dropped from a freight car, but he quickly recovered to a point where he could stand and fire the loaded musket at the enemy soldier who had shot him. With one arm, Conor balanced the musket and aimed high, hitting the Federal soldier in the neck. He then dropped the musket and moved his right hand to check his wounded shoulder, feeling the thick, sticky blood. The pain was immediate and severe, making him slightly nauseous. In an instant, a second ball knocked off Conor's hat and creased his skull, parting his hair on the left side and leaving a stream of blood running down the side of his face. His left arm was useless, and when he sat down and clumsily reloaded his pistol, he quickly expended those rounds without ever standing. He got up and searched for more loaded muskets among the bodies of his dead and dying troops. He found another, and after firing the rifle at a Yankee officer and hitting him, a third ball blew off the top two joints of the little finger on his right hand.

"Dammit!" he screamed when he looked at the bloody red mess at the end of his hand. *"You sons of bitches!"* He tried to climb up and over the embankment to get at the pistol the dead Union officer had dropped, but he struggled getting up the slope.

Sergeant Tanneyhill came over and steadied Conor when he began to stagger backward from the rise. "You've gotta get away from here, Captain. You're losing too much blood."

"I'm okay," he said. "See to the men. I'll be fine."

Conor's mouth was dry, and he was beginning to feel faint. Someone shouted that Colonel Gordon had been wounded and removed from the field. Meanwhile, the Yankees were pouring ever-increasing volleys into the Rebels' diminishing ranks. The fourth ball struck Conor on the outside of the right calf, passing through the flesh and muscle but not breaking the bone. He fell onto the body of a soldier who moaned loudly when the wounded man felt Conor's full weight on his own badly wounded leg. Conor heard someone call, "Get the captain out of here," before two of his troops grabbed him by his arms and legs to lift him, unleashing a torrent of pain that rushed through him as rapidly and forcefully as water surging over a breached dike.

The soldier holding Conor's legs was struck in the back by a bullet and fell forward onto him, fracturing Conor's left wrist. The soldier behind Conor pulled him free while another man came and lifted his legs. The two men struggled to climb out of the lane with Conor's weight in their grasp, and both fell at one point only to lift him again and proceed to the rear. Conor thought he could sense the sound of the firing gradually lessening, or perhaps it was his own consciousness giving way, but at any rate soon everything around him became quiet.

That is all he remembered from the Bloody Lane.

Conor awakened several hours later in a house in Sharpsburg that was being utilized as a field hospital. A doctor saw him attempt to sit up and walked over to check on him.

"I'm Doctor Whitmire, one of the regimental surgeons. Your wounds have been dressed, Captain, and your wrist has been immobilized. You should be fine in due course."

"Did you have to amputate anything?" Conor asked as he began taking an inventory of his extremities.

"No, nothing that wasn't already missing," he said with a point toward his hand, which was heavily bandaged. "You were only minutes away from expiring due to blood loss. And no, we didn't take your arm or leg off, and your scalp wound was sufficiently minor that we didn't take your head off."

"Sufficiently minor. All right, then," Conor said, feeling the bandage on his head. "With all due respect, Doctor, I find your humor so sufficiently minor that you'll forgive me if I don't laugh my damn self into a coma. Do you have any word from the field on the outcome?"

"It's stopped. Appears to be a stalemate, and a damned bloody one, at that. I've never seen anything like this."

"Where is Colonel Gordon? Do you have any word on his condition?"

"I haven't seen him here. I don't know where he is."

The surgeon then heard his name called and abruptly left.

Conor felt weak and nauseated. And in much pain. Sharp, piercing pain. Pain like he'd never felt before and didn't know was even possible. He tried to sit up again and look around the room, but he immediately fell back onto the blanket that covered the wooden parlor floor. He could hear moaning and screaming from other parts of the two-story house. An attractive, dark-haired woman in a blue

69

dress with a white cotton medical bib covering her front leaned over him and asked if he wanted a drink of water. He smiled and nodded appreciatively, and he detected the faint scent of the perfume on her hand as she propped his head and gave him a drink from a copper dipper.

"Is this your home, ma'am?" Conor asked.

"It is, yes," she answered softly.

"I'm sorry for all of this. Thank you for your kindness. God bless you."

She smiled slightly, saying nothing and then turning to leave.

"Oh, ma'am?" Conor called as she stopped and looked back. "Would you write the name Samuel Prescott on a piece of paper and give it to me, please?"

She nodded and left, returning moments later with the name inked on a slip of writing paper.

Therein is all that Conor remembered about his evening in the Sharpsburg hospital. However, it ended a day that he would never forget.

**

Monday, February 11, 1918

"Cappy, how did you leave Antietam?" asked Aaron.

"In a wagon train, with the army. Those who couldn't be moved were left in Sharpsburg to be cared for by the Yankee doctors. We crossed the Potomac on September nineteenth, and from there I was eventually sent to another hospital in Richmond to recuperate."

"Were you able to find out anything about the fate of F Company?"

"Yes. Sergeant Tanneyhill found me before I went to Richmond and gave me an update. He told me that F Company had lost thirty-one dead or wounded at Bloody Lane, leaving twenty-eight men standing from the total of eighty-eight we had crossed into Maryland with."

"That's a casualty rate of over two-thirds," Aaron said in astonishment. "I knew Antietam was the bloodiest single day in the war, but to lose two-thirds of your company is a pretty lethal campaign."

"Before I heard from Sergeant Tanneyhill, I had pictured in my mind that the entire company might have been lost, especially the way they were overwhelming and flanking us. I had even considered that the full regiment might have been torn to shreds."

"What about Colonel Gordon?"

"He was shot five times, and the last one struck him in the face. He eventually recovered, and I'll tell you more about him later."

"What about your brother, Sean? Was he wounded?"

"No. He didn't get a scratch, and he saw some very heavy fighting, especially in the early morning."

Aaron had a confused look. "Do you think it was wise for General Lee to have fought at Antietam, especially after the South Mountain battle had depleted his forces?"

"Well, it's always tempting in hindsight to judge the matter as a blunder since we suffered over sixteen-thousand casualties in the entire Maryland Campaign, a higher proportionate toll on us than what the Federals incurred. We didn't rally the Marylanders to our cause, as was hoped. And we didn't win a decisive victory, or a victory of any sort, for that matter. But Lincoln used the standoff to announce the Emancipation Proclamation, which was shrewd on his part, and which changed the war's objective from preserving the Union to preserving the Union *and* freeing the slaves."

"How did that go over with the Confederates?" asked Aaron.

"Not well, of course. It stirred up even more hatred of Lincoln from the people of the South."

"How so?"

"It was seen as another example of Northern meddling. It wasn't enough to invade us, but now Lincoln wanted to free what slave-owning Southerners viewed as their 'property.'"

"Didn't the South fire the first shots of the war?"

"Yes, but at Federal troops on Southern soil. Somebody told me that General Longstreet said we should have freed the slaves and *then* fired on Fort Sumter," Conor said, laughing.

Aaron paused a moment before asking, "What would that have accomplished?"

"Who knows? But there would have been no Emancipation Proclamation, not by Lincoln anyway."

"Getting back to the battle, Cappy, did Lee do the right thing, the smart thing in fighting the battle at Antietam?"

"Here's what you have to remember: We had an aggressive commander in General Lee, and if the South was going to win the war given the disparity in men and resources, then we had to take some risks. And give Lee credit for knowing that McClellan would not be as aggressive as maybe another Union leader might have been. And it turns out he wasn't. He had our battle plan and he had the resources to crush us. He didn't win the battle, and he did little to pursue us once we left out for Virginia. And he made an enemy out of Lincoln, which was not to his benefit. Still, Sharpsburg was a close run thing, as Wellington remarked about Waterloo. If we didn't hold the Yankees off at Bloody Lane for as long as we did, or if Robert Toombs' Georgians didn't delay the Federals from crossing Antietam Creek at the Rohrbach Bridge for as long as they did, or if A.P. Hill didn't show up at just the right time near the end of the day, then we would've no doubt been defeated and quite possibly destroyed."

Aaron shook his head, still not convinced of the advisability of the attack.

"But we didn't lose," Conor added.

"But at what cost? And for what clear strategic advantage?" Aaron countered.

"Those are fair questions, Aaron. And they're thoughtful questions. They should be studied and debated by men far smarter than me, men like yourself, the military professionals and historians. I don't know the answers, in all honesty. I just know what I saw as a soldier on the field there, and what we had hoped to achieve there. And especially how hard our men fought and died there. Those are the only things I know for sure."

"Oh, what about Private Prescott, Cappy? Were you ever able to contact his mother?"

"Sergeant Tanneyhill sent me her address and I wrote to her from my hospital bed in Richmond. Then after the war, I made it a point to visit her in Dothan. I told her of her son's bravery, how he had died at his post without great suffering, and how I was holding his hand when he took his last breath. I told her in his exact words the request he had made of me, and I gave her the piece of paper with her son's name written on it that I had carried with me the rest of the war. I confessed to her that I couldn't remember her son's name that day at Sharpsburg, but that I would never again forget the name of Samuel Prescott. And I haven't. And I won't. She was a fine lady, a very strong and courageous lady, and she was most appreciative."

Aaron stood and walked over to Conor's bedside and put his hand on his shoulder. "You were a brave and honorable soldier, sir, a commander of the sort I would be honored to serve under."

Tears welled up in Conor's eyes as he reached out and grasped Aaron's hand. "I would have been honored to have had you in my command."

"You look tired, Cappy. I don't want you to push yourself too hard. Maybe we should stop for today."

Conor shook his head. "No, let's just take a short break and keep going."

"You're sure?"

"Yes. Just a short break."

Aaron began laughing. "You're still one tough ole Reb."

Chapter Four

Victory and Loss at Chancellorsville

He's fighting for his own true love,
His foes he does defy,
He is the darling of my heart.
My Southern soldier boy.
"Southern Soldier Boy"

February-May, 1863

Once again Conor was in a Richmond hospital, this time for a period covering five months. His leg and wrist healed nicely, but his badly damaged left shoulder came around much more slowly, hindered by two infections, one of which very nearly killed him. There was also some nerve damage, and his grip was affected as a result.

On the war front, the Confederates won the Battle of Fredericksburg in December, 1862, by crushing the Union General Burnside. The overmatched Burnside sent repeated frontal assaults against the Southern troops posted behind a long wall, resulting in horrific Federal losses. General Lee sent the Yankees home once more in total defeat, and they were greatly demoralized as a result. Also important to note was that Union General U.S. Grant took command in the West, with orders to take Vicksburg.

In the meantime, Lincoln changed commanders from McClellan to Burnside to Hooker. General Joseph Hooker was nicknamed "Fighting Joe" Hooker, which prompted General Lee to refer to him sarcastically as "FJ" Hooker. Moreover, it seemed that FJ enjoyed the company of women, especially those ladies of the nighttime in the Washington area. Hence, the term "hooker" was coined, courtesy of an infamous Union general who couldn't resist the temptations and delectations of the night.

Conor had written to Colonel Gordon and informed the colonel that he wished to serve with him again. He heard nothing in return over a period of several weeks, however, and in the meantime the army gave him an assignment as one of several adjutants on the staff of Secretary of War James Seddon. So he stayed in Richmond from February until late April, doing very little apart from calculating how many rations the Army of Northern Virginia might require in the next ninety days; or how much rifle ammunition and how many artillery shells might be needed; or how much hay and grain would be required as fodder for the horses. Conor was bored, so bored that he badly wanted to get back into the war. He wanted to get back to commanding troops, the role he most enjoyed and the role he felt he had grown into nicely. Too, he felt strongly that the best way for him to contribute to the war effort would be as a commander in the field, leading his soldiers. He was bothered when he received a letter from Sergeant Tanneyhill informing him that F Company had already gone through three company commanders since Conor's wounding. He seriously missed F Company.

Greatly hoping for another job, Conor asked his reporting senior, a colonel, if he would be kind enough to arrange an assignment to an infantry regiment. The colonel curtly informed Conor that he would likely finish out the war in the job he now had. The colonel was overweight, arrogant, and cared little about what others thought of him. He had been a bookkeeper before the war and who, along with most of his crew, was lazy and incompetent when it came to military matters. The most highly honed skills in the colonel's possession were meeting with suppliers during the day and getting sideways drunk at night. The colonel tended to sweat a lot, and he would reek of liquor until well past noon on nearly every working day. Conor knew the colonel was jealous that he had served in the field and had fought and been wounded at Sharpsburg. Conor also knew the colonel would not have lasted a day in the infantry, or even an hour, and he suspected that the soft, flabby man bitterly despised most anyone who could. And so the feeling Conor held for the colonel was one of sheer contempt which he concealed only with the greatest of effort. Conor simply despised what he was doing and with whom he was doing it.

Then he met a young woman.

Her name was Penny Orr, and she was the beautiful, petite, auburn-haired daughter of a Confederate general who was on the staff of President Davis. She had attended Stratford College in Danville for two years, and she was intelligent, witty, and well informed. Privately, Conor was smitten with Penny, but since he was certain he would find a way to get back to the field and thus would not be in Richmond much longer, they mutually decided on a friendship rather than a courtship. On a night when Conor had supper at Penny's home, he asked her father, General David Orr, if he was acquainted with Colonel Gordon. The general answered that yes, he knew John and his wife Fanny, thought highly of them, and considered them to be good friends. Conor told General Orr that he had served with Colonel Gordon at Sharpsburg, and that he very much wanted to serve with the colonel again except that he was stuck in a mind-eroding desk job *counting* ammo instead of *firing* it. The general laughed and said he would see what he could do. Three days later Conor had the orders he was hoping for.

Conor was summoned by the obese colonel and told to pack his bags. He was immediately being transferred to General Stonewall Jackson's Second Corps, General Don Masterson's Division, and Brigadier General John B.

Gordon's Brigade. He was to report to General Gordon without delay in the vicinity of Fredericksburg. The colonel then sniffed and mentioned to Conor that he would not have gotten any more shell fragments in his ass if he had remained in his job on the colonel's staff. Conor informed the colonel that he had been wounded in the hip, shoulder, head, calf, and finger, the stump of which he held up for the colonel to see, but that he'd not yet been hit in the ass.

The colonel said, "Well then, I suppose there's always hope," in a condescending tone.

"What exactly do you mean, Colonel?"

"You're a captain and I'm a colonel, if you haven't noticed. I will ask the questions, not you. Now run along, sonny boy, and go play with your dirty, smelly little soldier friends."

Conor stared in hot, hard, wholehearted hatred.

"Did you not hear me, Captain Rafferty? I said *run along!*" the colonel bellowed as he motioned with his hand.

"Colonel, you're a drunken, crooked, arrogant jackass, and no doubt a coward, too. You should be court-martialed for being a conniving rat. And then you should be jailed and maybe hanged. You are nothing more than a big ole can of useless lard, and you have the odor of a week-old corpse. I only wish that you were on the other side so we could meet in the field. Then you could see what real soldiers do."

The colonel reached into a desk drawer and produced a revolver. "You are under arrest, my good sir. How dare you speak to me that way. I will have you in the brig for gross insubordination before nightfall. You have finally crossed the line, Captain."

"If I don't see my close friend sometime in the next two hours, he'll deliver by hand the letter I've written to Secretary of War Seddon detailing your long habit of accepting bribe money from unscrupulous government suppliers. It wasn't hard to figure out, Colonel. You always seem to have lots of cash. You eat and drink for free all over town with those well-dressed and freshly groomed gentlemen who are often in your office. Very often, in fact. If a guy like me can see it, I would think others could, too. You might want to note that. So put the revolver away before you misfire and shoot half your dick off. Who knows? You might need that other inch someday."

"You have nothing, Rafferty. You're a liar. A damn liar."

"Colonel, I may be lots of things, but I'm not like you. If someone were to snap you open like a green bean, there would be nothing there but stinking black ooze. You are wasting a military uniform of the Confederacy, and you'd look far better in a prison outfit."

The colonel cocked the pistol. "You have nothing, Rafferty."

There was a long pause. The colonel had begun sweating even more profusely, and his hand gripping the revolver was shaking noticeably.

"I have all I need, Colonel. I saw it all. I know what you've been doing. And I know who is in it with you. I know the names and the dates. And if I knew for sure that the money you were being paid in bribes was resulting in inferior shells or fuses or powder being shipped to my fellow soldiers, I'd take that pistol away from you and shoot you myself."

"You have nothing."

"Put the pistol away, Colonel, and we'll call it even. I'll leave, you'll stay, and we'll part as if nothing ever happened. No letter released, no harm done."

"I should kill you, right here and now."

"And you'll be the one in the brig before nightfall. And the Confederate government will be on to your bribery scheme. You'll never have another day of freedom for the rest of your life. Not one day."

"Get out of here," he snarled. "I hope you die in the stinking damn mud, Rafferty. And very, very slowly. *Now get the hell out of here!*"

There was no letter, but Penny's father, General Orr, had been made aware of the situation in exacting detail. Six people were arrested two weeks later, including the fat colonel.

It was nearing midnight on Thursday, April 30, 1863. Conor had taken the train from Richmond to Guiney's Station, and from there hitched a slow, bumpy ride to Fredericksburg with a group of resupply wagons, finally finding the encampment of General Don Masterson's Division. It took some time asking around before he was finally pointed in the direction of General Gordon's tent. He opened the flap and peered inside, seeing the general seated alone, drinking a glass of red wine and staring intently at a map spread out on a table made from pine logs. There was a cot on the far end, with a hat and some uniform clothing piled atop it, and two hanging lanterns providing the light inside.

"I've been ordered to report here, sir. My orders say Brigadier General John B. Gordon, so I should start by offering my congratulations."

The general smiled broadly and stood, his hand outstretched. "I've been expecting you, Conor. How the devil are you?"

"Good as could be expected, sir. The feeling's not quite back in my left hand, but other than that, I'm healthy and happy to be here. What about you, General?"

He pointed to the red puffy scar on his cheek. "It took a while to get over this thing, along with the other scrapes and scratches, but I'm fine now."

"Scrapes and scratches? You were shot five times, General Gordon."

"And you were shot four, my good sir. Let's not have this become a contest, shall we?"

They enjoyed a good laugh. The general slapped Conor on the back, looked him over carefully, and then poured him a glass of wine. They spoke briefly about Sharpsburg, about their recovery from their wounds, and the progress of the war since the Maryland Campaign. They spoke of common friends and talked like old friends, sort of, always with an awareness that one now wore stars and the other didn't. The general pulled another chair over and they both seated themselves at the small table.

"Here's our situation, Conor: The Federals are on the move, in large numbers as far as we can tell, and we're just not sure of what their intentions are yet. They seem to be concentrating near our location but on the other side of the Rappahannock, with Sedgwick's Sixth Corps for sure, possibly another. It could very well turn out to be a feint. General Lee has split the army so he can meet any attempt Hooker may make to get behind him, but for now General Masterson's Division, to include us, will remain here and be ready to repulse any attempt on the part of the Federals to move on Fredericksburg. Or, of course, be ready to move elsewhere, as the situation dictates."

"What do we know about General Hooker, sir?"

"Ole Fighting Joe might be a little more calculating than Ambrose Burnside, but I really don't know very much about him. Some of our senior commanders tell me he's a courageous fighter, but they're not sure what he'll do now that he's in command of an entire army. He has a big job now, a very big job, and he's facing General Lee, which I'm sure weighs on him. I suppose we'll find out soon enough."

Conor wasn't sure what General Gordon had in mind for him, so he left it to the general to bring up the subject as he saw fit.

"How is Mrs. Gordon, General?"

"She's well. She helped me so much during my recuperation, I don't know what I would've done without her. And when she found out you were going to join my brigade, she wanted me to pass along her regards. She's visiting kinfolks back in Atlanta. Now, let's talk a bit about the job I have here for you. I have no slots open for a company commander, but I already know you can do that. So I have something else in mind. I want you to become a member of my staff, and I want you not only to function as an adjutant but act as a liaison officer, as well."

There was a pause and Conor could see that the general was measuring his reaction. Conor shifted nervously in his seat.

"I'll gladly take it, sir," Conor said with a slightly embarrassed smile. "But what exactly will I do?"

"You'll do what I need you to do, essentially. If I need you to attend a meeting for me, then you'll go. If I need some direction from General Masterson on a non-urgent matter, I'll send you. If I need your opinion on some of our company commanders, I'll ask you to spend some time with them and evaluate them. I have a large brigade— six regiments—and they're all Georgians, God bless 'em. However, I know nothing about them, nothing at all. And I'm told many of the troops are green and therefore untested. Furthermore, if I need a fresh set of eyes on a battle plan I'm developing, I'll want your honest opinion. I don't expect you to be a strategic expert, Conor, but you know how to fight, how to use terrain, and you know what makes a soldier fight long and hard, even when greatly outnumbered. I don't yet have that expertise on my staff, but now I'll have it with you."

"I'll do my best, sir," Conor said. "And here I thought I'd be assigned to the worst company in the brigade. Thank you for bringing me into your command."

"I'm delighted to have you. And there's not a doubt in my mind that you'll do well."

"I appreciate that, General."

"So, what do you think, Major?"

82

Conor was momentarily taken aback. "Begging the General's pardon, sir, but I'm—"

"Not so. You are a captain no longer. I'm promoting you to major, effective immediately. I have a horse already selected for you that you can collect in the morning." The general handed Conor a small box. "Here's your new rank insignia. You can sew them on your uniform tonight. Congratulations, Major Rafferty."

Later that night Conor wrote to his mother and gave her the news of his promotion, and provided her with his new mailing address. She had fussed over his health when he had last heard from her, and she seemed to be getting gloomier in each successive letter. Conor had become increasingly concerned about her worrying about Sean, Daniel, and himself. He hoped the news of his promotion would cheer her, maybe his father also, but he also knew that his being back in the field would bring about a new wave of anxiety on her part. He mailed the letter anyway.

The next morning, Friday, May 1, Conor sat in on General Gordon's meeting with his regimental commanders from the 13th Georgia, 26th Georgia, 31st Georgia, 38th Georgia, 60th Georgia, and 61st Georgia. The regimental commanders then congratulated Conor on his promotion to major. General Gordon spent time with General Masterson while Conor went around on foot to meet and visit with several of the company commanders. A supply sergeant tracked him down and delivered his horse at mid-morning. The horse's name was Shannon, which Conor took as an Irish sign of good luck. She was strong, even-tempered, and easily ridden, and he immediately liked her.

Conor rode Shannon to a slight rise to the north of the brigade position that overlooked the division encampment. She responded naturally and handled well as they galloped to the crest of the hill. Escaping Conor's notice at first was another solitary rider positioned atop the rise, but when he drew closer he instantly recognized

General Stonewall Jackson. General Jackson cut an impressive figure in his gray uniform, faded forage cap, white gloves, and black, knee-length boots. The sunlight caused him to squint, revealing the crow's feet in the corners of his eyes. His field glasses were on one side, his sabre dangling at his other side as he sat on his horse and surveyed the throngs of tents and campfires of the Confederate forces arrayed to his front. He seemed fixed in deep concentration, sitting upright and perfectly still, barely noticing Conor when he approached.

"I'm sorry to intrude, General Jackson," Conor said when the general finally turned and looked at him. "I'll take my leave, sir. My apologies."

Conor turned Shannon and started away.

"Have we met before, Major?" the general called.

"We have, sir, at First Manassas," Conor answered, turning back. "I approached you and passed along a request to cover the withdrawals of Colonel Bartow and General Bee. I was on Colonel Bartow's staff before I assumed command of B Company."

The general nodded. "Brave men, honorable men."

"That they were, sir. It was an honor to serve with Colonel Bartow."

"So what have you done since that day, Major?"

"I was wounded at Seven Pines, General, and when I got back I commanded a company in the Maryland Campaign with General Gordon's Sixth Alabama. After that I spent five months in a Richmond hospital after encountering what seemed like an endless number of Yankees at the sunken road at Sharpsburg."

General Jackson smiled slightly. "There were enough Yankees to go around, yes indeed."

"And I just joined General Gordon's Brigade staff last night, sir."

General Jackson stared at Conor for a brief moment, though it seemed much longer. His bright blue eyes seemed to penetrate all the way through Conor's skull and out the other side. Conor said nothing, his only noise being the sound of a loud swallow. Stonewall Jackson finally nodded, patted his horse's neck and said, "God be with you, sir," before riding off. Conor sat atop Shannon and watched as the famous general slowly made his way back to the encampment.

There were more meetings between General Gordon and General Masterson on Friday, May 1. The tension around the camp was palpable, and there was an urgency on the part of the top commanders to discover the enemy's intentions. It seemed once again that there was an interminable number of Federals moving about, this time nearing Fredericksburg and its environs.

"I'm about to find out if my brigade can fight," General Gordon said to Conor as they sat on the ground near his tent and drank coffee with a wee splash of Irish whiskey.

"By the way, where did the whiskey come from?" the general asked, nodding his approval.

"One of our soldiers traded a Yankee for it, sir, and he gave me a small sample. He said with a name like Rafferty my cousins had probably made the damn stuff."

"What did he trade for it?"

"Some good Virginia tobacco."

General Gordon laughed softly. "Ah, yes. Some would call that exchanging one vice for another."

"Sir, some would call a vice anything that might produce even the slightest amount of pleasure."

"You wouldn't be talking about Southern preachers, would you, Major?"

Conor smiled. "Why, of course not. And by the way, General, my strong feeling is that your brigade will fight like tigers."

"What makes you say that?"

"I've met all of the regimental commanders and almost all of the company commanders, and I like what I see. And besides, they're Georgians. They'll fight well."

The general shrugged. "We'll soon see."

On Saturday, May 2, Sedgewick's Union troops crossed the Rappahannock and occupied Fredericksburg in another bloody fight. General Gordon's Brigade was not engaged, and Conor could easily detect that the general was growing anxious to get into the fight. General Barksdale's Mississippi troops were in the heaviest fighting around Marye's Heights and the Stone Wall, and the Federal troops were too strong in numbers for Barksdale's men to prevail. There was lots of fighting around Chancellorsville to the west, on the Confederate left, and unbeknownst to the men of Gordon's Brigade, Stonewall Jackson was wounded that night after executing a brilliant flanking maneuver that sent the Union right fleeing the battlefield in panic.

Since the Confederates had more ground to cover than they had in available troops, they set up empty tents, built campfires in the rear, and kept their artillery pieces in view of the probing Union eyes. General Masterson's plan for the recapture of Marye's Heights and perhaps even the town of Fredericksburg was put in motion on Sunday, May 3. General Gordon was assigned to lead the attack, and Conor could tell from his behavior that he was tense, that he'd been away from commanding troops long enough and been hurt badly enough that there was a natural apprehension. Conor, too, felt it, even though he wasn't leading a company. In fact, he wasn't leading anyone.

General Gordon climbed onto the front of a supply wagon and spoke to the men of the 31st Georgia who had gathered around in a semi-circle. The 31st Georgia would lead the attack column. "Let every man raise a yell and take those heights. Will you do it? I ask you to go no further than I am willing to lead." The men responded with enthusiastic yelling, and soon they were off in the attack.

The brigade column rushed off down Telegraph Road before the rest of the division could get into position. Midway during the assault General Gordon received orders to halt, but his lead companies were taking sporadic fire and his temperament at that point was not to stop in mid-attack. Lee's Hill was not occupied and Marye's Heights offered only nominal resistance. Conor rode with General Gordon until the general ordered him to check on the progress of the trailing regiments, who Conor found were maintaining the proper intervals and proceeding as expected. Upon reaching Marye's Heights and after driving the Yankee skirmishers away, they found a half-dozen Mississippi scouts from Barksdale's Brigade and several kind-hearted Fredericksburg women searching the field for any wounded.

"Have you seen any Confederate casualties, ma'am?" Conor called to one of the women.

"No, there aren't any," she replied.

The Federals soon began firing artillery at the Confederates from the banks of the river. Meanwhile, the 31st Georgia moved toward Plank Road and captured a Yankee supply train before getting into a brisk firefight. General Gordon said nothing to General Masterson about the confusion concerning the attack's commencement that morning. He confided to Conor that he was uncertain whether he had misinterpreted the order or that the order was poorly written and confusing. The fact that his brigade had taken the heights without a casualty, the general observed with a sly smile, would probably keep him from being court-martialed. The day ended with the Confederate battle line extending twelve miles, from Fredericksburg to Wilderness Church, west of Chancellorsville.

General Lee visited General Masterson on the morning of May 4. Soon afterward, Gordon's Brigade attacked northward toward Taylor's Hill, moving generally parallel to the Rappahannock. The men were shouting and screaming with such energy that the occupying Federals left without much of a fight. They took Taylor's Hill right after which the Union artillerists opened up from the heights across the river at Falmouth. Afterwards, the Rebels were checked by a strong Union infantry counterattack.

General Gordon and Conor peered through their field glasses at the Union positions both to their immediate front and across the Rappahannock to their right.

"Tell me what you see, Major Rafferty."

"I see no massing of troops preparing to attack us. I see campfires, tents, and weapons stacked. I see infantry troops leisurely preparing their meals as if we didn't exist over here. I see no activity in their artillery batteries—no ammo being brought up, none of the guns manned, no one looking back at us in search of targets. It seems to me they are content to stay where they are as long as we seem content to stay the same way. I see nothing that tells me they are interested in bringing battle to us in the next several hours. That's what I see, General."

"So should we move off this hill and strike them?" the general asked.

Conor glanced over and noticed his slight smile. "If you're not content to remain here, sir, then I would say this might be one of those perfect times to introduce ourselves."

"There is but one problem with that approach, Major," the general said with a sigh.

"And that problem would be what, sir?"

"My orders are very specific: Remain in this position until notified further. I have no discretion in the matter. Billy Yank can enjoy his lunch. I swear, it's almost as if they know what my orders are over there."

They remained on the hill the rest of the day.

The larger battles were occurring around Chancellorsville, where Lee kept Hooker off balance with his bold flanking movements and daring assaults. Hooker later admitted that he lost faith in himself, and by May 6, his Army of the Potomac was in retreat. It was another stunning Confederate victory against a foe of vastly superior size, perhaps the boldest of Lee's conquests. But it was not without significant cost. General Gordon's Brigade had a modest loss of 17 dead and 178 wounded, but the total losses to Lee's Army of Northern Virginia were over 13,000 out of a 60,000-man force. Union casualties for Hooker's Army of the Potomac were 17,000 from a force of 134,000.

Stonewall Jackson, his left arm amputated and his lungs overtaken by pneumonia, was giving orders to A.P. Hill in his fevered delirium before finally calming and uttering, "Let us cross over the river, and rest under the shade of the trees." He then died in the house of a friend at Guinea Station, Virginia. It was Sunday, May 10, 1863.

Stonewall Jackson's loss to the army was devastating—undeniably, irreversibly, and somberly. The entire South felt it.

***

Monday, February 11, 1918

Conor quietly watched as Aaron reviewed his notes, made a few other remarks in the pages' margins, and then accepted a cup of coffee, a smile, and a wink from a cute nurse.

"Cappy, when Stonewall Jackson died, was it the thought among the Confederate soldiers that the war would be lost as a consequence?"

"No," Conor replied. "We knew it would be more difficult, and perhaps far more difficult, but as long as we had General Lee we still thought we would win."

"And by winning, did you mean nothing short of a Northern surrender?"

"Winning would mean that the Confederate States of America would remain in place, whether by an outright military victory or with some sort of negotiated settlement, maybe even aided by a foreign intervention on the Southern side. I didn't necessarily think we could achieve such an overwhelming military advantage that Lincoln would find no other recourse but to surrender, but we thought we could win enough to reach a point where the general public in the North would decide that the war had to end and the killing had to stop. And that point was actually closer than any of us realized."

Aaron looked up from his notes, a peculiar expression on his face, his hesitation showing. He finally swallowed and asked, "Do you think Chancellorsville was a pyrrhic victory for the South?"

Conor pondered the question for a moment. He had considered the same issue many times before in discussions with friends and former soldiers. Like much else, there were two sides to the story. "I suppose you could make that argument, but I'm not convinced it's accurate. There was little choice in the matter since they brought the fight to us, intending to destroy us. And if they had been able to get behind us, they might have done just that. But instead we outfought them, outthought them, outgeneraled them, and beat them in the end. And yes, we lost a lot of experienced troops that we couldn't replace as easily as the Federals. We didn't pummel their army with great losses so much as we broke the will of their leader, Hooker. So, even though they left the field in defeat, they suffered comparatively fewer losses. And unless we could have figured out some miraculous way to defeat them by taking far fewer casualties, then the imbalance was always going to be there, and not to our ultimate advantage. But in defeating them, we forced Lincoln to change commanders once again, this time with George Meade who was a more able, competent general, as it turned out. And of course we lost Stonewall Jackson, which was the single most devastating casualty of the war for the South. So I'm not so sure that a description of a pyrrhic victory is appropriate in this case.

For us, it was a victory for the ages. Lee took his drastically smaller army, split it, and then launched a series of risky movements that only a fool or a military genius would dare to take. And R.E. Lee was no fool."

"Sweet and bittersweet," Aaron added.

"I would agree."

"So, what's next in this saga for Major Conor Rafferty?"

"The invasion of Pennsylvania and a town called Gettysburg."

"Ah, yes. Start again first thing in the morning?"

"Yes, of course."

Chapter Five

On to Pennsylvania

> *Just before the battle, Mother,*
> *I am thinking most of you.*
> *While upon the field we're watching,*
> *with the enemy in view.*
> *Comrades brave are 'round me lying,*
> *filled with thoughts of home and God;*
> *For well they know that on the morrow,*
> *some will sleep beneath the sod.*
> *"Just Before The Battle Mother"*

June-July, 1863

"What's the objective in invading Pennsylvania, sir?" Conor asked General Gordon as he stood in the general's tent and studied a large map.

"First, to get the Yankees out of Virginia so the Virginia farmers can start to replenish the food stores and livestock that the Yankees have been plundering. Second, to lure the Union army into battle at a time and place of General Lee's choosing, and then to destroy it."

It was Tuesday, June 16, 1863 and the Confederates were camped at Winchester in the Shenandoah Valley after liberating the town from the Union garrison there. Lead elements of the Southern army were already on the move into Pennsylvania. General Masterson's orders had his division moving through Maryland to York and eventually linking up with General Ewell's other divisions in taking Harrisburg.

"My expectation," said General Gordon, continuing, "is that we will draw the Union army to us in pieces as they figure out where we are and how we pose a threat to Washington, Baltimore, or Philadelphia. They won't know for sure what our objectives are until we choose to make it known to them. And we will then be able to pounce on and destroy the individual pieces until the task is finally completed. Jeb Stuart and his cavalry boys will keep General Lee informed about the Union movements, and we'll subsist mostly off what the countryside offers, courtesy of the generous citizens of the Commonwealth of Pennsylvania."

They both laughed.

"They're about to get a taste of their own medicine," Conor added. "They've plundered Virginia for two long years now, so we'll return the favor with a little pillaging of our own."

"All done in the spirit of fairness, of course. And in keeping with the Commanding General's orders, I should also add."

General Gordon suddenly became serious. He cleared his throat and stroked his beard for a moment, suggesting to Conor that something important was about to follow.

"I expect a bitter struggle at some point. As hard as we fight on our Southern soil, I expect them to do the same on theirs. To think otherwise would be folly, in my opinion. I believe in my bones we will prevail, but not without a fight, and a hard fight at that."

"Understood, sir."

"Which leads me to you, Conor. I have six regimental commanders, and I believe them all to be excellent men and fine, brave soldiers, even though we've seen limited action together thus far. What I have seen, and what the regimental commanders have confirmed for me, is that there are only three company commanders who might be able to assume the duties of leading a regiment. I don't know the three captains in question, so I can only go on the advice of their superiors. Obviously, I would greatly prefer to have seen more of them in battle, but that hasn't happened. And so once the shooting begins on this campaign, if it follows to the magnitude that I think it might, then the chance of at least one of those regimental commanders becoming incapacitated is a real possibility, if not a probability. Can you see where I'm headed with this?"

Conor swallowed hard. "I think so."

"I will not hesitate to put you in command of the first regiment where such a loss occurs. I thought you should know that before we get underway."

"Yes, that's where I thought you were headed, General. And I appreciate your letting me know in advance."

After the meeting, as Conor was walking back to the staff tent, he felt a sudden onset of queasiness. He stood outside the tent for a moment, his mouth watery, his face flushed, reviewing again what he had just learned. That is, they were about to launch a largescale invasion into Pennsylvania; there was a near certainty they would be engaged in a critical battle; and in that large battle there was a strong possibility that he would become a regimental commander before the battle's conclusion. His breathing accelerated and he leaned forward to keep from vomiting on the tops of his boots. He remembered how he would sometimes talk softly to himself in battle in an effort to control his emotions, and he began to apply that same approach as he fought off the nausea.

"Are you okay, Conor?" one of his fellow staff officers called as he approached the tent.

"I think so. Just a little stomach flutter. Must've been something I ate," Conor replied without making eye contact.

After a few minutes he was mostly okay.

The brigade moved up the Cumberland Valley on June 22, then separated from General Ewell's other 2nd Corps divisions and followed along the western slope of South Mountain. They passed through Waynesboro, Quincy, and Mount Alto before making an eastward turn toward York. From there, they were to cross the Susquehanna River at Wrightsville and await the arrival of Ewell before taking Harrisburg.

Before reaching York, however, they arrived at Gettysburg on a rainy Friday, June 26. There was a report of Pennsylvania militia ahead whose strength was unknown. At about noon, General Masterson assigned General Gordon's Brigade to move along the Cashtown Pike toward Marsh Creek to locate the militia and promptly deal with it. There was no battle and the Rebels collected nearly 200 prisoners from the militia and the home guard. One of these irregulars was shot and killed by Confederate cavalry troops and hence became the first Federal battle death at Gettysburg.

The small town of Gettysburg in the south-central portion of Pennsylvania was distinguishable by the ten roads leading into it. The Southerners entered Gettysburg and found the citizens wary of them, even with their assurances that they meant no harm. The children on the street stared at the Confederate soldiers whereas the men avoided them altogether, while the women stole quick glances out of what seemed equal parts curiosity and amazement. There was little hostility directed at the Rebels, but from the looks they received it was clear the citizens were not overjoyed to have them in their midst.

General Gordon and Conor scouted the town on horseback, noting the shops and other buildings just off the main square, also called the Diamond. A man who appeared to be in his thirties was standing outside his office, carefully observing them as they rode by. The inscription on his office door identified him as "Garland H. Belkin, Attorney-at-Law."

"Good afternoon, sir," General Gordon called out to him. "What sort of law do you practice?"

"General practice. Wills and probates, mostly. Some real estate. Why? Are you in need of my services?"

General Gordon laughed. "No, I'm afraid not. I'm an attorney myself, actually."

"Then why the hell are you in that uniform and engaged in making war on us instead of practicing law?"

The general sat up straight in the saddle, his head cocked slightly, his eyes narrowing, the grin gone from his face. "Well, sir, given the indisputable fact that there is indeed a war on, I could turn that question around and ask you why the hell are you *not* in uniform?"

"Go to hell," the man muttered as he turned and went back into his office.

"Could you sue him for that, General?" Conor asked, grinning.

"No, but if he comes back out holding a weapon, I'll provide his heirs a reason to sue me."

Later, General Gordon and Conor climbed the steps of the cupola at the Lutheran Theological Seminary to have a look at the surrounding terrain. An older gent, perhaps a professor or school official of some sort, approached them and told them they were not permitted to be on school property, much less in the cupola. They were trespassing, the man said in a louder tone than necessary, and he insisted that they leave immediately. Conor informed him that the entire town, and thus the school and its cupola, was now under the occupation of the Army of Northern Virginia. Conor drew his pistol, cocked the hammer, and advised the man that *he* was the one who was trespassing, and as such he should turn around and leave immediately. The man swallowed, then turned and left immediately.

General Gordon, who had paid little attention to the man, began laughing. "I'd like to hear the stories at his supper table tonight."

There were no signs of Federal troops as far as they could observe on any of the main roads. In particular, there was nothing to the south, no indications of a large enemy force moving up from Maryland. There were several long-running ridgelines that caught the general's eye, along with the heights which were referred to as Big Round Top and Little Round Top by the locals.

"There's good ground here, and if a battle occurs in this place," General Gordon commented as he gazed through his field glasses, "whoever controls those heights will probably be the victor."

Two young women spotted them as they climbed down from the cupola and walked toward their horses. They were among several clusters of curious young people gathered about and staring as intently as if the Confederate officers had just arrived from the moon. The two young women approached, seemingly unafraid, and Conor tipped his hat.

"Why are you here?" one of them asked.

Conor glanced at General Gordon who instead nodded slightly for Conor to answer.

"We're here expecting to meet the Union army," Conor answered.

"Are you going to destroy our town?" the other young woman asked.

"No," General Gordon answered forcefully. "Just your army."

General Masterson made some demands for food, shoes, and clothing to the city fathers of Gettysburg, none of which could be met in the quantities sought by the general. The general then curtly informed the Gettysburg officials that they would just take what they wanted.

And they did.

On a tip from a local resident, Conor rode Shannon up to the northeast portion of Gettysburg, along the Harrisburg Road, with four of his fellow staff officers. There he found a cattle ranch and farm about a mile distant from their regimental bivouac area. The cows were huddled together in the rain in a nearby part of the pasture, at least thirty in number. The five officers, with their Confederate battle flag held aloft by a lieutenant, approached the white, two-story house.

A sturdily built, middle-aged farmer stepped out onto the porch while putting on his hat with one hand and holding a single-barrel shotgun with the other. A woman remained inside, peering out a window.

"State your business," the farmer said in a brusque tone.

Conor removed his hat and nodded. "Good afternoon, sir. I'm Major Rafferty from Gordon's Brigade. We didn't come here to cause you any harm, but these gentlemen with me are all battle veterans and all carrying weapons, as am I. So I would strongly suggest that you point the barrel of that shotgun away from us."

The farmer noted the sidearms the officers carried, noting as well that each man had his hand resting on his pistol's handle. The farmer hesitated only briefly before propping the shotgun against the porch's railing and taking a step back.

"I am informing you, sir, that ten of the cattle in your pasture are about to become the property of the Army of Northern Virginia. I am also advising you that in accordance with the directive of our Commanding General, you will be paid in Confederate currency for your property."

"That money's worthless. Take the damned cows and get the hell off my land," the farmer said defiantly, his hands on his hips.

"As soon as we complete this little campaign we're on, sir, that money you so wrongly describe as worthless will be used as legal tender from Maine to Florida to California and everywhere in between, including Pennsylvania," Conor replied.

Conor dropped a leather satchel containing $500 in Confederate currency.

The farmer stiffened in anger. "You're going to run into my son and my son-in-law out there sooner or later, Major, and when you do, you won't be happy with what you'll get from them. May God have mercy on your souls."

Conor saluted the farmer and then proceeded to the pasture to select the ten cows he was commandeering. They had brought sufficient rope and soon the Rebel officers had the cows on the road to the regimental cooks.

"I grew up around cattle," Conor told his fellow officers. "This reminds me of home."

Later, back in camp, General Gordon informed Conor that the regiment had somehow come into the possession of ten cows, and they would be having beef that night.

"You wouldn't happen to know anything about that, would you, Major Rafferty?" he asked.

"Courtesy of the generous citizens of the Commonwealth of Pennsylvania," Conor answered with an attempt at a straight face. "Along with a Confederate commissary officer who was willing to finance the undertaking," he added under his breath.

And of course, the beef was superb.

The Confederates released the teenage militia prisoners before leaving Gettysburg. General Masterson gave them an order to go home to their mothers before they "get hurt running around out here with muskets facing professional soldiers," to which they eagerly complied.

From Gettysburg, the Rebels moved on to York along the York Pike. The scenery along the way was awe-inspiring, with large fields of grain, oats, rye, and barley. The farms were generally well kept but smaller than was the custom in much of the plantation South. There were miles of white fences, and the barns were large and imposing. It was beautiful country with a richness and wellness that stood in stark contrast to so many of the overworked farms in the South.

"The landowner's plots are typically smaller because they don't have the slave labor to work the bigger parcels. They size the property in accordance with their ability to attend to it," General Gordon said as Conor rode alongside.

Their arrival at York on June 28 was peaceful. A small group of citizens met them on the outskirts and offered to surrender their town. Upon learning the news that there had been no resistance, General Masterson then ordered General Gordon to move quickly to Wrightsville and gain control of the Columbia Bridge, the large railroad bridge over the Susquehanna River that linked Wrightsville with Columbia on the other side. As they approached, they found a slight rise where they could observe a line of blue-clad soldiers awaiting them.

"What've we got here?" Conor asked, staring ahead through his field glasses.

"Militia, probably," said General Gordon. "This shouldn't take long."

And it didn't. At about 6:30 pm, Confederate companies sent out lines of skirmishers that began trading shots with the picket line to their front. General Gordon eventually fired his artillery in their direction, and the shooting soon quieted. It then became clear that the Federals were intent upon destroying the massive bridge, which was over a mile in length and the longest roofed bridge in North America. Several explosions were heard and dozens of torches were then observed.

"I'll be damned," one of the muddy soldiers of the 38th Georgia remarked as he passed by Conor. "They're gonna take the whole sumbitch down."

The bridge burned all night. Embers being blown by the wind ignited houses and stores in Wrightsville, and when the citizens and store owners produced dozens of pails, General Gordon had his soldiers extend lines from the river's edge into the town where they filled the pails and passed them up to the front. They saved several homes and businesses with their efforts, and one appreciative woman even invited General Gordon and several staff members, including Conor, for breakfast the following morning. Conor stood in the bucket line and worked for hours, thinking of the wicked irony that the homes the Confederates were sparing might never again be seen by the Wrightsville boys they could be killing in battle soon.

New orders were delivered on June 29, conveying a surprising change of plans. Instead of moving to take Harrisburg as planned, the Confederates were returning to Gettysburg. General Masterson's Division would move east, through East Berlin, and link up with Ewell's Corps around the Heidlersburg/Middletown area.

"Something big seems about to happen, sir," Conor remarked to General Gordon after a meeting with the regimental commanders to establish the order of march.

"Yes, indeed. We've found the enemy, or the enemy's found us," the general replied. "And Gettysburg makes perfect sense to me. With it being a road junction, General Lee can concentrate three corps there more easily than any other place I've seen in this region."

"Do we know the size of the force we might be facing there?" Conor asked.

"No, but I know if Gettysburg makes sense to General Lee to concentrate several corps there, then it also makes sense to the Union commander coming from the opposite direction to concentrate there, as well. And if all of that happens, we'll have ourselves one hell of a fight there."

For not having been trained as a professional soldier, General Gordon's intellect and instincts had always been impressive to Conor. Unlike many officers who had the benefit of military education and training, the general could see the bigger picture as quickly and clearly as many of his longer-tenured contemporaries. He tended toward being more aggressive than calculating, but he was hardly reckless. And his indisputable bravery had already been repeatedly demonstrated on the battlefield. If the brigade was about to fight an epic battle that might decide the outcome of the war, Conor was especially pleased to find himself under the command of John B. Gordon.

"The roads are muddy from the rains, so the going will be slow and tedious," the general noted. "I expect to be there in two days, probably not earlier. What day will that be?"

"Wednesday, July first, sir," Conor answered.

"Then let's make our way to Gettysburg, Major Rafferty."

***

Tuesday, February 12, 1918

"What was the feeling among the troops when they entered Pennsylvania, Cappy?"

Conor smiled at the thought. "The morale was exceptional. I don't know if it had ever been better. They marched hard, often at times when the sun was boiling hot, or in the rain and mud, but they kept a great spirit about them. They still cheered their hearts out when General Lee passed among them. The desertion rate was low, which was a great relief to the commanders. They weren't smart-alecky when they marched past the young Pennsylvania women who would sometimes line the road just to get a good look at them, unless the young women were unusually unattractive in which case I have to confess there might be some snickering in the ranks. They didn't deliberately kill or hurt any civilians, to my knowledge. They didn't steal a lot. Well, I should amend that. In all honesty, they stole a great deal, but nothing they couldn't consume or take with them 'for military purposes,' of course."

"What were they stealing?"

"Food, mostly. Chickens, eggs, vegetables. One man stole an apple pie. Another got a German chocolate cake. And, of course, whiskey somehow came into our possession on several occasions. Strangely, there were several puppies with us after we left Gettysburg the first time, and I don't know if the troops stole the dogs or enticed them to come with us by feeding them. There were even a few cats, too. Anyway, the commanders made them get rid of all the dogs and cats when we got to York. I'm sure the good people of York appreciated our greatly increasing the animal population in their town. And for sure our troops ate better in Pennsylvania than they had in months. In fact, they ate so much that some had problems with, well, let's just say they couldn't march for long without running off into the weeds. We had one company eat their weight in cherries when they came upon an orchard near York, and they were so sick they were in the weeds for a couple of days. Their commander almost got relieved."

"How do you feel, Cappy? We've done a lot today. Do you want to stop?"

"No. So much of this is coming back to me. Let's talk Gettysburg some more."

Chapter Six

Gettysburg — First Day

Beneath the cedar and the pine,
In solitude austere.
Unknown, unnamed, forgotten, lies
A Georgia Volunteer!
"A Georgia Volunteer"

July 1, 1863

Gordon's Brigade was positioned at the front of Masterson's Division as the long snaking column moved down the Harrisburg Road. It was 1:00 pm on Wednesday, July 1, when Conor pulled out of the line and moved ahead to get a look at what lay to their front. He moved at a gallop with two staff lieutenants and a sergeant and reached a point about a mile from the center of Gettysburg where, to his right-front, he could begin to see the developing battle. He saw where the Confederates were positioned to the north, northwest, and west of Gettysburg. Artillery fire was heavy, and the various unit and battle flags were visible. He noted with eagerness that the Harrisburg Road, on which they were traveling and which moved out from Gettysburg in a northeasterly direction, would position Gordon's Brigade on the Union right flank in a very advantageous position.

"Do you see what I see?" Conor asked one of the lieutenants while looking ahead through his field glasses.

"I see an opportunity, Major. I see one hell of an opportunity."

"We'll be slamming into their extreme right," Conor noted as he carefully studied the scene. "I can distinguish four Federal brigade flags near to, and slightly west of this road. And I can see General Doles' Division guarding our extreme right flank. I swear there could not be a better place on the entire field for us to join the battle. We'll have a chance to come in hard and roll up their right. Unless they're reinforcing with troops I don't yet see, we'll have a distinct advantage."

They turned and started to leave.

"Is that the place where we took the cows?" said a lieutenant, pointing to the right.

Conor glanced over and saw the familiar white house set back off the road several hundred yards. The family had a large Stars and Stripes flag flying from the porch. He wondered briefly if the farmer's son and son-in-law would be on the field facing them today. "Yes, that's it."

They rushed back and provided the good news to General Gordon. He went immediately to report the findings to General Masterson.

A messenger brought word that the Federals had pushed the Confederate left hard, and while the Rebs were slowly giving ground, they had not yet been broken. A Federal counterattack had given the blue-clad troops new momentum, and there was concern that the Confederate left flank was in peril. General Gordon's troops reached the field by 2:30 pm in what was yet another example of perfect timing, and quickly deployed in a battle line three brigades wide. The lines extended nearly a mile and overlapped the Federal front on both flanks. Confederate artillery was unleashed in a large-scale bombardment of the area to the front, unsettling and further confusing the Federal troops. General Gordon pivoted his brigade to the right and conducted a frontal assault against Blocher's

Knoll, fixing those Union defenders in place. Two other brigades turned the Federal right flank.

General Gordon removed his hat and waved his screaming troops forward in three lines of battle. They splashed across Rock Creek and met the mostly German soldiers of von Gilsa's Brigade in what became in several places a close, hand-to-hand struggle. The battle was intense, but the strength and aggressiveness of the Confederate attacking lines, and the well-coordinated flanking movements on their left and right, soon sent the enemy scampering off in defeat toward the town of Gettysburg. Conor stayed mounted on Shannon near the center of the brigade while General Gordon rode to all portions of his line, directing and shouting encouragement to his regiments, a virtual whirlwind of activity. Since Conor had no particular duties apart from those directed by General Gordon, he followed the lead companies toward the knoll, firing his pistol at any inviting targets and sending messengers to the artillery requesting specific target locations. Conor fired at a Yankee captain and missed what should have been an easy shot, then discovered to his great trepidation that his pistol was empty when he attempted to fire again. While he was reaching behind him for the second pistol he kept in his belt, the Yankee officer calmly walked several paces toward Conor to get a better aim with his own pistol. He took one step too many, for as soon as he raised his weapon to fire at Conor from a distance of no more than five paces he was felled by a shot from one of the Confederate troops. Conor quickly reloaded his pistol and made a mental note that his marksmanship could stand some improvement.

Conor glanced to his right in time to see two flag bearers fighting for possession of one another's flag in a ferocious encounter. The Confederate soldier began beating his Federal counterpart with the flagstaff just as another blue-clad trooper intervened and attempted to bayonet the

Southerner. Conor fired his pistol and struck the musket-carrying Yankee in the chest, dropping him, and then fired low at the Union flag bearer, hitting him in the knee and ending his interest in holding on to his flag. The Confederates were taking artillery fire from Blocher's Knoll that was slowing their advance until their own cannons blasted the annoying Union battery out of action. The Rebs made steady progress in driving the Yankees, and it was becoming obvious that the Union divisions opposing them were nearing a breaking point.

The piles of dead and wounded Federal troops were so dense that it became difficult to maneuver Shannon around them. Conor saw when Union General Francis Barlow was discovered seriously wounded by General Gordon, who then dismounted and called over several of his soldiers to move General Barlow back to a Confederate surgeon. Conor also dismounted Shannon and handed the reins over to a slightly wounded soldier with instructions to follow from a distance of one-hundred yards.

Suddenly a fierce Federal counterattack came plunging into the brigade and caught the Rebels at a moment when they were pausing to reorganize and straighten their lines. A ball clipped Conor's uniform at the top of the left shoulder but took nothing more than a strip of cloth. Another ball hit him in the midsection and knocked him over, leaving him feeling as if he'd been punched in the gut by a burly blacksmith. He reached for his belly, feeling for the blood and knowing that such a wound might very well be fatal. Yet there was no blood, only a large dent in his thick metal belt buckle.

A relieved Conor rose and gathered his hat and pistol, which had dislodged when he had fallen so abruptly. He began moving forward again, over and around the bodies, hearing the snap of the bullets passing near his head. He was attacking with the 61st Georgia as they continued to pour lethal volleys of lead into the ranks of the

Federals. Still, the tough Yankees kept advancing in spite of their losses.

Confederate artillery shells soon began crashing into the Federal lines with great accuracy. The slaughter was now coming from three sides as the Reb infantry pressed them from the front and both flanks while the artillery shifted to the area at the rear of the Union lines, inhibiting their ability to reinforce. Several Union artillery shells landed nearby and inflicted casualties, but the Southern soldiers continued to press forward. The last remaining Yankee battery to the brigade's front fired canister at the Southerners—shells loaded with round lead balls that cause horrifying damage to tightly packed infantry. The canister balls ripped into the Rebels with indiscriminate deadliness, and Conor was following close enough behind that he was sprayed with the blood of several victims. Confederate artillery soon eliminated the Yankee battery, but not before it had done its damage and thinned the brigade's ranks.

The lead elements of both lines soon met in another vicious hand-to-hand encounter that lasted perhaps three minutes before the outnumbered Federals broke off and started moving to the rear in a running retreat. One stubborn Yankee turned and thrust a bayonet at Conor, but a quick step to the right barely avoided his being gored. A single shot from Conor's revolver ended the confrontation. Confederates were now swarming over the battlefield like locusts, screaming and firing at the backs of the panicked Yankees.

My God, I almost got myself bayoneted! Conor thought in horror as he kept advancing. He had personally never known a Confederate officer who had been so wounded, and he was greatly relieved he had missed such a dubious distinction, if only barely.

A lone, frightened, unarmed Federal soldier stood with his arms raised in surrender in the center of the Rebel attack formation. Confederate soldiers ignored him and quickly moved forward in hot pursuit of his retreating brothers-in-arms. What Conor guessed to be a Yankee ball fired in their direction suddenly struck the Federal soldier in the middle of the back, passing through his torso and exiting at the very center of his chest. The man fell over just off to the side of Conor, unmoving, having survived in the attack only to die in surrender.

Fresh Federal troops gathered in the near distance for another counterattack. Their numbers appeared to comprise at least three companies, but they were slow in forming as the many retreating Federals passing through their lines distracted and unnerved them. Several consecutive volleys from Rebel soldiers thinned their lines by half, and the remaining Yankees soon broke and ran without having fired a shot.

General Gordon came riding up, waving his hat and shouting, "Push 'em, boys."

"This could be a good day," Conor shouted.

"This could be a *very* good day," he replied.

A courier came galloping toward General Gordon, coming quickly to a halt and passing a written order to the general. General Gordon read it and slapped his hat against his leg in anger.

"No, this is impossible. This can't be," the general shouted.

"It is accurate, sir. The order is clear," the courier, a lieutenant, said forcefully.

General Gordon quickly turned his horse and rode off.

It started as a trickle of Federal troops running from the field in panic. Conor concluded that while it's always heartening to see the enemy in a state of shock, it's unwise to judge a shift in momentum as an end result. Battles ebb and flow, he knew, and good commanders can often steady a shaken unit and have them back in the fight when moments before all seemed lost. Within thirty minutes, however, it became far more than a trickle when entire Federal regiments began collapsing and running toward Gettysburg. Conor could see that many had dropped their muskets and were literally running for their lives, against the desperate urging and pleading of their officers.

Conor's heart was pounding when he realized his fellow Confederate attackers had gained such an advantage in strength of numbers that they were overwhelming the Federals on as many parts of the battlefield as he could see. The Southern brigades had entered the battle at a faster rate than that of the enemy, and while the Federals fought with great spirit, the Confederate mass was enabling them to control the battlefield.

The knoll and surrounding area was finally cleared by 4:00 pm, and the final few Union defenders were likewise running away in panic. Several lines of Federal skirmishers were firing back at the Rebs to protect the general retreat, but once the Confederates turned their lines and started toward them, those Yankees similarly fled for the town.

Gray-clad troops were screaming the Rebel yell to a near deafening level as they were sweeping the field with remarkable success. Hundreds of prisoners were coming to them, and Conor quickly organized a detail to move them to the division rear. When he looked across the battlefield he could see Union troops in all directions either surrendering or fleeing toward Gettysburg. Conor had again been in that deadly space, that place where the opposing lines draw close and take dead aim, where the devil himself spreads unspeakable carnage before all who have dared to enter, where suffering and barbarous death become common, the sum total of which defies human expression. He had not experienced it to this extent since Sharpsburg, but he had survived it one more time, and the elation he felt not only in persevering but also in prevailing was exhilarating.

Conor noticed a wounded Union captain who was lying face-up on the ground nearby. The captain raised his hand and called to Conor as he walked by.

"Major, please," he said.

Conor leaned over the injured officer and noticed the gunshot wound to his lower abdomen. His face was pale, and the wound was seeping a steady flow of blood. His sabre was still in its scabbard on the ground beside him. His left hand was placed over the wound and he reached his right hand toward Conor, which Conor took in his own hand.

"I'm shot in the spine and my legs are paralyzed, Major, and the pain is intolerable. Please shoot me. I don't want to have to live like this. Will you do that for me, sir? Will you kindly shoot me?"

"No, Captain. I'll get you to our doctors, but I won't shoot you."

"Please, Major. I don't want a life with no use of my legs. I'm begging you, sir, shoot me and end my misery. If you can't do it, then get one of your men to put a bullet in my brain. Please, sir, have some Christian mercy on me."

Conor motioned for two Confederate soldiers who were walking nearby.

"Find a stretcher and move this officer to a medical tent. He needs to be seen quickly."

The two men called "Yessir" and ran off in search of a litter.

"You're not going to shoot me?" the captain asked dejectedly. "Then will you let me have your pistol so I can do it myself?"

"Of course not. You are still alive, Captain. Count your blessings."

"It's no blessing to not be able to move your legs."

"You're out of the war now. You can go home and get away from this insanity. If you still want a bullet in your skull, then you'll have to decide that for yourself later on. But it won't happen here, not with us, not now."

The captain took a deep breath and exhaled slowly. "Where are you from, Major?"

"Atlanta, Georgia."

"I grew up in Atlanta myself."

"Then what are you doing in that blue uniform?" Conor asked.

He managed a slight smile. "I call Boston home now. I've lived there for the past five years. Went to college there. Harvard. Was planning to become a doctor but this damned war changed everything. I couldn't go back to Georgia and join the Confederacy. My heart is with the Union, with Massachusetts, although all my uncles and cousins are fighting on your side. Who knows? Maybe one of my kinfolk put this ball in my spine. Now I have nothing to live for."

One of General Gordon's staff officers rode up and pointed to a stand of trees where the general was meeting with his commanders.

"He wants you over there, sir. Now."

Conor nodded, and then leaned down close to the wounded officer.

"Captain, we'll get you some medical attention as soon as my men return. We're not going to shoot a prisoner—a wounded one, at that—and you damn well know it. So don't make such a request of my soldiers. Goodbye and good luck to you."

The Union officer gave a salute with what little strength he had remaining, which Conor smartly returned.

General Gordon was standing underneath a large hickory tree, conferring with several of his regimental commanders as he motioned for Conor to join them. Conor was certain they were about to receive orders to pursue the fleeing Yankees through the town of Gettysburg and beyond, effectively ending the battle before nightfall. What he saw instead was General Gordon looking as glum as he'd ever seen him, and Conor's first thought was that someone of high importance, perhaps General Lee himself, had been killed.

"We've been ordered to halt," the general said dejectedly. "I ignored several of the orders that were sent previously, but I can't ignore it any longer. We're halting here."

Conor's facial expression changed to complete shock, as if he had just discovered a venomous snake in his rations. "General Gordon, that's got to be a mistaken order, sir. It had to be meant for somebody else, not us. For God's sake, we can't halt now. Somebody's got it all wrong."

"No, the orders were meant for us," the general said, shaking his head in obvious disgust. "I was advised personally by General Masterson that there is no mistake."

"But the enemy's disorganized and running away in shock. We can push on from here and maybe get in their rear. We can win this damn thing today, General!" Conor said, much more loudly than needed. "It's right there for us to take. We *can't* stop now."

"I've made that argument, Major Rafferty, and I've been ordered to halt."

"Dear God, sir! Is nobody else seeing what we're seeing? They're breaking and running! The field is wide open to our front. Wide open. Even a fool could see that, and a damn fool, at that."

"I know that, Conor, but we've got our orders. Those orders call for us to halt in place, and there is no room for argument. And I might suggest that you more closely watch your tongue, sir."

"Dammit!" Conor screamed with clenched teeth and fists. *"Dammit to hell!"*

Suddenly Conor was having difficulty breathing from the mixture of high excitement and utter frustration. He felt lightheaded as he reached for the canteen on his hip for a quick drink, only to discover that the canteen had been shot through and was bone dry.

"Well hell," Conor said disgustedly as he tossed the canteen aside. "This canteen's not the only thing not doing its duty right now."

The regimental commanders, all older than Conor, smiled among themselves but said nothing. Their comments were unnecessary, Conor concluded, for he had not only succeeded in making his point, but he'd had equal success in making an ass of himself. The thought crossed his mind that he was about to become a wagon driver.

"That will be all, gentlemen," the general said to the commanders. "I'll advise you when we have new orders. Keep your regiments ready to move at a moment's notice."

General Gordon was soon by Conor's side, extending his own canteen to him. "Are you all right, Conor? My God, man, that was a first-rate hissy fit if I've ever seen one."

Conor took a drink and followed it with a deep, refreshing breath. "I'm fine, sir. My apologies for the outburst. It won't happen again, I assure you. But where the hell is Stonewall Jackson when we need him the most?"

General Gordon smiled. "Don't think that thought hasn't already crossed my mind. Are you sure you're okay?"

"I'm positive, General. I'm fine."

Conor noticed General Gordon looking him over much more carefully than usual. After a long pause, the general finally straightened and said forcefully, "Then go and find the Thirty-eighth Georgia right away. Lieutenant Colonel McLeod has been killed, and I'm appointing you as its new commander, effective now."

Conor, surprised, had failed to notice McLeod's absence in the staff gathering just concluded. He took another drink before he returned the general's canteen.

"I'm on my way, sir."

"And Major, our orders are to halt," the general said, unsmiling and staring hard at him. "Look at me and tell me you fully understand what that means."

"Understood, General. We are halted."

Conor located the 38th Georgia and began receiving verbal reports from the company commanders on the condition of their respective companies. In addition to Lieutenant Colonel McLeod, two lieutenants from the regimental staff had also been killed, along with a number of non-commissioned officers in the various companies. Casualties in the regiment were the highest in the brigade with 16 dead and 54 wounded from a force of 341 men at the beginning of the day. First Sergeant Barrymore, of whom Conor had immediate doubts when he hesitated to tell Conor what he had done during the battle, took his new commander to the makeshift regimental hospital where Conor met the doctors and checked on the wounded soldiers. There were piles of amputated limbs outside the main tent that caught his attention and momentarily stunned him. He certainly knew that amputations were common from the bone-shattering wounds created by the Minie balls, but he had never actually seen the residue of those operations. Amid the grisly sounds and sights, he remembered Dante's phrase, "Abandon hope, all ye who enter here," before turning away and leaving.

"Ugly, ain't it?" First Sergeant Barrymore remarked.

Conor said nothing.

A courier on horseback arrived from General Gordon's staff. "Major Rafferty, General Gordon would like you to mount up and meet him at that same tree location, without delay."

Conor found the general in an even further state of agitation. "C'mon, Conor. We're riding into Gettysburg to make another argument that we attack Cemetery Hill immediately. If I don't make the case once more, I won't be able to live with myself."

They quickly started out toward the town, with barely an hour of daylight remaining.

"And if we can get authorization to attack tonight, I'm sending your regiment among those who will go in first. So see if you can take a look up there and find out as much as you can."

The town was chaotic with Confederate troops moving about in the streets while still exchanging fire with straggling Yankees. The town's citizens, taking refuge in what they hoped was the safety of their homes, were unnerved over what they had seen happening to their battered Union army. General Gordon located the house with the Confederate battle flags planted in the yard where Generals Masterson and Ewell were debating the wisdom of an evening attack. Conor went on ahead, riding Shannon south along the Baltimore Pike toward Cemetery Hill when suddenly a Confederate corporal stepped out onto the road and signaled for him to stop.

"Sir, they's Yankee snipers all up in them houses yonder. We've had three men shot at in the last half-hour."

"I need to get a look at Cemetery Hill. What do you suggest?"

"That thing's crawling with Yankees, sir. Listen and you can hear 'em diggin' in up there."

"I need to do more than hear them, Corporal. Is there a house close by that has a rooftop I could get on?"

The corporal pointed to a house across the street. "I've got a sniper on the roof of that house right there. A good bit of Cemetery Hill's in view from up there. Follow me, Major."

Conor tied Shannon to a post outside the two-story home and followed the corporal inside. There were at least a dozen wounded soldiers from both sides being treated by several women. He stepped around and over them and followed the corporal to a staircase that led to the roof. The sniper on the roof glanced at Conor but otherwise kept his eyes ahead in search of targets.

"Might wanna scrunch over, sir. Don't make yourself—"

The Confederate sniper suddenly fired at an opposing shooter on a rooftop across the street, perhaps seventy-five yards distant. The Yankee soldier slumped forward and dropped his rifle, his arms dangling and his body nearly tumbling off the roof. Blood began streaming down the side of the house.

"Good 'un, James," the corporal said. "I'll bet that's the same sumbitch tried to pop ole Red while ago."

Conor scrunched over.

As he looked through his field glasses in the fading light, Conor could see the Federal soldiers who had been running for their lives earlier in the day now furiously digging holes and piling rocks and fence rails in front of their positions. A tall, imposing officer on horseback moved about the men in a calm, deliberate manner, giving orders to other officers, occasionally personally directing the placement of cannons or troops. He would sometimes stop and say something that would cause a group of soldiers to laugh in that particularly loud, rowdy way that soldiers cackle at lewd comments. It was clear that these men had retreated as far as they intended, and they were now preparing a defensive position that would take an exacting toll on any attacker. Conor made a sketch of what he could see and an estimate of the number of Federal soldiers he thought were occupying the hill. He then got up to leave the rooftop.

The corporal noticed the missing little finger on Conor's writing hand. "Yankee ball take off that finger, sir?"

"Yep. I suppose it's still out there somewhere on that sunken road at Sharpsburg."

"We was both there," the corporal proudly announced with a point toward his sniper buddy. "Now *that* was a fight."

"You goin' up that hill, Major?" the young sniper asked Conor as he was leaving.

"I think so," he answered. "Better now than later."

He gave a reluctant nod. "Good luck, whenever you do."

There was an attractive young woman on the second floor of the house who was leaning back and resting in a chair when Conor came back inside. She appeared to be about his age, with blond hair and blue eyes, of medium height and build. She glanced up at Conor with a tired expression as he approached. When she saw his uniform, she quickly avoided eye contact.

"Do you live here, ma'am?" Conor asked.

"It's my mother's house, but I live here, yes," she replied, still without looking at Conor.

"This has been some day, huh?"

She frowned, but said nothing.

Conor reached an outstretched hand toward her. "I'm Major Conor Rafferty."

She hesitated a moment, staring at his hand and then noticing the missing finger. She soon relented and gave him a firm handshake, finally making eye contact. "Amanda Wiedenour."

"Thank you for looking after these wounded men, Amanda. I was injured at Sharpsburg and I'll always appreciate the help I was given in the home of a private citizen."

"I would have much preferred that you and your soldiers had never come to our peaceful little town. Things will never be the same for us now. This is going to become nothing but a disaster, a disaster on a huge scale, thanks to you," she said, her voice breaking. "My brother's out there somewhere, and this man you've got on our roof could be aiming his gun at him, for all I know."

"My brother's out there somewhere too, Amanda. I'm sorry you and your mother had to be pulled into this. I truly am."

"I'm sorry any of us in Gettysburg had to be pulled into this," she said, her tears streaming down her cheek.

Conor attempted to change the subject. "What do you do when there's not a war going on in the middle of your town?"

She looked at him in disgust.

"Yes, you're right. Those were poorly chosen words. I apologize, ma'am. I promise you I didn't mean that to be as callous as it sounded. Please forgive my rather clumsy attempt at humor."

She looked away.

"Let me try again. What do you do to make a living?"

"I'm a seamstress," she said, wiping her eyes with the bottom of her apron.

"Ah," he said. "I'm sure you're a good one."

"I am a good one. Are you good at what you do?"

"Well, I try to be. I had expected to become a lawyer but things obviously changed for me, as they did for most of us. I've spent nearly six months recovering in hospitals since I joined the army, so the lawyering way of life has an even greater appeal to me now."

She laughed out loud but quickly caught herself, cleared her throat, and resumed her rigid demeanor. "What were you doing on our roof?"

"Looking for a good restaurant. I haven't eaten in days, it seems."

"I believe that, sure."

"Of course you do."

"Did you see what you went up there to see?"

"I think we should talk about other things, ma'am."

"Like what? Like how much we're all enjoying our daily lives here in Gettysburg since your army showed up?"

"That wouldn't be at the top of the list of the things I'd care to talk about. Maybe I should just leave."

She took a deep breath. "So where is your home?"

"Georgia, near Atlanta. I haven't been home in two years."

"That's a long time," she said softly. "Did you leave a girl behind?"

"Well, not really," Conor said with a chuckle.

"Is she pretty?"

"Uh, yes, very. Her name is Patricia Welch. She's a schoolteacher."

"So what happened?"

"She wanted to get married, and honestly I was just about to propose, I really was. But then the war started and I cooled on the idea."

"So you just up and left?"

"Pretty much, yeah," Conor said with a chuckle as he remembered his conversation with Rebecca Gordon in Richmond.

"Boy, you're a real prize."

"I know. I'm not sure anyone will ever have me now."

"Oh, I'm sure you could have your pick of those pretty Southern belles," she said in an exaggerated accent.

Conor smiled. "What about you? Are you married or spoken for?"

"No, neither. That is probably the only thing we have in common, but not for the same reasons. Your Rebel army at Fredericksburg, Virginia killed my boyfriend. We were making plans for after the war."

"I'm very sorry."

She gave him a hard stare.

Conor again decided to change the subject. "Our regular soldiers who are coming into your home, like the men on the roof, are they being respectful?"

She shrugged. "They're polite, yeah. But I'd rather not have them here at all if you want to know the truth about it."

"I understand. They're just doing what they're told, Amanda, like the rest of us."

"Then tell them to go someplace else."

"I'm sorry, but I can't do that."

She sighed. "I just hope this whole nightmare ends soon."

Conor nodded. "We agree on that. Well, I really should go now."

She looked at him with reddened eyes and said, "Yes, you probably should."

Conor turned to leave but then stopped and asked, "Do you have enough food and water?"

"No," she answered quickly. "We'll be out of both soon. And we need bandages. We've used up all the sheets in the house. But we're really starting to feel desperate about the food and water. Please, help us if you can."

"I'll see to it right away. I can't promise anything, but I'll do what I can."

Conor held out his hand again and she took it.

"God bless you, Amanda Wiedenour."

Conor walked down the stairs and back through the open part of the house where the wounded were lying. He stopped and spoke briefly to the three wounded Confederates, all of whom were conscious and aware, and then started toward the door.

"Major?" she called from the top of the stairs.

He turned and heard Amanda say, "Please don't forget about the food and water."

Conor returned to the house where General Gordon was meeting with the other senior leaders. He waited outside, sitting in a rocking chair on the porch and wishing he could sleep for an hour. When an adjutant came out for a break, Conor gave him his sketch and his estimate of the enemy force. The adjutant took it back inside immediately.

A commissary sergeant Conor recognized passed by on foot in front of the house.

"Sergeant, I need your help in a big way. I need you to get me some rations and water. You can do that, can't you?"

"Depends, sir. Gimme a number."

"Enough for twenty people for say, five days. That's a hundred rations and water. Can you get those for me?"

"If you don't mind me asking, sir, who are you and what is your job?"

"I don't mind. I'm Major Rafferty, and I'm a regimental commander in Gordon's Brigade."

"That's good enough for me, sir. I should be able to do that. We just got our hands on some Yankee wagons full of rations. Do you want them delivered here?" he asked, pointing to the house behind Conor.

"No. I want you to deliver them to that gray, two-story house down the street there. We have wounded in that house, men from both sides, and they're running out of food and water. And if you can find something they can make bandages from, bring that along also. Deliver them to a young woman at the house named Amanda. Can you do that tonight?"

"Yessir. Deliver to Amanda. I'll do what I can."

"Thank you, Sergeant. And Sergeant?"

"Yessir?"

"There are Yankee snipers in the houses at the far end of the street. Don't make yourself an easy target. Move quickly and scrunch over."

General Gordon emerged from the house twenty minutes later, his expression still dour. "Nothing's happening tonight." He shook his head in disgust, then walked over and climbed onto his horse.

Conor said nothing on the ride back to camp. He had a hasty meeting with the company commanders when the orders were received placing the entire brigade on the York Road to guard the division's rear. A report of Union reinforcements moving toward Gettysburg from the northeast had been forwarded, and the brigade was deployed to intercept any such movement if it were to materialize. Conor pointed out his regiment's assigned place in the camp and the company commanders then went about moving their troops to their respective areas. Conor then spent time watching the company commanders as they oversaw the placement of their soldiers, and he later dined with them when their rations arrived. A few of the company commanders, a mix of captains and lieutenants, were suspicious of Conor, but he wasn't concerned. They would have a chance to get to know one another better in the coming days.

General Gordon summoned the regimental commanders to his tent once they had set up along the York Road.

"I argued hard to take this brigade up Cemetery Hill tonight and send those Yankees running, but General Masterson and General Ewell wouldn't give an inch. Some of us were terribly upset and disappointed with that decision, but in the end, there was little we could do about it. The Federals lost a corps commander today, John Reynolds, and they have been run off the field in defeat. Now they are digging in up there on Cemetery Hill, and we are going to leave them alone tonight and pay a big price for it tomorrow. We've missed our best chance, I'm afraid."

The meeting lasted less than thirty minutes since there were no orders beyond the current assignment of protecting the rear of the division.

"Any idea where Semmes' Brigade might be, sir?" Conor asked as he was leaving.

"That would be McLaws and Longstreet, to the west of Gettysburg. Why?"

"My brother's with the Tenth Georgia."

"Oh yes, of course," the general said. "Write a note to him in care of General Semmes' Brigade and I'll get it in the courier package in the morning. But don't go trying to ride over there in the dark tonight. You'd likely be shot before you got halfway there. That's not the way I want to lose a regimental commander."

"I won't do that, sir."

"By the way, Conor, you'll become a lieutenant colonel as soon as I can process the promotion."

"And I was just getting used to being a major, sir."

***

Tuesday, February 12, 1918
"Did you have any idea after the first day, Cappy, that Gettysburg would become such a consequential battle?" Aaron asked.

"Yes, I thought it would be the biggest battle we had fought to that point. Both armies were arriving in force to fight it out there, so yes, I knew it would be a big one. And even though we made the huge tactical blunder of not maintaining our pursuit of the Yankees on through to Cemetery Hill and beyond, I was confident we would win the battle and very possibly end the war at Gettysburg."

"For sure, it was a huge tactical blunder not to press the attack when your side had the clear advantage. Even still, you didn't seem to think at the time that it would affect the outcome in a negative way, did you?"

"No. I saw it as an impediment, but only that."

"Do you think Stonewall Jackson's presence would have made a difference?"

Conor smiled. "Of course. His presence almost always made a difference. There would have been no hesitation on his part to attack through the town and up Cemetery Hill before they could reorganize and dig in. If he had seen what I saw when we were clearing the field of Yankees—and he certainly would have seen it—he would have pursued them with all the speed and aggressiveness that was his custom. His absence was greatly felt at Gettysburg, and never more than on that first day."

"Do you think the war would have ended if the Confederacy had won the battle?"

"Quite possibly, yes."

"And do you think that would have been the best result for the country?"

Conor stared at Aaron before finally saying, "How do you expect me to answer that? At the time, of course I would have thought it was the best result. The killing stops and we all get to go home. But the way things have worked out with the country being reunited, the elimination of slavery and so forth, well, how can I say with any honesty that that has been a bad result?"

"That's probably an unfair question, Cappy," Aaron said apologetically. "It's always easier to look back and say, 'what if?' I didn't mean to put you on the spot."

"You ask what you want, Aaron. I'll do my best to answer, even if I get a little sore."

"Thanks. This is great stuff. Do you feel well enough to keep going?"

"Sure."

Chapter Seven

Gettysburg — Second Day

Get out of the way old Dan Tucker
You're too late to get your supper
Dinner's gone and supper's cookin'
Old Dan Tucker's just a-standin there lookin'.
"Old Dan Tucker"

July 2, 1863
Gordon's Brigade moved into its assigned position at the base of Cemetery Ridge for the anticipated attack upon Cemetery Hill. It was the afternoon of Thursday, July 2, and Conor had his regiment on the brigade's right flank as they assembled to the northeast of the enemy's position. General Masterson formed a two-brigade front, with Gordon's Brigade in reserve, and a fourth brigade kept on the York Road to protect the rear. General Rodes was to the right, to the northwest of Cemetery Hill, while on the left General Johnson faced his brigades toward Culp's Hill.

The larger plan was for Longstreet's 1st Corps to take the heights on the Union left which were seemingly unoccupied, then turn their left flank, with A.P. Hill's 3rd Corps threatening the Union center, and finally having Ewell's 2nd Corps roll up the Union right at Culp's Hill and Cemetery Hill. The effect would thus be a compressing and crushing of Meade's Army of the Potomac, ending the battle and perhaps the war itself.

Longstreet's attack was late in starting, so the assaults on the Union right against Cemetery Hill and

Culp's Hill were likewise delayed. Conor chose not to ride into battle since he wanted to be close enough to his companies to gain a better appreciation for their skill and temperament once the shooting began. He had spent time with all of his company commanders and found them to be intelligent, resourceful officers who were serving the regiment well.

The older, wiser Colonel Evans of the 31st Georgia had spent several hours with Conor off and on over the past twenty-four hours, providing his youthful understudy his unselfish advice on the business of running an infantry regiment. Conor considered the colonel to be the best regimental commander in the brigade by a substantial margin, and his counsel was not only wise but also greatly beneficial. The colonel was forthcoming enough to tell Conor that some of the officers in the regiment saw him as being General Gordon's personal favorite—his "lap dog," as it were. Colonel Evans told Conor he didn't see it that way himself, but several other officers who considered themselves more deserving had thought Conor's appointment to regimental commander wholly unfair. Conor thanked the colonel for his advice and honesty.

Conor had to admit he was a little stung at being referred to by some as a "lap dog." Even though he didn't know for sure which specific officers held that opinion, he did have some idea. However, he decided that his best course was simply to let the matter pass. He knew his performance in battle had long ago shown his worth as a commander, and he decided to ignore the pettiness of others. That he was close to General Gordon was an undeniable fact, but he felt strongly that their relationship had been built in large measure upon his own demonstrated competence. While the general was extraordinarily loyal, had he ever come to feel that he could no longer count on Conor or trust him to do the right thing, Conor knew the wagons would immediately gain that high-ranking driver.

Conor walked with Captain Willingham among the men of A Company as they spread out and rested on the grass. Some ate from leftover rations; some slept; most just sat and waited with the sort of equanimity that had been finely honed in the army over countless such hours of sitting and waiting. Even though they were young by their chronological age, they were battle-tested veterans who looked older than their nineteen or twenty years. Conor had directed First Sergeant Barrymore that, while it was okay for him to be beyond his physical reach, he was to make certain that Conor was never out of his view. He did not trust Barrymore, and he suspected that Barrymore had a strong propensity to be where the action wasn't. Barrymore was clearly unhappy about such a directive, as Conor had anticipated, but he followed along as ordered.

One of the privates held up a dark substance as Conor walked by. "Like a little chaw, sir?"

Conor leaned over and stared at the contents of the pouch for a moment, sniffed it, and then said in a loud voice, "Good grief! I swear I'd rather chew on Widow Brown's wrinkly old ass that put *that* stuff in my mouth."

The troops within earshot erupted in raucous laughter. Others began repeating the line to those who had heard the laughter but not the words. It instantly reminded Conor of the Union officer he had seen the night before on Cemetery Hill, whom General Gordon later told him had very likely been General Winfield Scott Hancock.

The Longstreet attack on the Union left commenced around 4:00 pm when his artillery barrage began as a precursor to the infantry assaults. Before long, the Confederate attacks on the Union right at Cemetery Hill and Culp's Hill were underway, and Conor quickly judged that the attacks were becoming especially intense. Union artillery was blasting away at two Confederate brigades attacking up Cemetery Hill, and the volume of musketry indicated that the Yankees were hotly contesting the objective.

Conor checked with his company commanders to ensure the regiment was ready to move ahead when ordered. With their assault plan established, they would move up to join the other regiments already engaged. Conor could see through his field glasses that the going was slow and tedious, that the Federals were opposing every foot of progress the Confederate soldiers were making. Conor couldn't spot an obvious weakness in the Federal position, so he concluded they would just have to force the attack and create a weak spot.

"May I speak with you, Major?"

First Sergeant Barrymore stood alongside Conor who was sitting and looking through his field glasses at the activity at Cemetery Hill.

"Sure. Take a seat. What's on your mind?"

"I don't think we've gotten off to the best of starts," Barrymore said as he plopped on the ground.

"What makes you say that?"

"Well sir, I had an arrangement with the previous commanding officer that I would keep things moving from an administrative standpoint when the regiment went into battle."

"What sorts of things are you referring to that would need to be kept moving?"

"Paperwork and so forth."

"In the rear?"

"Yessir, back at camp."

"And so when you say you think we've not gotten off to the best of starts, did you mean it's because I saw no reason for you to be anywhere but with the soldiers when we went into battle?"

"You're making me out to be some sort of coward, Major," Barrymore said defensively.

"That's not what I said, First Sergeant. I only told you that I expect you to be on the battlefield with us, and that I would prefer you to stay close enough so you can help me determine our level of casualties, make sure we get the wounded to the docs, and gather any other pieces of information I may need."

"Sir, I'm thirty-six years of age with a wife and five kids. I'd like to live to see them again when this thing is over."

"Would you prefer that I arrange a transfer to something less risky?"

"Again, Major, you're making me out to be a coward."

"I'm not making you out to be anything, First Sergeant. Do you want out of this regiment? Yes or no?"

There was a long pause, a deep breath, and a sigh before Barrymore finally nodded and answered, "I would like that transfer, yessir."

Conor nodded and said, "Then you have my word that I'll see to it as soon as possible."

Barrymore rose and saluted. "Thank you, sir."

General Gordon rode into Conor's position several times during the extended wait, each time reminding Conor to remain at the ready, that they would soon be getting the order to move forward. Minie balls were whizzing around the position, prompting Conor to order the troops to the ground. At one point, a solid-shot artillery shell came hurtling their way, passing so close to Conor's head that he distinctly felt the heat from it. Then he heard the sickening thud behind him of the shell hitting a soldier, and when he turned he saw First Sergeant Barrymore lying motionless on the ground. Barrymore had been struck flush in the upper chest and killed instantly. Two soldiers picked up the body and took it to the rear of the position. Conor felt a tinge of guilt for having ordered Barrymore to remain close by, especially when he thought of Barrymore's now five fatherless children. Then he reminded himself that good soldiers move toward the sound of the firing, not away from it. The guilt soon passed, but not without Conor questioning if the war was changing him into an unsympathetic, uncaring shell of a person he truly didn't want to become. After a few moments, he swallowed hard and forced himself back into his role as a troop leader about to go into battle.

It was difficult for Conor to determine at any given moment exactly what was going on to his front. The volume of firing told him little, though he kept an ear attuned for the wild, almost maniacal yelling and screaming of the Rebel troops that usually accompanied a breakthrough. He wondered several times what action Sean might be seeing on the other side of the field. Conor had sent him a letter earlier that morning, at General Gordon's suggestion, and he hoped to get a note back from him in case they were unable to meet after the battle's conclusion.

Meanwhile, they continued to wait.

Masterson's Division had some modest success, but by nightfall the Confederate troops had failed to dislodge the Federals either from Cemetery Hill or Culp's Hill. General Gordon's Brigade saw no action on July 2. General Masterson told General Gordon that he found it inadvisable to send in his brigade when the outcome would have changed little, if any. General Masterson blamed General Rodes for not being aggressive enough in attacking Cemetery Hill from the west, which caused the Southern troops to come under even heavier fire. It was a failure of Rodes' execution, Masterson declared, not his own, making Conor think it was somewhat akin to tossing a man from a ship and blaming the ocean for his death. Conor noticed there was a tendency on the part of general officers to blame one another when the outcome of an attack was less than desired. He could not easily remember an occasion where a general had taken full responsibility for a battlefield failure, that it must have been a common occurrence for as long as there had been battles and generals. He kept that little morsel to himself, however.

The brigade stayed in the same position for the rest of the night to counter any unexpected move by the Federals. The sporadic gunfire continued in the dark as pickets and skirmishers took shots at one another.

At about 9:00 pm, General Gordon sent word that he wanted Conor to accompany him into Gettysburg. Conor had Shannon brought forward and then rode into town with the general to the Corps headquarters house.

"There's someone here you need to see," the general said with a slight smile.

Sergeant Tanneyhill, who had served with Conor at F Company in the 6th Alabama, was waiting on the steps of the house.

Sergeant Tanneyhill saluted as they dismounted.

"The good sergeant here contacted me and asked if I could find a job for him in our brigade," General Gordon explained. "He got wounded a little after Sharpsburg and when he came back to his old outfit, they wanted to put him in the artillery. I remember what you said, Major Rafferty, about how good he had been with F Company, so I worked it out where he could come here. Major Rafferty, say hello to First Sergeant Tanneyhill. He now belongs to you and the Thirty-eighth Georgia."

The two friends shook hands enthusiastically.

"Where's your gear?" Conor asked.

First Sergeant Tanneyhill bounded up the steps and retrieved his knapsack, haversack, musket, and cartridge box from the porch.

"Do you need me here any further, General?" Conor asked.

"No. Take your man back with you before the Sixth Alabama finds out he's missing. Welcome to the brigade, First Sergeant."

Conor mounted Shannon and then pulled Tanneyhill up behind him. They stopped at the nearby two-story house up the street that Conor had visited the previous evening. Sporadic gunfire was still coming from the direction of Cemetery Hill, and when the dirt flew up between the two of them, Tanneyhill noticed immediately.

"We're getting shot at, sir," he offered calmly. "Snipers in the houses up yonder."

A sudden shot rang out from the roof of the house they were about to enter. First Sergeant Tanneyhill flinched and muttered, "Dammit!"

"Good one, James," Conor called.

They could only barely see him in the dark, but the young sniper from the previous evening leaned over from the rooftop and looked down at them, smiling. Conor and the sniper tipped their caps.

"C'mon, this won't take long," Conor said as they climbed the steps and knocked on the door.

A middle-aged woman opened the door and peered out at them suspiciously.

"Mrs. Wiedenour?"

"Yes. What do you want?"

"I'm Major Rafferty and this is First Sergeant Tanneyhill. I was here last night and I wanted to know if the water and rations were delivered to your home as I had directed."

Amanda quietly moved beside her mother and opened the door fully. "Come in, please," she said.

The three of them stood in the foyer as the mother stepped away. The wounded were still spread out on the floor, but now in twice the numbers.

Amanda smiled and nodded. "Yes, the food and water came late last night. Your solider even brought some sheets and blankets that we've been able to put to good use. We've taken in several more wounded men today, and all but one came from your side. One of your doctors came by the house late this morning and checked on all of the wounded. He said three of the men would have to have immediate surgery—two Confederate and one Union—and he sent for an ambulance wagon to transport them to one of your places where the surgery could be done. The doctor told us we were doing a great job taking care of them. He asked me what we were feeding them, and I showed him the rations. Then he asked where they came from and I told him a Confederate major had kindly arranged for it."

"What did the doctor say then?" Conor asked, chuckling.

"He laughed and said, 'I'll bet his name is Rafferty.' And I told him, 'Yes, that's him.' I hope I didn't get you in any trouble."

"No. In fact, the doctor is one of my regimental surgeons. I had asked him to stop in and check on y'all."

"Thank you again for everything, Major. I realize we're not on the same side, but I'm grateful for the help you've given us. You're very considerate."

Conor could have stood in the foyer and gazed into the blue eyes of that beautiful Pennsylvania girl for another hour, but he understood his priorities. He stepped out onto the porch.

"Well, Miss Wiedenour, please be careful and take good care of yourself. I truly hope everything works out for you and your family. Thank you once more for taking care of our wounded soldiers. I shall never forget you or your great kindness."

Conor saluted and then left with First Sergeant Tanneyhill.

"I won't ask how that happened," Tanneyhill commented.

"Ah, it's not as it seems. She's a nice girl, and she's caught up in something that's overwhelming her and her town. So naturally, she's startled by it and frightened by it.

But she's a brave and kindhearted lady, and I admire her for that."

"And she's a Yankee."

"And she's a Yankee, you're right. That's why I won't be sending my doc there again. I would trust her, but I don't know about her mother."

First Sergeant Tanneyhill and Conor spent most of the rest of the night catching up from when they had last seen one another at Sharpsburg. Conor set out his expectations for Tanneyhill in his new role, and concluded that it was a stroke of good fortune to have the exceptional Tanneyhill working with him again.

"I gotta ask, what happened to the guy I'm replacing?" said Tanneyhill.

"It was one of those wicked solid-shot projectiles that ricochets off the ground and—"

"Say no more."

***

Tuesday, February 12, 1918

Aaron shook his head in disbelief. "There were so many 'almosts' for the Confederates on July 2. They were right on the verge of victory much of the day. Were you aware of what had gone on at Little Round Top, the Wheatfield, Devil's Den, and so forth, Cappy?"

"Not until later. We were concerned about what was going on in front of us, and whether we would join the assault on Cemetery Hill. I had a regiment that I would presumably be taking into battle, so I was paying close attention to that, obviously. But later on when we started hearing reports about how close we had come to taking the heights, and about the overall terrible coordination of the attacks across the entire front, it was disheartening."

"Were you nervous about being a new regimental commander?"

"Lots, yes. It wasn't that I was overly concerned about getting hurt or even killed, even though I didn't want that to happen. But I was far more concerned about being the competent commander that hundreds of men were counting on. And remember, I was just twenty-three. So yes, I was plenty anxious."

"Was there still a sense of optimism even after the disappointments of the second day?"

"Of course. We had come within a whisker of turning the Federal left flank, and had we done that, the third day would have been very different. So yes, we were still optimistic that we would defeat Meade and gain the victory."

"We visited the Gettysburg battlefield in the summer of my second year at West Point, so I'm finding it fascinating to hear you tell stories about the place I visited and the battle I've studied, even the exact same terrain I walked over. It's really captivating to hear a firsthand account, especially knowing now that you were there the entire three days."

Conor felt energized by Aaron's keen interest and his obvious passion to learn.

"Keep going, Cappy?"

"Let's keep going."

Chapter Eight

Gettysburg — Third Day

Amazing Grace, how sweet the sound,
That saved a wretch like me,
I once was lost but now am found.
Was blind, but now I see.
"Amazing Grace"

July 3, 1863

"Begging your pardon, sir. Top of the morning to you, Major Rafferty."

Conor was awakened in his tent two hours before sunrise after a mostly fitful attempt at sleeping. An enlisted aide to General Gordon, lantern in one hand and a cup of steaming hot coffee in the other, apologized for the early hour. The aide put the coffee and lantern on Conor's small makeshift desk and then retrieved an envelope from his shirt pocket.

"This letter just came in with the courier package. Also, sir, General Gordon would like to see you in his tent as soon as possible," the aide added before leaving.

Conor wiped at his eyes and sat up, alone in his cramped tent. He got up and went to his desk, to the coffee, hoping the strong brew would chase the blurry haze from his head. He glanced at the envelope in the dim light of the lantern but didn't recognize the simple handwriting. It was addressed to "Maj Rafferty," with his brigade and regimental addresses apparently added by a clerk.

He opened the letter.

137

Jul 2 '63

Deer Maj Rafferty sir –

    My name is pvt Amos Caldwell, 10th Ga. CSA. I am sorry to writ to you that yor brother sgt Sean Rafferty was kilt to-day in the fight at the wheet field. He was shot with a ball at the top of his lef leg and bleed to deth. I was with him to the end and he ask me to writ to you to let you no he was kilt. I tell you sir Sean was a brav man. A better man they never was. I am sorry for you and yor famly. God bless.

Amos Caldwell

P.S. I have done a loc of Sean's hair in this for you.

    "You sent for me, General?"

    "Yes," the general answered, pointing toward a chair. "We have something important to discuss. Take a seat."

    Conor's eyes were bloodshot and puffy. "Okay," he said softly.

    The general took a deep breath and handed Conor a copy of a newly received order directing that one of General Gordon's regiments be temporarily assigned to General A.P. Hill's 3rd Corps. Generals Ewell and Masterson had endorsed the directive. Conor read over the order once, then once more, and handed it back to General Gordon.

    "Send me," Conor said curtly.

    "The word is we're launching a major assault today. Since you were not in command of your regiment during the heaviest fighting on the first day, and since we were in reserve yesterday, I thought you deserved the first chance at this. I don't know what you'll face out there today, but I can guess we may very well be headed toward another major battle. You should know what you might be getting yourself into in this assignment. You will be with commanders you don't know, with other regiments you've never worked with before, and on top of that you're not even familiar with your own regiment yet. And if that's not complicated enough, you'll likely be under fire, and probably intense fire. If you don't want this, for whatever reason, then I'll send Clement Evans. But I wanted to give you the first choice."

"Send me."

"Are you sure?"

"Yes, sir, entirely sure. Who should I report to?"

"General Ambrose Wright. He has three other Georgia regiments in his brigade and he'll be glad to have you."

"When should we get moving?"

"Now. They're expecting you."

Conor stood, a grim expression on his face. General Gordon also stood and extended his hand.

"Good luck, Conor. I have every confidence in you. Get back here as soon as you're done."

"I will, sir."

"And the letter you got this morning? Was it from your brother? Is he okay?"

"He was killed in battle yesterday, General."

General Gordon's face showed his surprise. "Oh dear God no, Conor. I'm so very sorry. I can't imagine what you must be going through. My God, I had no idea you were dealing with this. Look, this changes things. I am not sending you out there under these circumstances. I'm just not going to do this to you. I'm going to send Colonel Evans to this 3rd Corps assignment. You shouldn't have to deal with this on the day you've gotten the news of your brother's death."

Conor raised his hand in objection. "Actually, sir, this is the best possible thing I could do today. Please believe me. And this is the best thing you could do for me today. I need this assignment, General, more than you could ever know."

"For heaven's sake, Conor, think of your mother. You don't want her to—"

"It's fine, sir. I appreciate your concern, but I want very badly to do this. Now, if there's nothing else, General, I need to get my regiment on the road."

General Gordon took a long, deep breath and then placed his hand on Conor's shoulder. "If you're sure this is what you want, then I won't change it. I am truly sorry that you've lost your brother. You can let me know later if there is anything I can do. Until then, God be with you, Conor. God be with all of you."

Once on the road to 3rd Corps, marching in the dark, Conor confided to First Sergeant Tanneyhill that Sean had been killed the day prior.

"I'm sorry, sir. A chance to help even the score today might help," Tanneyhill remarked.

"That's exactly what I'm thinking," Conor replied.

By daybreak, Conor had moved his 38th Georgia from the Cemetery Hill region to the area around Seminary Ridge where he found the 3rd Corps headquarters and the nearby command post of General Ambrose Wright.

"My orders direct me to report to you, General," Conor said when he joined General Wright and his senior officers at their outdoor command center. "I'm from 2nd Corps, General Gordon's Brigade."

General Wright introduced Conor to the other officers, all Georgians, and all of whom were gathered around a large map atop a table. A campfire with its glowing embers was burning down nearby.

"Rafferty, my orders have changed," said General Wright, "and consequently so have yours."

Conor nodded his understanding. There was nothing odd or out of the ordinary for things to change in a military organization, no matter the meticulousness of the planning or the extent to which the changes might bring about additional complication or confusion. The irony was that an institution thought to be so organically resistant to change did, in fact, change all the time.

"My adjutant will direct you over to the 1st Corps headquarters where you are to be assigned to General Pickett's Division."

Twenty minutes later Conor was introduced to Major General George Pickett and his three brigade commanders, Generals Armistead, Kemper, and Garnett, all Virginians. They were standing outside General Pickett's headquarters tent, enjoying a breakfast of ham and biscuits.

"Would you join us with a bit of this absolutely delightful cuisine, Major Rafferty?" asked General Pickett, looking his swashbuckling best with his shoulder-length brown hair in long ringlets, his well-fitting uniform, and a riding whip in one hand with the other holding the thick, fluffy biscuit.

"Thank you, General. I'd be delighted to join you."

"What about your soldiers?" asked General Armistead. "Shall I arrange breakfast for them?"

"I would very much appreciate that, sir."

"Attention, gentlemen," called General Pickett as General James Longstreet, the famous 1st Corps commander and arguably General Lee's most trusted advisor, approached the group.

"At ease, gentlemen," said General Longstreet, a powerful-looking man with a heavy, untrimmed brown beard, a weatherworn uniform with mud-stained boots, and a heavy black felt hat. "It's been pointed out to me, George, that I might find the best breakfast in the whole of General Lee's army right here at your headquarters."

"You have been advised accurately, General Longstreet. But permit me, sir, to introduce Major Conor Rafferty who has kindly put his 38th Georgia at our disposal."

After returning Conor's salute, General Longstreet's handshake more than matched his vigorous physical bearing. His piercing, blueish-gray eyes gave off an aura of both intelligence and seriousness of purpose. He had a presence about him—all the great ones did, Conor thought—that caused every eye in sight to follow him, every ear to carefully listen to his words, and every mind to enable its powers of observation to determine his mood, his intentions, his actions and reactions.

"Major, you've come to the right place if you want to be a part of the biggest story of the day. Glad to have you and your Georgians with us. Tell John Gordon I owe him one."

"I will, General."

Conor's 38th Georgia was assigned to the brigade of General Lewis Armistead, and would be positioned in the middle of the second rank of the brigade's line. Armistead was positioned behind Garnett's Brigade, with Kemper's Brigade to Garnett's immediate right. This would constitute Pickett's Division, with Pettigrew's Division on its immediate left. Some 15,000 Confederate soldiers would participate in the frontal assault upon the center of Meade's Army of the Potomac, which was concentrated mainly along Cemetery Ridge.

By 11:00 am, Conor and his regiment were positioned in a swale near Seminary Ridge, looking to escape the heat and seeking some last-minute rest in preparation for the assault. General Armistead went over the attack plan with Conor once again, and both enjoyed a cup of coffee brought by one of the general's staff officers.

General Armistead pointed to Generals Lee and Longstreet as they rode nearby, with Lee stopping and pointing in the distance to the Federal positions on Cemetery Ridge.

"This battle could decide the fate of the war today, Major," said the general. "By the end of this day the war could well be over, God willing."

Conor nodded. "That's the hope of everyone who came here as part of this army."

The two officers then made a few minutes of small talk about families and hometowns and plans for after the war. Conor mentioned that his brother had been killed the previous day in the wheatfield fight. General Armistead offered his condolences and then summoned the brigade chaplain. When the chaplain arrived five minutes later, he offered a short but warmhearted prayer that deeply touched Conor, whose eyes inadvertently filled with tears. It was the first outward emotion Conor had permitted himself since receiving the news earlier that morning.

Conor later took out the small Bible given to him by Rebecca Gordon, which he always carried into battle with him. He read aloud Psalm 18:39, "For thou hast girded me with strength unto the battle: thou hast subdued under me those that rose up against me." He then said a silent prayer for Sean, for his family, and for his regiment.

By 1:00 pm, the Confederate artillery barrage began. The batteries stretched for more than a mile in width, 150 guns in all, and the concussion from the fusillade was well beyond anything any of the soldiers had ever experienced. Within 15 minutes, 75 Union guns commenced firing in return. The explosions were killing and wounding the Southern troops in their various staging areas, bursting on the ground, in the trees, and in the air. General Armistead got up and moved about, encouraging his soldiers to remain calm, that one place was no safer than any another. Conor was impressed with the general's unflinching courage under fire, and inspired by his command presence.

There was lots of smoke, obscuring the Confederate positions and making it virtually impossible to judge the results of the shelling of the Union positions. Conor was covered in dirt and debris as several of the bursts came within a matter of yards from him.

First Sergeant Tanneyhill ran over and plopped down beside Conor.

"How did we get so lucky to find ourselves in the middle of all this?" Tanneyhill said with a forced chuckle. "And if this ain't enough, we've only got to cover a mere three-quarters of a mile over open ground to attack an entrenched, reinforced enemy. God almighty, sir. Did I volunteer for this sort of damn crazy soldiering?"

"No," Conor replied. "But you hitched your wagon to a damn crazy soldier, I'm afraid."

"Would that be you, sir?"

"It would be me, yes. Definitely me."

By 2:30 pm, the cannonade had ceased and the smoke had largely cleared.

It was now the infantry's time.

"Remember Old Virginia," shouted General Pickett on horseback as he rode into the brigade position. "Up, men, and to your posts. Don't forget today that you are from Old Virginia."

As the animated General Pickett rode away at a gallop, General Armistead raised his sabre, faced his brigade, and shouted, "Men, remember what you are fighting for. Your homes, your firesides, and your sweethearts. Follow me!"

With that, the assault was underway. Tanneyhill and Conor shook hands, "See you on the other side," and placed themselves well apart from one another in the line of advance. Almost immediately, the brigades had to make continuous adjustments to keep the formation squared. By the time the lead elements had moved perhaps 300 yards, Union artillery let loose from Little Round Top and Cemetery Ridge with percussion shells that were instantly effective in killing and wounding large swaths of the Confederate attackers.

Conor was encouraged at the sheer number of Confederates in the attacking lines who were holding forth with great courage and discipline even as their ranks were being progressively thinned by the raking fire from the Federal cannons. He marched at the head of his regiment, and when he glanced behind him he saw a growing stream of wounded Rebs making their way back to Seminary Ridge. The ground was littered with the bodies of what seemed hundreds of soldiers. Union skirmishers began falling back when the lead Confederate brigades began nearing the Emmitsburg Road and the chest-high, sturdy plank fences which awaited them on both sides. It was then that Union cannoneers commenced firing canister, which cut into the lines at a diagonal, killing and maiming dozens of men. Conor was splashed with the blood and tissue of soldiers to his front. Some of Conor's men were falling but his advancing troops quickly closed the gaps in the line. There was fire coming from the right, from the vicinity of a red barn, and Conor could look straight ahead and see the line of blue soldiers on Cemetery Ridge and the stone wall along the crest.

By the time the Confederates began climbing the first of the two fences at the Emmitsburg Road, the Federals commenced with deadly musket fire. Conor managed to climb the first fence, then the second, with bullets whizzing past him and often striking others still climbing. The Confederates then swung to the left and realigned toward the center of the Union line. The brigades of Generals Kemper and Garnett were suffering dreadful losses as the Confederates kept pushing closer to the Union defenders. Wounded Rebs were limping and even crawling to the rear in ever-greater numbers, but the remaining Southerners continued to thrust toward the Union center.

Federal artillery then began firing solid shells at the Confederates, aiming low so that the heavy shells would skip along the ground and crash into the advancing lines. The damage to those caught in the path was usually dismemberment and most often death. Severed arms, legs, and heads were quite literally sent flying into the air, an altogether shocking sight even for the veteran soldiers.

Conor was stunned at the devastation when the solid projectiles began smashing into the lines to his front. He could actually see the shells after they had been fired, bouncing along the ground before colliding with and killing large clusters of soldiers. More than once Conor glanced behind him to make certain his troops were still following, which they were. He kept his attention directed toward the objective, the Union center, and pushed ahead one step at a time. The Confederates, Conor thought, needed to close with and defeat the enemy quickly before their entire attacking force was destroyed en route.

Still, despite the percussion shells, the canister, the solid shot, and now the Yankee musketry, all of which were tearing large gaps in their lines, the Confederates kept coming. The opposing forces could now clearly see one another's faces.

Conor saw General Armistead up ahead, his hat on his sabre, nearing the stone wall. Conor then glanced to the rear, hoping to see the remainder of General Lee's army joining the battle, but saw only dead and wounded soldiers strewn across the open field in startling numbers. The Confederate attackers were no longer a disciplined line but a mass of frantic men pushing forward, the struggle becoming hand-to-hand at the point where the forces merged. Conor was one-hundred yards behind General Armistead when he saw the general jump over the stone wall and attempt to turn the Federal artillery back on the Yankees, only to be hit and lurch backward. Union officers were superbly reinforcing their weak points and their soldiers were now swarming over the diminishing Rebel attackers. It was clear that the Confederate penetration was being repulsed and the brigades of Kemper and Garnett had virtually melted away. It was as grim a sight as Conor had ever witnessed, almost as if he were ensnared in a nightmare.

Some few of the Confederates still pushed ahead, but many were either stopping in confusion or turning around in retreat. General Armistead could no longer be seen, and there was no visible momentum left in the attack. Viewed from the Southern portion of the field, it was a ghastly, discouraging scene.

First Sergeant Tanneyhill arrived beside Conor, his face flushed and the front of his uniform covered with splotches of the blood of others from the devastating Union artillery fire.

"We gotta get the hell out of here," Tanneyhill shouted to Conor. "We'll either be shot or captured if we don't get what's left of our boys away from this. They've stopped us, sir, our attack has failed. And we won't help it none by continuing forward. We've got to break off now."

Conor looked ahead and saw the Confederates at the stone wall being captured, clubbed, bayoneted, or shot at close range. He and his men were a mere thirty yards from the wall, with Union bullets still slicing his way. Yet even more Union troops were arriving, and the fate of the grand Confederate assault was essentially sealed now. He looked at Tanneyhill and nodded.

"Thirty-eighth Georgia to the rear," Tanneyhill began shouting. "Move, boys. Face about and move to the rear, quickly."

Conor motioned with his arms for his soldiers to reverse their course. Some of the men were struck in the back as the Federals kept up their musket fire at the retreating Confederates. With each step he now took, Conor anticipated being struck and most likely killed by one of the many bullets still being fired in his direction. He could only hope that the result would be without excessive pain, that he would be dead by the time he hit the ground. His legs felt heavy and he became short of breath, his ears still ringing from the near-deafening, unrelenting noise of the battlefield. He looked around and tried to gauge what was left of his regiment, but there was no order to things anymore. His world was now upside down, and all he could do was to keep moving, one step after another. Dozens of images flashed into his mind—his brothers, his mother, his father, his soldiers, the consequences of the failed attack. More than a few of the retreating soldiers were in tears, and Conor had to fight off the impulse himself. He could hear the Union soldiers behind him on Cemetery Ridge shouting in unison, as if in one fearfully loud, ethereal voice, *"Fredericksburg! Fredericksburg! Fredericksburg!"*

By the time Conor crossed the Emmitsburg Road he could see General Longstreet in the near distance, sitting atop his horse with several of his staff, quietly watching as the survivors flooded back toward Seminary Ridge. Longstreet noticed Conor and nodded in his direction, the general's calm and stoic demeanor revealing little. Conor saluted and kept walking.

Up ahead, Conor noticed General Lee consoling the seemingly inconsolable General Pickett. "General Lee, I have no division," Conor overheard Pickett say in a voice saturated with emotion. Conor saluted and kept walking.

General Kemper returned on a stretcher, critically wounded. Generals Garnett and Armistead did not return.

Of the 38th Georgia's 271 soldiers Conor had brought that morning to General Pickett's Division, First Sergeant Tanneyhill reported that 179 were ready to make the march back to the Oak Hill area where General Gordon's Brigade was bivouacked. Conor sent his regiment ahead while he stayed and gathered information on as many of his wounded and dead soldiers as could be determined.

The sheer number of Confederate dead, wounded, and missing made it a slow and tedious process to gather the identifying data, and Conor finally left at 11:00 pm to return to his headquarters. He was in constant danger of being shot by Confederate sentries on the return trip, but after what he had endured throughout the agonizingly arduous day, he was almost too fatigued to care. He eventually reached his tent just prior to midnight.

***

Tuesday, February 12, 1918
Conor showed Aaron the original letter announcing Sean's death. The paper had yellowed over time, but the written words were still clear. Aaron read the fragile single page and then delicately placed it back in the envelope.

"I'm sorry, Aaron, but I think that's about all I can do today."

Aaron passed the letter back to Conor and sat quietly for five minutes, staring at the floor. He sniffed and wiped at his eyes several times before finally standing and reaching for his coat. "Me too, Cappy."

"No, wait," Conor called before Aaron was out of the room. "Look, we've got a limited amount of time. Let's finish with Gettysburg today. Sit back down and ask your questions, Aaron."

"You sure?"

"I'm sure, yes."

Aaron finally took a seat and looked over his notes. "July third is the day that ended the Confederacy's chances for victory in the war. Do you agree with that, Cappy?"

"Not until we got the news that Grant had taken Vicksburg did I start to think that victory might be slipping away. We still had a lot of fight left in us, and the morale of the army was good. General Gordon was optimistic and ever the fighter, but I could sense he felt that we had let a great opportunity get away from us at Gettysburg. And while none of us could be certain of what was in store, we knew that Gettysburg was not only a battle we could have won, but should have won."

"Did the fault for the failure ultimately reside with General Lee?"

"He was the overall commander, so yes, of course the fault has to be placed on General Lee. It was his plan, those were his handpicked senior commanders, and it might have been his belief in his army's invincibility that clouded his judgment, especially regarding the assault on the third day. Now, having placed the blame on General Lee's shoulders, I have to add that we still had great confidence in him."

"Lee's orders could have been more forceful, more clearly communicated, from what I've read."

"Aaron, make this a learning lesson for you: If you want a specific outcome, then give a specific order. General Lee left a lot to the discretion of his commanders, which he could do with commanders like Stonewall Jackson. But with others, his 'if practicable' guidance left too much discretion in the hands of those who needed more clear-cut direction. The afternoon of the first day comes to mind. How someone could have ordered us to suddenly halt when we were sweeping the field will forever be a mystery to me."

"I've read that some of the Confederate generals lost their nerve at Gettysburg. Did you sense that at the time?"

"I didn't see a loss of nerve so much as confusion or poor coordination. Maybe some were cautious at fighting on unfamiliar ground. But based on what I directly observed in the field on July third, I've never seen a more courageous group of general officers."

"Did Lee listen to Longstreet's objections about a frontal assault on the third day?"

"I'm sure he listened. But it also appeared that his mind was already made up. One of the great ironies of the war is that General Lee, in my opinion the greatest military strategist in our nation's history, seemed to have lost sight of the bigger picture when he sent his army up against an entrenched Union force on July third that he *had* to know would be extraordinarily difficult to overtake. It was a day I'm sure General Lee would have done differently if he could have done it all over again. "

"Do you think Jeb Stuart should have been reprimanded or even relieved of his command for showing up too late to influence the outcome?"

Conor shook his head and sighed. "That's a tough one. He was greatly talented and had served our army so well, but there is no getting around the fact that his absence at Gettysburg was damaging. General Lee still needed him badly afterward, and I'm sure that's why he didn't relieve him. And we'll never know how the results might have changed if Stuart had been there early on. Stuart's presence would have been useful, I do know that. He was good at what he did, really good, and the information he provided was usually accurate and well-reasoned. Now, if you ask me if his presence would have made a difference in the outcome, I would say maybe, but I can't say for certain. Nobody could."

"His absence was enormous, Cappy. If he had been providing solid information to General Lee on the first day, the second and third days may have been far different. I don't know that I'd go so far as to say that his dereliction cost the South the battle, but his not being there doing his job helped create a chain of events that cost the Confederacy dearly."

"I can't disagree with that."

"Speaking of the third day, I can't believe you were right in the middle of Pickett's charge and lived to tell about it."

"I can't believe it either, now or at the time it happened. I was never as certain of meeting my maker as I was that third day at Gettysburg. I just knew it was going to be a hard day for mother when she found out she had lost two of her sons in that campaign."

"There was a lot of bravery involved in that charge."

"Aaron, there was an enormous amount of bravery all over that battlefield from both sides. The boys from Pennsylvania and New York and Michigan didn't break. The boys from North Carolina and Georgia and Virginia moved across almost a mile of open ground, under deadly fire for much of it, and kept on advancing. There was American heroism all across the field, and that ground at Gettysburg should be preserved forever so the story of those brave men of both sides can be told to every generation."

"I agree. So, how do you sum up the Battle of Gettysburg, Cappy?"

"Well, the outcome wasn't what we had expected on the Southern side. We had come to Pennsylvania planning on winning a great victory, and we didn't. We came so close and yet it got away from us, due in no small part to all the mistakes we made that started to pile up in the end. But look, give the Yankees credit because they had plenty to do with the way things turned out. They fought hard, they were resilient and resourceful, and their commanders got better as the battle progressed. It's no small thing that Meade's army got a huge morale boost from Gettysburg."

"Anything else?"

Conor nodded. "I suppose for me personally, July third was a hard day, a very dark, brutal time. And apart from the day I was notified that your father had been killed at San Juan Hill, it was the darkest day of my life. I wouldn't wish a day of that sort on any human being."

"It took enormous strength to get through that."
Conor shrugged. "I had no choice, really."
"Thanks, Cappy. We should stop now."

Chapter Nine

Back to Virginia

When Johnny comes marching home again,
Hurrah! Hurrah!,
We'll give him a hearty welcome then,
Hurrah! Hurrah!
"When Johnny Comes Marching Home"

July, 1863

There was no panic on July 4, no feeling of impending doom among Conor's tired soldiers who otherwise had ample reason to feel dispirited. The Army of Northern Virginia dug in and awaited General Meade's anticipated attack. The brigade had shifted back to the Oak Hill area with the rest of Ewell's Corps, prepared to renew the fight. On the previous night, General Lee had ordered General Imboden, a cavalry commander, to organize the wagons into a long train in preparation for the redeployment back to Virginia. The vehicles began moving on July 4 with over 8,000 Confederate wounded and 3,800 Union prisoners. Another 4,500 Confederates who were so seriously wounded that they were unable to be transported were to be left to the mercy of the Union doctors.

Once the wagon train was stretched out on the road, the line extended for 17 miles in length. Then the hard rains came, and the muddy roads greatly slowed the progress of the withdrawal.

General Gordon advised Conor that the division would leave its position on July 5, the last to do so, and would thus become the army's rear guard. A.P. Hill's

Corps would lead, followed by Longstreet, then Ewell. Conor, like most of the rest of the Confederate soldiers, was eager to return to Virginia and their Southern homeland. Pennsylvania had been a hard host, to be sure.

At noon Rebel cavalry brought in a trio of prisoners who had been captured near the brigade position while keeping a close watch on the Confederates. Conor stepped outside his tent to light a cigar when he noticed the three Yankees—a major and two sergeants—standing nearby and waiting to be sent to a holding area. Two Confederate soldiers kept their muskets trained on the prisoners.

"Why are their hands tied behind their backs?" Conor asked the guards.

"That's the way they came to us, sir."

"Untie their hands. You can shoot them just as easily if they try to run."

The guard untied the ropes and the three men sat on the ground and immediately began rubbing the circulation back into their wrists and hands. "Much obliged," a burly sergeant said with a nod in Conor's direction.

"So what were you doing to get yourselves captured?" Conor asked the Yankee major after taking a seat on the ground beside him. The officer was short in height, dark haired, mustachioed, and looked to be in his late twenties.

"What do you think we were doing? We were finding the far left of your line."

"Well I'm happy to inform you that you've found it," Conor said with a nod. "And furthermore, you've now become a part of it. Welcome to the end of the line, for us and for you."

"What do you plan to do with us?"

"Sorry, but I don't decide those things. I'm sure you'll find out soon enough."

"You're whipped, Major," the Union officer snapped. "Your whole Reb army has been routed here on the field at Gettysburg."

"Oh, I beg to differ with you, sir. We may have been repulsed, but we were by no means routed. There's a very big difference in the two. I declare to you that this army has plenty of fight left in it. If your General Meade decides he wants to challenge my declaration, then he will get to see for himself just how 'whipped' we really are. And so will you."

"You'd better hope General Meade doesn't come this way in full force."

"Listen, we still have General Lee in our position. That will cause your guy to think long and hard before he orders his soldiers forward. Your army has a growing list of former commanders who thought General Lee could be easily disposed of. I'm sure General Meade would greatly prefer to stay off that list."

"General Meade is starting his own list of the Reb commanders he's defeated. And guess whose name is the first one on it?"

"Don't get too far ahead of yourself, Major. Your arrogance is misplaced and your ability to evade capture speaks to your overall professional competence. Forgive me if I see you as something other than the authority you seem to think you are."

"Let me ask you a question, Major."

"Go ahead."

"How can you people fight for such a dreadful cause?" he asked spitefully.

"What dreadful cause is that?"

"Keeping black people enslaved."

"When did you join the Union army, Major?"

"Sixty-one."

"And for what reason did you join the Union army?"

He said nothing.

"My guess is, like so many others like yourself, you joined the army because you wanted to see the Union preserved. Isn't that correct?" Conor asked.

The officer finally nodded. "Of course."

"Well let me share something with you, sir: Just like most of the men in my regiment, I own no slaves. Never have, never will. So I didn't join my army to *keep* slaves any more than you joined yours to *free* them."

"Then why *did* you join the Reb army?"

"I joined the Confederate army to throw your asses out of the South, plain and simple."

The officer smiled. "And now we're throwing your asses out of the North."

Conor shrugged and smiled. "Give, and it shall be given unto you."

A Confederate captain appeared with two soldiers and took possession of the prisoners. "On your feet. You men will follow me," the captain directed.

The Yankee major and Conor made eye contact as the group started to leave.

"See you in Richmond, Reb," he offered.

"I'll see you in Washington, Yank," Conor replied.

Meade never attacked in full force. He offered a cavalry probe, but nothing that was not quickly repulsed.

Conor left Gettysburg at noon on July 5. His regiment had endured more casualties than any other in the brigade. In fact, the Army of Northern Virginia had suffered over 20,000 casualties, with more than 2,500 dead. Conor glanced over in the direction of where the battle in the wheatfield had occurred three days earlier, and said a silent prayer for Sean as he marched past. He was going to miss his brother greatly, and he had so hoped they could somehow find a way to live a normal life after the war had ended. He would write to his mother about Sean's death once they had safely crossed the Potomac and settled in on the Virginia side.

As they slogged their way toward Virginia, Conor thought of the many wounded who were being jostled about in the wagons, some of whom would likely die as a result. It had to be dreadful beyond description for those poor men, and Conor said a silent prayer for them. Then he thought of the wounded being left behind who were not only badly injured but who were also prisoners now. He wondered about the fate of the Southern wounded at the Wiedenour house and all the other houses and buildings in town serving as makeshift hospitals. He said a silent prayer for them also. Then he thought of General Lee and how the strain of the past several days must be weighing heavily upon him. The general was no longer a young man, and the accumulated burdens from all the years of soldiering had to be catching up with him. Conor said two silent prayers for him.

The Confederates received cavalry probes on their flanks, and there were several cases where armed citizens shot at them or tried to damage their wagons. The going remained slow, with lots of starting and stopping, lots of waiting and worrying, which was draining for the soldiers. Conor expected to see Meade's army come barreling into them each day, but a force of any significant size had yet to materialize.

The lead portions of Lee's army began filing into the Williamsport, Maryland area on July 7. A pontoon bridge at Falling Waters was destroyed, much to the dismay of the tense Rebels. Additionally, the Potomac was rain-swollen and impossible to ford, so another solution had to be found. As the army's arrival continued, Lee's men established a defensive line along the river to meet what was being reported by cavalry scouts as a significant Union thrust approaching. Over the next three days, the defensive line was strengthened into such a formidable position that the Rebel soldiers actually hoped that Meade would attack and provide an opportunity for revenge. General Lee was actively involved and could be seen inspecting the line and directing the placement of cannons. General Gordon thought Lee looked particularly tense, and both he and Conor agreed that under the arduous circumstances his anxiety seemed justified.

Ewell's Corps was holding the far left of the line, near Hagerstown. Conor and his regiment left at dusk and made a night movement in the rain, mud, and fog to the Williamsport ford. Lanterns provided the light, and by the time they were ready to cross, the river depth was three to four feet. There was a great bonfire on the far Virginia bank, the very sight of which warmed the hearts of the troops. A line of taller soldiers with their muskets interlocked was established downstream to ensure that no man would be swept away and drowned.

By midnight, the soldiers were fording the Potomac River.

The men placed their knapsacks high on their shoulders with their cartridge boxes placed atop the knapsacks. They held their muskets high as they entered the brown water, often slipping in the mud or on the rocks. Most men of average height were in water up to their armpits and the smaller soldiers were being continuously doused as the water passed just beneath their chins. The smallest soldiers were carried across by others, which brought about a fair amount of ribbing. Conor breathed a great sigh of relief when he was told that all of his soldiers had made it to the far bank. The wounded and the prisoners were ferried across in boats, and the pontoon bridge was repaired well enough to enable the wagons to cross.

They were back in Virginia.

Thankfully.

They moved through Front Royal and Culpeper to a large encampment along the Rapidan River. The threat from Meade still existed, but clearly he had missed his chance to engage the Rebels before the river crossing. The tired troops of Lee's diminished army welcomed the chance to rest, and the companies whose strength had been so dramatically reduced were hopeful that fresh replacements would fill their ranks.

General Gordon found Conor at his regimental headquarters and handed him a box. "You are now a lieutenant colonel. Congratulations. Now let's have a look at your position."

The general gave Conor a well-needed and blunt critique after a half-hour inspection of his positions. It became clear to Conor that his area was sloppy and far short of the high standards and crisp military appearance the general expected.

"You're a regimental commander, Lieutenant Colonel Rafferty. I will expect you to lead like one in the field *and* in camp. Failing to maintain high standards will undoubtedly creep into everything we do and set us up for disappointment in battle. Set the standards high and make sure your officers and troops meet them. But it all has to start with you. Your regiment is looking to you for leadership, and so am I. Do you understand?"

"Yes, sir."

"Do you have any questions?"

"No, sir. I'll get it fixed."

So much for a promotion celebration.

One by one, Conor's company commanders stopped by his tent to review the issues from General Gordon's inspection. They also expressed their condolences when they heard the news from General Gordon about the death of Conor's brother, which Conor had largely chosen to keep to himself. Conor's fellow regimental commanders likewise dropped by when they heard the news. Even General Masterson came by with General Gordon to pass along some words of encouragement.

"If you didn't already have enough reasons to want to win this war, you certainly do now," General Masterson said. "You have my deepest sympathies, Lieutenant Colonel Rafferty."

The coffee that First Sergeant Tanneyhill brought to Conor's tent had been made from acorns, roots, and some other substance, and its dark color was the only similarity to real coffee that Conor could discern. They sat in chairs facing one another from across Conor's makeshift desk constructed from wooden ammunition boxes. It was gray and drizzly outside, with a bit of a chill in the air.

"Ain't bad, though," Tanneyhill observed after taking a noisy sip.

"Compared to what?" Conor replied.

"It's the best I could do, sir. By the way, has your mother been notified about your brother?"

"I wrote her, yes."

Conor handed the letter written by Private Caldwell to Tanneyhill.

"Oh no! Got that big artery. He never had a chance with a wound like that. Damn! Once again, sir, I'm sorry."

"Thank you. I'm just glad I won't be there to see my mother when she reads the letter if she hasn't found out already. It's hard for me to grasp that Sean is gone. It won't seem like home without him. I still can't believe it."

Tanneyhill sipped from the cup. "Do you ever worry about that, sir?"

"About dying, you mean?"

"Yessir."

"Rarely in camp, and never once the shooting starts. But I have to confess that I gave it some thought on the assault at Gettysburg on July third, and about how bad it would be for Mother if Sean and I were both killed. Daniel's out there too, somewhere in Tennessee, I think. But worry about it? Nah, it wouldn't do any good. It'd be like complaining about not having any decent coffee."

"It's been found, sir, that complaining in an army has done exactly zero good for thousands of years. Yet every soldier in every army in every war in history has complained. It makes no sense but it does give us a connection to the past."

"I suppose so. How about you? Do you ever worry about dying?"

"No."

"Why not?"

"I was an orphan, sir. My daddy left us and worked over on the river in New Orleans, and my momma was a prostitute in Mobile until some greasy merchant seaman stabbed her to death. An aunt and her second husband raised me, and he owned a tavern and surely must have drank all the profits away. He would come home drunk and beat her or beat me, sometimes both of us. I was probably ten at the time. I was scared of him, hated him, and wanted to kill him before he killed us. My aunt finally got enough of him and blowed a very large hole upside his head. And she shot him with the revolver that I 'borrowed' from a retired navy captain who kept lots of guns in his house across the street. She just beat me to it, that's all. I would have done it, I swear. And she knew it. Anyway, the court let my aunt off when she claimed she done it in our self-defense. Right after it happened, I went straight to the captain and told him about me breaking in and getting the gun so we could protect ourselves, and he went along with a story about having loaned her the pistol so she could protect us. And I returned the revolver to the captain as soon as my aunt got off in court. I almost joined the damned navy because of him. My poor aunt had another seizure and died four years ago—they said it was probably due to the damage to her brain from all the beatings—and I haven't seen my daddy since I was six. So I've said all of that to say this: I spent so much of my childhood worrying about what was going to happen to me that I've used up the entire ration of worry that I came into this world with. I don't worry about nothing no more, sir. Not dying, not being terribly wounded, not even the coffee."

"That's quite a story," Conor said. "I had no idea you came from such privilege."

They both laughed.

"Because I grew up without much family, sir, the army's become my family. And this regiment is my home."

"I'm glad you're where you are," Conor said, adding, "but you should know that I got a large portion of my backside chewed off today by a certain general we both know who wasn't happy with my attention to detail in building out our camp site."

"Uh oh. Bad was it?"

"Yes, very. Let's take a walk in the rain and I'll show you what we need to do to avoid it from now on."

"Following your lead, sir."

***

Wednesday, February 13, 1918

"Were you concerned that Meade would cut off the retreating Confederate army and destroy it before you could get across the Potomac, Cappy?"

"We were all concerned about that, sure. When he didn't attack us on July fourth, we guessed that maybe he had tired of it and didn't want to risk what he had already gained. Then General Gordon mentioned that the bigwigs in Washington would probably be yelling and screaming at Meade to catch up to us and finish us off. So sure, we were on edge during the entire march back to Virginia."

"Cappy, the parallels of McClellan squandering his opportunity at Antietam to follow up with overwhelming force and Meade at Gettysburg failing to do the same thing, stand out to me like a sore thumb."

"Well, I'm sort of glad they didn't," Conor said with a chuckle. "I was across the field from those two gentlemen in both cases."

Aaron's face blushed in embarrassment. "You know I didn't mean it in a bad way, Cappy. What I am saying is, from a purely academic standpoint, they both missed a chance to use their huge advantage in numbers to finish off a weakened foe, and probably end the war if they do it correctly. And it seems to me that they both froze at the moment of truth."

"And why do you think they froze?"

Aaron hesitated briefly before answering. "I think it was because Lee was opposite them. Had it been someone else, the Federals might have been more inclined to act. But Lee seemed to have a mystique about him that made them uncertain and hesitant. I seriously doubt that either McClellan or Meade thought they could outgeneral Robert E. Lee. They both knew the results of Fredericksburg. They weren't stupid."

Conor smiled and nodded his agreement.

"How did you think the Confederate army was going to replenish its depleted ranks? Where were those men going to come from?" asked Aaron.

"That's a good question, and in fact that was the same exact question we were asking one another. After Gettysburg, it seemed less likely we would get any foreign help, and most of the men in the South in the military-age range were already in uniform. So there wasn't an untapped pool of available young men who could come in and make a sizeable difference. Unless, of course, we armed the slaves."

"What about arming the slaves?"

"I supported it. We'll talk more about it later."

"Feel okay to keep going, Cappy? Not too tired?"

"I feel great. Let's continue."

Chapter Ten

Winter Quarters

We're tenting tonight on the old camp ground,
Give us a song to cheer
Our weary hearts, a song of home,
And friends we love so dear.
"Tenting On The Old Camp Ground"

January-May, 1864

The brigade's winter camp in Virginia was located near Clark's Mountain, on the south side of the Rapidan River. The tents and huts were set up in rows with crisscrossing lanes, the white smoke of fires twisting skyward in the chilled Northern Virginia air. The soldiers were still ragged in dress, and while generous women from many parts of the Confederacy were sending heavier clothing to the troops, the demand always far exceeded the supply. Their depleted ranks were augmented only slightly by new enlistees or the returning wounded, and conversely offset by those who became sick and died or those who just decided to walk away.

The monotony of winter camp, combined with the harsh weather, was always a challenge. The soldiers drilled as often as they reasonably could, and the officers would sometimes engage in spirited discussions on tactics, but still there was always the boredom that seemed to fill more than its share of space in a typical day. The men played card games, spent time in the upkeep of their living spaces, and attended religious services if they were so inclined.

Liquor would somehow make its way into the camp on occasion, and its effects were largely predictable. Snowball fights would often include company versus company, the end results of which were usually the source of lively arguments. The men thus had a chance to bond in the winter living conditions, much more so than in the warmer weather when they were constantly on the move.

Conor received word that his youngest brother Daniel had been captured by the Yankees at Dalton, in Georgia. Weeks later, Conor's mother received a single letter from Daniel, informing her that he was being held in a prison camp near Chicago. His commanding officer had earlier written to apprise Mrs. Rafferty that Daniel had fought bravely before his company had been overrun by a larger force. Several Confederates had witnessed a group of Federal soldiers taking Daniel away as their prisoner.

The news made Conor physically ill for an entire day, and he couldn't get it out of his mind for weeks. He kept seeing Daniel's boyish face in his dreams, hearing Daniel's voice and laughter, and then awakening to another day of uncertainty and fear.

Staying busy was the only thing that helped.

The Union army was located across the Rapidan and their camp was far larger and more expensively constructed than was the Southern version. But the Southerners didn't care. They weren't battling the Yankees, they were battling the cold. The muddy, slick roads and mountain passes, combined with the bitter temperatures, made it difficult to conduct military operations in the wintertime. Campaigns were thus conceived and planned in the winter and then executed in the fairer months.

Disease was a problem that worsened in those winter months. Many soldiers in the Confederate army had grown up in rural, sparsely populated agricultural communities and had yet to develop the natural immunities that their urban counterparts had most likely acquired.

Illnesses like measles and chickenpox could thus become lethal when outbreaks periodically swept through the ranks. Respiratory ailments were common, as was dysentery, or "quick step" as it was affectionately called. Clean drinking water was always a priority and always a challenge. After his earlier session with General Gordon, Conor made sure his officers strictly enforced the established procedures concerning latrines and sanitary conditions. In addition, body lice in clothing and bedding tended to aggravate more than incapacitate, but like much else, the soldiers just learned to deal with it.

Mail was important, and the receipt of letters and packages from home was always restorative. They all looked forward to the delivery of mail.

January 12, 1864
Dear Conor:

I just wanted to let you know that your friend and classmate Tom Easton died from Typhoid fever in Dalton, Georgia, where he was serving in the army. His funeral was yesterday. I'm not sure whether I let you know that Billy Stanton who went to our church was killed at Gettysburg, but he was. Anyway, his family is still in mourning like ours is. We have not heard anything further from Daniel, so we assume he is still being held as a prisoner in Chicago. I cannot bear the thought of losing another son to this war, so please take care of yourself, my dear sweet Conor. God be with you always.
With love,
Mother

January 25, 1864
Dear Mother:

Thank you for letting me know about Tom and Billy. Please pass along my condolences to their families when you see them. I will try to find out about the prison

camp in Chicago, but in the meantime please write to me when you hear something from or about Daniel. God bless.
Love,
Conor

January 16, 1864
Dear Conor:

I thought I would write to you and tell you that I was married last month to Richard Davenport. Richard is from Macon and we met last November while he was on leave in Atlanta visiting his kinfolks. He is a <u>CAPTAIN</u> in the army! I am so proud of him and how he has advanced. He was able to get another leave for us to get married and have a honeymoon in Savannah. Sometimes things just have a way of working out for the best. Meanwhile, I am still teaching and enjoying it greatly. I hope and pray this war will end soon. Anyway, please take care of yourself, Conor. You are still important to me. God bless you.
Love,
Patricia

January 26, 1864
Dear Patricia:

Please accept my sincerest congratulations on your marriage to Captain Davenport. I wish you both many years of happiness, health, and prosperity. God bless.
Your obedient servant,
Conor Rafferty, Lieutenant Colonel, CSA
Commanding Officer, 38th Georgia Regiment

After meeting with General Gordon on a clear, crisp, mid-February morning about a training agenda they were scheduling for the following week, Conor rode Shannon to the top of Clark's Mountain to give her some exercise and to take advantage of the dry day. When he reached the crest, he noticed four Confederate officers already there, one he quickly recognized as General Lee.

Conor saluted and gave an enthusiastic, "Good morning," which drew return salutes and greetings. "I hope I'm not disturbing you, General. I just wanted to give my horse a bit of exercise."

"No bother," General Lee replied. "Fine looking animal. And who might its rider be?"

"I am Lieutenant Colonel Conor Rafferty, sir, commander of the Thirty-eighth Georgia under General Gordon."

General Lee placed his field glasses back in the case and quickly looked Conor over. "What is your age, sir?"

"I'm twenty-three, General."

"I was a lieutenant in the Corps of Engineers at that age. In fact, I was thirty-one when I made captain," he said, grinning. "Things have changed a might since then. It takes young men now to do this hard wartime work." He pointed to his staff members—a lieutenant colonel Conor recognized as Walter Taylor, Lee's chief aide, and two majors he didn't recognize. "Look at how young these boys are. Being around them makes me feel young," he said, pausing and adding, "sometimes."

They all laughed.

"The simple truth is, these young men here do wonderful work, as I'm sure you do, Lieutenant Colonel Rafferty."

"When I don't, sir, General Gordon has a way of letting me know about it."

"You can learn a lot from General Gordon. He's a splendid officer."

"I was with him at Sharpsburg, Chancellorsville, and Gettysburg, sir. He is very much a splendid officer."

Lee's eyebrows rose. "I would say with those battlefield attainments, you've passed through the crucible of fire in some of its hottest locations."

"Yes, sir. My splendid First Sergeant Tanneyhill refers to it as 'that deadly space.'"

"Deadly space," Lee repeated, his approval evident. "That's as simple and valid a description as I've ever heard. All of us who have ever found ourselves in that deadly space know exactly what your wise First Sergeant Tanneyhill speaks of."

The staff officers also gave their nodding approval.

"General Lee, may I ask you a question, sir?"

"You may indeed."

"Do you know anything about a Federal prison camp in Chicago? My youngest brother was taken prisoner at Chickamauga and my mother has only received one letter from him. My other brother was killed at Gettysburg, so she is understandably concerned. We all are, sir."

General Lee squinted and turned his head slightly, as if trying to recollect. He ran his hand over his white beard and stared off into the distance for a moment. "Condolences to you and your family. As for the camp, as best I remember it's called Camp Douglas, and it's just south of Chicago. We don't know for sure how many of our soldiers they're keeping there, but we reckon it's at least two, three thousand, and most of those are from the engagements in Tennessee and Georgia. We have some friends up there in the Chicago area who send Richmond a piece or two of information every now and again, but I rarely see any of it anymore. I wish I could tell you more, but that's all I know."

"That's very helpful, General. Thank you, sir. And General Lee?"

"Yes?"

"Thank you for what you do for this army, sir. It's an honor to meet you and equally an honor to serve with you."

General Lee nodded self-consciously. "That's very kind of you and very much appreciated. And I wish to thank you, Lieutenant Colonel Rafferty, for your service to this army, as well as that of your brothers. My best to you and the fine Thirty-eighth Georgia. Good day, sir."

Conor saluted as General Lee and his staff turned and rode away.

The next day Conor got a letter from his mother telling him that she had received further word from Daniel. The youngest Rafferty sibling had written to tell her that he was with nearly 4,000 other Confederate prisoners, many newly arrived, and he requested that any heavy clothes his mother could spare would be put to good use in the harsh Chicago winter. Daniel's mailing address was included in her letter, and Conor immediately wrote to him.

Two weeks later Conor got a letter from Daniel explaining that he was trying to get over an illness that had been afflicting him for weeks. There were many other prisoners who were also sick, he noted.

A week later Conor got a letter from a farm neighbor in Atlanta writing at his father's behest. She told him that Daniel's friend and fellow Confederate prisoner Robert Frye had written to inform the family that Daniel had died from smallpox and been buried in the prison cemetery.

Two days later, Conor got another letter from the same neighbor informing him that his mother had died in her bed the day after receiving the news about Daniel.

His two brothers were gone. His mother was now gone. His father would not even write to him, if even to remind him of his prophecy that Conor's joining the army would bring disaster upon their family. Conor was devastated. Was it his entire fault? Was his father right? He felt heartsick and guilty. He had his fellow soldiers to support him and keep him company, thank goodness, but there was still a dreadful, knawing emptiness that he could not completely elude. The thought crossed his mind to request a leave and go home, but he was concerned about leaving his regiment. Besides, his family's size had shrunk from five members to two. He wasn't even sure now that he wanted to go home and be reminded of what they had been but no longer were, nor would ever be again. Too, he wasn't sure if he'd even be welcomed under the circumstances. In many ways, for both his father and himself, it already seemed too late now.

Therefore, Conor concentrated on the war and the task before him. He was ready to get back into the field and resume the fight. He was prepared to kill as many Yankees as he could find and do his little part in bleeding the Union army so severely and decisively that it would leave the South and never come back. He wanted to avenge the deaths of his brothers and mother, and he had a powerful tool in the 38th Georgia to exact that revenge. He was seething inside, and he was growing impatient for the killing to begin anew.

The regimental chaplain, Franklin Yancey, stopped by Conor's hut and found him sitting alone and warming himself beside the fireplace on a chilly evening. Chaplain Yancey had only joined the regiment in January, replacing the previous chaplain who had been transferred to a post in Petersburg. It was now March, and there had been snow flurries in the early morning. The men were all tired of the cold, the boredom, the hardtack, and especially the coffee made from God-knows-what. They were all ready to break camp and become fighting soldiers again.

"Would you like some company?" the chaplain called from the doorway.

"Sure, why not," Conor replied with little conviction.

Chaplain Yancey took a seat in a chair beside Conor and began rubbing his hands together near the fire. "Nice and warm in here." The chaplain was in his early thirties, short, stocky, and balding on top, with a round face and a broad smile. He had a deep, booming voice, one that could easily be heard from outside the tent when he was bringing his chapel sermons to a climax. He was popular with the soldiers, and his core nature seemed to be unpretentious and affable.

"Would you like a taste?" Conor asked. "A girl from Richmond sent me a bottle of Irish whiskey with the stipulation that I must not drink alone."

The chaplain laughed. "Sound advice. And well, uh, yes, I'd enjoy a taste of Ireland to go along with the odor of burning maple. Good for the senses. Erin go bragh."

Conor smiled. They had a drink and talked about a random range of subjects, to include the war, the weather, and their families. When the chat came to a discussion of their fathers, Conor abruptly changed the subject. They had another drink and talked about their respective Georgia hometowns of Atlanta and Vidalia. It was nearly an hour later when Conor emptied the bottle into their cups for a third round, and he could sense the chaplain had something else on his mind.

"When we're not in the company of others," the chaplain said deliberately, "would you mind terribly if I call you Conor?"

"Of course not."

"Thank you. Listen, Conor, before I drink so much that somebody has to escort me to my hut, I just want you to know that I appreciate the way you support me and the way you encourage your officers and soldiers to attend my services. And I appreciate the way you make sure I'm one of the first people summoned when one of your boys gets some unpleasant news from home. I hear from my chaplain colleagues in the other regiments, and I have to tell you they are envious when I share with them how much support and cooperation I get from you. I wanted to tell you that personally."

"I'm just doing my job. I don't know if God has a preference as to who is going to win this war, but if He's still undecided at this point, I want to do all I can to swing Him our way. With God and the soldiers of the Thirty-eighth Georgia, I like our chances. And thank you for what you just told me."

The chaplain took a deep breath and exhaled slowly. "I know you've had some personal difficulties to deal with in the past few months, and I admire the way you can put those heartaches on a shelf someplace and not let it affect your job. But I also know it has to hurt to lose one family member, much less the three that you've experienced. I simply cannot imagine how difficult that must be. I want you to know that I'm always here to help in any way I can. I want to support you as diligently and faithfully as you've been supporting me."

"I'm doing fine. I'll keep your offer in mind, but really, I'm doing just fine."

"One final request then, if I may."

"Sure."

"I'd like for you to attend my services."

Conor chuckled. "And why would you like for me to do that?"

"I think it would set a great example, for starters. I am sure your boys would notice that their leader is in attendance. And I'm interested in your soul, Conor Rafferty. You may be the highest ranking of my parishioners, and you're certainly one of the most notorious officers in the entire brigade with all you've done, but you are still a sheep in my flock. And so I care about you and your spiritual well-being."

Conor stared at the fire and said nothing for a long, uncomfortable moment. He noticed the problem immediately—that he had encouraged others to do something that he himself had chosen to ignore. It was a leadership blunder, one that he should not have made, and he felt foolish for not seeing it beforehand.

"Then again, you don't have to do anything you don't want to do," the chaplain added when the silence became too awkward. "It was just a well-meaning request."

Again, Conor paused. It may have been the strong drink, but he suddenly wondered for the first time about the souls of his brothers. And his mother. And he wondered if even his own soul was so covered with mud and blood and killing that it had become crusted over and irredeemable. He stared at the fire, warmed and transfixed by the flame and the effects of the whiskey, and thought about what he might say when he found himself in His presence. Or whether He would even allow him in His presence to offer his feeble account of things.

The chaplain cleared his throat and got up to leave, but Conor motioned for him to remain seated. It was another long minute before he spoke.

"You know something, Franklin? You're exactly right. Now that you've been kind enough and brave enough to point out my obvious hypocrisy on the matter of church attendance, I'm embarrassed by it, plain and simple. I *should* be at your services. And as long as I'm encouraging my soldiers to attend, which I will continue to do, then I'll be at your services. You reserve a chair for me on the front row, and I'll be there from now on. And this is not a whiskey promise, this is the real thing. I mean it. I'll be there where I should have been all along."

"I wasn't trying to be quite as blunt as you, Conor, but I very much appreciate your commitment."

"And I appreciate your candor. Your predecessor never made such a request, but he probably felt the same way. You were honest with me. I need that. You may not always get what you want, but I'll always listen to you. You have my word on that. You're a member of my staff and you can serve me best by giving me your honest, wise counsel, especially if it involves an area you see as a shortcoming of mine. Not everyone has the strength to do that, but I believe you can. And now I believe you will. Do we have an understanding?"

"We have an understanding," the chaplain said, extending his hand.

They shook on it.

"One other thing, Franklin," Conor said. "Am I going to hell?"

The chaplain paused and cleared his throat, his eyes wide with surprise. "I'm afraid that's not a decision God would give me access to, Conor. Why? What makes you ask?"

"Probably the damn whiskey. Maybe we should talk about this over coffee instead. You think about my question and we'll discuss it on another occasion."

"I'd be happy to. And yes, coffee would be the wiser choice for such a discussion."

"Then I look forward to it," Conor said.

"Very well, sir. Thank you for the libation and the conversation. I have thoroughly enjoyed your gracious company. I'll see you at the service tomorrow."

"And what will your message be?"

"Hypocrisy."

Conor paused for a second before leaning back and laughing loudly.

With that, the chaplain made his way to the door and departed with only the slightest of wobbles.

And Conor was at the service the next night, on the front row. Chaplain Yancey was really quite good. And Conor felt better for being there with many of his men. The soldiers appreciated Conor's presence, and afterwards he stayed and made small talk with the young soldiers for nearly an hour.

The topic was not hypocrisy, but faith. It was a message they all very badly needed.

***

Wednesday, February 13, 1918

"Cappy, I'm not sure I could have endured the loss of my family the way you did. That took amazing strength."

"You would if you had to, Aaron. And I had no choice. The losses hurt deeply, still do for that matter. And always will. But the chaplain gave me reason to hope."

"Speaking of the chaplain, did you have the discussion with him about going to hell?"

"Yes, and over coffee. After we had a long talk, he said that while he could make no guarantees, he felt good about my prospects in the afterlife. And after our little talk, so did I."

Aaron laughed loudly. "By God, I'm glad I was born a Rafferty," he said with obvious pride.

"I'm glad you were, too."

"Keep going?"

"Yes, let's keep going."

Chapter Eleven

The Wilderness – First Day

Come, stack arms, men. Pile on the rails,
Stir up the campfire bright;
No matter if the canteen fails,
We'll make a roaring night.
Here Shenandoah brawls along,
There burly Blue Ridge echoes strong
To swell the brigade's rousing song
Of Stonewall Jackson's way.
"Stonewall Jackson's Way"

May 5, 1864

The anticipated confrontation between Lee and Grant finally began at the Battle of the Wilderness at Spotsylvania, Virginia. Once the fighting was underway, the two armies shot at one another virtually every day for the next year. With Grant's overwhelming numbers in men and resources, his intention was nothing less than to force an end to the war by annihilating the Confederate army.

The Confederates could see from Clark's Mountain the increasing number of white tents in the Federal camp. Every day their troop strength grew, and every day the Rebel strength would either stay the same or decline from sickness or desertion. The Southerners were hungry, ragged, and cold. It was not an especially happy condition.

The aptly named Wilderness was fifteen square miles of underbrush, briars, and vines. The leafy trees made it difficult to see any movement to the front, but even if one could see, it was still difficult to advance through the tangled woods. Grant, whose army crossed the Rapidan at its lower crossings on Wednesday, May 4, was well disguised from the alerted Confederates. Grant wanted to lure Lee from his strong defensive line out into the open where the advantage in sheer numbers would favor the Union. Longstreet's Corps was due back from Tennessee where it had participated in the Battle of Chickamauga, but still the Army of Northern Virginia was badly outnumbered, as was so often the case.

Gordon's Brigade set up camp on the night of May 4 at Locust Grove, in the rear of Ewell's Corps and on the extreme Confederate left. They were also facing Grant's center, whose line overlapped both the Confederate flanks.

First Sergeant Tanneyhill found Conor in a small clearing that several soldiers had made by hacking away the brush with shovels and knives. Tanneyhill, as usual, had coffee.

"How do you do that?" Conor asked.

"You mean, how do I manage to find coffee even under the most primitive of conditions?"

"Yes, exactly, even though some of the stuff you've called coffee would be giving it the benefit of considerable doubt."

He passed a tin cup to Conor. "Try this."

"Not bad," Conor commented after sipping.

"You're very welcome, sir."

Conor sighed. "Well, we're back on the line and badly outnumbered. Everything's back to normal again."

"What does General Gordon think will happen?"

"That they'll attack us at daylight," Conor answered. "Grant's been building to this all winter. It's time to get it going."

The firing started to their front at 7:00 am on Thursday, May 5. Conor's regiment remained in its position for two long hours until it became clear that the Confederate lines were being driven back. The ubiquitous Rebel yell had suddenly ceased, and the retreating gray troops were beginning to pass through Conor's ranks at far more than a leisurely pace. The scene was one of steadily increasing chaos—the Rebel formations breaking and their troops heading in the opposite direction, an always dispiriting and unnerving sight. Conor could not see far enough ahead to know what might be headed his way apart from the retreating Confederates, but of course he knew the pursuing Yankees were following close behind. Grant's center was relentlessly pushing the Rebel forces who were yielding large sections of the field.

General Ewell hurriedly rode up and shouted out, "General Gordon, the fate of the day depends on you, sir."

"These men will save it," General Gordon replied, who immediately turned to Conor and called, "Move your men forward, Conor, and quickly."

Conor immediately wheeled his regiment in line and moved off in the attack. He was at the front of the regiment, on its extreme right, traveling on foot with his new adjutant, Lieutenant Michael Post, walking beside him. The thick underbrush impeded their movement at first, but soon enough the thicket gave way to a partial clearing where they could see the assembled Union forces to their front. The 38th Georgia fired volley after devastating volley into the Federal line, abruptly stopping their advance and inflicting far more casualties than they were taking. Confederate casualties from the initial encounter were light, and Conor's companies were gaining the initiative. Behind him he heard General Gordon shout *"Forward!"* and thus knew the rest of the brigade was lined up and drawing closer to him.

Lieutenant Post caught up to Conor as they moved ahead. "We're doing good, aren't we, sir?"

"We're doing fine so far, Lieutenant."

"How many Yankees do you think are in front of us, sir?"

"Lots. We won't be able to see all of them until we get closer, but there will be plenty, I assure you."

"Do we have enough troops to win, sir? Can we whip them?"

Conor turned and saw that Post was red-faced and breathing heavily. "Take a deep breath and relax, Michael. You're doing fine."

"What do you want me to do, sir?"

"Stay close. Go ahead and draw your pistol. Fire at any target where you have a clear shot, but only if it's clear. In other words, don't shoot me in the damn back. Are you okay now?"

"I'm okay, sir," Post said as he removed his pistol from its holster.

The Rebs were beginning to take casualties as they entered into that deadly space, and Conor could see ahead that his troops were likewise inflicting casualties among the Federals. He glanced to his side to see that his lines were moving up in unison, but when he looked back he couldn't locate the other regiments. The volume of fire and the overall noise levels were increasing at a greater rate, causing Conor to have to scream at his nearest company commanders to be heard.

He turned to instruct Lieutenant Post to drop back and see how close the other regiments were following when the first ball struck Post in the throat, followed a split second later by another hitting him just beneath the breastbone. Post fell backward into an awkward position with his legs bent underneath him. His first experience in battle had now become his last. Conor stopped and leaned over him for a moment, but his wounds were fatal. He took Post's pistol and placed it inside his own belt.

Conor quickly discovered that it was the famed Iron Brigade to his front, the mostly Wisconsin men in the black hats who had distinguished themselves in so many previous engagements. Conor remembered that Union General

George McClellan had once observed that they were "the best troops in the world," and several times Confederate soldiers opposing them would have offered little argument. They had a reputation as fierce, disciplined fighters, and as soon as Conor noticed the black hats, he braced himself for an especially hard struggle.

The 38th Georgia kept advancing steadily. The Federal line was unmoving and seemed to be awaiting a close confrontation and a likely hand-to-hand struggle. Conor's pistol was already drawn, and he reached behind him to bring out the second gun. They were now close enough to hear the Yankee officers calling out instructions to their soldiers to hold their positions. Sensing the chance to get at the men in the black hats, the Confederates fired a deadly volley and then picked up the pace, slamming into them head-on with great momentum and an even greater uproar from the deafening Rebel yell. The Iron Brigade resisted bitterly at first, as Conor expected. They met the 38th Georgia aggressively, but the Rebel regiment's own attacking fury seemed to unnerve and confuse the Yankees. Conor and his men were quickly standing in front of them, screaming like mad men and firing volleys from a distance of only ten paces. Suddenly, the Federals to their direct front broke and moved away to the rear, creating a wide gap in the Federal line which, oddly enough, the Rebels filled as they kept advancing. Conor consequently expected that the Yankees on either side of their collapsing center would also break, but contrary to all logic, they did not. Conor was astonished at his sudden tactical predicament.

"What the hell's happening here?" Conor's nearest company commander called out to him.

He was not the only one who immediately sensed their bizarre tactical dilemma. The enemy to their front had vanished but the enemy to either side had not. Someone looking down from the top of a tree would have seen a straight, continuous line, but with the Confederates in the middle facing in the opposite direction from the Federals on either side.

Conor's regiment very neatly filled in the gap in the Federal battle line. He had neither seen nor heard of any similar situation ever existing on the battlefield, and he knew he couldn't keep advancing or the enemy would encircle and destroy his entire regiment as soon as they recovered their wits. The Yankees seemed as confused as the Southerners, and fortunately for Conor they did nothing but remain in their line like the disciplined soldiers they were. Conor looked to either side again before issuing orders, as much in disbelief as anything else, and once again what he saw was the retreating Federal force in front of him, showing him their backs, and a line of Federals to either side of him, standing their ground. He gave the order to halt, then at the double-quick he ordered them to file from the center to the right and left. They were now lined up perpendicular to the Federal line, half the regiment facing right, the other half facing left. Conor clearly noticed one Yankee officer, sabre in hand, staring at them dumbfounded and calling out, "What are they doing?" as the officer tried to think of an appropriate countermove.

The 38th Georgia then immediately began to attack in either direction and thus gained the initiative. They pushed the two Federal lines further away from what had been their center, but in so doing further separated the two wings of their own regiment. Conor kept expecting the center of the Federal line to reform and attack on what were now his exposed flanks, but he could see they were still moving away. The remaining black hats on both sides finally gave way and retreated, following after their center element already in flight. The field was now cleared of the Iron Brigade, and Conor's officers and soldiers were dumbfounded at what they had just accomplished.

General Gordon moved up and ordered Conor to halt his attacking companies and reform the 38th Georgia, noting that the brigade would pursue the Federals with his other regiments.

"Remain at the ready in this location until I send word where I want you next."

"Yes, sir."

"What the hell did you just do?" he asked with a mix of awe and puzzlement.

Conor shrugged. "Works every time, sir."

The Confederate troops who had retreated earlier now returned and got back into the fight. The ground they had yielded in the morning was now recovered. And for the first time in its storied history, the Iron Brigade had broken and left the field in a panic, all courtesy of the 38th Georgia.

First Sergeant Tanneyhill, who had been watching to make sure the companies kept their proper intervals as they moved into the attack, found Conor at the front as the men took a break and rested on one knee after establishing a defensive line.

Conor grinned and said, "Don't ask me, 'What the hell was that?' because I'm pretty sure I can't explain it."

"I kept asking myself, 'Is he really doing that? Am I really seeing what I think I'm seeing?'"

"Same thing the Yankee commander was probably asking."

The regiment's casualties were light—three dead and nine wounded, with none missing.

"We lost Lieutenant Post," Conor said to Tanneyhill.

"I know. I stepped over his body. Seemed like a nice kid. Where was he from?"

"LaGrange. His father is a Confederate colonel who lost both legs at Second Manassas. I'll write to his folks."

One of Conor's soldiers, a private from A Company, recovered two silver bugles the Iron Brigade had dropped in their haste to leave the field. He also wore a black hat that had been lifted from one of their casualties.

"We just whipped the black hats, sir," the private said, raising the trumpets in triumph.

"That ain't happened a lot," Tanneyhill observed. "The black hats usually stick around to the end. When I looked ahead and saw we were going up against them today, I thought we'd be in for a much tougher fight."

One of Conor's company commanders came running up and asked, "Are you smelling that smoke, sir? I think the woods are on fire."

Conor turned and then noticed not the smell of battlefield smoke from the powder of rifles and cannons, but the odor of burning brush.

"The damn woods are on fire!" someone shouted from the thickly entangled area they had recently occupied.

"We've got wounded all over the ground back there," Conor said to Tanneyhill. He called for the other company commanders and directed them to provide men to find and move the wounded away from the danger of the fire. The commanders moved quickly when a wounded soldier suddenly screamed out, *"For the love of God, please help me!"*

General Gordon rode up and asked why they were forming groups to move into the woods.

"There's a fire back there, General. We've got wounded on the ground screaming for help. We've gotta get those men out of there."

"Keep most of your men at the ready here while you're also doing that. I'll send more men to help," he said as he galloped off.

They got many of the injured to safety, but not all. Conor would never forget the blood-curdling yells of wounded and disabled men frantically trying to escape the flames. He thought it may well have been the most horrifying noise he had ever heard.

The brigade held its present position until nightfall when they were then ordered to move to the extreme left of the Confederate line. Grant's lines still overlapped their flanks, and there was always a concern that he would launch a flank attack. Conor's regiment spent most of the rest of the night constructing obstacles and breastworks as thoroughly as they could.

General Gordon inspected Conor's position at around midnight and found it much to his liking.

"How did you find all these logs?" he asked as Conor escorted him around his line by the light of a single lantern.

"First Sergeant Tanneyhill noticed some Yankee breastworks earlier today when we pushed them out of their position. He had the logs removed and brought here, where he thought we might set up at the day's end. It was a good guess."

"Excellent work."

"Do you think they'll attack us in the dark, General?"

"I wouldn't put it past Grant. But it's more likely he'll start again at dawn."

Later, Colonel Evans from the 31st Georgia paid a visit to Conor's covered position and said, "That was a remarkable piece of soldiering today, Conor. We were directly behind you and saw it all. I thought for a minute you might attempt to keep going and march the Thirty-eighth right into Grant's headquarters."

"Can you imagine the look on Grant's face if that had happened?" Conor said with a chuckle.

"I can't imagine the look on *your* face if all of a sudden you were staring straight ahead at Grant."

Conor laughed. "And we're both pointing our pistols at each other, demanding the other's surrender. What a sight that would have been."

"I want you to know that I'm really impressed with your man Tanneyhill," said Colonel Evans. "He must have pulled a dozen or more wounded soldiers out of the fire in the woods. He did more than anyone else, I was told, and I'm sure he's got some burns on his legs. That didn't slow him down, but you might check on him and see if he got those burns treated."

Conor thanked Colonel Evans for the information and later found First Sergeant Tanneyhill with bandages covering what were minor burns to his lower legs.

"Doc fixed me up. I'm fine, sir," he said nonchalantly. "The important thing was to get our wounded away from those flames."

It was exactly what Conor expected to hear from him.

Thus ended the first day of the first bloody encounter between Lee and Grant. The Confederates would soon enough discover that Grant was not so much a sprinter but more of a steadily advancing bulldog who would bite down hard and not let go. Ever.

***

Wednesday, February 13, 1918

Aaron was grinning. "What were you thinking, Cappy, when the Iron Brigade broke and you found yourself in the middle of the Union line?"

"I didn't have time to think. If I would've stopped to consider all the options available to me, they would have shot me. I'm still surprised they didn't shoot me anyway."

"Can we move to the second day now?"

"Of course. But before we do, let me ask you something, Aaron."

"Sure."

"Is any of this going to help you become a better officer?"

Conor saw Aaron's expression instantly change. "Yes, Cappy, of course. I'm getting the equivalent of an advanced West Point course in Tactics and Leadership.

187

And my professor was present at virtually all of the major battles of the Civil War, and even had conversations with the likes of Robert E. Lee and Stonewall Jackson and James Longstreet. Why do you ask? Am I not paying close enough attention?"

"No, Aaron, to the contrary. You're a terrific student. I just wanted to make sure that the teacher was keeping up with the student."

"The teacher is exceptional."

Conor laughed softly and said, "Then let's go back to the Wilderness."

Chapter Twelve

The Wilderness – Second Day

We are coming from the cotton fields,
We're coming from afar;
We have left the plow, the hoe and ax
And are going to the war.
"We Are Coming From The Cotton Fields"

May 6, 1864

The Confederates had deployed scouts throughout the night and into the early morning, stealthily working their way through the thick underbrush to determine what faced them to their front. It was thought that Grant's right extended past the Rebel left, but the scouts were returning with the surprising news that in fact the extreme right of Grant's line did not extend beyond their flank. Further, from all indications there was no additional support located to the rear of the Federal line. The soldiers referred to a flank not grounded to any natural obstacle as being "in the air." And the Federal right seemed to meet that description.

General Gordon personally accompanied the scouts, confirming to his complete satisfaction that indeed the Union right flank was in the air, and unsupported. In fact, the Federal troops on the line were taking a leisurely breakfast and enjoying their morning coffee.

The general developed a plan of attack that would collapse the Union right and in all probability enable another stunning Confederate victory. General Gordon had difficulty convincing General Masterson that the Union right was unsupported, with Masterson insisting that a Union corps was believed to be in reserve directly behind their extreme right. The result, Masterson contended, would be that the attacking Confederate brigade would be repulsed or captured.

It was yet another frustrating battle of wills with General Masterson that General Gordon found so wasteful and unnecessary.

"Why can't he take my word for it?" the general said in disgust when he returned from the meeting. "It's not like I just came into this job yesterday. I know what I saw, and I saw the Union right unsupported and in the air. I didn't guess it and I wasn't relying solely on what someone else had told me. No, I climbed through the damned brush and briars and saw it with my own two eyes. And once again we might lose another chance to gain and then keep the initiative."

Conor shook his head in disgust but otherwise said nothing.

Meanwhile, Longstreet's Corps arrived and strengthened Lee's right, which was generally considered the focus of Grant's attention as the battle at the center and right intensified. Longstreet was soon thereafter seriously wounded and borne from the field on a stretcher, which was hardly good news for the Confederates. Still, nothing was happening on the left as Conor and his regiment waited to attack the Federal right, which inexplicably still remained exposed throughout the day. Finally, at around 5:30 pm, General Lee met with Generals Ewell, Masterson, and Gordon, with Conor standing and listening near the opening to the headquarters tent. Lee pointedly asked why something could not be done on the Confederate left to relieve the pressure on the right. It was at that point that General Gordon's plan was put before Lee, with Masterson objecting. The visibly aggravated Lee finally ignored the objections from Masterson and Ewell and directly ordered General Gordon to attack the Union right.

Colonel Evans' regiment led the attack, with Conor's 38th Georgia following close behind. First Sergeant Tanneyhill and Conor shook hands before they moved out and offered their usual, "See you on the other side."

Once the regiments were formed for the attack, Conor closed up behind Colonel Evans and moved quickly through the underbrush. There was little resistance, so Colonel Evans began turning his line perpendicular to the Federal line and preparing to attack their flank. To their great liking, the Confederates quickly noticed that the Yankees had yet to recognize they were in the process of being flanked. Conor moved his regiment across and began placing them behind the 31st Georgia to support their attack, but the 31st was slow in forming which in turn delayed Conor.

The attack was finally launched and the Union right collapsed easily, just as General Gordon had predicted. The Reb casualties were very light, but to their chagrin they began taking fire from fellow Confederates on the right of their line who were firing down the Union front. The bullets were whizzing past and a soldier three paces away from Conor was hit in the hip. Another had his hat shot off but was unhurt.

The 31st Georgia was again slow to consolidate and press the Federals after their initial success.

"Move deeper in. Quickly, men," Conor shouted when another ball kicked up the ground in front of him. "We're taking flanking fire. Move in."

Conor stood in the line of fire, waving his companies forward. First Sergeant Tanneyhill passed him.

"Don't stay out here in the open long, sir," he warned.

Conor nodded and kept waving the men on.

"Quickly, men. Move quickly."

Conor shouted to Tanneyhill to move up and encourage the 31st Georgia to be a bit more hurried in pressing the attack since the delay was consuming valuable time. The last of Conor's soldiers was by then crossing the open space and heeding his instructions to form up to the rear of the 31st Georgia. The 31st was still not moving, and Conor decided he needed to find Colonel Evans and determine the cause of the unnecessary interruption.

Suddenly a ball struck Conor on the inside of his left knee, digging across the very top of his kneecap and immediately dropping him hard on his left side. *"Dammit!"* he exclaimed as he struggled to regain his feet. He saw a musket on the ground in front of him, only six-feet away, and he was able to crawl over, take hold of it, and use it as a crutch to lift himself up. He felt his leg to see if the kneecap was still affixed, and thankfully it was. The blood was streaming down into his boot, dampening his sock. He continued to move forward, adjusting his lines, encouraging his companies to form up faster, when his painful and swelling left leg finally became unable to bear his weight any longer. He stood leaning against the musket, noticing the ground around him still being struck by balls. The stock of the musket was suddenly hit, breaking it in half and sending him crashing to the ground again.

One of Conor's company commanders helped him to his feet. The commander noticed the blood soaking through Conor's uniform trousers and called for another musket for Conor's use as a brace. "Stay where you are and I'll get some help to you."

"No, I'm okay."

First Sergeant Tanneyhill came over, raised Conor's trouser leg, and looked at his knee. "We gotta get you to the docs, sir. You can't stay out here on that leg."

"I can get around with it. I'll be okay."

Conor took one step with the musket as a crutch and promptly fell over.

"I can't bear any weight on it," he said in disgust.

"We're getting you to the rear," said Tanneyhill. "Who do you want to appoint as a replacement, sir?"

"Get Captain Willingham over here."

Captain Brent Willingham, an experienced and highly respected company commander, hurried to Conor's side and was appointed as the acting regimental commander. They quickly reviewed the plan, and Conor instructed Tanneyhill to notify the other company commanders and Colonel Evans of the change.

Darkness was only minutes away, and the Confederate attack had succeeded as well as General Gordon could have wished. There was still gunfire coming from the right, but now it seemed more concentrated at a specific point than along the entirety of the battle line.

Two young soldiers from Conor's regiment came running toward him. "We're gonna get you to the rear, sir."

Conor reached his arms around their shoulders as they lifted him several inches off the ground. They started slowly back into the thicket at the only pace the pesky undergrowth would permit. Twice the man on the right of Conor tripped and fell, causing the three of them to end up in a pile and prompting cursing tirades from both the young men on either side. As hard as they cursed one another, as vile as the names were they called each other, there was no anger involved. Conor was at least relieved that they weren't intent upon killing one another and thus leaving him in the weeds.

"I haven't heard some of those words in a long while. Where'd you boys learn to cuss like that?" Conor remarked after the second spill.

"From him, sir," said the one on the right, motioning with his head toward the one on the left.

"From my ole granny, sir," said the one on the left.

Dear God, I love my soldiers, Conor thought with as much amusement as his pain would allow. Amusement aside, he had truly come to love his soldiers with a deep, unbreakable, everlasting affection, a bond so intense and complex that he wondered if he would ever again experience anything like it. What he had seen them do in battle time after time had so often amazed him that he vowed never to take their valor for granted. When he had seen them exhausted and hungry and yet offering him some of the food or coffee they had scrounged, he had been humbled. When he saw them lying wounded or dead in the field or in the hospital, he would try not to dwell on it so he could continue to function, but he hurt for them. Mightily. Every single one of them.

Now that they were cursing one another for dropping him when they had been assigned to assist him, he loved them all the more.

It was dark when they finally reached the hospital tent. "We got Lieutenant Colonel Rafferty here," one of the duo of bearers announced in a loud voice with a surge of newly discovered authority. "He's gonna need some immediate attention, gentlemen."

Conor thanked the two boys and dismissed them back to their company. Doctor Reynaud, one of Conor's regimental surgeons, had him moved to a table where he proceeded to slice Conor's uniform trousers away at mid-thigh. His knee was swollen and turning purple, with the path of the ball visible from the entry and exit wounds barely above the kneecap.

"Tell me what you're thinking, doc. And it damn well better not have the word 'amputate' in it."

He kept feeling Conor's knee, above, below, and at the kneecap, and then tested its flexibility, which was painfully difficult.

"No," he muttered.

"No what?"

"No, I don't see a necessity to amputate. The femur may be fractured, and more than likely it is. But it's definitely not splintered apart. There are probably fragments of bone that the bullet shaved off on its path through, but we'll find those and remove them. The patella seems intact, but I'm not sure what it may have done to the joint."

"That's good, right?"

"Considering you've been shot, then I would say that's mostly good, yes. Let's get your leg cleaned up and we'll get started."

An orderly was soon removing Conor's boot and cleansing his bloody leg. Conor glanced around and noticed that the number of wounded was significantly less than what they had experienced at Sharpsburg and Gettysburg. Other regimental hospitals were far more crowded, however, with one not very far away treating the badly wounded James Longstreet.

Three critically wounded soldiers were brought into the tent and Conor asked Doctor Reynaud to treat him only after he had attended to the other three. The pain Conor felt was persistent but not unbearable. He had developed a high tolerance for pain over the past several years, so he relaxed with a deep breath and tried to think of other things. It was nearly an hour before the doctor returned to his side.

"Okay, you're next," the doctor said.

Conor suddenly heard the voice of General Gordon asking, "Where is he?" In a moment General Gordon was standing beside the table and bending down to inspect Conor's injured knee.

"I thought we agreed this was not to be a contest. Look at you, you've already abrogated our covenant."

"You're using lawyer language on me, General. I didn't willfully try to abrogate anything, sir. There was a degree of complicity in this from someone else, someone with a musket."

"How do you feel, Conor?" he said softly, leaning close.

"I'll be fine, sir. Nothing too bad this time. And it worked, General. Your plan worked."

The general tapped his fist lightly on Conor's shoulder. "Get some rest, mister. I'll see you soon."

The general turned to leave.

"General Gordon, sir?" Conor called, raising up and propping himself with his elbows.

The general stopped and looked back.

"The damn plan worked!"

The general smiled and left.

Chaplain Yancey was the next to visit.

"I was here earlier, but I came back as soon as I heard you were hurt. Are you going to be okay, Conor?"

"I should be, yes. But if I wake up and something's missing, then I'll need to go ahead and ask forgiveness in advance for all the things I'll be saying."

The chaplain laughed and then said, "You should know your soldiers are asking about you. One private told me that he was shocked that the man who sent the Iron Brigade running could ever get shot. Another told me that he hoped the regiment would be able to keep you until the end of the war."

Conor grinned, but the pain was drawing away more of his strength.

The chaplain ended his visit with a short prayer, which Conor appreciated.

Conor quickly entertained the thought of waking up and discovering that his leg had been amputated at the knee, but he just as quickly dismissed it. The thought returned, however. He had seen scores of men with missing legs, and they seemed fine, living their lives in spite of their handicap. General Ewell had a wooden leg, he knew, so there was obviously nothing about his military career that had been set back due to his wound.

Just the same, Conor was going to hold Doctor Reynaud to his original diagnosis that his wound could be treated without amputation.

"Have you had ether before?" the doctor asked as he returned.

"Yes, a couple of times."

"Did you try to wave your arms and fly away?"

"Nah. Got a little sick the first time, but other than that I was fine. And it never did interfere with my flying."

"Well then, here we go again."

"Don't take my leg," Conor said emphatically.

The doctor placed the cloth on his face.

"Did you hear me, doc?"

"Yes, I heard you."

"Don't take my . . . "

***

Wednesday, February 13, 1918

Dr. Seth Hamilton, the Atlanta physician under whose care Conor was being treated, came into his hospital room in the early afternoon. Aaron and Conor took a break while the doctor proceeded through the list of tasks he typically performed—listening to Conor's heart, taking his pulse, taking his temperature, looking into his eyes, making notations on his chart. This time when he completed the entries, Dr. Hamilton pulled up a chair beside Aaron.

"My father was a surgeon in the Confederate army during the war," the doctor said. "Have I told you that before, Conor?"

"No," Conor answered. "Where did he serve?"

"Oh gosh, some of the biggest battles of the war. Sharpsburg, Gettysburg, several others. He was with General Lee's army."

"Do you remember any of the regimental or brigade commanders he served with?"

"John B. Gordon," the doctor answered.

Aaron began laughing. "How's that for a coincidence, Cappy?"

The doctor gave a confused look. "What's coincidental?"

"My grandfather," Aaron said, pointing, "was a company commander and then a regimental commander under General Gordon. Your father may have worked for him in his regiment."

The doctor looked at Conor in amazement. "Then did you know my father? His name was Harold Hamilton, from here in Atlanta."

"Of course, with the Sixtieth Georgia," Conor said. "I'm surprised I didn't make that connection before."

"Yes, exactly. The Sixtieth Georgia. He talked about it a lot. And he spoke often of General Gordon," the doctor said, becoming animated. "How well did you know my father, Conor?"

"Not well. We were just acquaintances. Where is he now?"

"He passed away three years ago at the age of eighty-two. What a small world, huh? My father also became John Gordon's personal physician when John was Governor of Georgia. They could tell some stories, those two."

"The General enjoyed a good story as much as anyone," Conor said.

"Yes, either hearing or telling," the doctor added with a chuckle. "And Fanny, my gosh, she could tell a story with the best of 'em. Clean or otherwise, she loved a good story."

The doctor removed the stethoscope from around his neck and wrapped it around the bedpost. He pulled his chair closer to Conor's bed, then sat back and relaxed. "I have to confess I've been eavesdropping on some of your sessions by standing in the hallway just outside your door and pretending to be engaged in the practice of medicine. I must say I find it all very fascinating, Conor. Some of the experiences you talk about are riveting. You should write a book, sir. By the way, how long was your recovery when you were wounded in the knee?"

"I made it back to my regiment in eight weeks. I was sent to Richmond again, and my recovery was slower than I had hoped for. I just couldn't do much to hurry it along. I walked with a pronounced limp, but it got better as time went on."

"You were fortunate, from the sound of things. A half-inch lower and you would've looked much different, my friend," the doctor observed. 'Let me have a look at that knee."

The doctor gave Conor's leg a quick examination.

"Even a quarter of an inch and it would've been a much worse outcome. Does it still bother you?" he asked.

"Yes, especially in rainy weather."

"You're a tough old Reb, Conor, just like those men you commanded. Please, continue your conversation. I'll just sit and listen for a spell."

Aaron took a quick look at his notes. "Did Captain Willingham keep command of the regiment while you were hospitalized, Cappy?"

"No, for some crazy reason General Gordon appointed another company commander, a guy who thought he should've been given the post in the first place. He was a decent company commander, but I thought Willingham was the far better choice. Anyway, the new guy rode my horse Shannon into a fight at Winchester, sitting up there like he was Napoleon from what I was told, and he proceeded to get shot off my horse in the first five minutes with a ball to the head. He got himself killed and then Shannon ran loose and was probably corralled by the Yankees. Damn that guy!"

"It seems the Confederates missed another opportunity on the second day at the Wilderness," Aaron observed.

"Ah, you saw that, did you? Yes, we let another one get by. Uncertainty is a certainty in war, but there's no reason whatsoever to try to invent ways to convert certainty into uncertainty. We had a high degree of assurance that the Federal right was unprotected, and that should've prompted an immediate attack. Yet we waited, and by waiting, we lost a golden opportunity that fell into our laps so unexpectedly. So we ended up in a stalemate, much as if we'd never fought the battle at all. Except for the casualties, of course."

Dr. Hamilton excused himself to check on another patient.

"Let's call it a night, Cappy."

"It's a little earlier than usual. Is everything okay?"

Aaron grinned slightly and spoke in a lowered voice. "Everything's fine. Actually, I'm going out with one of the nurses. She doesn't want it known, so we're being sorta discreet about it."

"Very well, Captain Rafferty. Your secret will be safe with me only insofar as you tell me which nurse it is."

"It's Joan, the brunette who brings you breakfast and takes your pulse in the morning."

Conor smiled approvingly. "She's been my favorite nurse the whole time I've been here. She's a sweetheart. You have a nice eye for women, sir."

"See there, Cappy. Your influence is rubbing off on me in more ways than one."

"Then God help you," Conor said, laughing.

Chapter Thirteen

The Richmond Girl

Into the ward of the clean, white-washed halls,
Where the dead slept and the dying lay;
Wounded by bayonets, sabres, and balls,
Somebody's darling was borne one day.
"Somebody's Darling"

May-June, 1864
"Hello, Conor. Remember me?"

He had finished breakfast and was reclining in his hospital bed, his left leg propped by pillows, reading a week-old Richmond *Dispatch* one of his fellow patients had given him. There were thirty-three patients in total, all officers, at Richmond's four-story General Hospital Number 4, facing the east side of Tenth Street and just north of Marshall near the affluent Court End neighborhood.

Conor lowered the newspaper and saw a beautiful young woman standing beside his bed.

"Penny!" he said, surprised. "My gosh, how are you, Miss Orr?"

"I'm fine," she said as she leaned over and hugged him. "I'm amazed you remembered me."

"Of course I remember you. I've thought about you a lot. How are you?"

"I'm fine. I'm a volunteer nurse's assistant two mornings a week, and when I saw your name on the list, I thought it was you but I wasn't sure. The last time I saw you, you were a captain and now you're a lieutenant colonel. You've done well, sir. How's your leg?"

"It's sore, but I suppose that's to be expected when you get shot. I can't seem to learn that lesson any other way than the hard way. How's your mother and General Orr?"

"My mother's fine. My father kept asking for a command and they finally gave him one. So he's now in Georgia commanding a division in the Army of the Tennessee."

"I was just reading about that in the newspaper. The Yankee General Sherman is pushing out of Chattanooga and probably headed toward Atlanta. I sure hope your father can keep him away from my hometown."

Penny frowned. "Atlanta's not the only place I'm hoping we can keep the Yankees away from," she said, motioning around the ward with her outstretched hand. "I certainly don't want to see them here in Richmond. They're already in Petersburg."

"You look incredible, Penny, just like I remember. And believe me when I say I *do* remember you."

She pulled a chair over to his bedside where they spent the next half-hour catching up from the thirteen months since they had last seen each other. In addition to her hospital-volunteer work, Penny also worked as a secretary at the Confederate White House which was nearby on Clay and Twelfth Streets.

"It doesn't hurt to be a Confederate general's daughter when you want a job in the Confederate government," she said, laughing.

"When do you have time for a social life?" he asked.

"I have no social life, Conor," she said with a blush.

"Ah, how does an intelligent, friendly, stunningly beautiful young woman like you have no social life?"

"Well, first, there's not an abundance of eligible young men floating around Richmond. Most of the younger guys are off fighting the Yankees, like you. And second, if I wanted to go out on the town with all of the older and sometimes married men who come around now that my father has gone off to Georgia, then sure, I could have a full social calendar. But I assure you I have no interest in that."

Her smile and her blue eyes were as exquisite and enticing as ever.

"How are things with you, Penny?"

"Everything's fine except for this godforsaken war. Tell me what you've been up. You've been promoted twice since I've last seen you, so you must've been doing some excellent work."

Conor explained how he had been reunited with General Gordon, albeit with her father's kind assistance. He noted the battles he had participated in and how he had progressed to taking command of a regiment of Georgians. He spoke of the good men he now led, and how much he had learned about leadership from his own experiences and the wise teachings of several splendid officers and one brilliant non-commissioned officer. When Penny asked if he was satisfied with his decision of a year ago to return to the field from the desk job he had held in Richmond, he laughed and told her it was easily the best choice he could have made. He added that he could think of only one thing that would have made it better.

"And what would that have been?" she asked.

"If I could've taken you with me," he replied, again causing her to blush.

"You haven't changed a bit, Conor Rafferty."

"I swear you're more gorgeous than ever, Penelope Orr."

"How's your family?" Penny asked.

Conor paused and swallowed hard and tried to force a smile, but couldn't.

"Conor, what's happened?"

He paused before finally saying, "One of my brothers was killed at Gettysburg and the other died in a prison camp near Chicago. Then Mother died of what seemed like a broken heart after the news of Sean and Daniel arrived. Father's the only one I've got left."

"Oh Conor, no," Penny said softly as she reached for his hand with both of hers. "I'm so sorry. Oh my, I had no idea. My gosh, I don't know what to say."

"We couldn't have known that it would ever come to this. My brothers and I knew we would be at risk, obviously, but we never included our mother in that same category. I just try not to think about it. I think I'm better off just keeping it at a distance."

Penny shook her head in disbelief and squeezed his hand. "I'm really sorry, Conor."

The harsh news of his family soured the cheery mood, and Penny soon announced that she had to leave for her secretarial job.

"Do you want me to stop by for a visit tomorrow?" she asked.

"Yes, please. I'd really like to make this a habit."

Penny's enticing scent remained after she had departed. Conor took a ration of good-natured ribbing from the other officers on his ward who complained about his monopolizing the time of the beautiful young volunteer nurse. He provided some background of his previous friendship with Penny, but they wouldn't accept it as an excuse for his cornering all of her available attention.

"I'm deliberately keeping her away from you gentlemen. It's for her own good, ya' know," he explained.

He was roundly booed and hissed by the others.

Conor tried walking without crutches on his stiff left leg after that first week in the hospital, but he struggled. The more he tried, the stiffer and more painful his leg became. The doctor noticed a redness and puffiness not previously seen and promptly treated him for an infection.

Meanwhile, Penny continued to visit. During the third week of his stay, Penny began visiting Conor in the evenings. There was a small courtyard in the back of the building, and he would make his way there on his crutches and wait for her, where they would then sit on a bench and talk until darkness fell.

After four weeks, Conor was walking without the crutches, albeit with a pronounced limp. He received permission to leave the hospital for an entire Saturday, so he met Penny outside where she had rented a carriage and driver for the day. They first stopped at the south end of Twelfth Street at an overlook where they could observe the James River's Pipeline Rapids. They sat on a wooden bench and watched the fast-moving water as it made its way toward and around Mayo's Island. Penny became excited when she pointed out several Great Blue Herons searching for food amid the wetlands on the opposite bank. The early-June weather was mild, even a bit cool, and Penny's plaid day dress with its long sleeves helped ward off the morning chill. Still, that same morning chill gave Conor an excuse to slip his arm around her shoulders as they sat and watched the large birds.

Next, they toured the downtown portion of Richmond.

"It's a different place than when you were here before," Penny noted. "There have been food shortages that caused rioting, inflation is out of control, and much of the city has become so overcrowded that crime is a major problem. There are probably more prostitutes and gamblers in Richmond today than there were citizens twenty-five years ago," she said with a laugh.

They stopped at the Confederate White House where Penny gave Conor a brief tour of the first floor where she was a familiar presence. They paused at an office where Penny introduced Conor to General Lawrence Roundtree who was on President Davis' staff, and who had replaced Penny's father when General Orr left for duty in Georgia. The gray-haired General Roundtree asked about Conor's service, and they then proceeded to exchange war stories for a brief time. The general had commanded a brigade at Gettysburg and had participated in the Battle of the Wheatfield.

"Robert Rodes and I lost many a good soldier in that fight," the general said. "Our brigades went in together and fought side-by-side on July second."

"My brother, Sergeant Sean Rafferty, was killed in that battle, sir, serving with General Rodes' brigade."

"And my son, Lieutenant Jesse Roundtree, also died that same day, serving with William Barksdale at the Peach Orchard."

They offered their respective condolences, and then Penny and Conor left.

"Did you know the general's son had been killed at Gettysburg?" he asked once they were back in the carriage.

"Yes," Penny answered. "I just thought it might be helpful for you to meet someone else in uniform who lost a family member there."

As they rode along Richmond's streets, Conor said nothing for several minutes. He thought again of Sean, seeing his face and hearing his voice, both clearly, as if he were sitting with Conor in the carriage. He missed Sean greatly, as he did Daniel, but after a few more minutes he finally pushed away any further thoughts of his brothers, knowing those images would always be there for another day or another night. But no more on this day, he concluded. Not on this day.

Penny looked at him and said softly, "I hope I didn't cause you any pain, Conor. I really didn't intend to do that."

"No pain, Penny," he said, and then leaned and kissed her on the cheek. "You really are something special."

He kissed her again, causing her to blush. He kissed her a third time and she admonished him, if only slightly.

They had a picnic lunch at a shady corner on the large open space around the Capitol building. Penny spread a blanket on the ground and then opened the wooden basket that contained bread and several cheeses, along with a bit of sausage. There were also fresh strawberries. Conor carefully inspected each of the food items as if he were seeing it for the first time. He then savored the taste of the succulent fruit, slowly, adding a grin and a nod of approval. Penny noticed his delight and began giggling. Afterwards, Conor struggled to remain awake.

"So, here's a question for you, Conor," Penny said, noting his drowsiness. "If you could have one wish today, and only one, what would it be?"

He took a deep breath and quietly considered her question. "I suppose it would be an end to the war," he said finally. "The killing would stop, and that alone would certainly be a worthwhile thing. And if it wouldn't count as a second wish, I would of course want it to end in victory for us."

"That's exactly what I thought you'd say," Penny said with a chuckle.

"Okay, your turn. What's your wish?"

"I would wish," she said, then pausing before adding, "yes, that's it. I would wish that you would come back to Richmond when the war was over."

Good God almighty, he thought, now fully awake. Ironically, he was originally tempted to wish that she would still be unattached and in Richmond after the war, but he had lost his nerve.

Penny grinned and said softly, "Yes, that's my wish."

"I would say that's a wish that has an excellent chance of coming true."

She leaned and kissed him on the cheek.

They held hands for several minutes until Penny finally broke the silence.

"May I ask you a personal question, Conor?"

"Sure. Ask me anything you want."

"Why is it that you never talk about your father?"

She surprised him, and he hesitated in answering.

"You've talked a lot about your mother and your brothers, but you've never mentioned anything about your father except that he brought y'all to this country from Ireland, and that he's a farmer. I'm just curious, that's all. If you'd rather not answer, that's okay."

Conor forced a slight smile and took in a deep breath. "My father's a hard man to please, and even harder to understand. I was the oldest and he always expected more from me. I understand that, and I always tried to do more. We didn't agree on much of anything as I got older, and then the war became an area of great tension between us. He said some unkind things to me before I left for army duty that I don't understand and don't know that I'll ever forget."

"Why? Why did he say those things to you?"

"He never told me why. I can only guess that he thought once I joined the army, my brothers would follow, which they did. And he thought the war would end up destroying our family, which it has. And he told me I would be a complete failure as an army officer, which I'm not."

"So he was opposed to the war from the start?"

"Yes, very much."

"What did he expect you to do?"

"I don't know. I asked him that very question, and he never answered me."

"I'm sorry, Conor. I won't bring it up again."

"It's okay. It's in the past and I've learned to live with it. I'm no longer interested in proving my worth to Father. I've proven my worth to myself and my soldiers and my commander, and that's what matters the most to me now. And even though it's taken me a while to come to terms with it, it wasn't my joining the army that destroyed our family, like he said it would. I don't blame myself for that because it's just not true. I finally see that now, and if Father can't see it, or chooses not to, then there's really nothing I can do about it."

After an hour on the hard ground, Conor had a difficult time standing due to the stiffness in his leg. A Confederate sergeant was passing by, and Conor called for his help.

"Thank you, Sergeant," Conor said once he was standing. "Getting shot will do this to you. I don't recommend it."

The sergeant held up his left hand, displaying his missing ring finger and saying with a laugh, "You're right. I don't recommend it either, sir."

When Conor held up his right hand with its missing finger, all three of them began laughing.

"Where did you lose your finger, sir?"

"Sharpsburg. What about you?"

"Second Manassas."

Conor and the sergeant wished each other well and parted company. He and Penny then went to Penny's two-story home not far from the hospital and released the carriage and driver, with their thanks. Penny's mother was preparing supper for them, so in the meantime the two of them sat in chairs on her wide front porch.

"Mother got a letter from my father yesterday," Penny said, "and he wrote that the Yankees were pushing steadily toward Atlanta. My father has his troops in Marietta, north of Atlanta."

Conor nodded his understanding.

"Are we going to lose the war, Conor? Tell me the truth. Will the South lose?"

"I don't think so. As long as General Lee's on our side, I'm confident we'll find a way to win."

Penny leaned toward him. "There's only one of General Lee. There are thousands upon thousands of Yankees and they are no further away than Petersburg, which is twenty-five miles from this doorstep. How far is Marietta from Atlanta?"

"About twenty miles."

Penny sighed and shook her head. "See there? The wolf is at the door. I wish I could believe we're winning this war, but my deep suspicion tells me we're not. I probably shouldn't mention this to you, but I see lots of correspondence at work where there are problems with shortages all across the Confederacy in everything from ammunition to rations to powder to winter clothing. The longer it goes on, the worse it'll get, and not just for the army. For all the farms and the people in the towns all across the South, it will only get worse. It's an ugly picture, Conor. My father knows it, and so do you. You just won't say it."

"I won't say it because I don't believe it. Our army is still very much alive with a lot of fight left in it. I know that because I've seen it. I can only speak for myself, but I'm a long way from declaring our situation hopeless."

Penny reached across and held his hand. "I want to believe you. I *need* to believe you. Otherwise I'd probably go crazy from the worry."

They had a lovely supper, the three of them. Mrs. Orr was especially sympathetic when Penny told her of Conor's family tragedies. Mrs. Orr was curious about Georgia, its features and climate, and then she described her childhood and young adulthood in Northern California. When the evening ended, Mrs. Orr gave Conor a box of Cuban cigars that the non-smoking General Orr had received as a gift.

"Share them with the boys in the hospital," she said.

Conor walked the short distance back to the hospital, but not before kissing Penny again. And this time Penny kissed back.

The cigars went over especially well with the boys in the ward.

Conor and Penny saw each other often over the next three weeks, from her regular hospital visits to the weekend passes that allowed them to be together for hours at a time. Conor was within a week of being released for duty when he walked the short distance to Penny's home on a drizzly, overcast day in June. He still walked with a limp, but the pain had eased greatly and he was ready to return to his regiment. A recent letter from General Gordon promised that command of the 38th Georgia would still be his. The general even asked if he had been able to see "the Richmond girl," the daughter of his friend General Orr and the one Conor had spoken of so glowingly on previous occasions.

In truth, the Richmond girl had broken out all over him like a fever during the past seven weeks. While he was looking forward to returning to the field, he was having increasing difficulty over the prospect of leaving her. He had never felt this way before, never in his life, and it was not only exhilarating but even a bit scary.

They sat on the sofa in Penny's parlor while her mother was away visiting friends. The constant *tick tock* of the large grandfather clock and the noise of the driving thunderstorm outside filled in the gaps of silence from their uneasy attempts at conversation. For the first time since they had begun seeing one another, they were struggling to put their feelings into words.

"I don't want you to go," Penny finally said, sliding close to him and resting her head upon his shoulder. "I'm dreading it, Conor. It's all I think about now, night and day."

"I know. I feel the same way. I want to get back to my regiment and do my duty, but I don't like the thought of not being with you."

"What if I could get General Roundtree to get you ordered back to Richmond?"

"I couldn't do that, Penny."

"Why not?"

"I thought you knew me better than that."

Penny sighed. "Oh, I do know you, Conor Rafferty. And I knew that's exactly what you would say. It was just a nice thought, that's all. A nice little bit of hope."

"Speaking of nice thoughts, I've been thinking about something," he said.

Penny raised her head and looked at him. "Yes? About what?"

He paused a moment and took a deep breath in an attempt to throw off a sudden case of nerves. He could've used a quick drink of water, or better yet a snort of whiskey, but there was nothing within easy reach.

"Conor, what?"

He paused, smiling self-consciously.

"Well, Conor? What?"

"Okay, here goes," he said, clearing his throat and taking in another deep breath. "How would you like to spend the rest of your life with a shot-up ole Reb officer who could promise you nothing except his unconditional love for you every day for as long as he lived?"

Penny paused for a moment before asking softly, "What are you saying, Conor? Are you proposing?"

"No," he replied. "I mean, not in the down-on-one-knee, ring-in-hand kind of way. No, that would come later, after I'd had a chance to speak with your father. I'm not proposing marriage. Not now, anyway."

"Then just what is it you're saying?"

"What I'm saying to you, Penny, is that I love you and I want to spend my life with you after this war's over. I know the last time I was in Richmond when we were spending time with each other, we decided to keep things on a 'friendship' level. Well, what I'm proposing, uh, what I'm *saying*, is that I want us to be more than friends. I want us to be a couple, and I want us to be married after the war. I want you to know that I love you and I'll return for you. And if you feel the same way, then you can expect me to show up here in Richmond the day after the war's over, God willing."

Penny stared at him for a moment before reaching her arms around his neck. She began crying softly.

"You're the girl I want, Penny. I want to travel the world with you. I want to see your beautiful face next to me in the morning light. I want to see you gently rocking our baby to sleep—you're going to be a great mother—while you're singing a lullaby, maybe even an Irish one. I want to help you become the person you want to become, just as you will do for me. That's what I'm saying, Penny. That's what I've been thinking about. That's what I want."

"I love you, Conor," she said. "I love you so much."

"You don't have to decide anything tonight. You can take your time, even if you have to write to me after I've left Richmond. I don't want you to do anything you don't want to do. I don't want—"

"Stop."

"What I mean is, Penny, I want you—"

"Stop, Conor."

Penny kissed him so hard his vision blurred, and he felt lightheaded from the strain his overloaded senses were signaling. His heart was racing so hard he could feel it in his temples, and he could likewise feel Penny's beating heart as she pressed against his chest.

But there was nothing wrong with his hearing, especially when he heard her say, "I'll be waiting here for you, Conor Rafferty."

***

Thursday, February 14, 1918
"You were smitten, Cappy."

"How could you tell?"

"Did it ever cross your mind in the quiet of the night to take a desk job in Richmond and stay there with your sweetheart?"

"No, of course not."

"I didn't think so."

"Would you have considered it, Aaron, if you found yourself in a similar situation?"

"Not for a minute."

"I didn't think so, either," Conor said, smiling.

"You seem energized now. Feel good enough to keep going?"

"Yes."

Chapter Fourteen

The Grip Tightens

Brave boys are they!
Gone at their country's call;
And yet, and yet we cannot forget
That many brave boys must fall.
"Brave Boys Are They"

July – December, 1864

Conor's regiment moved into the Shenandoah Valley as part of the larger force under the overall command of General Masterson. The general had been ordered by General Lee to mount an offensive that would force Grant to send additional troops and thus slow his dogged pursuit of the main body of the Army of Northern Virginia. General Gordon now commanded one of Masterson's four divisions, of which Conor's regiment was a part. The Rebel army in the Shenandoah was considerably smaller than the large force they now faced under Union General Sheridan, a condition they had endured for much of the war but was now more disadvantageous than ever.

While Conor had been recuperating in Richmond during the month of June, the war elsewhere in Virginia had slogged along. General Grant had suffered an appalling 7,000 casualties at Cold Harbor in a mere twenty minutes. The siege of Petersburg had also commenced.

In July, Union General Sherman's siege of Atlanta also began, a situation that gave Conor not only a feeling of anxiety about his hometown, but a sense of helplessness as

215

he went about managing his own little piece of the war from his faraway Virginia post.

Conor's mail finally caught up with him when he returned to the 38th Georgia.

July 25, 1864
Dear Conor:

I hope this letter reaches you and finds you in good health. As I'm sure you know by now, Atlanta has come under attack by the Yankees. The city is being shelled daily, and many of the residents have left for Jonesboro or Macon. So far I have only seen Confederate cavalry near our farm, but I'm sure the fighting will reach us sooner or later. I can hear the guns firing almost every day now and the damage to the city is already great.

I say a prayer for you every day and night, Conor, and it might be helpful if you could do the same for us here in Atlanta. I also pray that this war will be over soon and you can finally come home, as I'm sure you wish the same.

You are the sole heir to the property now, son. The lawyer Wilton L. Witcher has a copy of all the important papers in case something happens to me.

I am truly sorry for the way I treated and spoke to you, Conor. I have now come to realize that in so many ways I have been a failure as a father. In spite of that, you have become the sort of man that I can only wish I had become. I could never take back all the harm I'm sure I have done to you. I just want you to know that I am terribly sorry. You deserved better from me, and I live with that regret every day now.

Be a good soldier, my brave son, and know that I am proud of you and love you very much.
Yours,
Father

Conor put the letter away and did his best to forget about it.

General Masterson's Confederate forces, to include Gordon's Division, entered Maryland in July and fought battles at Monocacy and Fort Stevens where they threatened the city of Washington until Grant hurriedly sent reinforcements there.

In August they were involved in engagements at Guard Hill, Summit Point, and Smithfield Crossing. None of the battles were conclusive, though they did have modest success in attacking and driving the Union forces to their front. The Rebs spent lots of time on the march, fighting off the attacks of Union cavalry and finding little rest for their worn and exhausted troops.

On August 24, the Rebels moved from their position on the Martinsburg Pike to Winchester to face a large Federal force. Confederate General Robert Rodes, a close friend of General Gordon, was killed in the heavy fighting. The Southerners attacked, but the Federals did not break. The Rebels continued to pour fire into the Union ranks, but the Yankees still would not break. The Federals then began to push the Rebs back until soon the Southerners were in full flight. They left wounded on the field in their hasty retreat, and Conor had never felt quite so empty after an engagement. They gathered their remaining troops and marched hard before they had enough distance from the pursuing Yankees to call a halt.

Conor's soldiers were tired to the point of complete exhaustion, and they were soon asleep in the damp grass, their muskets beside them. Some were barefoot with bruised and bloody feet. Most wore tattered clothing. And all were hungry.

Conor found a bare patch of ground and spread his blanket out after meeting with General Gordon about the next day's objectives. He had no horse, and he had no officers on his personal staff apart from Chaplain Yancey and Doctor Reynaud. His company commanders were captains and lieutenants, and several of those were new.

Chaplain Yancey and First Sergeant Tanneyhill found Conor in the dark and spread their blankets out beside his. They all sensed Conor's displeasure at having left the battlefield in such disarray, especially with their own wounded soldiers watching as they quit the field and left those fellow Confederates to the mercy of the Yankees. It was his first experience since Gettysburg at having had his lines broken and then being forced into a disorderly retreat—an inglorious one, to be sure—and he was not at all happy about it. In addition, his knee was swollen and painful to the point where he was considering riding in one of the supply wagons the next day.

"There's no shame in what happened today," Chaplain Yancey said. "We were faced with either retreating or being destroyed. There's not much of a choice when one is faced with extinction. Thank God so many of us made it out alive."

"Do you agree with that, First Sergeant?" Conor asked.

Conor knew Tanneyhill would be made uncomfortable with such a question, but the First Sergeant surprised him when he answered without delay, "Yessir, I do."

"Isn't this the same regiment that sent the famous Iron Brigade running to the rear?" Conor asked to no one in particular. "And the same regiment that marched under fire for nearly a mile over open ground at Gettysburg?"

There was a long pause before Tanneyhill spoke up.

"Things have changed, sir."

"Oh? How so?"

"Just look at these men, sir. They look like skeletons. They're so undernourished they don't have but maybe thirty percent of the endurance they had back at Gettysburg. Back then, they could march all day and then go right into a major battle and perform well. But they can't do that now. It's amazing to me they can still do what they do. These men still fight with hearts like lions, just as they always have. They still have the heart and the will, but it's the physical strength they've lost. And they're up against a tough enemy who also has the advantage in numbers in a bigger way than we've ever seen before."

"Anything to add, Chaplain?" Conor asked.

"I know you well enough to know that you'll vigorously disagree with me about my saying there's no shame in what happened today."

"And you'd be correct," Conor interjected quickly

"And given the fact that you're a commander of troops, of course you would take exception to ever thinking that losing a battle is acceptable. But keep in mind what the First Sergeant is telling you about the condition of your soldiers because I'm seeing the same thing. And while I know these men would willingly follow you into Hell, the fact is they don't want to be captured or killed any more than those Iron Brigade fellows did, or any of those other Yankee regiments you've sent running from the field. They're soldiers, yes, and darned good ones, but they're also thinking and feeling human beings."

"The truth is, it's my fault, not theirs," Conor said. "They'll perform in accordance with the leadership they receive. They always have. I failed them today, and I failed them badly. They were poorly led and they panicked and broke as a result. I should forgo my pay for today because I sure as hell didn't earn it."

"I can't agree with that, sir," Tanneyhill countered. "You were the same leader today that you've always been. There was nothing you could have done that would've made the odds better for us. We just got overpowered and whipped today."

"But we've lived to fight another day," the chaplain added.

And so they did.

The same overall setting continued as the Rebels had running battles with Union cavalry and near daily skirmishes with Union infantry. The tired Confederate troops still fought hard, still marched long distances, still did all that was asked of them, but Conor had been paying closer attention to how little they were being fed. The supply of rations and ammunition was unpredictable, and there were times when they went without food for two or three days. On one particular foggy, rainy day, having been tipped off by scouts, the regiment intercepted a Yankee supply car from the B&O Railroad with a brilliantly executed raid under Conor's leadership. They captured large amounts of rations and fruit that allowed the Rebel soldiers to eat their fill for the first time in months. The captured oranges were especially helpful in fighting off the scurvy that Doctor Reynaud had been treating. There were also uniforms and bags of currency among the items seized, but it was the food that held the highest interest.

August 31, 1864
Dear Conor:

The situation here in Atlanta is grim. The Yankees are in control of large parts of the city, and our army seems on the verge of collapsing. It will not be long before Sherman will have Atlanta and nobody knows what he will do with it.

The Confederates took half my herd of cattle. I can hardly afford to feed them anyway. The Yankees will probably take what's left. I hope you are well in Virginia. I say a prayer for you often.

By the time this letter gets to you, Atlanta will have fallen. I don't plan to leave the farm no matter what the Yankees say. This is our home.

I'm proud of you and love you very much, son. I want to sit down with you after this war is over and square

things with you. I have many things I need to tell you, and I want to do that in person. I can only hope that you will forgive me and give me that chance.
Yours,
Father

     Conor's hometown of Atlanta fell on Friday, September 2.
     General Masterson's Confederates took up a strong position after the Winchester defeat, with its left anchored on Fisher's Hill, south of Strasburg, and its right on the north branch of the Shenandoah River. General Gordon's Division was in the center-right portion of the line, along the Manassas Gap Railroad, with Conor's regiment placed on the division's right. On September 21, the Federals advanced, pushing back the Rebel skirmishers, inflicting casualties, and taking important high ground to the north and west of the gray line. On September 22, a Federal corps attacked the Confederates in the center while another corps advanced from Little North Mountain on their left, and by 4:00 pm it was apparent that General Gordon's Division was flanked. Conor's heart sank when he saw waves of blue-coated soldiers streaming toward him on his exposed left. The Reb army thus began collapsing like a house of cards, from west to east, and by the time the regiments to Conor's left started their scamper in the opposite direction, his own regiment began to follow them in retreat despite his best efforts to keep them in their defensive positions.
     The sick feeling intensified.
     By the end of the month, the Confederates had established a defensive line at Rockfish Gap, near Waynesboro. Battle deaths from the Fisher's Hill fight were moderate, but their already depleted army lost 1,000 soldiers taken prisoner by Sheridan's forces.
     Union General Sheridan began laying waste to the upper Shenandoah Valley by torching mills, barns, and

haystacks. Sheridan, consistent with Grant's intentions to destroy the region and thus deny its use to the Confederate army, was burning extensive amounts of property.

"Meeting us on the field is one thing," General Gordon said as he and Conor sat under a broad old oak tree and gazed out their field glasses to the north, looking for any signs of enemy movement. "But burning the property of private citizens is a damn crime. I would personally like to shoot Phil Sheridan between the eyes and send him on his way to a hot, eternal hell. He is richly deserving of such a fate."

"And I hope he finds it," Conor added.

"At the hands of my division, preferably."

Nothing else was said for several minutes. They could see nothing to their front, no lines of blue troops or wagons, no dust on the roads. For one more day it seemed the Federals were busy elsewhere, another welcomed reprieve for the Confederate soldiers to gain some well-needed rest.

"General, how do you stop a retreating regiment?" Conor asked.

General Gordon removed his field glasses. "The same way one would stop a retreating company, I suppose," he answered with a shrug. "Inspiring leadership and bold action. But I should add that once it starts, it's a very challenging thing to reverse, especially if the enemy is pursuing. Let me guess that this has been weighing heavily on you lately. Is that right?"

"I've not stopped thinking about it since Winchester. Now that it's happened more than once, I just wonder if the soldiers are starting to view breaking and running as just another choice if things become difficult, whereas before such a thing as leaving the field to the enemy wasn't a possibility they would ever consider. What's happened, sir? Is it me? Is it my lack of leadership that's causing my regiment to break and run instead of staying on the line and fighting it out?"

"You've probably noticed that yours isn't the only regiment affected."

"I know that, General. It's just so discouraging to see our men panicked and running away. We've gone through so much of this war by forcing the Yankees to be the ones who either skedaddled or fought us to a draw. We haven't won every battle, of course, but at least we haven't made a habit of dishonoring ourselves."

General Gordon plucked a single blade of grass and put it into his mouth. "We're up against a large force, Conor, and we're taking pressure off General Lee by keeping Sheridan occupied here. That makes Grant's job a little harder each day. We're doing the army a great service by buying it as much time as we can for General Lee to figure out a way to whip Grant."

"Do you think that's possible?"

"I do, yes. And when it happens, we will have played a big role in it. There is a larger picture here, Conor, one that you should take into account when you think about the performance of your regiment or this division. You're having a little crisis of confidence. I still have confidence in you, probably more than you have in yourself now. And your soldiers still believe in you. So you can put to rest any notion that you've somehow forgotten how to be an effective commander. Your leadership is fine, just as it's always been. If it wasn't, I would've already let you know about it, I assure you."

Conor laughed hard, and then General Gordon began laughing also.

"Just what is it we're laughing at?" the general asked somewhat self-consciously.

"General Gordon, you've just convinced me that I'm the reincarnation of Stonewall Jackson, sir."

"Splendid. Then you can start delivering the victories he gave us in this valley."

General Gordon kept laughing, but Conor didn't.

"By the way, whatever happened with you and the Richmond girl?" the general asked.

"Her name's Penny. We saw quite a bit of each other. She's writing regularly, so who knows? I might drop in on her in Richmond after the war ends."

"And take her to Atlanta with you?"

"I'd like that, yes. I'd really like that."

"Well, I'm confident you'll work all of that out in due course. I'm sure she's a terrific lady."

"She is," Conor said, smiling. "She's the best."

"And have you heard from your father since Atlanta fell?"

"No."

"Do you even care what's happened to him?"

Conor hesitated before answering, "He's my father. Of course."

There was a long pause before General Gordon finally said, "Yes, he is, Conor. You would do well to remember that, no matter what you two may have to work out after this war's over. You'll discover one day that being a father isn't easy. We all make mistakes, we're all human. And more often than not, the ones we hurt the most are the ones we love the most. We have to learn to forgive in this life, or we'll end up even more damaged. I don't need to tell you that he's the only family member you have left. But I will tell you that the two of you need each other more than ever now. Give that some thought."

General Gordon got up and left.

On Tuesday, October 18, the Confederates broke camp and moved out after dark. They followed a narrow path between the Shenandoah River and the northern tip of Massanutten Mountain. They could move only in a single-file formation for long stretches, and thus could take no artillery with them. They met up with Masterson's other divisions in the heavy fog and attacked the Federals in their campsite, achieving total surprise. Conor's regiment led the attack from General Gordon's Division, and they found many of the Yankee soldiers still half-dressed when they came out to meet their attackers. The Federal troops made a fighting withdrawal, but the Rebels won the field.

By 10:00 am, the Southerners had once again achieved what appeared to be a stunning victory.

The hungry troops stopped only briefly to pillage the Union supplies for all they could find. They had collected 1,300 prisoners and 24 cannons, but inexplicably the order to halt came just as they were readying to press the final assault. Conor immediately thought of the first day at Gettysburg where the order to halt had cost them dearly, and when he saw General Gordon ride into his position he, too, seemed perplexed.

"Why are we halting, sir?"

"Orders from General Masterson. I'm on my way to see him to discuss the matter. I want you to have your regiment ready to resume the attack, but in the meantime you are to halt in place. Do you understand?"

"Understood. We are halted, General."

First Sergeant Tanneyhill came forward and handed Conor a biscuit and some bacon. "It's still warm," he said as he licked his fingers from his own unexpected but nonetheless much appreciated Yankee-style breakfast.

"We're halting again at exactly the wrong time," Conor said in disgust. "Courtesy of General Masterson."

"Can General Gordon change his mind?"

"I doubt it. Just between us, General Masterson's nothing but a hollow uniform. If you tapped him on the shoulder you'd probably hear an echo. And arguing with him is like picking up a dog with bowel complaint. It's usually best just to leave it be."

Tanneyhill laughed. "Why do you suppose General Masterson's like that?"

Conor sighed. "That's just who he is. The reason a skunk's a skunk is because he has no sense of refinement. In the general's case, he has no sense of battlefield refinement, so he panics and orders us to stop. It's become a habit he can't seem to break. Whenever he sees us about to become victorious, he slams the door shut and halts us in place. It's like he's satisfied with partial victory. I'm going to start referring to him as General Partial Victory Masterson. How do you like that, First Sergeant? Ole P.V. Masterson has halted us again. What a surprise."

"You might want to lower your voice, sir."

"Yessir, ole P.V.'s gonna get us in position to partially win this damn war. And then he can go back to his partial home with his partial family and find some partial job and live the good partial life. And when he grows old he'll probably figure out a way to partially die."

"Sir, my advice to you is to lower your voice."

"Okay, I'll split the difference with you and partially lower my voice. Besides, what's ole P.V. gonna do about it if he hears me? Order me to pack my gear and send my insubordinate ass to the Shenandoah as punishment? Well guess what? It appears he's already done that."

Conor then turned his attention to the food and consumed it in two large bites. When a lieutenant courier showed up on horseback and told him to halt his regiment in place, per General Masterson's orders, Conor began gesturing and cursing so vehemently with a mouth so overstuffed that white bits of biscuit were sent flying.

The lieutenant could see Conor's red-faced agitation but could understand nothing that was being said.

"He's aware of that order, sir," Tanneyhill calmly told the courier who immediately turned about and galloped away, but not without looking back.

"What's the matter with finishing what we started?" Conor said to no one in particular. "Have we lost our nerve in partial victory as well as defeat?"

Tanneyhill stepped beside Conor, put his hand on his shoulder, and said in a calm, measured tone, "Easy does it, sir. This regiment doesn't need you serving time in a military brig for insubordination. It needs you out here in command. You've made your point, so let it be. Please, sir, no more."

Conor took in a deep breath and let the matter pass. After a few minutes he was greatly ashamed at his lack of maturity, and he thanked Tanneyhill for the abundance of his.

The Confederates pressed forward, but only after several hours had passed. The Federals resisted stiffly and the Rebels withdrew without much of a determined attack. The main Federal counterattack came at about 4:00 pm, with Sheridan's cavalry attacking the Confederate flanks and his divisions pressing against the Reb center. For an hour, both armies battled furiously north of Middletown, but then Masterson's left flank began to crumble and Union cavalry suddenly appeared in the rear of the Confederates. More of the gray army collapsed when the men realized that the Federal cavalry might block their path to Cedar Creek, their only avenue of escape. Rebel artillery delayed the Union advance, but only for a short interval. To make matters worse, a small bridge on the Valley Pike collapsed and made it impossible for the Confederates to cross a creek south of Strasburg with their wagons, including the captured artillery. Thus, they had no choice but to abandon the guns and the wagons.

As the retreat was underway, Conor noticed a Confederate major on horseback, from General Masterson's staff, frantically waving his sabre at a group of Conor's soldiers. The officer was threatening to slash a frightened private when Conor rushed to confront the major.

"Put that sabre away, you damned fool," Conor shouted. "If you can't use it on the Yankees, then give it to someone who will."

"These men are cowards," the major shouted in return. "They should be punished. General Masterson will be interested to know how your troops behaved in battle today, sir."

"Then go back and tell General Masterson to punish all of us since it's his entire army being routed from the field. What does that tell you about his leadership?"

"It's not his leadership, sir. It's a failure of execution on your part. What would that tell him about you?"

"General Masterson and his entire staff, including you, you dandy pompous ass, should be relieved of duty twice—once for incompetence and another for being too damn dense to know it."

"You are very badly mistaken, sir."

"No, sadly, I am not mistaken. And let me add one other thing: You threaten another of my men on this or any other battlefield and I will personally blow a very large hole in that thick but otherwise empty skull of yours. Now get the hell out of my sight. *Go!*"

The officer stared at Conor, but made no move. Conor quickly drew and cocked his pistol and then took aim. The wide-eyed major spurred his horse and sped away. First Sergeant Tanneyhill, who had observed the entire scene, shook his head but remained silent.

The Federals eventually gave up the chase at nightfall and the Southerners gathered again at Fisher's Hill. The next day they marched on to New Market.

As they were on the move, Conor fell back into the middle of the column and took a good look at the condition of his troops.

"Where are your shoes, soldier?"

"Had some Yankee shoes, sir, but they was way too tight. Better just to do without."

He was not the only barefoot Confederate on the march. And he was not the only soldier who had been thinned by malnutrition. Their torn and tattered gray uniforms were hanging loosely on many, if not most. Conor's own clothing was now several sizes too large. If there was one thing he could see that was in good working order, it was the condition of their muskets. He could not find a dirty or rusting rifle in any of the several he observed. First Sergeant Tanneyhill's influence was large in weapon care and maintenance, and the results showed.

"Where we gonna go next, sir?"

"Wherever we're told to go, Corporal. You know how that works. But just out of curiosity, is there someplace you would prefer to go if you were given a choice?"

"How 'bout California, sir?"

Another said, "I'd take Florida. It's an easier march."

Still another said, "I'd go for a hotel room in Richmond with a beautiful girl and a great big ole steak."

From further back came, "Or what about a great big ole girl and a beautiful steak?"

"That'd be okay too, sure."

Conor couldn't help but smile as he kept walking.

For the small Rebel army, the Valley Campaign was essentially over. The Confederate forces would no longer control the Shenandoah Valley and the vital source of provender it had provided.

Once the brigade settled in at New Market, General Gordon summoned Conor to his tent. Conor immediately noticed the general's stiff demeanor and dour expression. The general, seated behind his small desk, ordered Conor to stand before him at attention.

"Are you aware that General Masterson is strongly considering bringing court-martial proceedings against you?" General Gordon asked.

"I am not, sir."

"Well, you apparently threatened to shoot one of his staff officers."

"Okay."

"Okay what? Did you threaten the officer?"

"I did, sir."

"Did you draw your pistol and aim it at him?"

"I did that too, sir," Conor said, pausing before asking, "and is that the only charge?"

"Are you saying there's *more*?" General Gordon asked sharply.

"I should tell you, sir, that I expressed an opinion about General Masterson's leadership that could've been viewed as, well, unflattering."

"Good God, Conor. Tell me everything," General Gordon said with a sigh and a shake of his head.

Conor then recounted the entire episode in exacting detail. Afterwards, he promised not to shoot the offended major or, for that matter, anyone else from General Masterson's staff. He also promised to keep to himself his exceedingly low opinion of General Masterson's worth to the army. Finally, Conor promised to heed King Solomon's admonition that there is "a time to be silent and a time to speak." For his part, General Gordon promised that he would do his best to smooth things over with General Masterson, but only after glaring at Conor for several long, uncomfortable moments.

"We will *not* have such a conversation *ever again*. Do I make myself clear, Conor?"

"Very clear, General."

Conor never knew what was said or agreed upon between the two generals, but nothing further was made of the incident.

A few days later, the mail caught up.

November 22, 1864
Dear Conor:

I am writing to you from Griffin, Georgia where I am one of the volunteers who was involved in the treatment of your father, Seamus Rafferty. I am sorry to tell you that your father has died from the effects of a serious heart ailment. He reluctantly left Atlanta two weeks ago with several families after his property was overtaken by the Yankees, and he became very ill during the trip. He gave me your mailing address and asked that I notify you were anything to happen to him.

Again, I am very sorry to have to deliver this bad news to you.

Seamus asked that his body be transported back to Atlanta for burial on his farm, alongside his wife. Given the uncertain circumstances in Atlanta, I cannot promise that we will be able to do this. But I can assure you we will do our very best to accommodate his wishes.

May God bless you, Conor, and all of our soldiers.
Yours,
Gayle Blackbourne

Conor wondered that night if the Rafferty family was destined for extinction. Otherwise it was difficult to reconcile the callous fate each of his family members had been delivered. He knew he would never be able to untangle such divine mysteries with his own earthly notions, but still he could not help reflecting upon it. And in those moments of reflection, he always ended up considering what his own destiny might be. The world could be a cruel place, crueler in certain places than others, and over the past several years he had been particularly adept at finding the cruelest of those places. He sought Chaplain Yancey, told him of the news of his father's death, and asked that he say a prayer for the souls of his family members. After the chaplain finished praying, which he did masterfully, he and Conor talked for perhaps twenty minutes. Conor eventually returned to his makeshift hut made from branches and logs, and felt a peace that he hadn't felt in months. He also slept soundly for the first time in weeks.

General Gordon sent for Conor the next morning. Conor knew the chaplain had updated the general on the news about his father, and he joined the general in his tent.

"I'm very sorry, Conor. And I'm sorry your family's down to just you now. As brutal and unfair as it seems, the sad truth is you are now the end of the line. I know you know that in your mind, but I doubt it has hit your soul with full force, like it will. You still have a life to live and a lot to look forward to, and I want you to remember that. And if you decide you need some time to get away and sort all this out, then I'll be happy to arrange a leave for you."

"No, General," he said, shaking his head. "I don't need a leave. If I don't stay here, then I don't have a purpose in life. And I very badly need to hang onto this purpose."

General Gordon nodded and said, "I understand. Just let me know if I can do anything for you."

Conor nodded his thanks, his eyes filled with tears.

Orders from General Lee were expected any day, but the Southerners already knew they were going to Petersburg.

Before they left, Conor received one more letter.

December 2, 1864
My dearest Conor:
This will be the last letter I will write from Richmond. My father was killed two weeks ago in a battle south of Atlanta, but before he died he directed that if

anything happened to him, he wanted my mother and me to leave Richmond at once and move to Northern California where we have relatives. I didn't know anything about this until my mother told me last week, and I greatly resisted leaving because I wanted to be here for you after the war. But my mother's health is declining and I cannot allow her to make such a trip alone. We are hoping to be able to get past the Yankees and make it to California.

Conor, I will always love you, but I know this will change the commitment we had made. I cannot ask you to cross the continent and find me in California, so I won't. I will never forget you, and I will always regret not being able to travel the world with you and sing that Irish lullaby to our baby. You are the best thing that ever happened to me, and in some ways I would rather die than lose my chance to be with you. I just do not feel I have any choice now.

Please, Conor, please try to understand my situation. It would be impossible for me to tell you how badly I feel about having to leave you. I wish it were otherwise, but it's not.

God bless you, my darling, and know that I am thinking of you always.
With all my love,
Penny

This one Conor just kept to himself.
Dear God, what was next?

***

Thursday, February 14, 1918
"Was this the low point of the war for you, Cappy?"

"It was one of several low points, Aaron, for sure. They just seemed to keep coming."

"How did an officer like General Masterson keep his job?"

"Good question. I often wondered that myself. General Lee was a wise old bird, and when he ordered us to Petersburg, he left Masterson in the Shenandoah and eventually relieved him of his small command."

"Ah, so it did catch up to him."

"It did, yes."

"Your reckless conduct and insubordination could have cost you your command, Cappy. Would that have been worth it to you?"

"Of course not. And I was thankful it didn't."

"Do you think your comments about General Masterson were swept under the rug because you were a very effective field commander whose loss would have been damaging to the army?"

"I don't know."

"Did you think you could get away with such comments precisely because you were so highly thought of by the high command?"

"Good grief, Aaron, I don't know the answer to that."

"If one of your soldiers had said the same thing about you, would you have court-martialed him?"

Conor finally smiled slightly. "I get your point, Captain Rafferty. The obvious lesson for you here is to keep a close watch over your mouth. You might not be as fortunate as I was."

Aaron also smiled. "Would you have shot that staff officer if he had slashed at your soldier?"

"What do you think?"

"I believe you would have," Aaron answered.

They both laughed.

Chapter Fifteen

Petersburg

No one but Mother can cheer me today,
No one for me could so fervently pray.
None to console me, no kind friend is near;
Mother would comfort me, if she were here.
"Mother Would Comfort Me"

December, 1864 – March, 1865

Christmas, 1864 was a miserable affair. Since General Lee had ordered General Masterson to dispatch two divisions from the Shenandoah Valley to Petersburg, Generals Gordon and Peagram left immediately with their commands. Lee's Army of Northern Virginia was thinly posted along a thirty-six mile line from White Oak Swamp to Hatcher's Run at Petersburg. Conor's regiment was deployed on the left bank of Hatcher's Run, protecting the last commercial rail line that had not yet been cut by Grant. It was woefully cold for the poorly outfitted Confederate soldiers, and there were no turkeys or chickens or hams available for their holiday pleasure. Parched corn and hardtack were about all they could expect, along with a few ounces of beef, and for many soldiers their long descent into starvation was fast becoming literal. Southern farms were so ravaged from years of plundering by the opposing armies that neither citizen nor soldier could expect enough food to maintain a healthy condition. Even the horses were sadly underfed.

General Gordon became acting commander of Second Corps which now contained less than 9,000 troops, by far its smallest size since its activation and emblematic of the critically shrunken state of the entire army. Colonel Evans of the 31st Georgia was promoted to fill the division commander role vacated by General Gordon. At the age of thirty-two, General John B. Gordon became the first non-career soldier to command a corps.

The ingenious Federals dug a mineshaft and exploded it during July, creating a large crater and blowing a gap in the Confederate line. The stories from the Petersburg veterans who were present at the explosion were entertaining and enthralling, though often embellished for even greater effect. There were many Southern storytellers in the Petersburg trenches in search of audiences, such that rich embellishment became a sort of tradecraft.

On occasion Grant would deploy skirmishers to the Reb front, but the muddy roads from the rain and snow discouraged any larger-scale attempts by the Federals to cut the rail line and withhold the last line of supply. A thick pine woods made any infantry movement cumbersome, though each army would dispatch scouts to monitor the other. Confederate soldiers manned the miles of trenches that had been carved into the landscape over the months of confrontation. Conor would slip into his overcoat and hat and inspect his line multiple times during the day, more often finding shivering soldiers in their thin, tattered uniforms, huddling together trying to stay warm.

"Merry Christmas, sir," several men facetiously called to Conor on the morning of December 25.

"Merry Christmas to you, as well. You'll be happy to know that the turkeys will be here for the noon meal, along with the breads, vegetables, pastries, and of course those fine French wines. No expense will be spared for our boys in the line. Do you prefer dark meat or white?" Conor called out, his breath vaporizing in the frigid air.

"Dark," came one response.

"White," came another.

"Both!" came yet another, prompting laughter from all around.

Later, First Sergeant Tanneyhill motioned for Conor to join him at a campfire after the commander had completed his inspection rounds on Christmas evening.

"We've had three men in the regiment desert in the last twenty-four hours, sir. More of our soldiers are getting letters from family members begging them to leave and come home to help them avoid starvation. It's bad across the entire division, from what I'm hearing."

"What do you suggest?"

"I'm getting around to a lot of the men, checking to see how they're doing and if they have anything they need help with. Chaplain Yancey's doing the same thing."

"Did any of them open up and tell you about letters from home asking them to desert?"

Tanneyhill nodded. "Several did, yessir."

"And?"

"I reminded them that their first duty was here with their friends and fellow soldiers. They seemed to be okay after that, like they just needed to get it off their chest."

Conor thought for a moment about how he could help forestall the problem from getting any worse than it already was. "Here's what I can do: I'll go around with the company commanders and meet with every man in the regiment. You're right, maybe they will be okay by just having a chance at getting some things off their chest, with me listening. We can't afford those losses or you and I will eventually be standing out here by ourselves."

"No offense, sir, but I'd rather that didn't happen. And I think your getting around to speak to every man is a good idea."

Connor smiled slightly. "I hadn't thought of this before, but this reminds me of the Revolution when General Washington was struggling so hard to keep his small army together. Families then were writing to their soldiers and asking them to leave and hurry home, just like what we're facing now. The similarities are definitely there. I just hope our ultimate outcome is the same as the one George Washington's army achieved."

Tanneyhill and Conor glanced at one another but said nothing.

Over the next three days, the company commanders and Conor met with all of their soldiers and reminded them that every musket was greatly needed if they were to keep Petersburg and Richmond from falling into Union hands. Conor gave them the quick history lesson on how General Washington's little army held on and gained the ultimate victory, ending the war and securing the young nation's independence.

"Think about it, men. We're doing the same thing here," he explained. "We have to persevere, and we have to keep believing that on the other side of our perseverance is victory."

All but a few of the soldiers were receptive, and Conor and his commanders could detect that most of the men were committed to remaining to the very end. They guessed that maybe ten men had received such letters and were clearly struggling with the decision to stay on. The incessant cold, the scarcity of food, and the presence in their immediate front of more Yankees than they could count were all factoring into their decision.

Not all of Conor's troubles involved the departures of men. A black male in tattered clothing was brought into Conor's headquarters tent one cold night by a lieutenant and two soldiers who had apprehended the man near their position on the line. The man appeared to be in his early twenties, of medium height and slender build. He was shivering from the cold, and Conor could sense the anxiety in his demeanor.

"I'll bet he's a Yankee spy, sir," the lieutenant said. "He was sneaking around out there trying to get a good look at our positions. He's gotta be a spy."

"That will be all. You men are dismissed. Return to your posts," Conor directed.

"If he's a spy, sir, and I'm sure he is, then he needs to be shot," one of the soldiers added.

"You are dismissed," Conor said forcefully.

Conor glanced at Tanneyhill.

"What's your name and what were you doing in my area?" Conor asked.

"Name's Ezekiel Foster. I came into this area by mistake. I'm trying to work my way to Maryland."

"Are you working for the Yankees?" Tanneyhill asked.

The man shook his head vigorously. "No. I ain't workin' for nobody. And I shore ain't no spy. I ain't that stupid."

"Are you a runaway slave?" asked Tanneyhill.

"I'm headed to Maryland. I ain't out here in this cold aiming to do nothing but get to Maryland. I don't want nothing to do with you Rebs or those Yankees over there. If I'd known all of y'all was in here as thick as fleas, I would've gone another way. But I got lost and y'all caught me. That's the truth."

"What were you looking for out there?" Conor asked.

"A way out, that's all."

"What information did the Yankees want you to find out about us?"

"Sir, I ain't workin' for no Yankees. I swear before God."

"Did they tell you what would happen if we caught you?"

"I ain't talked to no Yankees. Not here, not nowhere."

"When did you last eat?"

"Yesterday."

"What kind of rations?"

"No rations, sir. I took some eggs from a hen house about a day's walk from here."

"How much money do you have in your pockets?"

The man turned his pants pockets inside out. "I ain't got no kinda money, sir."

"Where are you coming from?"

"North Carolina."

Conor stared at the man for a long moment before saying, "I don't believe you're a spy, so I'm not going to have you shot. However, my orders are to send you back to North Carolina. We don't let runaway slaves run away when they come into our possession."

"I'll just run away again when I get back there," the man said matter-of-factly, after which he glanced over at the kettle of soup on Conor's desk. He stood up straight, his shivering almost stopped, and looked Conor directly in the eye when speaking to him.

"Would you like some soup?" Conor asked.

"I'd be much obliged."

Tanneyhill poured some clear soup into a metal cup and passed it to the man, who nodded appreciatively. He quickly consumed the lukewarm fluid and then glanced over at the kettle again. Tanneyhill took the cup and poured the remainder of the soup into it.

"What do you suggest I do with you, Ezekiel?" Conor asked.

"Mind telling me your name, sir?"

"I'm Lieutenant Colonel Rafferty. This is First Sergeant Tanneyhill."

"You seem like a fair man, Mister Rafferty, a good man. You know I ain't no spy, but you could have me shot anyway if you wanted to, just by saying so. You give me some soup instead, and give me a few minutes out of the cold. I'm getting a good feeling that you're gonna let me go, let me try to get away from here and get to Maryland. You've probably seen enough killing to last ten lifetimes, so killing me won't make no difference to this war. But letting me go would make a big difference. You would be giving a man a chance. That's all I ask of you, Mister Rafferty, just give me a chance. Look at me as a man—a good man who is asking another good man for a fair chance. Will you do that, sir? Will you just give me that?"

Conor carefully studied the young man as he considered the request. He finally turned to Tanneyhill and asked, "What do you think, First Sergeant?"

"Our orders are clear, sir: We send 'em back. If you let him go, you risk disobedience of an order. Do you want to risk that? And over a runaway slave?"

Conor nodded his understanding and then turned his attention back to Ezekiel. "Do you think you could safely find your way out of our army's area if I let you go?"

"Yessir, I'll find my way out, for sure."

"Your most recent experience doesn't give me a lot of confidence," said Tanneyhill. "You need to get clear of here while it's still dark. Even in the dark you're gonna risk being shot if you're discovered. You know that, don't you?"

"Yessir. Just give me that chance."

"Okay," said Conor. "You are facing north as you stand in this tent. When you leave here, head west. Cross the railroad tracks, keep going another mile, and then turn north."

"God bless you, sir. Both of you."

"One more thing," said Tanneyhill. "If you get caught again, I'm counting on you not to mention anything about your visit here. Don't get this good officer in trouble for trying to help you. Do you understand?"

"You have my word."

"Good luck," said Conor. "Get going."

The next morning before a meeting with his commanders, General Gordon explained that a Negro spy had been shot and killed near the rail line. "Grant very badly wants to cut that last supply line," the general asserted. "I'm sure they're gathering information and developing a plan for it. Be alert."

"How did we know he was a spy, General? Did he have documents or maps or anything of that sort?"

"No. But why else would he have been in our midst?"

Conor shook his head but said nothing.

First Sergeant Tanneyhill reported in early January that another two of their men had deserted. They were in the group of ten who had previously been identified as the soldiers most likely to leave. In February, there were six more who left, except this time only one of that number had been thought to be a risk.

On March 5, 1865, General Gordon summoned Conor to his headquarters in a single-story house several hundred yards behind the trenches. The General's personal staff was with him, four majors and three captains whom Conor knew, but not well. They had a large map of the Petersburg area spread out on the table and there was a brisk discussion underway when Conor announced himself at the door. The general waved him over to the table and continued discussing the matter at hand for another several minutes. Finally, he ended the discussion.

"Well, Lieutenant Colonel Rafferty, do you know these gentlemen?" the general asked with a motion toward the others.

Conor went around the table and reintroduced himself to each of the staff officers. He greeted each man warmly, and he had a clear impression from previous observations that the Second Corps staff was highly professional and functioned well together.

"Gentlemen, excuse us, please. Lieutenant Colonel Rafferty and I need a moment alone."

The staff officers reached for their overcoats and hats and left the house with the map still spread open on the table. General Gordon pulled two straight-backed chairs over and the two of them took a seat facing each other in front of the crackling fireplace.

"I want you to become my chief of staff, Conor," the general said. "We're about to make some proposals to General Lee that will change what's being done here at Petersburg, and I need your expertise. You'll become the senior officer on my staff, and you'll be responsible for the planning of our corps' major operations. You've met my current staff. They are all splendid officers, and of course they know of your reputation as a troop leader. You'd be the missing piece that would make this the best staff in the army."

The general then leaned forward, closer to Conor. "I know the kind of work you produce, and I've thought long and hard about the possibility of taking you away from the Thirty-eighth Georgia—a regiment that I could ill afford to have slip into mediocrity under another leader—but I've come to the conclusion that your skills would be better utilized here. You would be doing this army and especially this corps and its commander a great service by joining my staff."

The general then leaned back. "I need to know your answer now, Conor. Circumstances dictate that this move be made today, one way or another."

"I want the post, sir. It would be a great honor. Sign me up."

General Gordon smiled, and they both stood and shook hands, sealing the arrangement. The general reached over to the side of the table and produced another box of rank insignia.

"Congratulations. You are now Colonel Rafferty. By the way, how old are you, Conor?"

"I'll be twenty-five tomorrow, sir."

"Then we'll have some of the coffee my wife has been hoarding for most of the war, and we'll celebrate your promotion and your birthday," he said, handing Conor the box.

They made small talk for the next five minutes until General Gordon pointed to the clock on the wall. It was 3:45 pm when he informed Conor that General Lee would arrive at 4:00 pm.

"General Lee? Coming here? Now?"

"Yes, and here's why: Two days ago I met with the general and he asked me for my recommendations for our army. I told him that I saw three choices. First, seek favorable peace terms from Grant. Second, slip out of Petersburg, link up with General Johnston in North Carolina and strike Sherman before Grant can reinforce him. Third, fight here with a plan for a major attack."

"Did he agree with the three choices?"

"He did."

"Which one do you think he will choose?"

"I don't know yet. We debated the merits and problems of each, but I don't know which way he's leaning."

Conor took in a deep breath and let it out slowly, his mind racing ahead to the prospects of a major attack.

General Lee and his chief of staff Colonel Walter Taylor walked into the house at the appointed time. General Gordon introduced Conor as his new chief of staff.

"We've met before, have we not, Colonel Rafferty?" General Lee asked.

"Last winter at Clark's Mountain, sir."

"Ah yes, I remember now. Do you still have that beautiful horse?"

"No, sir. I'm afraid not."

"What about your brother in the prison camp? Chicago, was it?"

"Yes, sir. He died from smallpox while still a prisoner."

General Lee lowered his head. "I'm very sorry to hear that, Colonel. Very sorry."

General Gordon offered chairs, but Lee preferred to stand.

"General Gordon, I am still considering the material you and I reviewed at my headquarters recently," Lee said. "I expect to have a direction on the matter by tomorrow, the day after at the very latest. And then we'll put Colonel Rafferty here to work."

Conor grinned but said nothing.

"And by the way, Colonel Rafferty, your hard-earned experience in 'that deadly space' will no doubt become useful to you in your new role."

Conor noticed the slight smile on General Lee's face and was astonished at the power of his recall.

"It will indeed, sir," Conor replied.

After General Lee and Colonel Taylor had left, General Gordon turned to Conor and asked, "Deadly space? What was that all about?"

Conor explained his earlier meeting with General Lee, and the background behind the term. General Gordon then asked Conor for a recommendation on his replacement.

"I'd promote Captain Willingham from A Company and give him the post, sir," Conor answered. "He knows the regiment, he's well respected by the men, and he knows his way around a battlefield. He's a good man, a fair man. I have had a high degree of trust in him and his judgment has always been sound. That's what I would do, sir. Willingham's the best man for the job."

"Colonel Baker will be asking for your recommendation since it's really his decision, but I've already suggested that he take a good look at Willingham in the event that I decide to pull you out of the regiment. I agree with you that he would be the best choice."

"When do you want me to report here, sir?"

"In the morning, bright and early. Happy birthday, Colonel."

They both laughed.

Saying goodbye to the company commanders was difficult. Saying goodbye to First Sergeant Tanneyhill was especially difficult. Conor promised Chaplain Yancey that he would attend as many of his services as possible, as he had been doing, and Conor thanked him for his support and friendship. The brigade commander, Colonel Baker, agreed that Captain Willingham would be the best choice as Conor's replacement, and the three of them met for two hours to transition the regiment.

In the late evening, Conor was walking the regimental line with Captain Willingham when three soldiers called out from their trench.

"We hear you're leaving us, sir. Before you get away, we'd like for you to join us down here."

Willingham and Conor jumped down into the trench with the three young soldiers. One man reached into his coat pocket and brought out a handful of shelled, roasted peanuts. He passed three of the peanuts to Conor, three to the others, and they toasted each other by tapping the shells together. "To the Thirty-eighth Georgia," they all repeated.

The peanuts were damp and stale, but Conor didn't care. It was the purest, most unselfish, most cherished gift he could remember.

"We'll miss you, sir. We walked a lot of miles together, didn't we?"

"We did. And I appreciate what you men have meant to this regiment, and to me personally. I'll ask you to give Captain Willingham the same great support you gave me."

"We will, sir. Good luck to you."

Conor mentioned to Willingham as they finished the inspection of the line, "Where did we get such men as these? How could I have been so blessed to command them? To have gone into battle with them, and bled with them, and watched so many of them die? These men have carried me from the field after being wounded. I have seen them march for days on dusty roads, wade fast-flowing, rain-swollen rivers, trudge through hard rain and thick mud, and lie down on the grass and be asleep in a matter of seconds. I have looked into their eyes just before we faced an enemy of superior strength and seen their determination, and knew they would be right there with me as we moved forward each time, every time. I have watched them freezing in the cold, half-starved, homesick, lovesick, physically sick, and yet they manned their posts. I have written to their mothers of their astonishing bravery and of how proud they should be of their dead heroic sons. I have listened to their ribald humor, their cursing, their sarcasm, and their prayers. I know that no matter how long I live, no matter what else I do in this life, I will never see their equal again. Just where did we get such men as these?"

Afterwards, when he got back to his hut and thought about those young, undernourished, loyal soldiers so eagerly sharing their few remaining peanuts with him, an act of extraordinary generosity matched only by their magnificent valor, Conor sat on the ground and wept.

He had been seated on the hard cold ground for about twenty minutes when a soldier walked nearby.

"Where are you going, soldier?" Conor called.

"I just need to piss. Who goes there?" he called back.

"Colonel Rafferty. Come closer."

Conor could not recognize the man in the dim light, though he could see that he had his knapsack with him but not his musket. "Yessir?"

247

"Are you running away, soldier. Are you deserting us tonight?"

"Oh no, sir. I just have to piss."

"Need your knapsack to do that? And not your musket?"

There was a long, awkward silence. Conor could see the man shifting from side to side.

"You're running away, aren't you?" he pressed. "You're going to leave your friends—probably the best friends you've ever had and may *ever* have—and run home. That's what you're doing, isn't it?"

"Sir, you don't understand."

"I don't understand what, soldier?"

"My papa's sick, sir, and they need me at home."

"And those friends I just mentioned, you don't think they need you, too? If you knew for a fact that your leaving meant one or two of those friends would be killed as a direct result, would you still leave them?"

"Well no, I wouldn't go then."

Conor heard the sniffing.

"That just might happen if you're not here with your musket when you're needed the most. And don't you dare insult me by telling me I don't understand, soldier. Both my brothers have died in this war, and my mother and father are now dead. I'm all that's left of my pre-war family of five. But I wouldn't think of slinking away like a rat in the middle of the night and leaving my fellow soldiers to their own fates. Our fates are linked, and I will stay out here with them and with you no matter what. And you should stay out here, too."

There was more sniffing, but the young soldier remained quiet.

"I could have you arrested. You know that, don't you?" Conor asked.

"Yessir."

"But I'm not going to. I'm not going to ask you your name or your company or anything else that might identify you to me. This will only be between you, me, and almighty God. And here is what I want you to think about: If you leave and run away tonight or tomorrow or some other time, you'll be ashamed of what you did for the rest of your life. Your children will someday ask you what you did in the war, and then your grandchildren. And what will you tell them? Will you tell them the truth? That you ran away and deserted? That you left your fellow soldiers in the cold with one less musket on their side? No, of course you won't admit to that. How could you? So the truth is you'll be lying about this for the rest of your life. And you'll never be sure that your leaving didn't get one of your friends killed. Or maybe more than one. Are you hearing me, soldier?"

"Yessir."

"And if you stay and do your duty, you might very well die out here in the cold before this war's over."

Conor paused, and then added, "So make your decision, soldier. Run away or go back to your company. Live a lie for the rest of your life, and all the shame and guilt that you'll feel, or go back and do your duty as you've done up until this point. It's dishonor or honor. The first one might seem tempting and easy, but it will come with a stiff price. And the second one is the hard one, and it will come at a price also, but it's the right one. And you know deep down that what I'm saying is true. Either way, you're a soldier and a man and I'm leaving the choice with you. I will not say or do anything further."

Conor could see the young man slumped forward, exhausted. The soldier finally said, "You're right, sir. I can't leave. I'm going back."

Conor stood. "You're making the right choice."

"Thank you, sir."

"No, I thank you, soldier."

The man saluted before returning to his company.

The next morning General Gordon delivered on the coffee he had promised. The odor alone was worth its weight in gold, and the taste was divine. And Conor was now twenty five years old and a colonel. A darn colonel, he kept thinking. How in the world has that happened?

General Gordon met with General Lee the next day and came back with a three-word summation: "We will attack."

The staff put together a conceptual framework of the plan during the next several days, but there were numerous details that needed attention. Each staffer took a share of the many identified tasks and started to work as quickly as possible.

General Gordon quietly and stealthily moved his corps into the trenches and fortifications around the city in the dark of night, with his headquarters located in the city. The staff developed a detailed map of Grant's fortifications, noting the areas of strength and weakness, the locations of possible opportunity, and the positions of the supporting artillery. Conor was fired upon by pickets, slipped and fell into open trenches at night, and dodged artillery shells as he scouted as much of the line to their front as he reasonably could. They interviewed Union prisoners and matched that information with what they had developed from their own scouting. General Gordon's guidance to his staff indicated that he wanted a fast-moving night attack with the element of surprise as their greatest advantage.

The staff began thinking that Fort Stedman, which was situated in Grant's line across from Colquitt's Salient, a bump in the Confederate line, would be the most advantageous target. There were significant obstructions built into the ground in front of the fort, but from the prisoners and their own scouting, they knew those exact locations. They then developed a pre-dawn attack plan that would employ speed and deception with a small initial group, followed by a general assault from General Gordon's three Second Corps divisions, two brigades from Fourth Corps in support, and two brigades from Third Corps in reserve. The total number of troops projected would be 11,500, nearly half of Lee's Army of Northern Virginia. They would capture three other forts behind Fort Stedman and create havoc in the Union rear.

Conor and the staff reviewed the initial plan with General Gordon who then made several key observations and suggestions. It took another week to have the plan finalized and ready for General Lee's review. Generals Gordon and Lee then met and discussed the attack in some detail, after which General Lee gave his approval.

The attack began on schedule at 4:15 on the morning of Wednesday, March 25. The lead parties of scouts, engineers, and sharpshooters got by the Union pickets and began removing the obstructions that would hinder the assaulting infantry. Three groups of 100 men each then moved toward the rear forts. The Rebels took Fort Stedman, and General Gordon notified General Lee by courier that the plan was progressing as expected. However, unknown to the general, the groups of 100 were unable to find their objectives and were instead wandering around in the Union rear. Confederate cavalry was thus unable to find its way and the Federals then began assembling for a counterattack. Further compounding the Rebels' problems was the fact that their supporting brigades had difficulty with transportation and were delayed as a result. Conor crossed the trenches with General Evans' Division which attacked Fort Haskell on the southern flank and was met with Union canister shells. When daylight came, it was clear the assault plan was in deep trouble as the Federals began vigorously counterattacking with substantially larger numbers of troops. The Confederates retreated under intense fire and suffered numerous casualties when General Lee finally ordered General Gordon to return his forces to their breastworks.

Conor helped a wounded and limping Confederate soldier cross back into their lines.

"Did you understand the plan for this assault?" the soldier asked through clenched teeth, the pain in his wounded leg intensifying.

"I thought I did," Conor replied.

"I thought I did, too. But once we got over there, nothing went like it was supposed to."

"What do you think happened?" Conor asked.

"Hell if I know. Maybe it was just too complicated. Night assaults are a bad idea, if you ask me. We work with simple plans in daylight assaults. You'd have to be dumb as a damn donkey to think that a complicated plan would work in the dark of night."

Conor said nothing, still holding onto and guiding the injured man.

"General Lee should get rid of the high falutin' blowhards that thought up this thing and get somebody in there with some horse sense," the man added bitterly.

"Yes," Conor replied. "He probably should."

Once they were out of danger, a Confederate hospital assistant came close enough to recognize Conor and offered to assist. "I'll take it from here, Colonel Rafferty," he said.

The wounded soldier looked at Conor and said, "Uh oh!"

"Good luck with that wound," Conor said as he left the man with the hospital assistant.

The attack ended in failure for the Confederates.

They had tried their best. Their men had been willing and able to move from the trenches to launch the attack upon the Yankees. They had performed boldly, as always. And they had demonstrated to Grant that they still had the capacity and the disposition to strike him. But the fog of war had tilted in a most unfavorable way for the Southerners, and they had failed. And with that failure, a feeling began building in the pit of Conor's stomach that the fate of their brave army had already been cast.

General Gordon and Conor sat in chairs on the porch of the house the general was using as his headquarters. His wife, who had traveled with him for much of the war, was feeling ill and remained inside. It was noon, March 25, less than eight hours after the failed attack on Fort Stedman. The weather was cold and overcast.

"We can't stay in Petersburg much longer," the general observed in a moment of rare despondency. "We're stretched too thin to hold this line. Our men are starving and any day now, Grant will pounce on us with all he's got and chop us up piece by piece. We'll have to abandon Petersburg and probably Richmond and move to the south or west, to a supply train."

"When do you expect that order, sir?"

"Soon. It's inevitable. Our situation here is impossible."

"What about arming the slaves, sir?"

The general gave Conor an odd look. "What?"

"Yes, sir. We should enlist the Negroes of Petersburg and Richmond and everywhere else. Enlist the slaves and issue them muskets. The Confederacy is already drafting Negroes on a limited basis. We should draft them all. Hell, Lincoln's bringing them into his army. Why can't we?"

"It's different with Lincoln."

"Not in the sense that he's trying to do everything he can to win the war, General."

"And what would we do with them after the war? Do you think they'd want to go back to being slaves when they've been taught to become soldiers, especially now that they know how to shoot and kill people with great efficiency?"

"Slavery's finished, General. It's done. So why not arm those men? I remember reading that at the start of the war there were over three-million slaves in the South. How useful could a force of tens of thousands have been to us?"

General Gordon shook his head, but Conor couldn't tell if it was from disagreement or exasperation.

"General, it's an idea we should consider. We're at a point where everything should be put forward for discussion."

"We can't even feed our own soldiers now."

"And that's because we're at a huge disadvantage militarily, sir. If we could change the numbers on our side, we could change the situation. And if we could change the military situation, we could influence the political situation in the North. They think they've captured the moral high ground with the Emancipation Proclamation, but if we freed the slaves and then had black men in our ranks shooting Yankee soldiers, how do you think that would go over?"

"Since when did you become a politician, Colonel?"

"I'm not a politician, sir. I'm making this suggestion as a military officer. To suppose that we can win this war doing the same things as always is to suppose that cows will stop eating hay and start eating deer. It's not going to happen. Not now, not ever."

"And how likely would it be that Southern politicians would endorse freeing and then arming Negroes? Most of the political crowd are slave owners, anyway. I'm afraid your suggestion wouldn't get very far. Arming the slaves wouldn't work, anyway."

"It seems to be working with them, sir," Conor said with a nod toward the Union lines.

The general pulled his chair around and faced Conor squarely. "Listen, Conor, we're soldiers. We don't make policy. And the people who do make policy would be no more inclined to set about a largescale arming of slaves than they would in moving the Confederate government to Iceland. Think about this: If General Lee thought that arming the slaves would be something he could actually persuade the politicians to enact, that there was a legitimate interest in authorizing it and funding it and so forth, don't you think he would've already done it? Is there anyone in the Confederacy looking harder at ways to achieve victory than General Lee? And your comment about slavery being finished, well, I think that is overstated. Were we to somehow find a way to forestall an outright defeat, you don't think we'd be so imprudent as to then free the slaves after so much blood and treasure has been expended?"

"Sir, on its most basic level, the Confederacy is not a normal nation. There would always be a constant tension between the Confederacy and the rest of the world. Southern slavery can't survive if the products from slave labor are boycotted by most of the other nations. How would the plantation owners go about keeping their slaves after the war ends? Under armed guard? That wouldn't last long. The entire economic model of a slave economy in a democracy is obsolete and gone forever, sir."

"But you're still willing to fight and quite possibly die for that system, are you?"

"General Gordon, with all due respect, sir, I've never seen it as my overriding duty to fight and risk my life or the lives of my soldiers to keep Negroes in slavery. That has never been my objective. And I personally don't know of any soldier in this army who would be satisfied being told beforehand that his death in battle was going to help keep black people in slavery. I'm willing to fight and die, and you damn well know that, General, but my reasons do not involve keeping people enslaved. And if that's what our politicians think we're doing out here, then they're crazy as—"

"It might be wise to close this conversation, Colonel, and get back to work," the general said with a tone of impatience.

General Gordon stood, after which Conor followed.

"Conor, you're a young man of great ability. You've grown enormously in the time we've served together, and I'm proud of you for that. But you are a young man, and you have a lot to learn about the ways of the world."

***

Thursday, February 14, 1918

"Didn't get any easier, huh Cappy?"

"No, Aaron. Those were hard days, about to get even harder."

"Let's stop for today."

"Spending some time with a pretty nurse?"

Aaron grinned.

Chapter Sixteen

Appomattox and the End

In Dixie's Land where I was born in,
Early on one frosty mornin,
Look away! Look away! Look away! Dixie Land.
"Dixie"

April, 1865

Conor knew the war was finished while they were still at Petersburg. Most of the Confederate officers did as well, Conor guessed. However, nobody wanted to believe it, much less say it. One of the first dead Confederate soldiers Conor had seen in a Petersburg trench was a fourteen-year-old boy. He knew then that, absent some miracle, they were approaching the end. But the Army of Northern Virginia was feisty and proud, and defeat was a hard thing to envision, much less swallow.

Grant's forces cut the final supply line of Lee's army on April 2 at the Battle of Five Forks. They also killed Confederate General A.P. Hill, one of the senior surviving officers to that point. Just after midnight on April 4, General Gordon's Second Corps was the final Confederate force to evacuate Petersburg. They filed out of the trenches of that dreadful place, away from the constant hazards of hunger, cold, and death, and began walking into an unknown fate. They knew Grant would follow and attack them relentlessly, but by that time most of the soldiers were more concerned with food than with Yankees.

They made it to the Amelia Courthouse but the rations they were expecting from Richmond failed to arrive. They moved south on April 5, but Sheridan's cavalry appeared ready to deny them that route, so they turned to the west toward Farmville with a planned rail resupply there. They fought running battles all during the day and marched much of the night. Finally on the morning of April 7, the train cars with provisions arrived. Grant's sudden presence to the east set in motion another battle, causing General Lee to order the supply trains to Appomattox Station.

The Southern soldiers had looked forward to those rations, thinking about little else for days over the many miles they had marched and the battles they had fought, and when the train pulled away, it was a devastating sight. Somehow, they braced themselves and looked forward to the next train. They eventually met up with the provisions, and Conor was thankful to see the smiling faces of his troops when they finally got a meal.

At Sailor's Creek, the Federals cut off and destroyed a Confederate corps. The Army of Northern Virginia numbered less than 30,000 soldiers and was being pursued from nearly every direction by Union attackers. On the evening of April 8, Conor accompanied General Gordon to General Lee's headquarters where there was a campfire burning but no tents erected. With Lee were Generals Pendleton, Fitzhugh Lee, and Longstreet, along with several staff members.

The mood was subdued, but General Lee's demeanor was calm and reassuring. He had received several recent overtures from General Grant about surrender, but it was clear the Confederate commander had yet to reach such a point. The generals discussed other options, but it was finally concluded that they would attempt to cut through Grant's lines the following morning. General Gordon's infantry and Fitzhugh Lee's cavalry would lead, with General Longstreet in support.

Conor watched carefully as General Lee wrapped up the meeting. He was businesslike and straightforward, perhaps even a bit introspective, and he looked very tired, as did all the top commanders. Nobody spoke of defeat, but it was clear that without surrender their small army would be finished off in a matter of days. They could no longer outfight or outrun the Union hordes except in the very short term, and that simple but unspoken truth was brutally evident to all of the senior Confederate leaders.

Conor was walking with General Gordon back to their headquarters when someone called, "Colonel Rafferty?"

Conor recognized the voice of First Sergeant Tanneyhill. He was seated on the ground beside an ambulance wagon, propped against a front wheel, with his left leg heavily bandaged. They greeted one another with a handshake and Conor took a seat on the ground beside him.

"I took a ball through the lower leg, but it didn't shatter the bone, thank God," Tanneyhill said. "It's sore enough that I just can't walk. Otherwise, I'd be out there with a musket."

"Fort Stedman attack?" Conor asked.

"Nah. A line of skirmishers rushed us three nights ago, and one of 'em got off a lucky shot."

"Well I'm glad they didn't leave you at Petersburg."

Tanneyhill glanced around to make certain they were alone. "It's over, isn't it, sir? I mean, we can't keep this up much longer. General Lee's not going to sacrifice all of us, is he?"

"No, he won't do that. He knows our soldiers are exhausted. My gosh, at this point they couldn't run out of sight in two days. And Grant's already pushing him to surrender. It's just a matter of days now, I think."

Tanneyhill leaned his head back against the wagon wheel and drew a deep breath, exhaling loudly. "What do you think will happen to us?"

"I don't know. For those of us who survive, I would hope Grant's treatment would be fair when General Lee goes ahead and surrenders. General Gordon told me that Longstreet and Grant were close friends before the war, so maybe that will somehow help us."

"Grant could start by sharing some food with us. That would go over well."

Conor chuckled. "I'll bet our little army could eat every ration they've got."

"No doubt, sir."

Conor stood. "I've gotta go, friend. Please take care of that leg."

Conor reached to shake his hand and could see Tanneyhill's moistened eyes in the dim light. "You were the best I ever came across," Conor said, suddenly feeling his own emotional tug. "It was an honor to serve with you, Gilbert Tanneyhill. I shall never forget you."

"And it was my honor to serve with you, sir."

"See you on the other side."

General Gordon, his staff, and the division commanders reviewed the battle plan for the next day in the light of the campfire at his headquarters. The general thanked his officers for their splendid service to his corps and wished them well for the next day's fight.

Conor had a hard time sleeping that night. His experiences in the war seemed to ramble across his brain, from the battles fought to the troops commanded to the months spent in hospitals. He wondered briefly about what he might do after the war, but he had been reluctant to think about postwar plans when he wasn't sure he would ever live to see a postwar. He concluded that night that if he were to die tomorrow or the next day, he had lived an exciting, interesting, and honorable life. He had been blessed to lead such wonderful men in battle, and he felt in his heart that he had been a good soldier. He had proven his father wrong about his fitness as a soldier and a leader, but by now he took little satisfaction in it.

The fact that Conor had no wife and children to return home to also meant that his family would not be in mourning over his death were he to step in front of a Yankee ball before the war ended. The harsh truth was he simply didn't have a family of any sort now. The Raffertys had sacrificed a great deal in the last four years, more than any one family he knew. He wondered whether one more sacrifice was in store.

His thoughts then turned to Penny, as they often did, and he wondered where she might be. Did she get past the Yankees and make it to California? Had she met someone else? Did she still think of Conor every day, as he did her? Had their original plan still been in play they would have been together in just a matter of days now, and the loss of her came back to him with such force that he had to get up and walk around. When that didn't help he sat on the ground for a spell, but that didn't help either. He dearly loved Penny, and he wondered if he would ever again love anyone as fully and completely.

Conor wanted very much to feel sorry for himself, to give in to his emotions and weep over his profoundly unfair life. He wanted everyone he knew to feel sorry for him, if only for a little while. And why not? He deserved it, he thought. Who else had been afflicted with as many wounds—physical *and* emotional—as he had experienced in the past four years? Anyone else in this army? Hell, anyone else in this world?

He was tempted to call out, "Why did all this have to happen to me?" but he was afraid a deep voice would come back saying, "That discussion would take more than one night."

He began laughing, and the despondency eventually eased.

He read from his small, well-worn Bible and then prayed that he would do his duty as best he could.

It took some time of reflection before that moment of clarity finally appeared before him, more like an unruffled sunrise than a sudden flash of lightning. Conor realized that by being spared, if that indeed became his fate, he would be the one who would have a chance at a full life with the hope that the good things, the full richness of love and happiness and peace, would follow. He would have a chance to start over after the war and make a life of his own choosing, unlike his brothers and so many of his fellow soldiers. He had known enough tragedy to be able to appreciate life even more, and in so doing make his remaining time a life of service to others. He would have been spared for a reason he could hardly grasp, but there had to be a reason nevertheless. And it would be up to him to discover that reason in the days and years ahead, once again contingent upon his surviving the next several days.

Conor's heart was full, and he finally slept.

By dawn the next morning the fight was on. Rebel cavalry sped around the Federal left while the infantry and artillery attacked the center. Union breastworks that had been constructed the night before were soon overtaken and Confederate battle flags were waving in victory once again. General Gordon had ordered Conor to stay in the rear, away from the front, but he ignored that directive and instead moved forward with the 61st Georgia, firing his pistol and adding his own feeble Rebel yell to the wild hollering all around him. Before long, however, Federal infantry began converging on them from the rear and the right. Yankee cavalry then threatened on the left, and suddenly the Confederates were fighting with every last ounce of energy, skill, and courage they could gather. Bullets were whizzing past Conor's head, and when he saw the regimental commander fall over wounded from shell fragments, he went to his side and asked about a replacement.

"Major Porter would've been next in line, but he's down too," the commander said. "It's gotta be you now, Conor. I appoint you to take command of my regiment."

Conor took command of the 61st Georgia and began issuing orders to the company commanders, filling the gaps in the line and shifting more troops to the areas of greatest concern. The officers followed his orders dutifully, and the soldiers were resisting the Yankee advances with volley after deadly volley. A soldier running beside Conor who was shifting positions at the double-quick, tripped and fell forward but in the process the stock of his rifle struck Conor squarely in the back of the head. As he was falling, Conor's first thought was that he had just received a bullet to the skull on his last foray into that deadly space. The young soldier jumped up and immediately came rushing to Conor, helping him to his feet and apologizing for what had happened.

"I'm not shot?" Conor asked, dazed but otherwise unhurt.

"No, sir. It was the butt of my rifle that hit you when I stumbled. I'm really sorry, sir."

"I'm okay. Go."

It took a moment for his head to clear. He smiled slightly and remembered the blow to his head in his very first battle at First Manassas. He was still a bit wobbly, so he dropped to one knee and took the time to observe the scene evolving around him, trying to assess the situation based upon what he could see and hear, and what his recovering senses were telling him. What he saw and heard was a regiment in very real danger of being swallowed up by a much larger force. His instincts were screaming at him to call for reinforcements with the highest urgency, but he knew from experience that with everyone else engaged up to their armpits in Yankees, the likelihood of gaining additional help was near zero. They were on their own to fight it out successfully, or die trying.

The fighting went on, increasing in intensity as the Federals threw even more men into the fray, squeezing the Rebels like a constrictor snake and drawing them ever closer to that point of suffocation. Conor was firing his pistol when he suddenly and strangely shouted out as loudly as he could, "Dammit to hell, you were all wrong about me!"

"What's that you're shouting, Colonel?" General Gordon said as he and the cavalry commander arrived behind Conor on horseback. "Who was wrong about what?"

"It was nothing, sir."

"I won't ask how you got here, Conor. I'll just advise you that Longstreet will likely not be able to support us. What we've got is all we're gonna get, it seems."

"This is not good, sir," Conor said. "We can't allow all these brave men to be slaughtered here like swine. There's nothing good about any of this."

Conor expected General Gordon to reprimand him or relieve him on the spot, or to raise his sabre and shout words of encouragement at him, but instead he just nodded slightly and mouthed the words, "I know."

Colonel Venable from General Lee's staff galloped toward them. He stated that it was urgent for General Lee to know if General Gordon could punch through the Union lines.

General Gordon replied, "Tell General Lee I have fought my corps to a frazzle, and I fear I can do nothing unless I am heavily supported by Longstreet's Corps."

"Hold your ground here, Colonel," General Gordon shouted to Conor as he prepared to leave. "If Longstreet can somehow, someway break loose, you should see him shortly. If not, then do what you can."

"The Sixty-first Georgia will hold this part of the field, sir. We're not going anywhere."

The general then caught Conor completely by surprise by smiling broadly, as if he were a boy on a playground rather than a corps commander in a desperate battle.

"By God, give 'em the cold steel, Conor my boy."

Conor smiled in return, and then went around to each of the regiment's company commanders for a status report. Each of them essentially said, "This is not good, sir."

"I know," Conor replied. "We're very nearly surrounded and cut off, so we've got targets in all directions. Make it a fight they'll remember."

They were still fighting frantically in every direction when word came from General Lee that a flag of truce was now in place between Grant and himself. The Confederates hastily put a white flag on a guidon and sent forth a mounted officer to notify the Union commander. Not long afterward, Union General Sheridan, whom they had come to loathe so deeply from the Valley Campaign, rode up to their line, again under a flag of truce. General Gordon rode out to meet him, and Conor kept thinking that General Gordon might make good on his previously stated desire to shoot and kill Sheridan. One of the Rebel soldiers standing beside Conor raised his musket and took aim at Sheridan. Conor grabbed the barrel and harshly instructed the man not to fire his rifle. He obeyed, but not happily. Conor kept his pistol at the ready, however, in the event Sheridan were to reel and tumble from his horse from a shot fired by General Gordon. But alas, military courtesy and professionalism prevailed. Sheridan was fortunately spared the wrath of a Confederate general long on memory but equally long on self-control.

There was no more shooting, but there were enough misgivings about the cease-fire that the Rebs kept their muskets at the ready. There was also a suspicion on their part that the Federals would use the break to gain a tactical advantage. However, General Gordon soon came around to each regiment and explained that it appeared to him that the shooting was over for good.

"The two top commanders are working things out right now," the general explained. "Until I give you further orders, you will stand down."

General Lee surrendered to General Grant on the afternoon of Sunday, April 9, 1865, at Appomattox Court House. The terms stated that Confederate officers could keep their side arms, while enlisted men were to turn in all of their military equipment and battle flags. The Confederates could also keep horses. And for Lee's remaining troops, Grant ordered 25,000 rations. The Confederates were paroled over the next several days, and on Wednesday, April 12, the Southern soldiers stacked their arms in a ceremony overseen by Union General Joshua Chamberlain. As the gray-clad troops passed in line to stack their rifles with bayonets attached, the blue-clad soldiers gave a salute to their tattered and proud former foe. It was a powerful moment, and later when Conor came upon General Chamberlain, he made it a point to thank him for his kind act of chivalry.

"We are Americans again, Colonel," said General Chamberlain in his thick Maine accent. "Let our salute be a starting point for our unification."

Conor found the ambulance wagons and began shouting for First Sergeant Tanneyhill until he heard a voice call out, "Over here."

Tanneyhill was sitting on a fallen pine log, drinking a cup of coffee and grinning at Conor as he approached. He pointed at the coffee. "It's the real stuff, sir, and I can get you some if you'd like."

"No, I just came to say goodbye. I'm shoving off for Atlanta in the morning, and I wanted to wish you well."

"I wish things had worked out so that you'd be stopping in Richmond first, sir. Have you had any word from her?"

"No, nothing."

"Are you going to try and find her in California?"

"No," Conor said, seeing her smiling face in his mind.

"Why not?"

Conor sighed and hesitated before answering. "Because I'm sure she's started a new life by now. She doesn't need me to come barging in to disrupt things. I don't want to put her through that. Hopefully she's found herself a good man out there who hasn't been damaged by this damn war."

"She had the man she wanted. Why do you think that would've changed?"

Conor smiled and said, "Time and distance."

"But you love her, don't you?"

"Yes, more than I could ever express."

"Then dammit, go find her. Take her away from anybody who has moved in on her. Bring her back home to the South."

Conor shook his head in resignation. "No, I can't do that."

"My gosh, those are words I can never remember hearing from you before, with all due respect, sir."

"I just can't, that's all."

"We've lost the war and you've lost your love. It's not the grandest of times, huh Colonel?"

Conor grinned. "There's a line in Shakespeare's *Hamlet* that goes, 'When sorrows come, they come not single spies, but in battalions.'"

Tanneyhill nodded thoughtfully. "You have a way with words, sir."

"As did Shakespeare."

"Well, on another matter, I heard what you did out there today. The word quickly got all the way back here to me about Colonel Rafferty taking over the Sixty-first Georgia and climbing right back into that deadly space. The thing is, the last damn bullet of the last damn battle could have killed you. Didn't anyone tell you that staff officers were supposed to stay back and do staff stuff?"

"Yes, I was told that, as a matter of fact," he said with a self-conscious smile.

"I remember that day when I thought I was going to have to hit you in the head and knock you out when we were in the Shenandoah Valley and you kept going on about ole P.V. Masterson. I could just see you being marched away in chains to the brig, especially when you threatened to shoot that jackass major."

They laughed.

"It's a miracle we're both getting out of this thing alive," Conor said. "And how did we ever live through that fight at the sunken road at Sharpsburg? Or the third day at Gettysburg?"

They shrugged, and then shook their heads in disbelief.

"How did we keep from getting shot when we lined up right beside the Iron Brigade that crazy day in the Wilderness fight?" Tanneyhill said.

Again they laughed, but this time harder.

"One of the happiest days of my life," said Tanneyhill, "was that day at Gettysburg when General Gordon brought me over to his brigade and told me he was assigning me to your regiment. I've never been an overly spiritual man, but I've thanked God every day since then."

Conor had a hard time saying anything after that.

"Come to Mobile, Colonel. I'm going back there and see if I can find something honest and worthwhile to do. Come and let me buy you a drink and show you around and bore you with stories about the best damn regiment in the Confederate army. You'll enjoy yourself, I promise."

"How will I find you?"

"There's a downtown saloon there called Rousseau's, and they'll know how to contact me. Jimmy Rousseau is one of my best friends, and he's always there. I'm counting on you for that first visit. Then I'll return the courtesy and come to Atlanta. Is that a deal?"

"It's a deal, friend."

They talked a few minutes longer before they finally embraced and shook hands. Conor then handed an envelope to Tanneyhill and told him to open it later.

"See you on the other side."

Conor left with a huge lump in his throat. When he got back to the headquarters site, Major Willingham of the 38th Georgia was awaiting him.

"Sir, I know we were supposed to turn in the battle flags with our weapons and military gear," said Willingham, "but the men decided that we should keep this flag and present it to you. It was their feeling that a great deal of the distinction this flag earned was under your command. And since this very same flag of the Thirty-eighth Georgia is the one that flew so proudly when you led us into battle, I consider it an honor to present it to you on behalf of all the soldiers who served with you."

The flag was wrapped inside a knapsack that Willingham ceremoniously passed to Conor.

"It has the bullet holes in it and the blood on it to show that it was in the thick of battle on multiple occasions, and I hope you'll take it and keep it as a source of pride and remembrance. The men really wanted you to have it, and they asked that you never forget them or the regiment," Willingham added.

"Thank you, Major. You can tell the men that for the rest of my life I will have no more cherished keepsake than the battle flag of my beloved Thirty-eighth Georgia."

Major Willingham then saluted and left.

Conor was prepared to return to Atlanta on foot if necessary, by train if possible. He had his pistols, blanket, and several days of rations in his knapsack. He had no idea how long such a journey would take, but he was anxious to begin. He only wished there would be someone at home to greet him. And a certain someone traveling with him.

He had survived. Whatever awaited Conor on the other side of this dark nightmare, he was eager to go off in search of it. His melancholy of the previous night had left, hopefully forever, and he was ready to close this chapter and begin another. They had lost the war, and in the process they had very nearly been obliterated as an army. He was quite sure that much of the rest of the South lay in ruins, not unlike their army. He and his fellow Southerners would have to live with the results that would most likely be humbling and humiliating, but he would enter his new life knowing he had done his best in the old one.

A chaplain led a brief service in the field that dozens of soldiers attended. He gave thanks for their survival, and he prayed for the souls of their brothers who didn't. He encouraged the men to go home and live in peace. When the service concluded, Conor turned and saw General Lee on horseback at the rear of the group, his hat removed, where he had been listening inconspicuously. Many of the men quickly crowded around to shake the hand of their famous commander, to touch him and perhaps speak to him and see him one final time. General Lee patiently shook every hand extended to him, often thanking his beloved soldiers for their service to the army. Conor saluted when he finally caught his eye, after which the general placed his hat back upon his head, raised himself in the saddle, and returned Conor's salute. They then nodded to each other before Lee turned Traveller and left.

Conor was alone at the corps headquarters campsite when General Gordon and Union General Chamberlain approached on foot, with Chamberlain holding the reins to a horse.

"General Chamberlain tells me that you two have met," said General Gordon.

Conor stood and saluted. "Yes, sir. I've had the honor of meeting General Chamberlain."

"Colonel Rafferty," said Chamberlain, "I'm making this horse and saddle available to you since I understand you're going home to Atlanta and could use a mount. Consider it a loan from the United States Army that you are under no obligation to repay."

He passed the reins to Conor.

"Thank you, General, for another kindness on your part. Once again, I'm grateful for your generosity. And he's such a beautiful animal. Does he have a name, sir?"

"His name is Topper. We spotted him from Little Round Top after the second day at Gettysburg, and we were pretty sure he belonged to one of the Alabama brigades. So in a sense he's going home just like you, Colonel. Good luck to you."

"Many thanks, sir," Conor said, saluting with General Gordon as General Chamberlain turned and left.

"Thank you, General," Conor said to General Gordon. "I know you arranged this, and I want you to know I appreciate it."

"Glad I could help. Well, I'm headed back to Petersburg to collect Mrs. Gordon. I'm hoping some Yankee doctor treated her and got her well."

"Please send her my best, sir."

"I certainly will."

"General," Conor said, his chin suddenly quivering and the tears welling in his eyes.

"I know, Conor. I know."

Conor's throat was constricted and the tears began dripping onto his uniform blouse. He wiped his eyes with his hand and cleared his throat. "Thank you, sir, for all you've meant to me."

"Oh, we're not finished yet, Mister Rafferty. When we both get back to Atlanta, if you don't come calling on me I'm going to send my scouts out looking for you."

They embraced, and then Conor saluted.

"See you back in Georgia, Conor. God be with you, my good and loyal friend."

"And with you, sir."

It was over. And he had survived.

Finally. Thankfully.

***

Friday, February 15, 1918

"How did you feel about the South losing the war, Cappy?"

"Humbled. Humiliated. Dejected. How the hell would you expect me to feel, Aaron?"

"I don't know. That's why I asked."

"We lost. We didn't like it, but that was our fate. They won, we lost. That was about it."

"You at least had to feel good about being alive, though. You had survived."

"I was glad to be alive, yes. I was sick over the outcome and about all of my soldiers whose mothers, wives, and children would never get to see them again. And I was certainly sad over the fate of my own family members. But sure, I was relieved and thankful to have survived, and a little guilty over it."

"Guilty? How so?"

"I led men into battle, walked them into that deadly space, and ordered them to do things that sometimes got them killed. And I survived. I was going home to start a new life and they weren't. Yes, believe me when I tell you there's a certain feeling of guilt about that."

Aaron nodded. "I can see that. And even though Grant was sometimes considered ruthless and demanded unconditional surrender, in the end he was considerate toward the Confederate soldiers."

"He certainly was. And I'd like to think our top commander would have been just as charitable if we had won. We fought each other hard for four years, but when it was finally over, that was it. It was done."

"And what was Joshua Chamberlain like?"

"He was awarded the Medal of Honor for his role at Gettysburg. He was gracious in victory which in my opinion should forever be an American standard of behavior, an American attribute that can be traced directly back to Appomattox with Grant and Chamberlain."

"You seemed concerned that someone might shoot General Sheridan during the ceasefire at the end."

"Well, we didn't need that to happen, not at that point. I have to confess, though, that if someone had blown Sheridan into the next county, I believe my heart would have leapt like a horse jumping a fence. I doubt if General Gordon would have shed any tears, either."

"That's pretty harsh, Cappy."

"I know. And I don't care."

Aaron laughed and then asked, "What were your thoughts about coming home to Atlanta after all that time?"

"It was mixed. I had no family to welcome me back. And I knew my town had been damaged, maybe even destroyed. But still I was anxious to get back home and start a new life."

"Did you have some idea about what you wanted to do, Cappy?"

Conor chuckled. "No. But I was open to anything except being a soldier."

They both laughed.

"Well Aaron," Conor said, grinning, "do you want to keep going or do you want to spend time with your pretty nurse?"

Aaron grinned. "Both, but let's you and I keep going for now."

Chapter Seventeen

Home to Atlanta

Who would whisper words of comfort,
who would soothe your pain?
Ah! The many cruel fancies, ever in my brain.
Weeping, sad and lonely, hopes and fears, how vain!
When this cruel war is over praying then to meet again.
"When This Cruel War Is Over"

April – May, 1865
It was a healthy distance of 400 miles from Appomattox to Atlanta. Conor was thankful he was not walking the entire way on what was still a tender left knee. After breakfast with several 38th Georgia friends, he rode Topper out of camp on Thursday, April 13, 1865, with the thought that if he could average twenty miles per day, he would reach Atlanta on May 2. He had no idea what awaited him on his journey home, but he was anxious to get started.

He couldn't help but think how different his trip might have been had Penny remained in Richmond. He might never have returned to Atlanta if their love affair had continued as before, as he had anticipated. As it were, he had no idea of Penny's current location, only that she had intended to move to California. He could only hope she was safe and well.

Conor stayed on roads that were nearest to the rail line. The commercial trains running throughout the South were coming under the jurisdiction of the U.S. government now, and he surmised their schedules would be erratic and their space limited. He had a brass pocket compass that he'd carried since First Manassas, and he knew enough about how to navigate from the position of the sun to stay moving in the right direction. His staff work had given him access to maps, several of which he carried in his haversack. Virginia, North Carolina, South Carolina, and Georgia maps would all come in handy.

Five miles out, he came upon a Federal cavalry column with a captain at its head. The captain saluted crisply as they passed, with Conor saluting in return. Several of the troopers nodded; others just ignored him altogether. He found it a promising start to see soldiers in blue and not have to dodge their gunfire.

During the Valley Campaign, one of the Confederate cavalry officers had come across several bags of Union currency when his raiding party seized a Federal train. The money, about $3,000 U.S., was eventually turned in to General Gordon who kept it in his possession and later used portions of it to buy food from Petersburg-area stores and farms to feed his starving troops. At Appomattox, the general took the remainder of the money and divided it equally among his staff, taking none for himself. Thus, Conor received about $300 in currency, $150 of which he gave to First Sergeant Tanneyhill and the remainder he intended to use for food and other necessities once his rations had been consumed. The Confederate money he had been saving was of course worthless now, but he brought it with him anyway to use as kindling.

After a week of traveling, his progress to date had been steady and uneventful. It was all too clear that the Southern countryside had paid a steep price for the four years of war it had endured. Farms were far from recovering and some of the single- and two-story buildings where manufacturing facilities had once operated had been razed. Conor had minimal interaction with the citizens of the small towns he passed through, but he couldn't avoid noticing the dazed expressions on many of the faces of the men and women he came across. Confederate veterans were returning home to the small towns across the South, and it wasn't uncommon for Conor to receive a wave or a salute from a gray-clad veteran or a legless young man in civilian attire. The war had touched every community, some worse than others, and some of it was difficult to look at. He would smile when he saw a Confederate Stars and Bars flying defiantly from a porch, snapping proudly in the breeze. He had advanced under that flag in more battles than he could remember, and it was still stirring to see it on display. It had been a symbol of bravery and fighting spirit, but he wondered how the Confederate battle flag might be perceived across the nation as the years went by. He knew he would always treasure his 38th Georgia flag.

Farmers were kind about letting Topper graze in their pastures, and more than once they provided grains and corn to supplement his feeding. Conor would regale them with stories of rousing Confederate victories and they would let Topper feed for free, sometimes feeding Conor as well. Their generosity in sharing what little they had was uplifting, and his faith in the good people of the South was renewed often. He slept outside mostly, often along streams or riverbanks unless the rains would challenge his ingenuity. In bad weather, he would sometimes find a barn or a smokehouse and invite himself inside to borrow some shelter for the night. He was certain that his uniform kept him from being shot on several occasions.

Conor reached Lexington, North Carolina in the late afternoon. The night before, he had used the last of his soap while bathing in a cold stream and washing his clothes of the smell that had been accumulating for weeks. There was a general store in town, and he bought some canned food and soap and a couple of stale cigars. As he was making his way out, an attractive young woman who was also leaving turned and looked at him.

"Well hello there. Where you headed, soldier?" she asked.

She seemed about mid-twenties, thin in build with piercing green eyes and a sweet, enticing smile. She wore her dark hair in a ponytail, and her blue-and-white checkered dress was slightly faded from age and use. She seemed lively and stouthearted in the way she spoke and carried herself, yet there was also something delicate and cultivated about her, adding to her physical attractiveness.

"Atlanta, ma'am."

"Oh, got a long way to go, do you?"

"Yes, well, I'm making progress."

"How long has it been since you've been home?"

"Four years."

She frowned and turned her head slightly. "Ouch! That must seem like forever. I'm sure you're excited about finally going home."

He nodded. "Sure."

"Wife or sweetheart back in Atlanta?"

"Nope, neither."

"Parents, brothers, sisters, dogs, cats?"

"My parents are deceased and my two brothers died in the war."

"Oh my, I'm very sorry to hear that. Please accept my deepest sympathies."

"Thank you. No cats, but hopefully my two dogs will still be there."

She laughed and then noticed his rank insignia. "What rank is that?"

"Colonel."

"Colonel? You're mighty young for that high a rank."

He grinned. "I'm old enough."

"My goodness," she said, her eyebrows raised. "You're a really big shot."

"No, not at all. I worked for a big shot, but that's hardly what I am."

"You probably knew Robert E. Lee."

"I did, yes."

"You swear? You swear to God?" she said, her eyes wide. "You really knew General Lee?"

"I really knew General Lee, ma'am."

"My husband Jimmy Toney was killed at Chancellorsville almost two years ago, serving in General Lee's army. It was a bad day here in Lexington when we found out that twenty-six of our boys had been killed in one afternoon. Needless to say, it was a bad day for me, too. Were you there? Were you in that battle?"

"Yes, but I was several miles away at Fredericksburg on our army's far right."

"Did you know Jimmy? Jimmy Toney?"

"No, I'm afraid not."

"He was a lieutenant with the Eighteenth North Carolina. Graduated from the University of North Carolina. We both came from farm families here in Lexington. He was going to be a mathematics instructor at Guilford College in Greensboro. We got married, but then the war started and all of a sudden Jimmy was in the army gone off to Virginia."

She followed Conor out of the store, telling him more about her husband. Conor placed his purchases in his knapsack and then untied Topper from a post in front of the store. "Nice talking to you, ma'am, but I need to be on my way."

"Where are you staying, Colonel?"

"Wherever I happen to stop and find a place on the road. I'm an old infantryman, so I'm used to it."

"You're hardly old. I'm curious about something: Is it true what we kept hearing about how our Confederate soldiers were nearly starving to death at the end?"

"It's the truth, I'm afraid. The soldiers in Virginia were in constant danger of starving."

"Y'all didn't have to resort to eating the horses, did you?"

"No, it never got to that, not where I was. Besides, most of the horses were so starved they probably discussed eating us."

She hesitated a moment and then burst out laughing. "At least you've still got your sense of humor," she noted.

"I've discovered that soldiers have the most well-developed senses of humor of any group I've ever been around. There isn't anything that's so sacred that a soldier won't make a joke about it."

"You swear you really knew General Lee?" she asked, grinning.

"I swear."

"What about Stonewall Jackson?"

"Met him, too. And James Longstreet, as well."

"God, you really *are* a big shot."

He laughed at her look of astonishment. "You're easily impressed. I could talk to you all day."

"Actually, I'm not. Or at least not usually," she said, slightly embarrassed.

"It's okay," he added quickly. "I was always in awe of those gentlemen when I spoke to them. They each had a presence unlike anybody I'd ever come across, especially General Lee."

"That is really, really interesting. I'd love to hear more. And you have my permission to talk to me all day."

Conor smiled. "I suppose I'd better be moving along now. I'll need to find a place for the night."

"So you're not going to stay at the Inn?"

"No, nothing as fancy as that."

"Do you have enough to eat?"

"Yes, I've got everything I need."

"Well, let me ask you something: When's the last time you had a home-cooked meal?"

He hesitated.

"Been a while, huh? Look, my neighbors and I went in together and bought a cow recently, and I still have some dried beef. I would like nothing more than to share it with a young Confederate colonel. And especially one who knew Robert E. Lee and fought in the same battle where my husband lived his final day. Please, would you join me for supper as a small token of my appreciation, Colonel?"

"My name is Conor Rafferty, ma'am."

"And I'm Teresa. Teresa Toney. So, will you take me up on my offer, Conor?"

He hesitated again.

"I'm not a damn Yankee, Colonel Rafferty. And I don't bite, but even if I did I'm not contagious with anything that I know of."

Conor laughed loudly. "I'd be honored to join you, Teresa."

He followed Teresa's wagon to her modest, single-story, wood-frame house about a mile away. Her property seemed to encompass several acres, part of which held a large garden while the rest appeared as if it had been unattended for some time. Conor had expected the house would be crowded with children, but there were none. He left Topper in the stable at the rear of the house, with her two horses and a mule. Teresa then escorted him inside and offered to open a bottle of red wine she had been hoarding for nearly a year, and when he politely declined she opened it anyway. While she prepared the meal, Conor took his wine to the front porch where he lit the last cigar from the three First Sergeant Tanneyhill had given him before they left Appomattox. The smell of cooking beef reminded him of home, and in many ways it had nearly an intoxicating effect on him. Or perhaps it was the red wine. In any case, both the aroma and the wine felt like long lost friends.

The food was delicious, and Teresa's company was equally agreeable. They relaxed and talked about many things, especially their respective families. Conor explained how his family had suffered so terribly during the war, and how mixed were his feelings about going back to Atlanta after four years and so much heartbreak. Teresa explained how she and her husband had lost a child to scarlet fever at the age of six months, and had yet to conceive again before his death in battle. She related how she had struggled to maintain the tobacco farm her husband's family had overseen for years before the war. Like many Southern women, life had been a constant challenge for Teresa during the war years. Conor guessed it would likely continue that way for the foreseeable future.

"I had never expected to become a widow at twenty-two years of age," she said.

"You're hardly alone in that condition, sad to say," he said as he thought briefly of the untold thousands of widowed women, North and South.

They sat at the table and finished the rest of the wine. Teresa was intrigued by his exploits, the battles he had survived, the wounds he had received, the people he had met. She especially wanted to know about Robert E. Lee and Stonewall Jackson, what they were like, how they dealt with their soldiers. Teresa was open and unpretentious, and she had a soothing manner that put him at ease and opened up his conversational apparatus. He became a free-flowing chatterbox for the better part of two hours, relaxed and renewed, unguarded in a way he had not been since Penny and Richmond. Teresa seemed awed by his rank and young age, and Conor didn't mind it a bit.

"You must have been an exceptional officer, Conor."

"No, I wasn't exceptional. But the men I served with were."

"What will happen now? What will the Yankees do to us?"

"They were generous to our soldiers when the war ended. I hope we can reunite the nation without the sort of bitterness that existed before the war."

"Did you ever think we'd lose the war?" she asked.

"Not until Petersburg, at the very end. Up until then, I thought General Lee would figure out a way to win."

A black-and-white cat appeared for the first time and jumped into Conor's lap, startling him.

"Jericho, mind your manners, please," Teresa called, laughing. "We got him from our preacher's family just before the war started, and he's turned out to be my best friend and housemate these past several years. He very rarely goes to strangers, so he must think you're pretty special, Conor."

He began petting the purring feline. "No, he must figure me for somebody else. General Lee, maybe."

"He's a proud Rebel cat, so he's just saying hello to a friend."

It was getting late, and Conor thanked Teresa for her hospitality. They walked out onto the front porch and noticed the lightly falling rain. It instantly reminded him of so many rainy nights in the field—the smell, the sound, the wet clothes—repeated so many times in so many places that now it seemed an almost natural condition. He stood for a moment and allowed his senses to take him back as he listened to the rain falling softly through the nearby pines.

"Where are you going to go?" Teresa asked, moving a step closer that he didn't fail to notice.

"I'll find a place in the trees. It's something the army gave me plenty of practice at."

She said nothing, leaving him to look off into the distance and summon up a procession of fast-moving memories with faces, places, and voices that had become so deeply embedded that they were now a permanent part of him. It was another of those strange new feelings, the realization that the war was truly over, that he need not worry about it further, somewhat akin to the sense of relief in awakening from a white-hot nightmare.

"I gotta shove off," he finally said after coming back from what seemed like a trance. "I've taken up enough of your evening. Thank you for your kindness. You're a beautiful, brave woman and a perfect delight to be around, Teresa. I only wish now that you lived in Atlanta."

"I have an extra room here. You'd be welcome to stay the night."

"I couldn't do that. You've been a wonderful hostess, but you've already done more for me than I deserve."

"I've done nothing but provide you with a meal, and you're certainly deserving of that. It's raining and it's getting late, and I just want to offer you that room for the night," she said, adding softly, "with no strings attached. You can take it or leave it, but for what it's worth, I'd very much like you to stay."

And for what it's worth, he did stay. He couldn't remember having slumbered in a real bed since his most recent hospitalization, and it was a complete joy. The comfort of the bed and the cool sheets, the sound of the rain on the roof, and the feeling of the wine and a full belly were all highly pleasurable, exceeded only when Teresa opened the door a half-hour later and joined him.

Conor slept very little that night, but a more agreeable reason to lose sleep over, he could not imagine.

"You wouldn't consider staying a little while longer, would you?" Teresa asked the next morning as he prepared to leave after breakfast.

"I can't, Teresa," he said, adding with a smile and a wink, "but you should know I'm highly tempted. I'm very highly tempted, in fact. You are a wonderful lady and if my circumstances were different, who knows what might happen? But I'm sorry, I have to go. God bless you, Teresa Toney."

The next several days took him through the South Carolina towns of Chester, Newberry, and Abbeville. The good citizens there made fodder available for Topper and a farm family gave him fruit to take with him. He crossed over a Savannah River bridge into Georgia early one morning while the white mist hung over the water like a protective cloud. He slept at Danielsville, near a stream, and Topper's unusually loud neighing and snorting awakened him just after first light. He opened his eyes to see an unpleasant-looking man standing over him, pointing a pistol at his head and gazing at his possessions.

"Well lookey here. Got myself a boy gen'ral," the man said as he glanced at Conor's uniform blouse, folded and placed atop his knapsack.

"Who are you and what do you want?" Conor asked brusquely.

"It's no never mind who I am. What I want is that revolver, for starters," he said as he picked up the belt with the attached holster and pistol next to Conor. "And I shore do like the look of that fine hoss you got there."

The man wore tattered clothing and an old floppy hat. His hair and beard were scruffy and unkempt, and several of his bottom teeth were missing. One of his eyes didn't quite move in unison with the other, and he was skinny and drawn. He seemed to be in his thirties, but the years had been hard and Conor quickly reasoned from his own recent experience with mean-looking men that this stranger meant to shoot him, take what he had, and never look back.

"Were you a Confederate soldier?" Conor asked as the man slung the pistol belt over his shoulder.

"No, I wasn't. You got any money?" he asked, keeping his revolver trained on Conor.

"Some, yes. Why weren't you a soldier?"

"Ain't none of your damn bidness, gen'ral. Now where's the damn money."

"Were you a deserter?"

He stepped toward Conor, the pistol uncomfortably close to Conor's head, and suddenly the smell of him was overpowering nearly to a point of gagging.

"Topper, I see what you mean, boy," Conor cracked.

"I'm 'bout to lose my temper, boy gen'ral. And I'm only gonna ask nice one mo' time. Where's the money at?"

"It's in my haversack," Conor said with a point to the satchel near his feet. "Down in the bottom."

The man stepped back several paces, leaned over and then opened the haversack. He began hurriedly fingering the contents in search of the money, alternately glancing at Conor and the opened satchel. Conor waited until the moment the man found the roll of currency to raise his second pistol from underneath his blanket and fire a single shot into the man's skull, directly above his left eye. He didn't fall right away but instead looked at Conor in a flash of disbelief before Conor fired again, hitting him squarely in the forehead. The dead man then toppled forward on his face.

"Big mistake there, friend. Always assume a second gun."

Conor rolled the man over and felt for a pulse, but there was none. He examined his pistol, found it poorly maintained, and then tossed it into the stream. He then considered what he should do about disposing of the body, but since he had no shovel or other means of digging a shallow grave, he covered it with leaves and pine needles, and left. He considered reporting the incident to whatever authorities he could locate, but he decided in the end to continue on to Atlanta. He doubted that anyone who knew the man would be surprised at his fate.

He was nearing Jefferson, Georgia at dusk when he began idly thinking about the contrast of making love to a beautiful woman one night and a few mornings later shooting and killing an armed robber whose foul odor his nasal membranes had still yet to overcome. Neither had been anticipated, both had generated an intense excitement that broke the monotony of the excursion, but only one would he prefer to repeat.

And he repeated that one in his mind more than once. All the way into and past Jefferson, as a matter of fact.

He reached Atlanta on May 3, a day later than planned. He avoided the center of the city and instead headed straight for his farm. There were still Union occupation soldiers in the city, and several cavalry troops had passed him on the road. There was destruction to many of the buildings and houses on the outskirts, and it had that all too familiar look of a place where a big battle had been fought. He had seen hundreds of Confederate soldiers returning to their hometowns throughout the course of his trip, but coming into Atlanta he noticed the roads were thicker with returning soldiers than any of the other places he had thus far seen.

"What regiment were you with, Colonel?" the men would call when Conor approached. Twice he dismounted and walked for a while with a group of returning veterans, sharing experiences and enjoying the camaraderie that comes so naturally to soldiers.

He finally reached his farm in the early afternoon. The red-dirt road leading to his house was covered in leaves and overgrown with weeds. He dismounted Topper and began walking up that homeward lane for the first time in four years, expecting the smells of the farm to fill his nostrils as it had for most of his life before the war. Instead, he sniffed the distinctive odor of charred wood, and then he saw the heartbreaking sight of the collapsed and blackened barn. He could feel the emotion surging through him as he stood in this once familiar, safe place, a place that had been transformed into something foreign and inhospitable to him. He walked toward his house, but the closer he came the more he could see through the windows into the empty rooms. The dwelling was in a state of disrepair on the outside, and he noticed several of the boards on the porch had either buckled or fallen though.

Even his two dogs who had always come running at top speed anytime he came walking up the road were gone.

"Dear God, this can't be," he said in a moment of crushing sorrow. "This can't be all that's left of us."

There were no cattle in the pasture. The crop fields were overgrown and the fences were missing most of the posts and boards. There was nothing left of the split-rail fence that had encircled the house in happier days. The grounds in the front were cluttered with the debris of an army encampment, and he could see evidence of the campfires the occupying soldiers had built. He looked past the house near the old oak tree and noticed two white headstones, one beside the other. When he approached, he could see the names of Emily Moynihan Rafferty on one and Seamus Ryan Rafferty on the other. He stood at the foot of the graves and stared at the names chiseled into the headstones, a bruising finality settling over him, wishing like a child he was dreaming but knowing as he stood there as a man he was not. He could see their faces and hear their voices as clearly as if they were tarrying under the old tree with him. He could hear their singing as they stood around the piano, and the laughter of Sean and Daniel when he would raise his voice and sing like a girl. He remembered the sound of Father's voice when blessing their food with the same prayer he always prayed. He could see his mother crying and wiping her eyes with her apron, waving to him from the nearby front porch as he went off to war.

He sat down and wept, letting go of his emotions and crying harder than he'd ever cried in his adult life.

"I forgive you, Father," he said through the tears as he stared at the headstone. "I forgive you. I'm sorry it had to be this way. I'm sorry for all the bitterness, all the pain. I'm sorry for all we're going to miss. I love you, Father. And I love you, Mother, so very, very much. I miss you both and I'm so sorry all of this had to happen to us. I'm so sorry."

He sat there until dusk, thinking about his mother and his father, then Sean and Daniel, until he was fully exhausted. He had no more tears left, and he could think of no other time in his life when he had felt such despair and helplessness. Now that he was home, it seemed like only yesterday that the childhood gatherings under the old oak had been a source of joy and comfort and stability. But not now, not ever again. He closed his eyes and said a short prayer, recalling the words of Chaplain Yancey.

Even though he heard no noise behind him, he got the distinct feeling that he was not alone. In one motion he drew the pistol from his holster and turned to look behind him. A black man of perhaps his own approximate age stood motionless twenty feet behind him, and twenty feet further back stood what Conor took to be his wife and two children, a boy and a girl.

"Please don't shoot, mister. We don't mean no harm," the man called in a soft tone.

"Who are you?"

"My name's Robert Banks, and this is my wife Thelma and my children William and Jennifer. Are you the owner of this property, sir?"

Conor put the pistol away and stood. "Yes, I'm the owner. What are you doing here?"

"We've been living in this house for about a week now. Came to here from the Hatcher plantation in Madison. Some of our people left when the Yankees from Sherman's army came through Madison, but we stayed on with Miss Hatcher. Well, when she didn't have no more money she shut everything down there and told all of us that was left to go somewhere else and be free people. So we left there and ended up here. We haven't hurt nothing or stole nothing, I give you my word. We've just been staying here and being free people but not knowing what else to do or where else to go. But we'll leave now if you want us to, mister."

"They told you to go and be free people?"

"Yessir, that's what she told us."

"Do you even know what that means?"

"I know what it means in words, sir. But I don't quite know what it means in real life. Not yet, anyway."

Conor walked over to Banks and extended his hand. "I'm Conor Rafferty. And no, I don't want you to leave now," he said as he nodded to the young woman and the children.

Conor began walking toward the house. "Y'all can show me around inside. I haven't seen it in four years."

The interior of the house was nearly empty, nothing like what he had left four years earlier. The furniture had been looted except for the kitchen table and two of the previous five chairs. Some of the kitchen utensils and cooking pots remained, but the silverware was gone. The furnishings and paintings had been removed, leaving outlines on the walls. Even the old piano and its stool had been taken.

"Is there anything left in the bedrooms?" Conor asked.

"No, sir. It's all gone, too. Nothing but bare floors."

"Who did this to the place? Who took all of our things?" Conor asked in exasperation.

"We don't know, sir. It was like this when we got here."

Conor was unfamiliar with the details of the Battle of Atlanta and the movements of the lines, but it seemed possible that either or both armies could have occupied the property. He glanced down and noticed the dark stains on the floors.

"Are the bedroom floors stained like this?" he asked, pointing to a spot on the parlor floor.

"Yessir," the young woman answered. "Is that from blood?"

"I think so, yes. The house was used as a hospital."

Conor noticed a rifle propped near the kitchen door. He pointed and asked, "Is that your gun?"

"Yessir."

"Where'd you get it?"

"Miss Hatcher thought it would be best that I have it, just in case."

"What have you used it for?"

"Squirrels and rabbits, mostly. One wild hog. And a dog foaming at the mouth."

"And people of bad faith, if necessary," Conor added.

"Them too, I suppose, but only if I have to."

Conor took a seat at the table and began contemplating how difficult it would be for him to become a farmer. He walked with a limp from his achy knee and the full feeling would likely never return to his left-hand fingers from the shoulder wound he had taken at Sharpsburg. He knew the physical demands that had been borne by his father throughout all his years of farming, and he concluded that he would have to find another calling.

Conor let out a big groan and rested his head on the table. "What now?" he mumbled mournfully, his mind and body fatigued nearly to a point of numbness.

"Is there anything we can do for you, sir?" Banks asked softly.

Conor raised his head and managed a slight smile. "No. But thanks just the same."

"Is that your momma and poppa out there, sir?" Banks asked with a point toward the oak tree.

"Yes. And my two brothers are buried where they died during the war. I'm the last one, the last Rafferty left."

Banks and his wife both sighed audibly and shook their heads.

"I'm sorry, Mister Rafferty. No man should have to live through what you have. I'm really sorry, sir."

"I suppose I could say the same thing to you. We seem to have something in common, Mister Banks."

"Are you hungry, sir? We have some stew here we'd be glad to share with you."

"Yes, I'd like that. And please, call me Conor."

"Thank you, Conor. You were in the army?"

"Yes."

"What was your rank, sir?"

"I was a colonel."

"That's almost a general, isn't it?"

Conor chuckled. "I suppose it is, yes. Have you been to school? Have you had an education?"

"Miss Hatcher hired some teachers to teach us, sir. Reading and some arithmetic. Some writing, too. And we've taught our children. She did that after Mister Hatcher passed away not long after the war started. He would never have allowed that, but she did, bless her heart."

"Well, let's have supper outside underneath the old oak, like my family used to do. Will that be okay?" Conor asked.

"That'll be fine, Conor. Out there with your momma and poppa."

"Yes, out there with my momma and poppa."

***

Friday, February 15, 1918

"So what became of the Banks family, Cappy?"

"I let them stay at the house with the understanding that they would make the needed repairs and generally fix things up. I gave them a budget for the materials and for their food. Then later we agreed that Robert would farm the land and start paying me a rent when he sold his crops."

"Where were you? Did you live someplace else?"

"Yes, I got a job in Atlanta learning the timber business and lived in town. I eventually became friends with a banker who I convinced to loan Robert Banks the money to buy the farm outright, and who then helped me finance the start of my own business."

"And the banker really loaned money to a black man?"

"Only after I threatened to take my own business to a competing bank, and only as long as I co-signed the loan, which I did. Robert got the farm back to health and kept current with his loan payments. He eventually repaid the loan in full."

"And so it all worked out for the good."

"Not completely, no."

"What happened?"

"Some white-trash crackers didn't like the idea of a black family farming the land near them, especially when Robert was farming circles around them. And so one night one of the fools fired a small-caliber rifle through Robert's front window and hit his daughter in the arm."

"Oh no! Was she badly hurt?"

"She eventually recovered, but she lost some of the use of that arm."

"Did they catch the shooter?"

"No, they didn't want to catch him. When I found out who the man was, I paid a drifter twenty-five dollars to shoot his horse and leave a note that said, 'I know you did it, and next time it will be your own daughter.' There were no problems after that."

"You wouldn't have harmed the man's daughter, would you, Cappy?"

"Of course not. But he couldn't have been certain of that."

Aaron started laughing. "How about this for an irony: A Confederate soldier returns from the war, sells his farm to a black man, and when a white man tries to intimidate the black family, the former Confederate soldier takes the side of the black family."

Conor shook his head in disagreement. "That's just basic human decency. Sorry, but I don't see an irony there."

Aaron nodded his agreement. "I see your point. Shall we keep going?"

"Yes."

Chapter Eighteen

The Aftermath

Way down in the meadow where the lily first blows,
Where the wind from the mountain ne'er ruffles the rose;
Lives fond Evelina, the sweet little dove,
The pride of the valley, the girl that I love.
"Sweet Evelina"

1865 - 1918

Four years of war left much of the South devastated and barely recognizable, its towns and plantations and factories in ruins, its slave economy eradicated forever, and an entire generation of young Southern men resting peacefully in cemeteries across the length and breadth of the Confederacy. It was a horror like no other Conor had ever known, and he often prayed to a merciful God that nothing of the sort would ever befall the nation again. The war was similarly difficult on the people of the North where the great loss of their boys was as real and heartbreaking as was the loss of so many Southern boys.

Conor was old at age twenty-five when the war ended. His parents and two brothers were all deceased, so he became the rightful heir to the family farm. He was the only Rafferty left of his immediate family—they the Raffertys of Cork, province of Munster, Ireland, and from there to their blessed America, to Georgia, which, much like his family, now lay in ruins.

Conor sold the farm in 1867 and started his own business in the harvesting of trees for lumber. It was rough at first, but over time he bought a sawmill and started to do well, eventually doing very well as the rebuilding of Georgia gained momentum. He worked hard, very hard, but sometimes found the time to play just as hard with a rowdy group of Johnny Reb veterans he befriended over the years. As for the ladies, well, there were lots of war widows in Georgia.

It was estimated that something on the order of 120,000 Georgians served as Confederate soldiers during the war. Estimates ranging from 11,000 to 25,000 represented the number of those soldiers who died from either wounds or disease. Conor had roughly estimated at one time that 15% of the men populating the Georgia regiments had been killed on the battlefields where he fought, which was within the range of the various estimates he saw of Georgia soldiers killed during the war. The war was undeniably a very large drain on the state's population.

Georgia underwent Reconstruction from 1865 to 1871. The state was war-ravaged, devoid of civil order, with food shortages and widespread disorder. Cotton fell from 700,000 bales in 1860 to less than 50,000 in 1865, while other cash crops were also meager. The coastal rice plantations would never recover from the war. There was little effective political leadership to govern Georgia's white population of 550,000 and the more than 460,000 newly freed slaves. Many former slaves migrated to larger towns where they found overcrowding and shortages of food, and large numbers of them died from epidemic diseases. The 13th Amendment abolished slavery, and the Freedmen's Bureau returned many of the former slaves to the fields by mediating a contract-labor system between white landowners and their black workers, often their former slaves. In July, 1868 Georgia was readmitted to the Union when the newly elected General Assembly ratified the Fourteenth Amendment.

Conor traveled extensively after the war. His business required him to travel throughout Georgia, but he also enjoyed visiting army friends in places both in and outside of the South. Conor and Gilbert Tanneyhill, his closest friend, exchanged regular visits between Mobile and Atlanta. Chaplain Yancey became the pastor of an Atlanta church which, when he became aware of it, Conor immediately joined and renewed their friendship. His 38th Georgia soldiers would have reunions in various locations across the state, and Conor would attend as many of those as his schedule allowed.

General Gordon and Conor continued their friendship after the war. The general ran for governor of Georgia in 1868 and lost, but his interest in politics grew. Conor did some work for his campaign by reaching out to Confederate veterans for their support. He shared many meals with the general and Fanny, and they would tell stories that would inevitably extend deep into the night. When General Gordon's name was mentioned in the newspapers in connection with an affiliation with the Ku Klux Klan, Conor immediately went to his office in nearby Kirkwood and confronted him directly about it.

"Is it true, General?" Conor asked.

"Do you believe the story, Conor?" he replied.

"I don't want to believe it, General, because if it's accurate then I would be greatly disappointed in a man I have come to admire so much. It's not who I think you are, and I hope like hell it's not what you've become, sir. Is it true? Are you involved with those criminals?"

"The story's not accurate, Conor. I am not involved with criminals of any sort. I am only interested in developing a new South that is better and stronger in every way than the old one. And being viewed as associating with such hooligans would not help in advancing that agenda. You know that. And you know me."

Conor would have preferred the general to have pounded his desk in anger and threatened to sue the newspaper for slander, but he did not. Still, Conor left his office feeling better about the matter. Or at least he *wanted* to feel better about it. And he did. Mostly.

A mutual friend introduced Conor to Mary McIntosh, and after a courtship of six months, they were married in 1869. Mary was of Scottish ancestry, tall and sturdy with long, flowing red hair and a highly spirited nature. Taylor came along a year later, an energetic bundle of pink, pure joy. They were a small and happy family making their way in postwar Georgia, minding their own business, tending to a successful business, and raising a smart, strong, enterprising son. Mary never seemed to enjoy Conor's army friends and their wives when they would periodically gather, though he never fully understood why. Maybe she thought them too loud and boorish, too drunken and offensive, or too glum and bitter over the outcome of the war. In truth, they were probably all of that, but it was also a way for men bonded by war to blow off steam and enjoy one another's company again.

General Gordon won election to the United States Senate in 1873. He would become in 1879 the first former Confederate to lead the Senate. He wrote Conor a letter in June, 1874 to come to Washington and speak to a Senate committee on how the "New South" was beginning to prosper and how such business entrepreneurs like Conor were reinvigorating Georgia and the entire region. Mary chose to stay in Atlanta, so Conor caught the train and traveled to Washington not really knowing what to expect but excited to see the general in his capacity as a U.S. Senator from Georgia.

Conor spoke to the committee and answered questions about the business enterprise he was involved with, its growth and success, along with questions about how white Georgians were dealing with the fact that black Georgians were free and equal and becoming more a part of the economic and social fabric of the state. The questions became testy after a while, as if all white Georgians were interested in nothing more than subjugating black people and denying them their legal rights to a full and productive citizenship. It was a combination of the arrogance of some of the senators and Conor's own headstrong Southern pride that made it difficult for him to abide such posturing and lecturing. He could see that General Gordon was nearing a point of summarily adjourning the session.

"Let me just say this, gentlemen," Conor finally said. "I lost my parents during the war, and my two brothers died in service to the Confederacy. I'm hardly the only person who has suffered great loss in his life, but in four years, I lost the four people who meant the most to me of anyone else in this world. Instead of being welcomed home with open arms, I came back to a home in shambles with the graves of my parents in the yard behind our house. Then I found that a family of black squatters had settled into my house on our farm because they had no other place to go and no one to turn to, like so many thousands of other former slaves. I befriended that family, and I ended up selling my farm to them by agreeing to co-sign the loan they used to pay me. They built that farm into one of the most productive in the area, and we remain friends to this day."

Conor paused and looked every member of the committee in the eye.

"Gentlemen," he continued, "we are still a work in progress in Georgia. We still have our challenges, and we still have miles to go. We are far from perfect, just as I am sure none of you would hold up your respective states as examples of perfection. We need your economic assistance, your manufacturing expertise, your access to capital and your extended hand of renewed friendship, but not your condescension and heavy-handedness. We Southerners have lost the war and been occupied, but we are not the murderous savages we are often depicted as being. We are people of faith and good faith and courage and industriousness. And while there are still people in my state who would act in bad faith, most of my fellow citizens, white and black, would prefer to deal with one another fairly and honestly. The truth is, we all have the same hopes, the same fears, and the same needs no matter what we look like. You just heard my story about my business, and you heard my story about my farming friends. We are rebuilding Georgia from the ruin that came to it from the war, and I believe we are doing it to the benefit of all of our citizens. Come and see for yourselves. Meet our friendly people, see our rise from the ashes, and sample our delicious Southern cooking. I'll be happy to show y'all around my town. And I sincerely thank you gentlemen for your time today."

The senators applauded vigorously. General Gordon winked and shook Conor's hand.

"Come with me," the general said, guiding him out the door.

The general showed him around the Capitol Building with its newly completed dome, the Senate chambers and House hall, the office spaces, and the view from his own office looking across the open space toward the Washington Monument. He pointed to their right-front, toward tree-lined Pennsylvania Avenue, where the White House was visible in the distance.

"Let's go. We don't want to be late."

The two of them took a carriage ride to the White House where they were met and escorted into the Oval Office. President Ulysses S. Grant got up from behind his desk and greeted them cordially.

"I've got someone I'd like you to meet, Mister President," General Gordon said. "This is Colonel Conor Rafferty who served with me in several capacities during the war. He's doing some great things back home to help our state's recovery, and I just wanted to stop in and introduce him."

"Pleased to meet you, Colonel," came the greeting along with the outstretched hand of the President of the United States.

President Grant spent twenty minutes with them, discussing everything from former military associates and foes, to the difficulties of curbing rampant corruption in government, to his high hopes for the nation as a whole.

"Everybody seems to know where to find the easy money, and nobody seems to be able to do anything about it. What does that tell you?" the president commented.

Grant was interested in how the former soldiers of the Confederacy were adjusting to civilian life. He mentioned his concern over organized acts of violence against blacks in the South, and he said his administration was crafting legislation that would carry stiff penalties for such activity. Conor mentioned that many former soldiers were starting businesses and operating farms and raising families all over Georgia. He acknowledged that there was still bitterness among some portions of the white citizenry, and he noted that while the passage of time would help, the most effective way to bring the South back into the mainstream would involve electing good leaders. Getting, and then keeping, a strong level of growth in the Southern states' economies was also important.

Grant finally stood, signaling the meeting's end.

"I'm counting on men of goodwill like yourself, Colonel, and leaders of great ability like Senator Gordon here, to help us make this country whole again, to make it better for all our people. Can I count on you, Colonel Rafferty?"

"You can, Mister President."

They left the White House and rode the carriage the short distance to the Willard Hotel where they met former Union General Joshua Chamberlain in the lobby. He was also former Governor Chamberlain of Maine, and his current role as President, Bowdoin College, his alma mater, was one he had held for two years. He was a recipient of the nation's highest award for combat valor, the Medal of Honor, for his leadership and gallantry at Little Round Top on July 2, 1863 at Gettysburg. When reminded by General Gordon, Chamberlain recalled having given Conor the horse at Appomattox at the conclusion of the war.

"Topper is still serving me well, General," Conor added.

"Topper served both armies, as I remember, and I'm sure he served both well," Chamberlain responded.

They talked and had a drink in the lobby before heading to supper in the hotel's restaurant. Fanny Gordon joined them for what turned out to be a delightful evening of entertaining stories and warm reminiscences shared by former foes but now fellow Americans.

"Come to Maine, Colonel Rafferty," Chamberlain offered. "Let me show you around Bowdoin College in the morning and then give you a taste of Maine lobster that night. My wife, whose name is also Fanny, would love to show off Brunswick to an old friend."

"I would love to come to Maine, General," Conor answered, which he did the following year.

Conor offered this toast at the end of the evening:

"How can a nation with such men of the character and abilities of John Gordon and Joshua Chamberlain, and women of the strength and dedication of Fanny Gordon and Fanny Chamberlain, become anything other than the leading light in this world. To our special friendship, and to the United States of America and all that she can become."

General Gordon returned home after his Senate service and was elected Governor of Georgia in 1886. Conor campaigned for him throughout the state, and as he prepared to take office, he offered Conor one of several important posts in his new administration. Conor declined and instead remained with his business which by then had become quite time-consuming but very lucrative. He did volunteer work on behalf of Confederate veterans and made several recommendations to the governor on areas of improvement for their health care, all of which were implemented.

Mary and Conor enjoyed lives filled with the sort of privilege and access that came with money. They were hardly excessive, but they had a nice home filled with nice things and admission into the political and civic circles that held the most sway in Atlanta and Georgia. Conor championed a number of causes, mostly involving veterans' issues, and always had the ear of General Gordon in this area. Mary sponsored an annual Christmas ball for twenty years to raise funds for the Atlanta orphanage she helped to create. They donated time and funds to publicize the works of many outstanding Southern artists with exhibitions all over the country. Mary had a large park built near a poor neighborhood to give the children a place to play. Conor's good friend John Pemberton, like himself a former Confederate colonel, asked Conor to invest with several others in the little company he named "Coca-Cola" which did quite nicely for their finances. Overall, Mary seemed happy, though Conor never remembered asking her directly. He just always assumed that she was.

But she wasn't.

The decree of divorce stated "incompatibility of temper and interests." Mary left Conor six years after Taylor had been killed at San Juan Hill, and he didn't hear so much as a single word from her in the ensuing fifteen years. Conor harvested all the timber, sold it and the sawmill and the rest of the land, sold the Coca-Cola holdings, and gave her fifty-percent of the proceeds. Conor later heard a rumor that she had married a dry-goods merchant out of Savannah, but he never knew that to be a fact. He just knew that she left and never came back. He supposed he was to blame for not being attentive enough, and he was sure he had handled many things inexpertly.

The plain truth is they just grew apart, slowly and undeniably, like a crack in a wooden plank that widens with pressure and age. Neither of them ever recovered from Taylor's death, not really. It was as if they both died a little inside, and that little bit of death on the inside took away the part that was familiar and comfortable about each other, making them seem more and more like strangers. The whole sad, sorry thing seemed to move along much like poison ivy—slowly, then suddenly. Thus, at the age of 64 and after 35 years of marriage, Conor was abruptly alone and on his own, much as if he were a widower. If there was a consolation, however, it was that there were still lots of war widows in Georgia. But a small consolation, at that.

So, Conor was married once, and that was enough. The thought of a second marriage was no more appealing to him than volunteering to be that fellow who follows behind the elephants with a broom and bucket during the circus parade. Lots of old soldiers were marrying young women, and one would venture a guess that such an arrangement would plant perpetual smiles on the faces of the old coots. But not so for the ones Conor knew. Whether he saw them limping along at the general store or worshiping at church or eventually lying in a casket, he never noticed that sort of smile. The young widows, on the other hand, often collected on the Confederate pensions of their deceased spouses. While the money wasn't grand enough to shout out with glee, a slight smile might have creased their young faces. Conor joked that it was a form of deferred earnings for the young widows, anyway. At any rate, Conor had his share of female acquaintances over the years, several of whom he became quite fond of, but even so marriage was no longer a condition he wished to visit upon himself again.

General John B. Gordon published his memoirs, "Reminiscences of the Civil War", in 1903. A year later he was dead at age 71. An estimated 75,000 people attended his burial service at Atlanta's Oakland Cemetery. Conor was one of them.

General Joshua Chamberlain died in 1914 at age 85 from his lingering war wounds. He was buried in Brunswick, Maine with a sizeable crowd in attendance. Conor was also one of them.

First Sergeant Gilbert Tanneyhill died from pneumonia in 1915 at the age of 76. He was buried in Mobile after a moving ceremony with his widow and two daughters, six grandchildren, and several dozen friends in attendance. Conor was one of them.

Tanneyhill's widow, Jeanette, came and stood beside Conor once the minister had completed his graveside remarks.

"Will you say it, Colonel Rafferty?" Jeanette asked. "Please, will you say it?"

Conor gave a confused look.

"Will you say what you always said when you had a memorial service after one of your Thirty-eighth Georgia soldiers had been killed in battle? It's so beautiful. Gilbert would have been pleased, and so would we."

Conor nodded. He looked around and took in the serenity and comforting simplicity of the small church and its neatly ordered cemetery. There was a slight breeze on his face, cooling the humid late-spring air, with birds offering their sympathies in song from the stately, moss-covered oaks in the distance. He noticed the distinctive scents of the freshly shoveled earth, the flowers in the arrangements, and the perfumes of the ladies. He glanced at the closed casket that now owned the body of the dearest friend of his life, draped with the stirring bright colors of a Confederate battle flag. He remembered for a fleeting moment some of what he and Tanneyhill had shared and endured together—just a very small slice of a much larger whole—that only the two of them could fully sense in either spoken or unspoken understanding. He noticed the well-dressed family members and friends with their hands clasped in front of them, their kindhearted, respectful eyes now turned toward him. He saw a small, curly-haired boy dressed in his Sunday best pull a dandelion from the grass, study it carefully for a moment, and then offer it up as a gift to his appreciative mother.

Conor took a deep breath and lightly cleared his throat. He then stood at attention.

"In memory of First Sergeant Gilbert Tanneyhill, Thirty-eighth Georgia Infantry Regiment: I walked more miles than there are grains of sand on a Savannah beach. I lost count of the many roots, wild berries, and crawling things I ate so I could find enough strength to move to the sound of the firing and join the fight, because I was a soldier. I chewed leaves for moisture when there was no stream. I drank the rain as fast as it would fall on my parched lips. My clothes were ragged, my shoes were scuffed beyond repair, my skin was cracked and burned and swollen from bites. I have been so hot that I forgot my own name, so cold that I was incapable of even mumbling my own name, so tired that I could fall asleep standing. But when the battle lines were formed, when the flag of the Thirty-eighth Georgia came onto the field, I was in my place in the line because I was a soldier. I fired my musket, reloaded and fired again. When all around me my brothers were falling, I stayed in the fight and gave it all I had. And when finally I did fall, when I could fight no more, I fell as a soldier. My blood hallows the ground where I fought and fell with honor and with courage. Being a soldier was not just what I did, it was who I was. And now as I go to my well-earned rest, I leave the fight to you, my brothers. There is no hardship you cannot endure, no battle you will not join, no greater love you can have than the love you have for one another. Remember me for the bravery and the spirit with which I fought, and for the price that I willingly paid. I leave you now as I step off the line and out of that deadly space, but I will see you on the other side."

Of all the friends who had come and gone in Conor's life, Gilbert Tanneyhill was the one he cherished the most, the one he would now miss the most.

The war ended at Appomattox in 1865, or at least the shooting between the armies ended that year. Bitterness among many Southerners over the war's outcome continued through the end of the century and on into the next. For most, it was not the sort of rancor that led to violence, although for some it did. Instead, it was more a sour taste over a costly defeat, a humiliating occupation, and a rebuilding of a region that made it so different and in some respects so threatening as to make many Southerners look back and yearn for what had been. That yearning was evident in many of the reunions Conor attended where The Lost Cause was draped in nostalgia and the antebellum South was fondly remembered as the best of times, when in fact it produced many of the conditions that led to the worst of times. Conor remembered what his father had predicted that a war would bring to the South, and it was with little pleasure that he was proven right, God rest his soul.

And so Conor grew old, lived alone, ate alone, sometimes drank alone, and reckoned that someday soon he would die alone. He had money but he would have been no more happy or sad had he been without it. He no longer worked at anything meaningful, and he stopped traveling for pleasure to visit friends and old army mates when the long train rides became too burdensome. He rarely awakened feeling anything other than pain, fatigue, and bleakness, sleeping only 3-4 hours a night. The hurt always seemed to move in a loop, sometimes presenting itself in a frontal assault, other times sneaking up behind him. He learned to count on it always being there, somewhere, like an unwelcomed guest.

Many nights he would lie awake haunted by the lingering memories of the suffering and death he had seen in the war. There was always the smoke, the gunfire, the screaming, and the piles of casualties, and often it was the hunger and the retreating and the loss of hope. Those horrific images never went away, probably never would, and over time it became much like a disease that searches for and then squeezes out all of the pleasant, peaceful thoughts that used to make the nighttime tolerable.

Consequently, Conor had no purpose in life and hence no particular incentive to carry on with it.

He was long in the tooth, to be sure, and he wasn't long for this world.

***

Friday, February 15, 1918

"Cappy, what do you think the nation learned from the war?"

"That it's always better to seek compromise than to kill each other over our differences. That our founding principles as a nation are unique to the world and worth preserving and protecting. That our Union could have been destroyed by the war, but its preservation will make it stronger and better as a nation."

"I agree with you. Anything from a military perspective?"

"Well, we know we are blessed with incredibly brave soldiers in America. We know that we produce great leaders at all levels who eventually rise to the top. And when we combine Yankee artillery with Confederate infantry, we can whip anybody's ass in the world."

They laughed loudly.

"And that's exactly what we've got now in our army," Aaron said with a laugh. "The grandsons of both

Rebs and Yanks in our infantry and artillery. We should be quite a potent force, huh?"

A nurse admonished them over the noise coming from the room.

Aaron shifted in his seat and cleared his throat. "Mind if I ask you a personal question, Cappy?"

Conor noticed Aaron's discomfort. "You may ask me anything you'd like, kind sir."

"Do you have any regrets about your life?"

Conor squinted slightly as he considered the question for a long moment. "Yes, of course I have regrets," he finally said. "I suppose there are many things I would do differently if I had the chance to do them over again. I've made my share of mistakes, for sure. I had a damaged relationship with my own father; I had a failed marriage; my relationship with my son pains me greatly. However, one of the things I figured out along the way is that life is not science. There is very little precision to it. There's not a lot of predictability to it. And it involves not things, but unique, complicated, imperfect human beings. Therefore, you do the best you can, and if you can be satisfied that you've done your very best, then the results are the results, the outcomes the outcomes. I've had both the good and the bad in my life, Aaron, the sum total of which is what you see before you now. I can't go back and change any of it. So do I have any regrets about the life I've lived? Sure I do. But it's all part of the mishmash that constitutes a life that I have come to terms with. It's my life—the good and the bad of it, the *whole* of it—and I accept it as it is. I accept the mistakes, the missed opportunities, and the foolish things I did, along with the things I'm most proud of. And I'm comfortable with all of it now. That's what I should emphasize, that I'm comfortable with what life has given me, and with what I've put into the living of my life. I hope that answers your question."

"That was a terrific answer, Cappy."

"One more thing," Conor added. "I believe that history will judge the Army of Northern Virginia to be one of the greatest armies in the annals of warfare. I know that's an unusual thing to say about an army that was defeated, but when you consider the numerical odds against it, the skill and boldness of its leaders like Lee and Jackson and Longstreet and Gordon, and its unmatched fighting spirit even in the midst of great deprivation, our army was extraordinary."

"It will be interesting to see how history judges it, Cappy. We studied Lee's army at West Point."

"And it would be well worth studying. Likewise, it would be worth studying the great army it took to defeat it."

"Let's stop for today," Aaron said. "I need to pack and get ready to leave tomorrow. And I will need to get your house ready for you to come home to when you're discharged. Thank you for letting me use the guest bedroom."

"I'll see you tomorrow," Conor said.

Chapter Nineteen

Thoughts of Taylor

Where do you hear that the preaching does begin,
Bend down low for to drive away your sin
And when you gets religion, you want to shout and sing
There'll be a hot time in the old town tonight!
"A Hot Time In The Old Town Tonight"

1870 - 1899

Taylor was born in Mary and Conor's Atlanta home on March 12, 1870. He had a normal childhood, did well in school, and showed at an early age an athletic aptitude as a runner. He was smart and strong with a natural leadership ability that Conor noticed when Taylor was around other children. He wasn't boisterous or bullying but instead had a presence, a knack that caused other boys to view him as a leader. As he grew older, his capacity for leadership likewise grew. Conor thought he might become a successful businessman when he observed how skillfully Taylor helped with the family business in the summers. Taylor understood how to control costs and make a profit, how markets were discovered and developed, and how hiring and then developing good people were key functions. He was a self-starter who needed little supervision, and he learned quickly. He had a head for business, Conor thought.

Conor wasn't entirely surprised when Taylor informed his father that he was intent upon seeking an appointment to West Point. He had always expressed interest in Conor's experiences during the war, and he read all he could find on military history. Mary wasn't happy about his preference for a military education and she was strictly opposed to a military career, but in the end, she knew the choice would rest with Taylor. Mary obviously knew of Conor's service in the war, his wounds and aches and nightmares, and she wanted nothing of the sort for her son. Conor advised Taylor that his mother would eventually come around, that she was naturally troubled by the thought of her son going off to a war in some foreign land. He offered Taylor his help with the appointment, but Taylor responded that he would call on his father if needed. So Conor left it all in his hands, and it wasn't long before he proudly showed Mary and Conor a letter confirming his appointment for the academy class beginning in 1888.

Taylor did well in all areas at West Point and showed a strong aptitude for the academy's rigorous academics. Then something changed. When Taylor came home for a visit after his first year, he kept his distance from Conor, inexplicably, almost as if his father was carrying a contagious disease. Mary noticed it and asked Conor what had happened between them. Conor finally asked Taylor what was bothering him.

"You are," he replied sharply.

Conor was taken aback, and when he asked what he had done to provoke such treatment, Taylor related that he was embarrassed by his father's service in the Confederate army. Taylor referred to Conor as an unrepentant rebel who had helped bring about the deaths of thousands of loyal American soldiers, and that he should be ashamed rather than proud. Taylor was distressed that his father could remain proud of his service in a war that might have destroyed the country forever. Taylor then explained that he was attending West Point to regain the Rafferty family's honor, and furthermore to *defend* the United States of America as opposed to rebelling against it.

Conor was stunned, to say the least. It was almost as if they had suddenly become strangers, that Taylor had discovered something new in something old, something so detestable and dishonorable that it made his father's presence repugnant to him.

"Would you like for me to explain again why I joined the Confederate army, Taylor?" Conor asked. "It's not like it's been a secret for the nineteen years you've been around me."

"No explanation would ever be sufficient, so no explanation is necessary," Taylor replied in such a cold tone that it staggered Conor.

And so began the difficulty Conor experienced in reaching his own son. Conor wrote several letters when Taylor returned to West Point, but none were answered. Mary continued to enjoy a warm relationship with Taylor, but his sudden contempt for his father puzzled her, as well.

It bothered Conor every day, and most every night.

Taylor graduated in 1892 near the top of his class and received his commission as a second lieutenant. Conor had a lump in his throat throughout the entire journey as Mary and he rode the train to New York to attend the graduation ceremony. Taylor received his commission and gold bars and then accepted Conor's congratulatory handshake, but otherwise said very little to his father while they were all at West Point. Conor couldn't remember another time in his life when he had felt such frustration and bewilderment. Even still, on that graduation day he was eternally grateful for, and proud of, his united country, its splendid army, and in particular one of its newest young officers. Conor cried that gorgeous day on the Hudson River, and when he would dwell on it afterwards—the difficulty of what should have been a joyous time—he would cry again.

Taylor and Julia Avant, the daughter of a prominent Philadelphia lawyer and former Union cavalry commander, were married in New York City a week later in an extravagant wedding held at the Hotel Astor in Times Square. Mary and Conor had stayed over in the city to attend, but under the circumstances Conor's heart was not in it. He supposed it was possible that he was beginning to see himself much as Taylor did, as unworthy and with little redeeming value. He certainly felt that way when he was in Taylor's presence.

Soon thereafter, U.S. Army Second Lieutenant Taylor Rafferty and his new bride reported to Fort Buford in the Dakota Territory at the junction of the Missouri and Yellowstone Rivers. The Great Plains post was isolated from other army installations, in the prime buffalo-hunting country of the Sioux. Conor was amused when Taylor's letter to Mary arrived and informed her that General Phil Sheridan was the post commander, the same Phil Sheridan that he feared General Gordon was going to shoot under a flag of truce at Appomattox at the end of the war. Taylor honed his horsemanship skills during this assignment, and he gained a strong understanding of cavalry tactics. Aaron was born in 1893, a wonderful addition. They remained at Fort Buford until 1894 when they received orders to Fort Leavenworth, Kansas for Taylor to become a cavalry instructor for new recruits.

Taylor and Julia also welcomed the birth of daughter Catherine in 1896, another wonderful addition. Taylor was promoted to captain and, with Spain's brutal repression of Cuba edging the United States closer toward a military confrontation, he was ordered to San Antonio, Texas in late 1897.

Taylor, Julia, and the two grandkids were able to spend several days in Atlanta prior to Taylor's reporting to San Antonio. Mary and Conor saw Aaron and Catherine for only the second time, and of course they proceeded to do all they could to spoil them. They were undeniably beautiful children with an energy level and an endless curiosity that reminded Conor so much of their father.

Conor enticed Taylor away from the others one evening and invited him to walk out onto the wrap-around front porch and take a seat in a rocking chair. They lit cigars and poured after-supper drinks and relaxed in the cool November air. Conor was exhausted from trying to keep up with the grandkids, who were fast asleep inside, but he badly needed this time with Taylor. His son's previous cold attitude seemed to have warmed somewhat, and he wanted to exploit that long-awaited opening.

"So what's going to happen in Cuba, Taylor?" Conor asked. "Are we going to war with Spain?"

"I'm not sure, but it seems we're headed that way. We're forming a cavalry brigade with volunteers because we don't have enough troops in the regular army to fill all the posts."

"What?"

"Yes. Colonel Leonard Wood has been slated to command it, and the volunteers are going to come from cowboys, ranchers, hunters, Indians, former soldiers, and God knows where, with a few regulars like myself to train them. The army's really shrunk since the war."

"You may have a challenge on your hands training those guys into a cohesive unit."

"I'm sure I will. I heard that Theodore Roosevelt, who was Assistant Secretary of the Navy, is also looking to be a part of the brigade. I just hope this Navy guy Roosevelt can learn something about the cavalry."

Conor paused, took a drink and a deep breath, and then leaned in to face Taylor.

"Taylor, can we just go ahead and clear the air over whatever it is that's been dividing us for several years now?" he asked, watching carefully. "Is there anything you need to hear from me that would help?"

"I suppose some remorse would be helpful."

"Remorse over what?"

"We've been over this before, but here it is again: Remorse over joining a rebel army and fighting against a country that had been so good to our family," Taylor answered, looking straight ahead.

"My God, son, how can you speak to me that way? What did they teach you at West Point that would turn you against a father who did nothing but love and care for you to the absolute best of his ability?"

"You made a huge mistake and you seem to have no remorse over it. You chose the wrong side. You turned your back on your country. You tarnished our family name. Your own father warned you against it. Why can't you see that?" said Taylor, still staring straight ahead.

"How did those of us who fought for the South become such despicable figures in your judgment?"

"Because you fought for a despicable cause."

"Taylor, I deeply resent the fact that you think I dishonored the family. I fought and bled with honor. Your uncles gave their lives in the war. I raised you with a strong moral code to do right and play fair, to work hard and be self-reliant, and for the life of me I don't understand why you're telling me I should be remorseful for being the man I am."

Taylor finally turned and looked at Conor, but said nothing.

"I would also add, Taylor, that you've become close-minded, ungrateful, and arrogant, a young man who thinks he knows everything but in truth knows very little. You'll have Southern troops under your command, good troops ready to follow a good leader, whose fathers and uncles also may have fought for the Confederacy. And as soon as they discover your lack of authenticity and your struggle to figure out *who* you are and *what* you are, you'll lose them. All of them, not just the Southerners. And it will be *your* great loss if that happens."

Conor paused and took another deep breath.

"As for being remorseful," he continued, "I wouldn't change anything about my past. I'm proud to have served in the Confederate army, and the fact that I served with honor is something you or anyone else should never challenge. I will never again allow you to cause me to feel shame over it. You would do well to remember that you, too, are a son of the South, whether you like it or not, and I cannot understand why you've been made to feel so uncomfortable over it. And I certainly don't know what has happened to turn you against me. But I will say this: If you want to be ashamed of me for doing what I thought was the right thing for me to do during a very difficult time, then it appears there's not much I can say or do to change your mind. And if that is truly the case, then so be it. However, I will always love you and be proud of you because you're my son. No matter what I am to you, I want you to know that you are, and always will be, the most important man in my life. And I hope you never forget that, Taylor."

Taylor got up and went back inside. They barely spoke during the remainder of the visit, and Taylor's efforts to avoid Conor were painfully evident to all. Conor only wished he could have somehow broken through to his son, but he failed in that effort, and he felt sick about it.

Neither of them had any way of knowing that their conversation on the porch that evening would be their last.

The battleship USS Maine was sunk in Havana Harbor in February, 1898, under suspicious circumstances, heightening the already tense atmosphere in Cuba. Spain and the United States declared war on one another in April, 1898, after the Americans had demanded a Spanish withdrawal from Cuba. The U.S. had a standing army of 27,000 troops, while 200,000 Spaniards were massed in Cuba. Volunteers were called for, and within weeks some 20,000 men had joined up. The 1st U.S. Volunteer Cavalry, which would come to be known as the Rough Riders, began training for war, with Lieutenant Colonel Theodore Roosevelt as second in command.

In May, 1898, Taylor left San Antonio for Tampa, Florida where the final planning would occur before getting underway to Cuba. Julia and the kids stayed in Philadelphia with her parents while Taylor was away. Taylor's letters to Mary indicated that he and Roosevelt had become close friends, with TR (as Taylor referred to him) relying heavily upon Taylor's cavalry expertise to train the men. Taylor noted that TR kidded him incessantly about not having had the foresight five years earlier to name his son Theodore. While still in Tampa, Roosevelt promoted Taylor to the rank of major.

The Rough Riders arrived in Cuba in late June after several logistical challenges forced the Americans to leave some of the cavalry in Tampa. The first contact they had with Spanish forces was at the outpost of Las Guasimas. The battle was short but intense, and many of the Americans received their first taste of battle. Six days later, the Americans attacked Kettle Hill at the San Juan Heights. Roosevelt led his men up the hill while waving his hat in the air and cheering, with his Rough Riders eagerly following. There were a series of short rushes, with the cavalry functioning largely as dismounted infantry, and within twenty minutes the Americans took Kettle Hill, though with heavy casualties. They took the rest of the San Juan Heights within the next hour.

One of his fellow officers described Taylor as fearlessly rallying his troops from atop his horse at a critical moment when it appeared the Americans were losing momentum. By his personal bravery and leadership, Taylor inspired his men forward. Within yards of reaching the crest of Kettle Hill, he was shot through the heart and died immediately. Roosevelt saw his dear friend fall from his horse, and he was devastated when he arrived and discovered there was no pulse.

Conor received the news several days later in the form of a telegraph, followed by a personal letter from Theodore Roosevelt. Taylor's body was buried in Cuba with the other American dead. He was twenty-eight at the time of his death.

In the days that followed the news of Taylor's death, Mary went into a depression from which Conor feared she might never recover. For his part, Conor certainly felt a truly indescribable grief, but with Mary it seemed far deeper and far more debilitating. Conor recalled how his mother had been so shattered and broken over the news of his brother Daniel's death that it had killed her. More than once he thought the same fate might befall Mary, but after two weeks she seemed to regain her footing and function in a mostly normal manner again.

It took longer for the finality of his son's death to affect Conor, but when it did it drove him into a deep, dark abyss that grabbed him by the throat and very nearly choked the life from him. Conor had so much regret and guilt accumulating inside him that it was burning through to the outside. Mary suggested that he see a doctor, but he declined and saw a bartender instead.

Theodore Roosevelt was distraught over losing his trusted protégé, Major Taylor Rafferty, and a year later in 1899, Roosevelt, now Governor of New York, visited Julia and the two children in Philadelphia. During that visit, TR presented Julia with Taylor's posthumous award of the Distinguished Service Cross, the second highest military award for combat valor that a member of the United States Army can receive. The Philadelphia newspapers provided front-page coverage of the wildly popular Roosevelt calling on the young Rafferty family.

Roosevelt was hardly the only one stricken with grief over Taylor's death. Mary and Conor received countless letters from Taylor's West Point classmates and instructors as well as from many of the men who had served with him in the United States and Cuba. Taylor was brave, brilliant, and ambitious to a fault. With his many connections, he may well have ended up as the top officer in the army. But the same Spanish bullet that stopped Taylor's heart, also broke Conor's.

And, as Conor already knew, he would never fully recover from it.

Taylor's widowed wife, Julia, eventually married a railroad executive and moved to Richmond. From that point on, Conor rarely saw his grandchildren.

***

Saturday, February 16, 1918

"I'm glad we saved this until my last day here in Atlanta, Cappy. I don't know that my attention span would have been quite as long afterwards had we covered this earlier. And I'm sure my emotions would have overtaken me, like they're about to now."

Aaron wasn't the only one struggling. Both sets of eyes were damp, not just at the remembrance of Taylor, but of their weeklong visit that was now ending.

"My greatest regret, Aaron, is that Taylor and I never resolved our differences before he died. If I could have had one more conversation with him, one more visit, one more letter, we could have worked things out. I know we could have, I just *know* it. But we didn't. And I'm still filled with a regret that I'll never get over, I'm afraid."

Aaron wiped his eyes with a handkerchief and then cleared his throat. He sat up straight, looking at Conor directly. "I will tell you now, Cappy, before I leave for my own war duty, that I don't see you the way you've come to think that my father saw you. I see you as the most decent, honorable man I've ever known. In addition, I think my father saw you that way, too. For whatever his reasons, he just wouldn't acknowledge it. So I'll do it for him. His

320

blood runs through my veins, I trained at West Point just as he did, and I wear the same uniform as he wore. I'm as proud of you as I can be, and I really, truly believe he was, too. I've come to understand from our time together what you did and why you did it, and my respect and admiration for you is great. You did your best and you should be proud of it, like I know you are. So please, let go of the regret. Like you told me before, you can't change the past so you may as well come to terms with it. My father's gone. You no longer have him, but you do have me. And, thankfully, I have you."

Conor reached out and hugged Aaron, holding on tightly for several moments.

"Let the regret go, Cappy. Look at what you have, not at what you've lost. Remember that when you lost your son, I lost my father. But I've discovered what you and I share is not only that loss, but also a bond between us that will never be broken. And I can clearly sense that you're as grateful for that as I am."

"For such a young man, you sure have a lot of wisdom."

"I'm a Rafferty, sir. All of us have a lot of good stuff."

They laughed again, finally.

"When do you leave for Europe?" Conor finally asked.

"In a week. I'll spend a few days in Virginia and then report to New York City to board the troop transport for France."

"Do you know what you'll do when you get over there?"

"I expect to command a rifle company. That's what I'm counting on. The army is drafting almost three-million men into service, and I've been directly involved in training hundreds of them. This war's been going on overseas since nineteen-fourteen, but with our draftees filling up the pipeline, we're about to get in, and in a big way."

"I'd appreciate a letter every now and again."

"I'll write, Cappy. I promise."

"By the way, do you have your father's Distinguished Service Cross?"

"Yes, it's one of my prized possessions. And do you know what else will become a prized possession?"

"No."

Aaron held up the folder of notes he had taken over the past week. "These papers. This is my written record of my grandfather's incredible experiences. His heroism. His sacrifice. And the lessons I've learned from him. I will treasure these pages for as long as I live. It's part of our family's legacy now."

Aaron had his two packed bags with him. His afternoon train to Richmond was leaving in less than two hours, and he would be traveling throughout the night. He was dressed in his army uniform, and more than once Joan, his favorite nurse, had walked past to look in on him.

"You should know, Aaron, that my health has improved to the point that I'll be discharged tomorrow. I'm not sure that would've happened had you not shown up when you did. You just might have saved this old man's life, young man."

Aaron shrugged and smiled. "Nah, Cappy. You're still a tough ole Reb. You've got plenty of miles left to march."

Thus, their reunion ended. Conor had been fortunate late in his life to resurrect a cherished relationship that might otherwise have gone unfulfilled. He was thankful for Aaron, for the Rafferty name Aaron carried, for Aaron's curiosity about his grandfather that had led to his visit, and for his rejuvenating presence that filled a void in Conor that had been growing bigger by the day. Conor felt joy and gratitude, but he also felt the same nagging knot in his stomach about Aaron going off to war in Europe that he had felt when Taylor left for Cuba.

Conor never had the chance to reconcile with Taylor, but the wise words of his grandson gave an old man a sense of peace he hadn't felt in many years.

"Here," Conor said. "I want you to have this."

"It's your Bible, Cappy, the one you carried with you during the war. Are you sure you want to part with this?"

"Yes. It needs to belong with you now."

Conor could see Aaron fighting back the tears as he looked at the worn, faded little book. "I know where this Bible's been. I'll treasure it for as long as I live. Thank you, sir."

When the time came and they shook hands in that hospital room, Conor was so proud he thought he might burst. He said a silent prayer for Aaron's protection, and he thanked God that he was so blessed to be his grandfather. They held the handshake a bit longer than usual, looking one another directly in the eye. Conor saw Taylor in Aaron's eyes, and he thought he could see Taylor looking back at him, nodding, with a proud smile on his face.

"I'll see you on the other side, Aaron."

"I'll see you on the other side, Cappy."

Epilogue

Thursday, October 17, 1918

Conor made his way by train from Atlanta to Washington, D.C., where he was met at Union Station by a young army captain and a leathery old sergeant. They escorted Conor to a horse-drawn carriage and provided him with a blanket to shield him from the chill. The captain said that residents of the city were being asked to avoid streetcars because of the influenza epidemic now present in Washington. Schools and churches were closing and businesses were staggering their hours to reduce the congestion on public transportation. Several thousand cases had been reported thus far, the captain noted, but the number of new cases seemed to be leveling off.

At age seventy-eight, Conor's old body ached from the long trip and the damp cold, but in spite of the aches and pains and the risks of flu, he was glad he had come. They arrived in due course at Walter Reed General Hospital where the captain led Conor up several flights of stairs to a doctors' lounge, which was adjacent to a ward filled with wounded soldiers.

Conor needed a moment to catch his breath.

"Colonel Rafferty?" called an army lieutenant colonel who was seated at a table drinking coffee with several doctors and uniformed army officers.

"Yes?" he answered, breathing heavily, seeing but not recognizing the man.

The officer got up and approached Conor, a wide smile on his face. "I'm Lieutenant Colonel Theodore Roosevelt, Junior. Thank you for coming, sir. Your grandson will be pleasantly surprised to see you."

The others at the table all stood as Conor approached. He was speechless.

"I spent some time with Aaron earlier this morning," said Roosevelt, "and I'm happy to report he's recovering nicely. Doctor Underwood will give you a more detailed medical briefing on his overall condition, but the important point is his wounds are healing. Aaron also told me about you and your experiences, and about the very special relationship his father had with my father. I'm so pleased you could be here today, Colonel."

"Well," Conor said, finally finding his voice, "I'm really pleased to meet you, Lieutenant Colonel Roosevelt. Your father meant a great deal to my son, Taylor. They did indeed have a very special relationship."

"I heard my father speak of Taylor on numerous occasions, and always with admiration."

Roosevelt introduced Conor around, after which he took a seat at the table with the others. Doctor Underwood proceeded to advise Conor that Aaron's shrapnel wounds had been concentrated in his right hip and leg, and the exploding German artillery shell had also peppered his right arm.

"No damage to any vital organs, but there's tissue and muscle damage to his upper and lower leg and his right elbow was fractured. I would foresee Major Rafferty being a patient here for at least another month, but given his youth and excellent physical conditioning, I don't anticipate anything other than a full and complete recovery."

"Can he move his hand and feel his fingers?" Conor asked.

"Yes," the doctor answered. "He has full feeling in all of the affected areas. You've had some experience with battlefield wounds, Colonel?" he asked, having noticed both his limp and his missing finger.

"There were some very good marksmen among those boys in blue, sir," Conor said, drawing laughter. "So, Aaron's been promoted to major?"

"Yes," answered Roosevelt. "The army promoted him yesterday and we're awarding him the Distinguished Service Cross today."

"Does Aaron know he's being awarded the DSC?" Conor asked.

"No," answered Roosevelt with a grin. "He knows he was nominated, but he doesn't know it will be awarded today. It will also be a surprise to him that you're here, Colonel."

Conor noticed the DSC medal Roosevelt was wearing.

Aaron's mother Julia, with her husband and Conor's granddaughter Catherine, along with her husband and young daughter, came into the lounge. They had arrived the previous day from Richmond and had been able to visit Aaron in the late afternoon. It had been far too many years since Conor had seen Julia and Catherine, and he greeted them warmly. His great-granddaughter was an adorable young girl of two whom he was seeing for the first time.

Conor noticed that his granddaughter Catherine had a slight resemblance to Taylor but mostly favored Julia. But his great-granddaughter Grace had a very strong resemblance to Taylor. Grace allowed Conor to hold her, and she looked him over as curiously as he did her.

"Hi, Cappy," she said in a voice so sweet that it very nearly brought tears to his eyes. He couldn't stop hugging her.

Julia told Conor that she had written Mary, his ex-wife and Aaron's grandmother, and informed her of the ceremony, but Mary had declined due to poor health. Mary had instead sent a letter to Julia to give to Aaron. Conor nodded his understanding, but said nothing. He had wondered on the trip from Atlanta whether Mary might turn up, and in some ways he was relieved that she didn't. Then he realized that this was Aaron's day, not his, and he wished then that Mary had chosen to come.

Soon Lieutenant Colonel Roosevelt led the group into the ward where they gathered around the bed of the surprised Aaron. He wore heavy bandages on his leg and a cast on his arm, but he was able to sit up and greet everyone. When Aaron saw his grandfather he became emotional, and they shared a long embrace before Roosevelt brought out a box and unfolded a citation. An army photographer positioned himself near the bed to take photos of the ceremony.

"Major Rafferty," Roosevelt began, "it is my distinct honor today to preside over your award of the Distinguished Service Cross. It is no small coincidence that this is the same high award that was presented posthumously to your father, United States Army Major Taylor Rafferty, by my late father. This award is presented for combat action that occurred in France last summer. If I may, let me begin by reading the citation. It reads as follows: 'While his Company B, Sixtieth Infantry, Fifth Division was crossing a canal near the Meuse River on nine July, nineteen-eighteen, the bridge over the canal was hit and destroyed by enemy artillery fire. One platoon of Captain Rafferty's command became isolated on the far bank of the canal and was immediately threatened by a larger enemy force. Captain Rafferty unhesitatingly waded across the canal under heavy fire, with his men following, to provide support to the detached platoon. Inspired by his leadership, Captain Rafferty's men quickly gained the slopes, repulsed the enemy, and linked up with the forward platoon. B Company then assaulted and overran the enemy position, sending the survivors into retreat. By his valiant personal example, he broke the enemy's hold on this key position. The exceptional courage and leadership displayed by Captain Rafferty made possible the control of the bridgehead and its immediate area by Allied forces.'"

Roosevelt then leaned over and pinned the medal on Aaron's gown. At least two-dozen wounded and curious soldiers, several on crutches, had crowded around to listen in. The entire ward broke out in loud, sustained applause when Roosevelt came to attention and saluted Aaron.

Conor stood back and savored the sight of Aaron and his immediate family taking in this special moment. He had been heartsick when Julia wrote to inform him of Aaron's wounding and hospitalization. She then followed with another letter soon thereafter to say that the DSC award had been approved, and expressed her hope that he would be able to travel to Washington and attend the ceremony. He immediately wrote back and confirmed he would make the trip. Julia didn't tell him that she had arranged for Lieutenant Colonel Roosevelt to present the award, which was a terrific surprise to both Aaron and Conor, and greatly fitting, as well.

Aaron's wide, bright smile let Conor know that he was going to be just fine.

"Aaron told me about your losing both brothers in the war, Colonel," Roosevelt said as he stood beside Conor near the foot of Aaron's bed. "I lost my younger brother Quentin last summer when he was killed in aerial combat in France as a pilot in the Air Service. He was only twenty when he died. I have some idea of what such a loss means."

"My sympathies to you and your family, sir. It's a hurt that never quite goes away."

"Well, we can talk more at dinner tonight. In case you didn't know, the Raffertys are being treated to what I anticipate will be a delightful meal courtesy of the Roosevelts. Julia has all the details. I'll see you soon, Colonel."

"Thank you, sir. It's been a special honor to meet you," Conor said in return.

Roosevelt soon left with his aides, and Julia and family eventually left for the nearby hotel where Conor was also booked. There were still a half-dozen young soldiers gathered around Aaron, laughing and joking.

A well-dressed gentleman who had come into the ward just prior to the ceremony, and who had spoken with Aaron and Julia afterwards, approached Conor.

"Colonel Rafferty, I'm Representative Henry Hodgson from Richmond, Virginia. I'm Aaron's congressman here in Washington."

"Ah, I'm very pleased to meet you, sir," Conor said, extending his hand.

Hodgson appeared to be in his late-forties, salt-and-pepper hair, tall and sturdy and well-groomed with a decided air of erudition about him.

"I want to thank you for coming. I'm sure Aaron appreciates your making the trip," Hodgson offered.

"Thank you, as well, Congressman Hodgson. Nice of you to take the time to come by."

"It's my pleasure, I assure you. When I found out that one of my Virginia constituents was being awarded the Distinguished Service Cross, I wanted to be here. Teddy Roosevelt had stopped in several days ago and told me about the ceremony, and I got here today as soon my schedule allowed. I'm sure you're tremendously proud of Aaron, Colonel Rafferty."

"I couldn't be prouder, sir."

"Well, I have to tell you that the name Rafferty rang a bell with me when Teddy told me about Aaron and a little about the service of Aaron's father, and then about your service in the Confederate army."

"Rang a bell? How so?" Conor asked.

"Do you remember the name Penny Orr?"

Conor paused a moment and then answered, "Yes, of course I remember Penny."

"Well, Colonel, she's my mother."

Conor blinked and felt the blood rushing out of his head, making him dizzy for an instant. He tried to speak, but couldn't. Nor could he act casual and unaffected, as hard as he tried. He was stunned into silence, and except for the revived images of a beautiful young woman streaming across his brain and the rapid pounding of his heart, the rest of him suddenly seemed inoperable. Conor finally thought to close his open mouth and take in a deep breath, all while Henry Hodgson chuckled at the sight of his complete and total surprise.

"I should tell you, Colonel, that when I told Mother I had happened upon one of her old beaus, Conor Rafferty, she had much the same reaction," said Hodgson, still laughing. "She has spoken of you many, many times through the years, always affectionately and always with a sort of twinkle in her eye."

"Where is she?"

"She's here, in Washington. She happened to be here visiting my family when I was made aware of Aaron's award and his connection to you."

"My God, I'm sorry if I seem a bit caught off guard."

"It's perfectly okay. She wants to see you. She and I will be joining you, Julia's family, and the Roosevelts for supper tonight. She didn't want to come here to the hospital and be a distraction, so she told me to tell you she's looking forward to seeing you tonight."

"It's been over fifty years."

"Fifty-four, according to Mother. And let me give you some quick background information: As you know, Mother and my grandmother moved to California near the end of the war. They took up residence in San Francisco with some of our kinfolk there. Mother eventually married a successful businessman, became Penny Hodgson, and over the span of eight years gave birth to two daughters and me. My grandmother died in 1871 and my father drowned in a boating accident in 1879. Ever the Southern girl, Mother moved us back to Richmond in 1880 and never remarried."

Conor shook his head in utter amazement. "This is astonishing, right out of a novel."

"She said much the same thing. Life goes on, does it not? Well, if you'll excuse me, Colonel, I need to get back to my office on Capitol Hill. The people's business never rests. I look forward to seeing you again this evening."

Conor stood alone for a moment to gather himself, and then asked a nurse for a glass of water when Aaron motioned him over to his bedside. The same nurse also brought Conor a chair. He took a seat next to Aaron's bed.

"You okay, Cappy? You look a little pale."

"I'm fine, Aaron. Couldn't be better, actually."

"I'm really grateful you made the trip. It meant the world for me to look up and see you standing there. And I have to say, you look mighty handsome in that suit, sir."

"The honor is all mine, Major Rafferty, I assure you. And I'm glad you like my new suit. Damn thing cost me almost forty dollars. It's outrageous."

Aaron laughed and gave Conor an affectionate slap on the leg.

They talked about Aaron's service in France, about his command of a company that was in the thick of many big battles. Several of his West Point classmates had been killed in action, including his best friend, and he was thankful to have not been killed or more seriously wounded.

"I was in that deadly space, Cappy. I know now what you were talking about when you referred to it. General Lee was right—once you've been in it, you know without any doubt the description is spot on."

Conor nodded his agreement. "You have a good memory, Aaron."

"Many of the lessons in leadership I learned from you during our visit, especially about leadership when things are not going well, were like a godsend to me. I thought about those lessons and examples very carefully and applied them when I took over my rifle company. This award of the DSC belongs as much to you, Cappy, as it does to me."

"No, Aaron," Conor replied, "I may have given you reason to think and learn, but it was you who had to act when the time came. I appreciate your generosity, but this award is for what you did when you had to do it. I'm proud of you for the leader you've become, and even prouder for the man you are."

"So what are you doing now, Cappy? Have you married again?"

Conor laughed. "No, I've not married again."

"Then what are you doing with your time?"

"I'm writing a book."

"Really? A book about what?"

"It's a book about a visit, about some wartime experiences shared by an old man with a wonderful young man. It's about how that visit gave the old man a new purpose in life, a great story to tell, and very probably kept him alive long enough to complete it. That's what the book is about."

Aaron smiled broadly. "Mind if I read it when you're finished?"

"Of course not. In fact, the very first copy will be yours, sir."

Aaron made Conor promise to visit him at his Richmond home where he would spend his convalescent leave.

"I might be able to work that out," Conor said, suppressing a smile. "In the meantime, I'll be back in the morning for a short visit before my train leaves."

They hugged and said their goodbyes, each adding, "See you on the other side."

Conor walked to the hotel, checked in and freshened up, and then walked the three blocks to the restaurant. He arrived early and was seated at the bar, alone and having an Irish whiskey before the others arrived. He was thinking about how truly fortunate he was to be the grandfather of such a fine young man as Aaron, and how proud he was of him as a soldier. His thoughts then turned back to Penny. He was anxious about seeing her again after five decades in time and a million miles down the road from a youthful romance that for a brief moment had been so full of promise. Their reunion now seemed such an improbable occurrence that he had to keep reminding himself that it was real, that this time it wasn't a dream. Oddly enough, dreaming had been the only way he had been able to spend time with Penny since 1864, and the prospect of the real thing was unnerving him.

The first whiskey helped very little.

He had another before someone lightly touched him on the shoulder.

"Hello Conor. Remember me?"

He turned and looked and there she stood, as if fifty-four years of his life had suddenly been rewound back to a distant time and place. She was striking, as beautiful as he remembered. There was a wrinkle or two and the hair was now gray, but her eyes and smile were as captivating and familiar as if he'd been whisked back to her Richmond parlor. Conor climbed off the barstool, kissed her on the cheek, and then hugged her tightly, bringing to the surface a rush of warm feelings that had been dormant for years. He could sense the emotions moving through her and into his arms and chest, just as he was certain she was feeling the same in return. After all the years, all the best and worst of times, all the many fleeting moments wondering what had become of her, she was now here with him. She was in his arms again, and it felt right. Part of him wanted to shout out with glee, another part to shed a tear. For a split-second he thought he might indulge both. It was all he could do to keep his feelings under control.

Conor took a deep breath and steadied himself.

"I would've come for you in Richmond. You know that, don't you?" he said as he looked at her lovely face.

She nodded, her eyes sparkling. "Yes, I know that. I've always known that."

"The Richmond girl is standing in front of me. I can't believe it's really you, Penny. And after all these years."

"It's really me, Conor. The Richmond girl."

He stood and admired her further, holding her hands in his. He felt energized and young again. And the way Penny looked at him made him feel attractive again.

"I never thought I'd stand in your presence again, or see your face and hear your voice again. I never thought something like this could ever happen," he said, shaking his head in disbelief.

"Nor did I. But I do believe everything happens for a reason."

"It has to be fate, Penny. How could it be anything else?"

"I just know I'm glad it happened, whatever it is."

"Listen, I want to catch up," he said excitedly. "I want to know everything about you. I want to meet your daughters. I want you to meet my grandson. I want to explain why I didn't come to California. I want to tell you what I'm doing now. I want to . . . "

He paused and stared into her eyes, feeling saturated with emotion.

"You want to what, Conor Rafferty?"

"I want to come to Richmond and finish what I started a long time ago."

Penny smiled and turned her head slightly, that same twinkle in her eye that he remembered so well. "I'll be there," she said, adding, "this time for sure."

THE END

About the Author

Gerald Gillis is the author of four novels. His books have been recognized by awards from the Military Writers Society of America and the National Indie Excellence Awards. Gerald holds degrees from the University of Georgia and the University of Tampa. After college, he served three years as an officer in the U.S. Marine Corps. Gerald had a successful business career in the medical-devices industry before becoming a full-time novelist and event speaker. He and his wife reside in the Atlanta area.

Read more about Gerald at www.geraldgillis.com.